RACHEL L. SCHADE

Forsaken Kingdom

SILENT KINGDOM SERIES
BOOK 2

RACHEL L. SCHADE

Forsaken Kingdom

SILENT KINGDOM SERIES
BOOK 2

DRAGON SHADOW PUBLISHING

Cover design by Chicklen.Doodle and MiblArt

Maps by MoorBooks Design

ISBN: 978-1-7364856-9-9

www.rachelschadeauthor.com

*For Sheree, who believed in my dreams even when I did not,
and for Julienne, who walked into Hell with me and never looked back.*

NESTED RUNES

CONDEMNED

DAUGHTER OF THE DEAD

PRONUNCIATION GUIDE

Characters

Halia (HAY-lee-uh)

Gillen (GILL-in)

Narek (NAIR-ek)

Velaire (Vuhl-AIR)

Avrik (Â-vrik)

Lyanna (LIE-ann-uh)

Elena (ELL-in-uh)

Captain Luiken (LOO-kin)

Haed (HAYd)

Iyleth (Î-leth)

Reylinn (RAY-lin)

Ilett (ELL-let)

Creatures

Sedwa (Sed-wuh)

Ichgor (ICK-gor)

Nestred (NESS-tred),
nestrae (Ness-TRAY)

Vilspen (Vill-spin)

Locations/Other

Misroth (MIZ-roth),
Misrothian (Miz-ROW-thee-un)

Toryn (TOR-in)

Alrenor (AL-ren-or),
Alrenian (Al-REN-ee-un)

Vorvinia (Vor-vin-YUH),
Vorvinian Mountains (Vor-vin-YUN)

Calidar (KAL-i-dar)

Vehgar (VAY-gar)

Nesrelle (NEZ-rell)

Elhalin (Ell-HAY-lin)

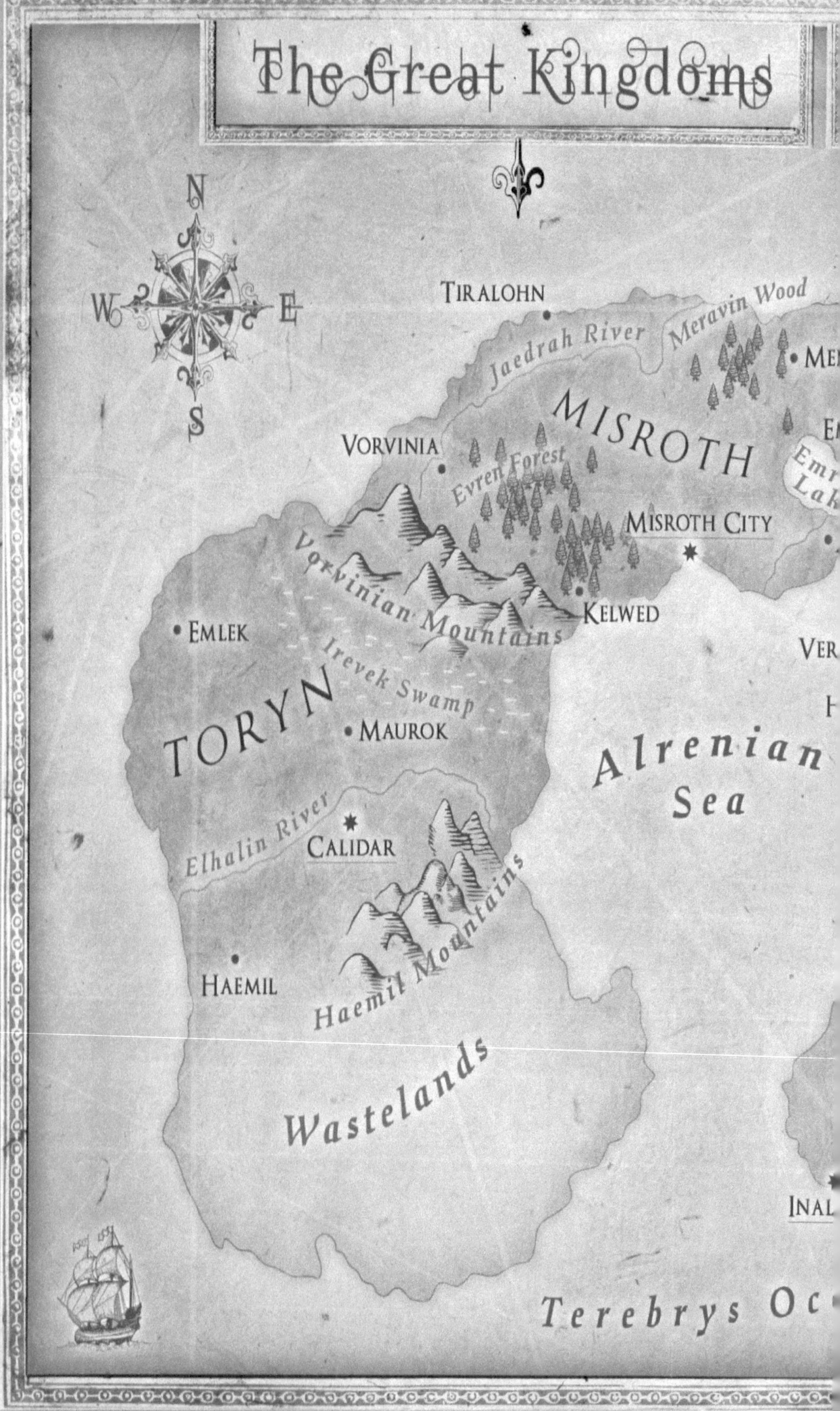

The Great Kingdoms
N
W
E
S
TIRALOHN
Jaedrah River
Meravin Wood
MER
MISROTH
VORVINIA
Evren Forest
Emr
Lak
E
MISROTH CITY
Vorvinian Mountains
KELWED
EMLEK
VER
Irevek Swamp
H
TORYN
MAUROK
Alrenian
Sea
Elhalin River
CALIDAR
Haemil Mountains
HAEMIL
Wastelands
INAL
Terebrys Oc

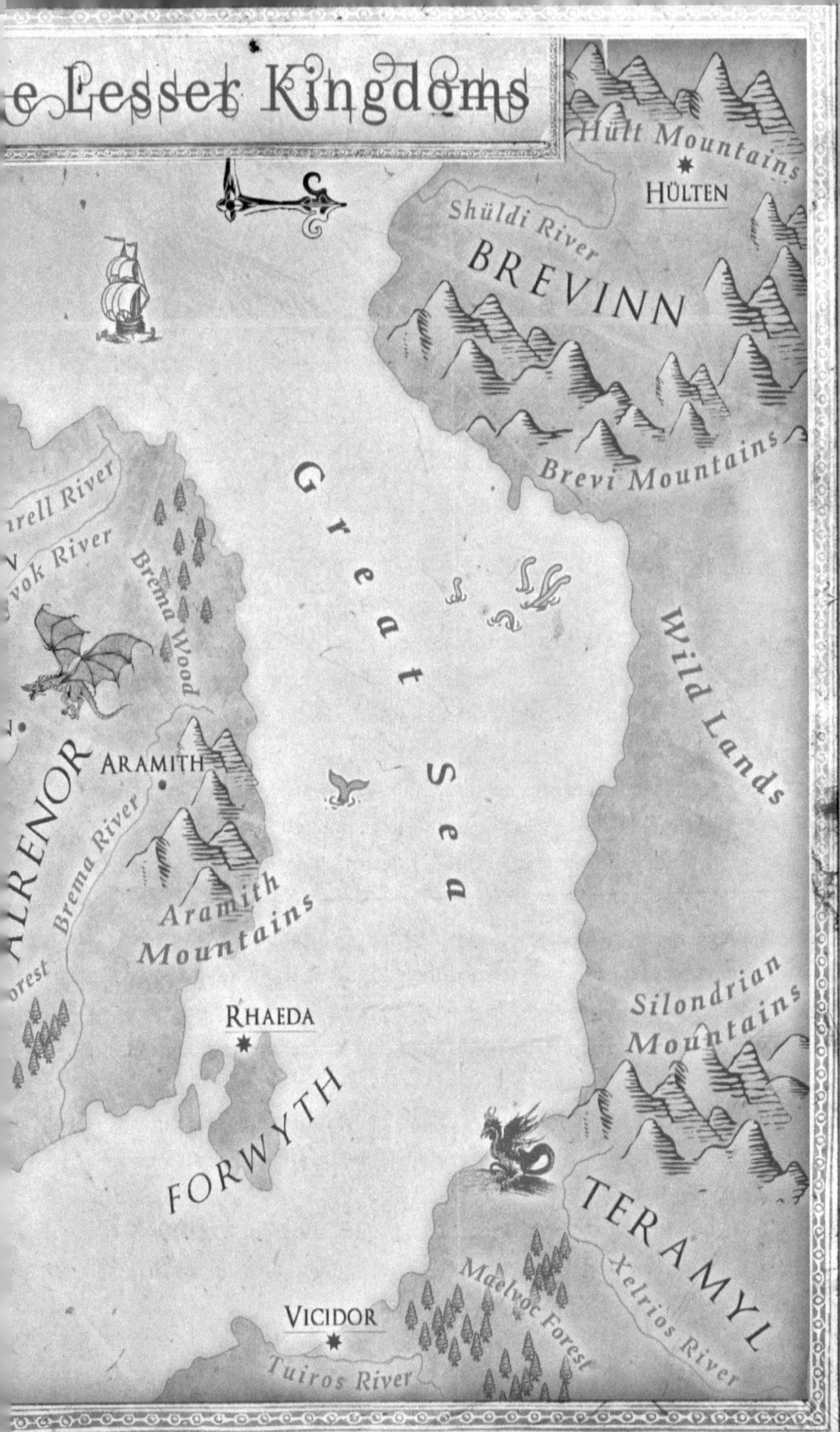

e Lesser Kingdoms
Hult Mountains
HÜLTEN
Shüldi River
BREVINN
Brevi Mountains
rell River
vok River
Brema Wood
Great Sea
Wild Lands
ALRENOR
ARAMITH
Brema River
orest
Aramith Mountains
RHAEDA
Silondrian Mountains
FORWYTH
TERAMYL
Maelvoc Forest
Xelrios River
VICIDOR
Tuiros River

CHAPTER ONE

THE PEOPLE OF MISROTH MARCHED my father's head through the streets. In a gleeful parade, men, women, and even children held their fists high in the air and shouted their victory, their freedom, and their release from tyranny and death. The patches of ice and snow littering the muddy cobblestones underfoot did nothing to slow their steps.

Kneeling beside my mother's memorial, I watched them stream through the streets below as anger and disgust stabbed my chest. Beside me, Jennah reached out and grasped my arm, her hand warm and reassuring.

I stared at her, a breeze off the Alrenian brushing its chill fingers through my hair. Her eyes were sympathetic, but her brow was furrowed into firm lines. In the daylight, the fresh scar cutting across her cheek contrasted starkly with the dark, gold-tinted skin that, along with her eyes, showed her Alrenian heritage.

"This needs to end," I said, plucking her hand from my arm and rising. The rebels standing behind us, acting as my unofficial Royal Guard, stirred uncomfortably.

Jennah didn't move, but continued to gaze at the stone altar. Words were etched into its side, words that left me cold and numb as they blandly recited facts:

Lady Ryn of Misroth,
Daughter of Lord Dievon and Lady Loella, Wife of Prince Zarev.
Born Year 159. Perished Year 201.

Prepared years ago for the former queen, with her death date added mere days ago, its charred surface was a heavy reminder of the night we burned her body. Contrasting starkly with the blackness were white sythrel petals scattered over the memorial, offerings to plead for the Life-Giver's favor toward the dead.

My fingers curled into fists. There would be no favor for the dead if there was not favor for the living first. And behaving as my father had was no way for my kingdom to earn it.

I turned my back to my mother's memorial and took a step back toward the city, my boots crunching on gravel and sand.

"Your Highness." Jennah's voice was low, smooth.

"Do not call me that."

Ignoring my comment, Jennah stood and joined me as I glared down at the streets. She studied me for a moment before quirking an eyebrow. "How do you plan to stop a mob—by running out into the fray and being trampled to death?"

I lifted my hands to massage my temples. "We must not be like him. We cannot stoop to this—this barbarism…"

Again, Jennah reached out her hand to touch my shoulder. Her face softened with compassion, the gold flecks in her brown eyes glittering with warmth. "What will you have us tell the people?"

"Tell them to burn the king's body. Scatter the ashes to the wind, or bury them to be forgotten forever. I don't care," I finished, "as long as the people return to their lives. It is time to rebuild. To forget."

I fingered the red armband of mourning adorning my right forearm, tracing the outline of sythrel petals etched into its smooth leather surface. It and the diamond star hanging from a white gold chain my mother had worn to honor her marriage to my father were the only symbols of bereavement I bore. It had seemed wrong not to follow Misrothian custom in the wake of my mother's death, even if she had failed me in countless ways. Jennah's eyes followed my movement, and I could read the question on her face: Was there a part of me that mourned my father?

Refusing to contemplate that possibility, I averted my gaze.

"Let's return to the castle, and I will pass on your orders," Jennah said.

We descended the dirt pathway leading to the streets. Now that the riotous crowd had passed, the surrounding city was quiet and empty. A distant bell tolled the time—half past the thirteenth hour—and a stray cat skittered along the cobblestones to avoid our path. Half the shops we passed, even those lining the main street that wound a path toward the castle, were closed, while the rest looked lifeless, vacant of all but their shopkeepers.

Our guards followed Jennah and me silently, a constant reminder that I was confined once again to the life of a royal, always being followed, always being watched. Always feeling constricted. Towering overhead, even the slate-colored buildings of the capital seemed to hem me in. I caught a glimpse of a woman peering from a window high above until she met my gaze and turned away. The eyes of an entire city—an entire kingdom—were on me, all the Misrothian people resting their hopes in my hands and waiting to see what I would do next. I couldn't fail them.

I swallowed as memories of open skies and friendly faces darted through my mind, as grief and regret rose at the reminder of how much I missed Lyanna and Rev and all the others I'd never even bid goodbye. But in a kingdom teetering toward anarchy in these uncertain days, I had no time to consider that now.

Mere days had passed since the rebels had taken possession of the castle, but these days had felt like a lifetime. I couldn't leave Misroth until a semblance of order was restored and my aunt was well enough to rule in her son's stead, but my heart ached to be journeying toward my cousin

Gillen, to find him and bring him home safely. Every moment I remained in Misroth was another moment I was abandoning him to an unknown fate in a perilous land.

We reached the castle, our footsteps echoing in the courtyard as guards let us pass with salutes. Two more pushed the main doors inward to reveal the gleaming marble floors and carved mahogany columns of the main entrance. My stomach twisted; I still wasn't used to the sight of my childhood home, a place that felt cold and empty with so many recent painful memories—and without Gillen's presence. After the years I'd spent in the quiet village of Evren with Lyanna and Rev, I felt like I was living a stranger's life in Misroth City.

Jennah turned toward me. "We need to prepare for your meeting with the Royal Council." She glanced back at the men accompanying us. "Gather more men and put an end to the riots, in the princess's name."

Ever since King Zarev had been overthrown, I'd found there were few I could trust within the castle. Most of his Royal Guard were locked in the prisons while the servants were questioned one by one. Because of this, members of the rebellion, including Jennah and her family, had moved into the castle with me to better serve as my unofficial guard and assist in the many changes I needed to enact. Jennah had already proved to be an encouraging supporter and advisor. But I wasn't as thrilled as she about my meeting to reconvene the Royal Council today.

I drew a deep breath as Jennah and I passed through the halls and up the spiraling staircases of the castle. Endless stone corridors, richly carpeted rooms, grand windows with breathtaking views of the gardens and sea, and dozens upon dozens of paintings and statues and tapestries commemorating Misroth's history—they all whirled by in a maze I could have walked with my eyes closed. When we entered my chambers, two servants were already laying out a gown the royal seamstress had prepared for the occasion. They glanced up at me expectantly, but I waved them away.

"That will be all, thank you," I said. The headache forming in my temples was growing more relentless, more insistent.

"It's beautiful," Jennah murmured, running the skirt's silken folds through her fingers.

Pressing my lips together, I studied the dress carefully spread across my bedcovers. It was scarlet, its flared sleeves accented with small jewels that cast small glimmers of light along the walls. The bodice was fitted and overlaid with silver lace; the skirt hung in loose folds that shimmered with further hints of silver—more lace or jewels or perhaps elegant embroidery, I could not tell. I didn't want to look and suppressed the urge to cringe.

Jennah spun toward me with a smile. "Now you can finally set that old dress aside."

"Yes," I said, turning away as I bunched folds of my wool skirt in my hands. It was travel-stained and faded, an old brown dress Lyanna had made for me. I had few possessions from Evren to hold on to, and I longed for even these simple reminders of the family and friends I'd left behind. Though I knew I had no choice, I was afraid if I discarded my old clothes for all the new castle attire the seamstress was preparing, the servants would burn them or use them as rags.

This isn't a time to be sentimental. Drawing a deep breath, I nodded. "I will change." I snatched the gown from the bed before Jennah could protest and dashed toward my dressing chamber.

"Do you want help...?" Jennah called hesitantly.

I repressed an urge to laugh aloud. Help? I'd lived as a commoner only a few years of my life, and I'd felt more comfortable then than I'd ever had within the castle walls. If only she knew how much I longed to return to that life now, as the Misrothian people turned to me in anticipation and hope. "I'm fine," I murmured instead.

The dress was as heavy as I'd imagined, but to the seamstress's credit, it fit perfectly, and the material was soft against my skin. And politically, to be attired in Misroth's colors—well, I hoped I would make the impression I strove to make with the Royal Council, because I knew what

I had to say was going to stir their anger. Drawing as deep of a breath as I could in my fitted bodice, I walked back toward my bedchamber and quirked an eyebrow at Jennah.

Jennah set her hands on her hips. "I was right. You look stunning." She smiled. "Like a princess."

I relaxed my shoulders somewhat and stepped forward, trying to ignore the way the dress swished along the floorboards around my feet. After years of sword practice and archery with Avrik in simple, more loose-fitting attire that let me move as I needed, it was hard to feel comfortable in a dress that restricted me. Even if my fight was over—for now.

"Good," I said, "then they will listen to me."

Jennah's gaze was level yet piercing, as if she were looking into my head and assessing my thoughts. "You are their leader; they will listen to you no matter what. You are the one who should be dead, if not for the Life-Giver's blessing. Have the people not sought blessings from our god all this time? To see one of their own, a member of the royal family, receiving his blessing and offering them freedom again as King Eldon did… It means something."

I caught a glimpse of myself in the floor-length mirror on the opposite wall and paused. My green eyes and dark hair were so like my mother's, but my jawline and stern expression were more my father's, traits that I could use to give me his same commanding appearance, if I wanted to. "Gillen is their rightful leader," I said.

In the mirror, Jennah's reflection was visible over my shoulder. Her eyebrow rose in understanding. "You mean to find him," she said. "You called this meeting to inform the Council or to seek its blessing." Her brow furrowed and she shook her head. "Ele—Halia, please reconsider. Misrothians will look to you during this time. You must be crowned queen regent in Gillen's absence and help the kingdom recover."

I tugged on the sleeve of my dress and stared down at my feet. "My aunt can do all of this in my absence."

"She is royalty by marriage only…"

"She is as capable as anyone. More capable than I am, certainly." I fidgeted with the folds of my skirt before I caught myself and stopped. "Trust me, Jennah, I've considered all of this. I know the objections that will be made. But if I don't go"—I struggled not to choke on the words—"if I send others in my place while I sit in the safety of this castle… I cannot do it. I can't leave him again."

Jennah's eyes met mine in the mirror and for several long seconds we said nothing. Determination spread across her face and her eyes sparkled with defiance. "If you go, I go with you."

"What about your daughters?"

"If this is for the kingdom's safety, it is for theirs." Jennah saluted. "Please grant me this. Let me stay by your side to protect you."

I hesitated, studying her strong features, her tall, slender form. A woman of Alrenian heritage with a warrior's heart would surely be an asset, but I hated to risk her safety and tear her apart from her family again. The jagged scar tracing her cheek, pale white against her dark complexion, reminded me of how much she had already given. But who was I to tell her no?

"If this is what you want," I sighed, "I will not say no. But do what is best for you and your family, not me. Think of them and then make your final decision."

Jennah lifted her chin. "I already have. I'll speak with my husband, but I know he'll see my point. It's too soon for him to travel again, when he's still recovering, and he's been away from our daughters all this time."

Bowing my head, I nodded.

Distant tolling marked the hour, and I jerked upright, straightening my back and holding my head high. It was time to meet with the Royal Council.

I leaned back in my seat, staring at the mahogany columns, carved in intricate vines and flowers and stretching up to a ceiling painted in dozens of scenes portraying Misroth's history. Looking up from the columns, I fixed my gaze on King Eldon, his stern countenance and fiery blue eyes staring back at me as he lifted his sword against Alrenor's armies and began the war that brought us independence from the old Alrenian Empire.

Sighing, I glanced around. To my left, a long table polished until it gleamed in the flickering light of the multiple chandeliers and candle sconces spaced about the room. It held enough papers and pens for me to sign a hundred proclamations into effect that day.

"Your Highness." Councilor Veren's voice cut into my reverie.

My eyes snapped to the old man's face. He and the other nine councilors were standing before a semicircle of hard-backed armchairs facing mine.

"We are honored that you have summoned us to reconvene," he continued, "but we must request that you explain your intentions in the wake of your father's death. It is our recommendation that you announce your intention to take the throne as soon as possible." He cleared his throat. "We understand that you are not yet quite of age, but we believe, given the circumstances, that an exception may be made. As…thrilled as the kingdom may be, it will soon fall into chaos if order is not restored."

Setting my jaw, I glanced down at my hands, folded carefully in my lap. With a deep breath I lifted my eyes to gaze at the councilmen. "The council may be seated," I said, and the men sank into their seats. "Thank you for your advice, Councilor Veren. However, I invited you here today for a different proposal." I forced my voice to remain steady. Though raised as a royal, I had never been groomed to lead a kingdom, and it had been a long while since any woman had led Misroth. I knew every one of these councilors would be watching me closely, waiting for me to make a mistake, waiting for me to reveal myself as weak-minded, ignorant, and naïve. Because I was a woman. Because I was my father's daughter, and I knew none of them fully trusted me yet, despite the sacrifices I'd made.

The men said nothing, shifting in their seats impatiently as they waited for me to continue.

"As you are all aware, King Regent Zarev took the throne from his elder brother after murdering him, on the pretense of ruling in Gillen's stead, until Gillen came of age. However, before Gillen came of age, Zarev sent him away, presumably to war." I sat up as straight and tall as I could, lifting my chin and staring each in the face in turn. "Gillen is the rightful king of Misroth."

Councilor Byor raised shaggy eyebrows. "But—"

Councilor Veren cleared his throat. "Your Majesty—"

"Don't call me by that title," I cut in. "I am not your queen, nor will I ever be. There will be no preparations, no coronation ceremony. Do not pretend to be dismayed by this. I know the only reason most of you want me here is because you hope a female ruler will be easily manipulated and let you hold sway over the kingdom."

Murmurs echoed throughout the room. They hadn't expected someone so blunt. They didn't know I was gifted with the truth, that even now my mind was flooded with clarifying visions that let me see into their private meetings held in the days before. They didn't know that I'd already understood the way they operated, that as a child I'd observed the Council meetings my uncle had invited my cousin and I to a lot more closely than they had realized. I knew these men, but they did not know me.

I pressed on, despite their murmurings. "You know as well as I, thanks to messengers to and from Argelon and many other secrets brought to light over these past several days, that Zarev lied to us about the war against Alrenor. I have learned that Gillen was sent into Toryn under the pretense of forming an alliance, and it is my understanding that he is in grave danger. Therefore, Velaire will rule for her son until his return. And I will depart to find him, to bring the true king of Misroth back to our kingdom."

"This is madness!" Councilor Lurok shouted. "You reconvened the

Royal Council for our advice, not to inform us that you will be abandoning our kingdom to disorder."

I forced my voice to remain smooth. "I reconvened the Council to keep you and the rest of the kingdom informed in this time of uncertainty. How would you propose to go against my decision? Will you imprison me in the castle walls? Compel me to accept the crown?" I stared openly at each councilor's face, studying their anger and fear and weighing my options. Did I outrage them further by revealing the remainder of my plan, or risk their wrath anyway by keeping it secret? As much as these men and their pretense disgusted me, I knew I should attempt to mollify them, for the kingdom's sake. They stared down at their feet, seething but quieted.

"I have made my choice with the people of Misroth in mind," I said firmly. "And," I drew a deep breath, glancing at the rebel guards stationed at the doorway and nodding to them, "I will be accompanied on my travels by the man closest in my father's counsel, a man who can help lead me to Gillen."

The men, still breathlessly quiet, glanced at each other. I could imagine their thoughts: the Council had been disbanded and no royal advisors had been kept close to the king or made privy to his secrets. Anyone who had been loyal to my father had been imprisoned, awaiting trial, or had gone into hiding. *Who?* If they hadn't been afraid to mutter, to sound like they were questioning me, the words would have fallen from their lips.

To our right, the guards pulled open the doors, their hinges creaking as they swung inward. In the doorway, outlined by the afternoon light, framed by two rebels, stood Narek, former Captain of the Royal Guard.

CHAPTER TWO

NAREK'S FACE WAS SMUDGED, HIS once impeccably clean and straight uniform disheveled. His short-cropped hair was unruly, greasy tufts curling near his ears and standing in tousled waves along his forehead. But when his black eyes found mine, they flickered with his usual confidence and a hint of amusement. As if this were all a game to him.

My pulse throbbed a warning in my ears, but I quelled my rising discomfort even as the councilmen leapt to their feet, crying out in anger.

"What is the meaning of this?" Councilor Veren shouted, his face red with rage. All pretense of respect had disintegrated.

The Royal Council turned wide, suspicious eyes toward me, but I refused to let my gaze waver. "Narek was Captain of the Guard under my father's reign and was deeply involved in many of his plans. He has information about Gillen and will help me find him."

Councilor Lurok pinched his lips together, barely concealing the trembling in his limbs. "Your Highness," he said, bowing his head rigidly and forcing his voice to sound steady, "this is unwise. This man should be returned to the dungeons—sent back to await his trial for the crimes he committed against our people."

I kept my voice even and cool. "I do not disagree with you. However, we must set Misroth's *true* king on the throne, and Narek can help me do that.”

“What if you never return? What if our land falls into chaos?” Councilor Emren was the youngest man in the group, his dark hair unmarked by grey, his eyes keen, and his body still strong next to the watery-eyed, withered men beside him.

I rose, forcing the few councilmen who had reseated themselves to follow suit. “Then perhaps you will find a king amongst our nobility—or yourselves.” Glancing over my shoulder, I saw some of the councilors’ eyes light up at my last words, as I’d hoped they would.

“We are not done here,” Councilor Veren said, his voice low and dangerously insolent. “This Council will not accept your alliance with an enemy of our kingdom without some indication that you are not a traitor yourself!”

I was halfway to the door when his words enveloped me, and I was tempted to storm out, leaving without their blessing. No part of me wanted this responsibility or their false allegiance. But I needed to keep my people’s welfare in mind.

Turning slowly, I kept my eyes narrow but my anger in check. “Councilor Veren, need I remind you that I have reconvened the Council after my father destroyed it, *and* refused the crown he stole? You have no proof that I crave the power he had. I’ve imprisoned his men, including Narek, and releasing him from his cell does *not* mean he is no longer my prisoner.”

“The people are restless and afraid,” Councilor Lurok replied, keeping his eyes low in reverence, his hands trembling visibly. He was nervous, not humble. “You cannot leave on this mission when our kingdom is vulnerable like this. Ugomath Prison is filled with men loyal to your father, but there are easily more still free, still threatening our kingdom’s safety. The throne is vacant, and many thirst for power. If you leave, we could fall to anarchy. To terror. The people see you as their savior, the one who defeated their tyrant. They chant your name; they call for *you*. You must give them…something.”

My gaze was steady. "I am not done in Misroth just yet. Velaire was your queen once, and as mother of the true king, she will be a suitable regent, someone the people can look to for security and hope. But until she is well enough, I will remain here and make decisions for my people, decisions that will start with justice for us all." I turned away again, weary. "You are dismissed." My eyes met the guards' impassive expressions. "Take Narek to his new chambers—ensure we have a constant watch and he's escorted everywhere."

Narek smirked, but I left the room before his expression could unnerve me.

Restless, I paced the length of the castle walkway—a long, narrow corridor on the first level lined with dozens of windows affording a view of the grounds. Evening had turned the sky red as blood and set fire to the snowy earth. Red and orange hues glinted off icicles hanging from tree branches and burned my eyes. Amongst the harsh expressions of chiseled statues and barren earth, a few hardy flowers poked their heads: sythrel nearly lost amongst the snow, silver-gilded velaire, and blue embyth.

From here, the Alrenian was not visible, but even within the castle I could hear its distant roar. I closed my eyes and leaned my forehead against the nearest windowpane, feeling the cold glass against my skin. How many times had Gillen and I walked past these windows, our shadows stretching along the polished floor as we discussed what our tutors had taught us, how we imagined life away from the responsibilities of the castle? Sometimes we had stopped to peer out at the grounds and Gillen would point out different wildlife, squirrels darting through the garden or birds lighting on nearby branches, and ask me why the Life-Giver created such beauty if it was a distraction, as the priests insisted it was.

Gillen, with his good heart, was in the land of our enemies now. *Because of me. Because I left him behind. Because I never returned for him, never warned him about my father.*

Footsteps echoed behind me and I jerked back from the window.

"Apologies, my lady…" Layk, my friend and fellow member of the rebellion, stood behind me, his posture set in the rigid stance of a guard. As one of the few rebels officially trained to guard, I had given him the unofficial title of captain. Despite his usual confidence, he seemed uneasy as his bright blue eyes scanned my face. "Narek insisted on seeing you. We've escorted him to you…but we will send him away at your command…"

I looked over his shoulder at three more approaching figures and shook my head. "I'll speak with him."

And then Narek was before me once more. Freshly cleaned and in new attire, a plain white shirt and brown trousers, he still carried himself like a guard. Stopping a few yards away, he pried himself free of the guards to press a hand to his chest. His lips curled in a smirk and I swallowed my anger.

I nodded to the guards beside Narek. "You may leave us," I said.

"But, princess, you said he is to be guarded…" Layk protested.

"You may stay."

He settled himself next to me, shuffling his feet uncomfortably as the other men saluted and left. Narek raised his eyebrows.

"Why are you here?" I demanded.

"If you hope to find your cousin alive, I suggest we leave as soon as possible…princess," Narek said.

I noticed the sidelong glance Layk cast in my direction and I averted my gaze.

"I agree." I turned to stare out the window again, in the direction I knew the sea was. A memory flashed through my mind: a black night, rough waves, the open maw of the sea rising to envelope me forever. My breath caught in my throat, but I forced the words from my mouth. "We will sail for Toryn as soon as my aunt is well enough to lead in my stead."

"No, we must head for the Vorvinian Mountains. It is our surest path into Toryn."

I hated to travel by water, but I hated to delay finding Gillen more. "But the sea is the most direct route to Calidar," I protested. "Why would we waste time?"

Narek raised his eyebrows. "Who says he has even made it into Calidar? Your father sent the prince and his men into Toryn on foot to…as he said, disguise Gillen's identity."

I crossed my arms, my suspicions flaring. "But you said he traveled to Toryn under the guise of creating an alliance."

"Yes, and your father suggested that he shouldn't announce his heritage right away." Narek smirked. "He claimed he wanted your cousin to meet with the people on his journeys throughout Toryn and reveal who he was only after establishing some level of trust with the people. Gillen traversed the Vorvinian Mountains and was likely killed somewhere in northern Toryn."

I bit back my retort. In my mind's eye, I could see the vision I'd had of my cousin more than once: a dark night full of men cowering before a swamp. Irevek Swamp was in northern Toryn, not toward the southern regions of the kingdom where Calidar lay.

"Besides, if you fear the Toryn people are hostile toward Misroth, do you expect they would let you make port near the capital? We could enter their kingdom unmolested and begin our search without the Toryn knowing of our presence." A slow smile crept across his lips. "Or are you afraid to take the path that leads through Evren Forest?" His eyes were like onyx, gleaming with mirth in the fading light. He could have been handsome, if I hadn't wanted to kill him.

Drawing a deep breath, I stepped closer, staring up into his face. "If you lead me astray, you'll wish you had remained a prisoner here," I snapped.

A smile flashed across Narek's face. "There is the queen I pledged my service to."

I curled my fingers into fists. "You pledged nothing."

Narek cocked his head to the side. "You could say I made a pledge to you in blood when I slew your father. But, however you choose to see it, my helping you find your cousin does secure my freedom, even temporarily."

"You are still a prisoner. Do not count on any freedom." I paused, again thinking of my vision of Gillen and the creatures that lurked in Toryn, creatures that had somehow, at least for the most part, not entered Misroth. "If you were so deep in my father's counsel, then what of the rumors about the borders?"

"About King Eldon's barrier around Misroth?"

Not trusting my voice to hold steady, I nodded.

"Why would your father share information about King Eldon with me? If the barrier somehow does exist, it must be a well-kept secret indeed."

I watched him narrowly, wishing my gift for truth would operate on my command. "How can I trust anything you say?"

He ran a finger along his jawline, scratching at the stubble there. "I have as much of a desire to be trapped within Toryn amongst its horrors as you do, my lady. As I said, I only want to earn my freedom, even temporarily." He shrugged his shoulders casually, but I couldn't shake my unease that he was withholding information. There was something else motivating him beyond an effort to save his own life, I was sure of it.

Trying to erase the memories of my visions, I approached the window to gaze at the soft evening light and the beauty of the gardens, even in winter. If only the beauty in the world could erase its ugliness forever. "If you don't believe Gillen is in Calidar," I said at last, turning back to Narek, "and you truly expect the Toryn people will be hostile toward us, we will head for the mountains. We will follow in Gillen's footsteps until we find him."

Narek flashed me another smile. "I think we can safely assume the people of Toryn despise Misroth. Two hundred years is a long time for ire to grow, and according to history, the Toryn weren't overjoyed that King Eldon closed the borders of Misroth and refused to aid them in their own revolt against Alrenor. It's doubtful they have forgotten."

I flicked my eyes toward Layk, and I could see the questions dancing in his eyes, all the words he longed to say. "You can escort Narek back to his chambers," I said, and swept out of the hall.

The vision struck suddenly as I was climbing one of the staircases leading to my chambers. Head reeling, I stumbled to the landing and pressed against the wall to try to keep myself on my feet. The cool stone was firm beneath my cheek as I stared at the torches flickering in their sconces over my head. Then the castle vanished, and I was immersed in a black night.

It was the same vision that haunted me in both my sleeping and waking hours: a cold, starless night filled with the screams of Gillen's dying companions as an unseen predator attacked from the sky. This time I felt even more physically present in the vision than ever before. The tall grass rustled around me, brushing against my cheeks and arms as I threw myself to the earth and pressed into the dirt, willing myself to become invisible. Overhead the heavy beat of wings pulsed through the air, drowned out only by the screams. As the ground beneath me grew soggy and the scent of blood filled my nostrils, I squeezed my eyes shut and clamped my teeth together to block out the world and prevent myself from screaming.

A hand grasped my shoulder and I opened my eyes. I was back in the castle with the concerned face of a servant girl peering down at me. When had I fallen to the floor?

"Are you all right, princess?" the girl asked, her eyes wide. When I jerked away, she pulled her hand back and fidgeted with the folds of her dress.

I blinked, assuring myself the castle walls weren't about to disappear again. Slowly, I stood and brushed at my gown. "Yes…I—I'm fine," I said. "Thank you."

"Should I summon the Royal Healer?" the girl asked doubtfully.

"No, I'm not ill."

She continued to stare at me for a moment until I became uncomfortable.

"You may be on your way."

As if recollecting herself, she straightened hastily and pressed a fist over her heart. "Yes, princess," she murmured, and was gone in an instant, her hasty footsteps echoing behind her.

Breathing deeply, I pressed my forehead against the wall to reassure myself everything around me was still solid. *It was only a vision.* Yet the men's screams continued to resonate in my ears; the scent of blood was still fresh in my nose. *How many have already died?*

I refused to entertain the possibility that Gillen could be one of the fatalities, that my coming journey could already be in vain.

I wasn't surprised when Jennah knocked on my door later that evening, accompanied by Layk and Gare. Seated in the private study adjoining my bedchamber and dressing room, I called for them to enter. They filed in and watched me silently from my position by the fire, where I was huddled in an armchair with one hand clutching Lyanna's sprig of dried lavender. As soon as I bid them to sit, Jennah sank into a chair beside mine, but Layk and Gare clustered before the mantel so they could face me.

"I assume you are here because you're unhappy with my decision to leave," I said. I stared down at the lavender. I knew my chambers were high enough within the castle that if I crossed the room to peer through the window overlooking the grounds, I would be able to catch a glimpse of the sea far below. Although my windows were closed tight against the cold, I could still smell the Alrenian's briny scent clinging to everything, a scent that both reminded me of happier days and nightmares, a scent that now felt heavy and suffocating. I wished the lavender's aroma could drown out that of the sea.

Gare dipped his head. "We are here, princess, to offer our companionship on your journey."

I lifted my eyes to him, unable to conceal my surprise.

"You need guards to ensure Narek does not fall out of line." Layk said his former captain's name with a growl.

Jennah smiled at me softly. "We have already faced impossible odds undertaking bold—even foolhardy—tasks. You said yes to me. Don't deny them the chance to risk their lives for their kingdom again."

"Benor would be here too," Gare added, "but his wife has fallen ill and we all agreed his place is by her side."

"The Council felt that I was abandoning Misroth," I said after a long moment. "But Gillen is the rightful king. He was trained all his life to take the throne, and he is like his father: he is kind and wise and prepared to make sacrifices for his people. And his mother is more fit to rule as regent than I am." I sighed, my gaze flitting to each of my friends in turn. "I cannot ask anyone else to make this journey unless I'm willing to go myself. I won't abandon my cousin again."

"I do not understand the risk, if the war was a farce," Gare said. "Do you believe the Alrenians hold your cousin hostage?"

I repressed a shudder. "I've seen visions," I murmured, drawing a deep breath. I wondered if they would begin to think I was mad now. "Like Marke, I have a gift from the Life-Giver, only mine reveals the truth in visions. Those I've had of Gillen are all nightmarish. He's in Toryn, a land Narek said is overrun with creatures from the Wastelands, monsters like the sedwa…and—and worse." I gulped, trying to repress the memory of the shadowy vision and the screams that continued to haunt me, day and night.

"It's true I cannot do this alone," I continued, "but from what I have seen, Gillen could be the last surviving member of his company. I don't know if I only see visions of the past, or if they could sometimes be of the future. All I know is that their journey has become, or is doomed to be, a bloodbath." I paused, drawing a breath. "There is also the chance, even if we survive the dangers of the land itself, that we cannot leave it. I do not believe in the rumors about Eldon's barrier, but it is a risk we must all weigh in our considerations. I want you to understand what you would be going into."

Studying each of my friends in turn, I tried to weigh the fear in their eyes against the courage.

But they hadn't seen what I'd seen.

Jennah's lip quirked slightly. "What do we have to fear when we have the invincible princess on our side?" She winked at me.

Gare shifted on his feet, almost as if he were impatient to be on his way already. "I am a soldier untested in true war. Perhaps this is to be my war, not that skirmish we had with your father and his men."

Layk's face was still solemn, set apart from the more lighthearted attitudes of his friends. "I know now that the Giver of Life protects you and that you can hold your own in a fight, but that doesn't mean you don't need help to keep you safe. Someone must defend you from that wretched excuse of a guard," he said fiercely, his blue eyes flashing.

I wasn't sure if I felt more relieved or troubled. I'd planned to recruit rebels without loved ones depending on them to return home—not Jennah with her husband and daughters, Layk with his younger brother and sister, and Gare with his wife and son. Yet it was comforting to think I'd be with friends.

If I agreed, what regrets would I face later? How many times in the future would I wish to return to this moment and refuse to let them join me?

I inhaled deeply, hoping I was making the right choice. "You may come," I said.

Gare shot me a toothy grin. "Good," he replied, "because we wouldn't have accepted no for an answer. You won't rid yourself of us so easily!" He chuckled before remembering himself. "Princess," he added with a quick salute.

Smirking, I shook my head. "Don't be so formal around me. We are still friends. And princess or not, I am still Elena." I fingered the lavender in my hand once again, breathing in its scent and remembering my home in Evren.

Gare's brow furrowed in disagreement. "You are much more than that, my lady."

CHAPTER THREE

WEIGHED DOWN BY THE HORROR of my visions and the hopes of an entire kingdom, it was hard to find sleep that night. I lay in bed wishing myself back in my room in Evren with Rev's gentle snoring in my ears, but instead I listened to the guards' pacing outside my door while watching dark shadows linger in the corners of my too-spacious chamber.

It was too easy to recall my mother's face in this castle, her soft words and careful glances toward my father, always eager to please, always quick to apologize when he rebuked her. It was too easy to remember the way I'd also bent myself willingly to my father's will, craving his rare smiles of approval so much I would have forgotten my own desires if not for Gillen. Gillen was the one who helped me continue to dream, to disobey even in small ways by sneaking away from lessons or teaching me to swim, a skill that my father deemed unladylike for royal women. The memories were vivid and painful now: our laughter as we'd chased each other along the shoreline, splashing one another until we were both soaked; his encouragement and pride when I outshot him during one of our archery lessons; our secretive, knowing glances when we passed notes and planned to steal away from our tutors and our dull studies.

Slipping from bed, I pushed a wave of hair from my cheek and brushed aside the heavy curtain covering one of my windows. Starlight made the Alrenian's churning, distant waves look silver and mysterious. Dark clouds hovered on the distant horizon, suggesting an impending storm.

Who would I have become without Gillen? Would I have ever had the strength to stand against my father, if not for my cousin's influence when we were children?

I will find you, I thought into the night.

Hearing a floorboard creak behind me, I spun on my heel, all senses alert. A knife flashed through the air and hurtled toward my face. I dove for the floor, reaching for my bow where it lay beside my bed. As the knife thudded into the wall, I hazarded a glimpse up toward my attacker. Almost concealed in shadow, a figure in dark clothes leered toward me.

He was swift. Before I could nock an arrow to my bow, he was upon me, slicing with another knife. I clutched his arm mid-swing and grunted against the solid muscle bearing down on me. Hair clung to my sweaty neck and my breath hitched in my throat. I felt my arm waver and weaken. The man pulled away from me and tried to swing again, but I kicked him hard in the shin, thrusting him off balance, if even for a moment. A moment was all I needed.

I strung an arrow to my bow, aiming the point straight for my attacker's chest. "Stop or I'll shoot!"

"You'll execute me anyway," the man snarled, and flung his weapon at my head.

I dropped backward, away from his blade, and shot. His knife nicked my forehead and clattered to the floor, but my arrow struck his heart. He toppled forward and fell in his own blood at my feet.

Shaking, I stared down at the body, then looked away. Squeezing my eyes shut, I tried to block out the image of the blood splattering my bedroom floor, but it seemed imprinted in my mind.

"Princess!" Layk's voice rang out over his pounding footsteps outside my door. An instant later he flung it open, his bow in hand while his wide eyes scanned the room to find me standing and wiping the blood trickling toward my eyes. Gare and Jennah ran up behind him and breathlessly peered over his shoulder, their faces pale, their blades drawn.

"Are you all right?" Layk demanded.

Panting, I nodded.

Layk stepped in quickly, ushering the others in behind him, and closed the door.

"Some of your men are restraining assassins who infiltrated the castle and killed some guards. Including the men posted outside your door," he added somberly. "I would like to hope there are no other attackers lingering in the castle, but until we can be sure they've all been caught, you should not be alone."

Raising my eyebrows, I glanced at the body lying on my floor.

Gare's smile was warm and proud. "As capable as you are, it is our honor to protect you."

Jennah strode forward, sheathing her dagger as she approached. "Let's clean the blood from your face and bandage that wound," she said.

"It's nothing," I protested.

"Still." She set a hand on her hip.

Within moments she had filled a basin with water and gathered a cloth, aluera—a cleansing medicine—and some bandages from the washroom adjoining my bedchamber. She guided me to the chair at my dressing table and began dabbing gently at my forehead to clean away the blood before applying the aluera, which stung until my eyes began to water.

"How did these men manage to infiltrate the castle anyway?" Jennah asked, her eyes flitting over to Layk.

"Most of the rebel volunteers aren't trained guards and are still unfamiliar with the castle layout." Layk hesitated. "These attackers…they are trained men who know their way around these hallways. Some of my more capable men fended off a few of the attackers; I heard them on my rounds and ran to help. But once noise broke out they had the upper hand. More guards arrived, and I left to find you." He smiled and turned to me. "Jennah and Gare heard the fighting break out as well and joined me." His smile faded. "We didn't know what we would find—any number of men could have made it to your rooms, considering how many were scattered about the castle."

"The attackers are probably former guards of my father's," I said as Jennah wrapped the bandage around my head.

Gare's face was solemn. "Who is to say how many men served your father loyally and are still free, wishing you harm?"

"I imagine half this city wishes me harm," I muttered.

Jennah cocked an eyebrow at me.

"The people are afraid and have every right to be suspicious of my motives for returning to Misroth City and overthrowing my father's rule. The Royal Council hates me and would eagerly claim an opportunity to gain power." I shrugged. "There is chaos everywhere, and when it is common knowledge that most of the *trained* guards have been imprisoned, I am vulnerable to anyone who wants to try for the throne."

"Perhaps many do wish you harm," Gare agreed slowly, crossing his thick arms across his chest, "but there are also a great many who look to you as their hero. They chant your name in the streets. They tell stories to their children of the girl who died and came back to life. You are a living legend to them, more revered and miraculous than King Eldon himself."

I shuddered at his words. "I do not want this responsibility."

"This attack will only instill more fear and uncertainty in the people." Layk's cool eyes watched me steadily, his fingers fastened securely on his bow. "It will be a difficult time to leave Misroth when they are clinging to you so desperately."

"There will be unrest whether I stay or go, but the only choice for me is to go," I said firmly.

"Yes, but will they let you go peacefully?"

I frowned at the empty hearth in the corner opposite me. "If they truly revere me so much, they will respect my decisions as their…temporary ruler."

Layk nodded slowly.

Gare winked. "And if they do not respect your decisions, we will help them to."

As the night drew on, falling quiet around us, Gare and Layk lifted the body and carried it from my chambers, dropping it unceremoniously in the hallway. Jennah scrubbed the blood from my floor with a restless energy that made me think she had to keep her hands busy for her own peace of mind. I turned away from these sights, trying to forget the fact that I had just killed a man.

My friends and I gathered in my private sitting room, clustering together on the settee and overstuffed chairs. Gare started a fire and with a grin, turned to Jennah and requested a song. In my friends' cheering company, I felt the tightness in my chest slowly ease away.

We spent the remainder of the night there, waiting for dawn to creep in through the curtains. Layk and Gare took turns pacing my chambers, peering out the windows, or listening at the doors. Jennah sang us songs in the New Language as well as Alrenian, happily translating those in the forbidden tongue for us when we asked. Gare and Layk took turns telling us about their training regimens for their positions as soldier and guard, pointing out differences and similarities in their experiences. As the hours slipped away and the threat vanished, sleepiness stole over me again.

At last, a knock at the door jolted me fully awake. Jennah paused mid-song.

"Your Highness?"

Layk answered the door, opening it to two rebel guards.

"All of the men have been caught and imprisoned in the castle cells." The man saluted.

"And the castle has been searched?"

The man gave a single nod. "Not a sign of any others. We've captured them all."

"For now," Layk said under his breath.

"Thank you," I said.

The guard saluted again. "We await your sentencing of the attackers. They will be closely guarded until then." He and his companion left swiftly, leaving me to stare down at my hands.

I knew what I had to do.

A brisk wind swirled my cloak and skirt about my ankles as my boots thudded a steady rhythm on the cobblestone street. Once again I was clothed in red. The color of blood, of justice, of damnation. The air about me was unnaturally silent, as if the entirety of the city, perhaps even the whole kingdom, was holding its breath and watching me. I passed the row of new members of the Royal Guard, including Layk, and gave them a brief nod to acknowledge their salutes. Beyond them stood the Royal Councilmen in their finest garb, their fur-lined cloaks billowing about them as they pressed reluctant fists to their hearts and watched me with uncertain eyes.

My shoulders tensed and an uncomfortable weight settled in my stomach, but my body easily remembered the lessons my parents and tutor had given me. With my eyes straight ahead, never wavering, and my steps sure, I kept my mouth quirked in a confident look that was not quite a smile for this solemn occasion, yet far from a frown. Misroth would not see me falter. I was not their true leader, not the one they desperately needed, but for this short time I would offer the sense of security they craved. I owed them this.

Just as I had on the day my father tried to kill me, I climbed the scaffold's steps with steady feet. The executioner, a rebel man who had stepped forward so willingly for the job that I'd almost refused him, shifted back and forth on his feet, slowly swinging the axe from hand to hand. I felt small gazing down at the citizens staring up at me, their pale faces and wide eyes reminding me of children. These were grown men and women, some who had weathered far more seasons than I, watching me with hope and awe—even reverence. A chill crept along my arms. I was not a savior, only a fortunate soul saved by the Life-Giver when I should have died.

"Citizens of Misroth!" My voice echoed throughout the town square. I hesitated, studying the faces before me. An elderly woman nodded her head slowly, her lips moving as if in silent prayer. A broad-shouldered man stood with arms crossed, anger furrowing his brow while he scanned the row of men gathered beside the scaffold. The Royal Councilors' faces were composed, set into expressions of regard that only I knew were disgustingly false.

"You have suffered too long under tyranny and injustice." I raised my voice, sharing in the emotions I saw written across the people's countenances. Though I was not accustomed to these sorts of speeches, I could speak the truth, so that was just what I would do. "You have been deceived and manipulated, maimed and bereaved, ill-used and terrorized. A member of your own royal family betrayed you and his own blood, and we have all paid too high a price."

Murmuring erupted amongst the crowd. More heads nodded. I could almost smell their rising indignation and lust for vengeance.

I lifted my hand to call for quiet and just as quickly as the noise had risen, the crowd fell still. "But we are not ruled by cruelty and barbarism, as my father was. Our kingdom's long era of peace was born because our people chose to be free of a harsh and greedy empire. My father thirsted for power and blood; he gained his position and his following through murder and deceit." I drew a breath and shouted, "We seek justice!" The crowd responded with uplifted arms and shouts of their own.

"These men attempted to assassinate me and have confessed their loyalty to Zarev," I continued, gesturing toward the shackled men guarded by my rebels. "For their crimes, they are condemned to death."

Cheers erupted around me.

"Anyone still loyal to Zarev and his tyranny is a threat to our kingdom and will be punished!"

Even the councilors were applauding and throwing their fists in the air, making an appropriate display of enthusiasm. They could approve my choice this time, but since I had made the decision without their counsel, I knew I had hardly gained their goodwill.

Good, I thought. *Let those power-hungry fools remember their places.*

As I descended the platform and took my place in front of the Royal Council, surrounded by guards, more of my men jostled the prisoners up the steps. The weight in my stomach felt like a fist now, squeezing ever tighter.

Cold morning sunlight glinted off the executioner's axe as he adjusted its weight on his shoulder and shuffled forward. The prisoners were shoved to their knees and laid on the chopping blocks. A hush washed over the square. My hands were clammy; my shoulders so taut that I could feel Layk's eyes drift in a sideways glance toward me as he noticed my discomfort. I stiffened more and clasped my hands, refusing to let my gaze wander from the prisoners. Royalty always unflinchingly watched the punishments they pronounced.

From this angle, I couldn't see the men's expressions as they died. The axe fell once, twice, seven times with a dull thud and a nauseating amount of blood. My men caught the heads in baskets. I bit my tongue and tasted blood. The citizens of Misroth cheered. To them, this was vengeance; to the rebels surrounding me, this was justice.

But to me, it was more bloodshed.

The next three weeks passed slowly. Layk, Gare, or Jennah were constantly at my side now, taking turns to watch my surroundings and anticipate any new threats, even though I already had several rebel guards in rotation to protect me. Layk and I personally interviewed and selected guards to watch over Velaire, both now and in our absence, to ensure we could trust them. I could not live with myself if I left my aunt, and therefore, my people, in unsafe hands.

Each night my sleep was interrupted with nightmares and the sounds of guards pacing outside my bedroom. Each day I filled with countless meetings and efforts to revoke Zarev's laws, and each evening I visited Velaire, reading her books or reminiscing with her about better days, when Gillen and I were children and Reylon was alive.

Over this time, I found dozens of instances in which all evidence pointed to Narek telling the truth: the war had been fabricated by my father. Men in my father's custody had been framed as foreign spies with falsified Alrenian documents, a general visiting from Argelon admitted he knew the war was a lie, and I came across correspondences in my father's personal study from other members of the army that validated this story even further. My father and his loyalists had carefully crafted false evidence and rumors of war that had robbed the kingdom through steep taxes and sewn fear throughout the people. It had been the perfect excuse to steal young men away from families to be indoctrinated in Zarev's army and to let additional guards and even soldiers stalk city streets throughout Misroth, enforcing the law.

More men were imprisoned as this evidence came to light, some to be questioned further, some to be promptly executed. I met with the Royal Council more times than I ever wanted to see those pompous old men in my life. For the most part, I politely ignored their recommendations. I stormed Ugomath Prison with Layk and other trusted rebels and released innocent men and women my father had imprisoned and tortured. I revoked Zarev's curfews and lowered the exorbitant taxes he had set. Night upon night I sat in my father's study, shivering against the cold and against the discomfort I felt there, as if his ghost lingered in the shadows. For long hours I pored over documents and books and searched for journals, sure there would be so much more to learn about him and his deceit. Perhaps his exact plans and methods to poison and murder my uncle. Or maybe information about Toryn, where he'd sent my cousin to fight his false war.

But it was impossible to sort through and read everything in his study in the short time I had, and I could hardly undo all my father's wrongs in a few weeks. So I did what I could, knowing Velaire would continue my work once I left.

On the evening before we were set to depart, we held a ball to celebrate Velaire's recovery and Misroth's restored freedom. Only a regent who was expected to hold the throne for a period of years required an official coronation ceremony; for Velaire, who we hoped would only wait a few months for her son's return, a royal ball would be enough.

"How many potential suitors do you think I will dance with tonight?" I said, rolling my eyes as Jennah finished lacing the bodice of my gown.

Her laugh was light as she stepped round to face me, her curls dancing loosely about her face. She was clothed in a scarlet dress that complemented her dark complexion and would remind the nobility in attendance tonight of her prominent position in the rebellion. "Well, you certainly look royal now."

She spun me to face my mirror. Servants had plaited my hair around my head and draped a diamond necklace about my neck. Intricately designed silver earrings wrapped about my ears. My gown was silver overlaid with layers of lace and countless glistening crystals and beads. I spun, letting the skirt folds swish around my ankles, and looked over my shoulder to see a shimmering blue imitation of Vehgar stretching across my back. Sheer sleeves of silver and blue sparkled with crystals and stretched to my wrists, where the fabric become lace and covered the backs of my hands like gloves. Spinning around again, I squinted at the front of my gown, where the fitted bodice flashed in a complex pattern of blindingly bright crystals, like the seamstress had stitched an entire sky of stars into my dress.

"She made me look…queenly," I said, haltingly. My hand grasped in vain for my armband, forgetting I'd removed it earlier. The token of mourning held no place in a celebration.

Jennah shook her head. "She prepared the dress to your orders: she gave you an outfit worthy of a great celebration, for the woman who has brought us our freedom and will find us our king."

As we left my chambers and a cluster of guards joined us, I repressed a sigh. Jennah saw my look and squeezed my arm. "We leave tomorrow," she whispered.

Music and murmuring from the crowds greeted us long before we arrived at the ballroom. The guards standing at attention in the doorway saluted and one turned toward the crowd and raised his voice above the din. "Princess Halia of Misroth!"

The noise fell silent. I drew a deep breath, preparing myself for the stares, the questions, and the dancing I would have to partake in tonight, and entered the room with my head held high. This time, I was not under my father's relentless scrutiny. As I entered, every person froze and saluted until I smiled and nodded, giving them my release. Slowly, the music and then the conversations recommenced.

Dozens of torches blazed along the walls, chandeliers glistened like miniature suns suspended from the ceiling, and candelabras clustered at every table and window ledge in the space. The light was so brilliant compared to the hall outside I had to blink several times before I could take in all the sights. It was almost impossible to see out the glass double doors at the far end of the ballroom, but I caught a glimpse of the torch-lined walkway leading through the grounds as the doors opened and closed to admit more guests. Everywhere I looked inside, glasses were filled to the brim with a supply of wines and juices the servants kept in constant supply. Endless pastries, meats, cheeses, fruits, nuts, and chocolates were spread at the side tables, where noblemen and noblewomen gossiped and flirted. No one would dance tonight until I did.

At the far end of the room, Velaire was seated in a comfortable armchair near her own table, surrounded by several servants, some holding dishes of food, others clutching glasses. They fretted and fawned over her like anxious mothers no matter how she waved them away. Her gown was pale blue and shimmered in the countless flickering lights. Frothed in lace, the fabric leant her an elegant, poised look as she reclined in the chair. A healthy glow had returned to her eyes, and her auburn hair was glossy and swept back perfectly over her shoulders.

When I approached her, she rose and embraced me. Jennah hovered at my heels.

"It is good to see you so well," I murmured in my aunt's ear.

She pulled back and beamed, but the smile didn't quite reach her eyes. Her hands squeezed mine. "You look lovely in that gown. So…grown. So like…" She let her words fade instead of saying *your mother.*

Before I could respond, a man cleared his throat behind us. I suppressed a grimace and turned to face Councilor Veren, adorned in his silk finery.

"My lady," he said, hand on his chest in a casual salute. "Since you are to begin the ball with the first dance, might I suggest my grandson Myrent as your first partner?" He gestured toward a young man beside him.

I knew the nobility would push their sons upon me, each in the hope that their family would make a royal match, but I hadn't expected anyone to begin this soon and interrupt my aunt's and my greetings. Not for the first time, I wished Layk and the other guards would have agreed that inviting common citizens alongside the nobility would have been acceptable and safe, but they had all pointed out the impossibility of gauging the trustworthiness of countless strangers.

With a plastered smile, I studied Myrent, who was fidgeting with his jacket sleeves. By his face I guessed he had seen a few more years than me, but his stature was as gangly as a young colt's. His ears were too large for his head and his wide mouth wore a lopsided grin radiating nerves and uncertainty.

"Very well," I said through my teeth, grabbing Myrent's hand and leading him toward the dance floor.

Quiet fell over the people when they realized the dancing was about to start. The music halted as the musicians prepared to play something befitting my first dance of the evening. Jennah clung to the edges of the crowd and flashed me a smirk. I resisted the urge to roll my eyes at her. As the first notes began to play, I let my eyes scan the crowd, finding Gare and Layk each stationed at different corners of the room.

Misrothian tradition called for the male to lead in dance, but as the first notes of a slow, sweet melody began, I gently tugged Myrent in the direction we needed to go. "I—thank you," he stammered. "I've never been much for dancing."

I almost cringed at the memory his words recalled: A much smaller, homier room and my friend Bren's cheerful tune on the jiadro as Avrik stumbled through a dance with me. His closeness, his swift smile, the warmth of his hand…

"You look…quite stunning, my lady," Myrent continued, cheeks pink.

I nodded once, acknowledging his words with a smile.

Taking encouragement in this, his bravery grew. "I've wondered about your intention to leave Misroth, princess. I am surprised that you would give up the enjoyments of ball dancing and lovely gowns."

My temper flared. "Lovely gowns and dancing were rather scarce in my father's prison," I snapped. "You need not wonder about my intentions. I know full well what I am doing."

Myrent's eyes widened and he clamped his mouth shut. "Forgive me, Your Ladyship," he mumbled at his shoes.

We finished our dance in tense silence. The music ceased, the people applauded, Myrent kept his head bowed low, and I forced a grin when I turned to see the long line of young noblemen waiting to ask for a dance.

The evening passed at an agonizingly slow pace. Some of the men attempted to charm me while others spoke condescendingly, gracing their speech with polite words to thinly mask their insolence. A few were so shy they scarcely spoke at all, too embarrassed in the presence of a royal to know how to even attempt to woo me. Only one praised me for retracting some of my father's laws already and lifting the capital's curfew, and even he did it with an attitude of condescension, as if surprised at my abilities. All the dances and interactions were painful, a long stream of reminders of all I hadn't missed during my life in Evren.

At last, stomach growling, I snatched a moment to take a few bites from a plate of meats and cheeses a servant brought to me. I wiped at the sweat gathering on the back of my neck and realized I'd forgotten how exhausting balls could become.

"A drink?" I looked up to see that Layk had drawn close, putting himself between me and a cluster of nobles waiting to speak with me. He held out a glass of water, which I gratefully accepted.

"Do you still worry much for my safety tonight?" I asked, raising my brows pointedly at the way Layk hovered nearby. I sipped my water, fighting to maintain a royal appearance and not gulp the entire glass in one breath.

"A few of the other guards reported some men loitering outside the castle gates earlier. They appeared like a few drunken men who had strayed from the people's celebrations in the streets. None seemed to be armed and they all were cheering and crying out your name. They left without opposition when the guards sent them away, but I find it a bit suspicious."

"You find everything suspicious, Layk."

"It's my job, princess. And so," he added, "I think it's best that I stay near."

"Oh," I said, inspiration striking me. I deposited my plate and glass at my aunt's table and turned back to Layk. "Then you can dance with me next."

Layk couldn't mask the shock and anxiety on his face. "What?" He cleared his throat. "I mean, my lady…that is… Guards are not trained to… Why?"

"I need a minute away from the noblemen," I said, taking his hand just as a new song began. "Don't worry; I can lead you through the steps."

As we stepped onto the dancefloor, I saw a woman frown and turn to her friend. A few of the councilors were watching me with dark expressions. My choice of dance partner certainly went against all expectations, but they couldn't say much. As heir to the throne, I could choose to dance with whomever I wished tonight.

"So…everything is ready for us to depart tomorrow…my lady?" Layk asked stiffly. Every movement he made looked uncoordinated and graceless, no matter how I pulled or prodded or nudged him. His expression had returned to a guard's usual impassive gaze, trying to cover his discomfort. I stifled a laugh.

"Yes, although the nobles are still opposed, according to all they've been telling me tonight."

Layk frowned. "They have no right to question your decisions."

I shrugged. "Many are part of the Council or the Council's family. That is *their* job."

But my friend's face remained dark. "I don't like the way they look at you, princess. Their attitudes are…"

"Insufferable?" I suggested.

Layk allowed himself a chuckle. His blue eyes brightened when he let himself relax and enjoy the moment. Then the next he stiffened and stared at a point over my shoulder, toward the glass double doors.

"What is it?"

"I don't like the looks of the men outside," he said. "I think we should end the ball and have guards escort you and Velaire back to your chambers." I opened my mouth to protest, but he ignored me and gestured for two of the guards posted along the ballroom's perimeter. As the men approached and Layk leaned forward to give them instructions, the music wavered and people around us began to murmur anxiously. "Gather two more men and tell them to escort Velaire back to her chambers and set up post to protect her tonight. You will escort Halia to her chambers and then guard her until you receive further orders from me."

As the men led me from the ballroom, pausing to whisper to the guards near the entrance, Layk turned toward the crowd, still murmuring and upset. "The ball is over!" he called. "The princess and Lady Velaire are weary and must retire. Please gather your things and head home."

The crowd's uncomfortable chatter faded away as the guards escorted me down the winding hallways and staircases that led to my chambers. Outside my door, we scanned the empty hall and stepped forward silently.

"Wait here, my lady," one of the guards whispered, drawing his sword and nodding to his companion as he turned the knob. As the first guard flung open the door, the second man drew a knife, grasped his companion's shoulder, and slit his throat.

# CHAPTER FOUR

M Y CRY HADN'T EVEN ESCAPED my lips when the guard spun on me, bloody knife whirling toward my face. I dropped to the floor and the knife swung high, dripping blood as it flew over my head. The guard pulled away as I rolled back and launched a kick at his groin, one too fast for him to evade. He grunted and punched me in the face, slamming me back on the floor. Sparks flashed across my vision. I looked up to see the knifepoint driving toward my face. Rolling to the side, I escaped the man's attack again, but I knew I couldn't outmaneuver him for long. Unarmed, I had low chances of survival.

Before he struck again, I lunged toward the fallen guard, reaching for his sword. Kicking me in the back, my attacker dropped me flat on my stomach and pressed me into the floor. I groped for the sword hilt, just out of reach. I was helpless, waiting for the death strike.

No. Keep fighting.

Squirming against his weight, I stretched my arm as far as it could go. My fingers brushed the metal but could not grasp it. Sweat trickled down my face.

The man behind me laughed, his pitch high and unnatural.

"You're a fellow rebel!" I snarled. "Why kill your own people?"

His heel dug into my spine as he leaned forward, hot breath on my neck, and pressed the knife's cold edge to my throat with a shaking hand.

"I was a spy, planted by King Zarev, and I hold no allegiance to a peasant princess who tried to murder her own father," he whispered. "Now you can die in disgrace, you treasonous wench."

I heard the arrow just before it struck him. His knife clattered to the floor and his dead weight collapsed on top of me.

"Forgive me," Layk said breathlessly, kicking the dead man off me. He helped pull me to my feet. "Are you all right, my lady?"

I nodded, rubbing at my cheekbone, swollen and bruised beneath my fingers. My head throbbed and my back ached.

"I never would have expected… I thought for sure these men were all trustworthy—I never thought…" Layk stammered. He shook his head, still at a loss for words.

"It's not your fault," I said slowly, "but you may need to gather those you trust absolutely and tell them to start questioning our own. I cannot leave my aunt with guards who will as soon kill her as defend her."

He nodded, his lips a tight line. "The number I trust shrinks every day. I won't leave her with anyone I don't trust implicitly, and I'll begin more questioning tomorrow." He gestured to my entryway. "Let's check your rooms, my lady."

I lifted the first guard's sword as Layk entered my chambers, another arrow already strung to his bow. My sitting room was dark and quiet, for the servants hadn't even lit a fire in the hearth yet. Beyond lay my small dining room, where moonlight streamed through the windows and reflected in the table's polished surface. Nothing was out of place. Finally, we entered my bedchamber, washroom, and study, which were all empty.

"Gare and Jennah are on their way," Layk said, running a hand across his brow.

"And Velaire? Is she safe?" I asked.

"I asked them to check on her before joining us."

Still clutching the sword close, I sat on my bed. This was the second unexpected attack in the short space since my father's death, and that fact made it hard to feel safe anywhere. Layk's presence was comforting, but with adrenaline still coursing through my body, I felt coiled tight like a wire. Sleep would not come tonight.

At last, Jennah and Gare arrived, their weapons at the ready.

"What happened?" they cried, eyes wide at the bodies they had passed.

"Is my aunt Velaire safe?" I demanded, ignoring their question.

Jennah studied my face closely, noting the swelling. "Yes, but are *you?*"

"She was attacked by one of her guards. He was a loyalist to Zarev all this time, and I'd thought him trustworthy," Layk said bitterly.

Gare strode toward me. "We will keep you safe. Just as before, none of us will leave you tonight."

I smiled and nodded. "Thank you."

"Are you sure you're all right?" Jennah asked.

As I watched my friends gather close, my smile widened. "I am now."

"This is the last uneasy night we will have to spend here," Gare added. "Tomorrow, we leave."

For other dangers, I thought darkly.

I woke early in the morning to the sound of distant waves crashing on the shore, reminding me of all my fears. It was a surprise to me that I'd managed to fall asleep at all. Tumbling out of bed, I found that Layk and Gare had already left and Jennah was asleep in the armchair opposite me.

Letting Jennah sleep, I crossed to my dressing room and found that the servants had already laid out the new clothes the seamstress had made for me. There were shooting gloves and a traveling cloak, along with a pair of black leggings and tunic adorned with Misroth's crest: Vehgar, the dragon constellation. As I slipped the clothes on, I smiled at the genius of the outfit: not only was it comfortable, but also it resembled the uniform of the Royal Guard. It even bore embroidered silver stars along the right sleeve, matching the Captain of the Guard's marks of rank in a clear statement that I, not Narek, was captain of this venture.

I pulled on my boots and slid my armband over my sleeve. Rather than wake Jennah, I decided to let her sleep longer, while she still had some time to rest. Sweeping out of my chambers, I wound my way through the castle halls to my father's study. Layk met me there with several guards we questioned together to assess their trustworthiness. None of them had suspected the traitor in their midst either and seemed just as shaken as Layk had been.

At last, when Layk and I were both satisfied that we could still trust the handful of men we'd assigned to Velaire in our absence, I walked to my aunt's bedchamber. She answered my knock immediately, swinging the door inward and smiling softly when she saw me.

I stepped inside and studied her as she closed the door behind me. She was dressed in a lilac gown that hung a bit loosely over her frame. Without the powder she'd worn to the ball, there were still dark circles under her eyes, but they looked as lively as ever. Her hair was gathered in elegant plaits woven with sythrel, the only sign she was in mourning. She didn't wear a band as I did.

She pulled me into a tight embrace. "Oh, Halia," she murmured against my hair. In our years apart, I still hadn't grown tall enough to match her graceful stature. "I wish you would send someone else to find Gillen. It's so hard to part with you again."

My throat burned with unshed tears. "I can't sit by while he is in danger," I said. "I can't entrust anyone else with this mission."

She held me a moment longer, her body feeling frail against mine. "Come home. Come back to me." She pulled away and stared into my eyes, her own shining with tears. "Even if...even if it is too late for Gillen, promise me you will return. I cannot bear to lose you both."

I pressed my lips into a firm line and wished I could make that promise. But there were too many dangers and I couldn't foresee the future, couldn't know I would live to make it home. I embraced her again. "I will do everything I can to ensure Gillen and I both return," I whispered.

Her hand slid over my armband and lingered there. Stepping back, she studied it, running her fingers over its smooth surface. "Your mother…" She shook her head and sighed. "Whatever the knowledge is worth, know even as she believed your father's lies, she loved you. She may have believed your father was innocent and that you plotted to kill him, but she mourned for you."

I fidgeted with the armband, memories of her pale, horrified face flashing before my eyes, of her crumpling into my arms as she bled out onto the castle floor. Her lips had moved in an unfinished sentence, words I'd never hear her say, though I often imagined what she had tried to say. Did it matter anymore? I blinked the images away. "Does that mean I should *truly* mourn her?"

Velaire moved her hand to my cheek and brushed back an unruly strand of hair. "No. It means you are a better person than her. You are willing to do anything to save someone you love, no matter the cost. You are prepared to undo your parents' wrongs." She smiled sadly and brushed away her tears. "Be safe, Halia. My love goes with you."

I reached out and grasped her hand, my tongue stumbling for words. "I love you," I choked out.

Before I could give in to sorrow, I turned and left without a backward glance. There was no time to waste.

Great crowds had gathered along the main street to bid my company and me farewell. We could see them as we descended the last steps of the cliffside path from the castle, all waiting quietly for us to pass them by. Staring out at their solemn faces, I wondered how many hated me for leaving them after, in their eyes, I'd returned their freedom to them. Had

Misroth forgotten her true king so soon?

I glanced at my friends, clothed in attire like mine. My chest tightened when I turned to Narek, standing between Gare and Layk. Stripped of his rank, he was dressed all in plain black without any royal insignias, but his lack of a uniform did not make him any less imposing. I'd insisted to my friends that, considering the dangers we were venturing toward, his sword be returned to him for the journey, but seeing it at his side still made me uneasy. He watched the crowd impassively until his eyes caught my stare and some emotion I couldn't place darted across his face. Was he still laughing at me inwardly? Or plotting how he could finally drown me successfully? What secrets did he hide? I longed to be able to conjure my visions at will.

I tightened my hands into fists. It was too late to second guess my plan. After days of considering my moves, of conversing with Jennah, Layk, Gare, and even Narek, and of packing supplies, there was nothing left but to find Gillen. And trust that Narek could lead me to him.

As we adjusted our packs and stepped down into the street, Jennah shot me a soft smile. The morning sunlight sparked in the gold flecks in her eyes and I thought of fireside stories of Alrenian warriors, of blazing sunshine and fearless deeds, of far-off lands and adventures, and I felt my courage rise.

The waves of people seemed endless. Men, women, and children clustered along the road, around buildings, and at windows. Everywhere I looked there were eyes gazing back at me, some filled with anger and others fear. Only a few looked at me with hope.

At the forefront of the crowds, clustered in the shadow of the cliff we'd just descended, was the Royal Council, their faces solemn and barely concealing their disapproval. Wind rippled through their fine cloaks and ruffled their beards. I tried to ignore Councilor Veren's beady eyes on me as I faced the assembled Misrothians.

"My people!" I cried. I hesitated, searching for words, suddenly keenly aware that I had not been raised to make speeches like this. The emotions that had carried me through my execution speech felt distant after many more long days, weighed down by responsibilities and fears. The people looked to me for hope, for security, but they were looking to the wrong person. "I know…I know that our kingdom has fallen into uncertainty and many of you now look to me for leadership. But I am not first in line to the throne. You see…my task was not to rule you, but to free you. I must…"

I wavered, then caught sight of Jennah, who shot me a sidelong glance and smiled. Courage rose in my heart and I remembered the purpose that had led me here. In that moment I wasn't the silent, reserved girl who had hidden in Evren. I wasn't the child who had balked at the thought of royal dinners and crowded ballrooms. I was Princess of Misroth, daughter of Eldon. My voice rang out clear and strong in the heavy quiet, and my people listened. "My purpose is to restore the crown to the true ruler of Misroth. That title belongs to my cousin Gillen, the rightful king, who was groomed and trained for the role since his birth. Misroth's best hope for the future is with him."

My friends stood close to my side, Layk constantly scanning the area for potential threats. He didn't trust the other rebel guards that surrounded us, some clearly visible and others hidden amidst the throng. Gare hovered near Narek and shot him a threatening glance whenever he so much as breathed too loudly. Councilors Lurok and Veren scratched at their beards. The crowd remained quiet, uncertainty etched across every face I studied. This was not the speech they wanted to hear, but it was the truth, the one they needed to hear. I believed this with everything in me.

Gesturing toward my friends, I continued. "These are some of the companions who helped me win back Misroth, and they have pledged to help me find our king, whom my father sent to the land of Toryn under the pretense of building an alliance in a false war. We have a prisoner who was in my father's counsel and will guide us to King Gillen. In my absence, Velaire, mother of our king and wife to our beloved King Reylon, will be more than capable to lead you and hold our Royal Council together."

The silence stretched on.

"I know many of you are afraid." I searched the faces of men and women filled with fear and anger, keeping my own expression composed and confident. "I know many of you are doubtful." I spared a glance toward the Royal Council, and several of the councilors frowned deeply. "I know most of you have lost much and sacrificed far more than I could ever repay." I studied my friends' loved ones, waiting in the crowd to bid them goodbye. "I cannot thank you enough. I cannot guarantee what our future will hold, but I can reassure you that the Giver of Life is on our side and has heard our cries for justice and peace. He, not I, has freed our kingdom, and so I have faith that he will aid us in our quest to restore the throne."

I drew myself up taller, squaring my shoulders and raising my voice. "We who are true to Misroth have no reason to fear, for we have already shown those loyal to my father's memory and those greedy for power that they are outnumbered. We have overthrown tyranny and we have slain assassins. We have sent a clear message that any who oppose peace in Misroth will be punished for their treason. We stand united and strong, true people of Eldon's cause. We are the descendants of those who defied imperial rule and defeated conquerors. We laughed in the face of a great empire and we were victorious. How could we now be afraid?" I cried.

Finally, the people were responding, nodding their heads to my words and letting glimmers of hope and pride reflect in their eyes. "We are Eldon's people," I continued. "We are brave, we are strong, and we are triumphant!" I threw a fist into the air and the throng joined me.

"We are triumphant!" they shouted, a chant rising around us.

In the din, Jennah turned toward me with a smile dancing across her lips. "Oh, how the people love you," she laughed. There was pride in her smile, making my confidence swell. We would find Gillen. My cousin and my people would be safe. "They will miss you, but after all you have done for them, your words hold power and they will trust you."

Gare clapped me on the shoulder. "I hope you don't take this the wrong way, but if Gillen ever refused the crown…I would be honored to have you as my queen."

Layk spared a smile in my direction. "Well done, my lady."

Layk's brother and sister were running toward us, flanked by Gare's and Jennah's families. I nodded at Layk. "Take your time with your goodbyes."

The farewells were painful to watch and reminded me of Lyanna and Rev and the words I'd never said to them. Did they miss me, or did they feel as betrayed as Avrik had? Did Shilam, Jaren, and Bren ever hope for my return, or had they sided with Avrik and turned against me? Did anyone stand waiting by a window or stir hopefully at every knock at the door?

Gare and his son, a tall young man, embraced and patted one another firmly on the back. "I love you, Keriv," Gare said gruffly, voice barely restraining his emotion. Keriv's whispered response escaped my ears. Then Gare turned to hold his crying wife. "Be strong, Loae," he murmured against her hair. "I will be thinking of you every day, every moment."

I watched Layk hug each of his siblings in turn.

"Dalen, Fia. Take care of one another," he said, his usually stern voice trembling. "If you need anything while I am away, the rebels can provide for you."

His brother and sister blinked wordlessly up at him, their faces drawn and pale with sorrow and concern. I didn't even know them, and yet it felt like I was the reason for their sadness. My chest tightened, and I considered ordering my friends to stay. But I knew that would be pointless; they had made their choice.

"I *will* come back," he vowed, pulling them into another tight embrace. "I will."

Turning away, I noticed Jennah's husband Marke and mother Kam standing near. Her daughters, Laydin and Avalee, darted into her arms. She laughed and enveloped them both in an embrace. The girls, however, were straight-faced and wide-eyed.

"Mama," Laydin began breathlessly, "when will you come home? Will you be gone a long time like Papa?"

Sadness passed over Jennah's face, but her smile did not waver. "Perhaps even longer," she said. "But you must care for him and ensure he recovers properly while I am away. The time will pass faster that way."

"You have to go?" Avalee's tiny face crumpled into a frown and her eyes filled with tears.

Jennah reached out to brush her daughter's cheek. "Do not cry. Papa and Grandmama will keep you safe while I am away. I must go, to make sure our kingdom stays safe as long as you are both alive."

The girls stared up at her, uncertain of her meaning, but they made no further protests. Kam and Marke approached, the first pulling her daughter into a hug and whispering tearful words in her ear.

Then Jennah turned to Marke, and the look they shared made me feel like I was intruding on something intimate. Without a word spoken between them, he kissed her and held her close.

Cheeks warming, I lowered my gaze to my boots and thought of a time that felt so distant now, when I had hoped for something like what Jennah and Marke shared. Even with the bow he'd given me strapped to my back and his smile still vivid in my memory, it angered me to find myself sparing another thought for Avrik. With a shrug, I jostled it away.

When Marke and Jennah parted at last, he said softly, "Return to me." She grasped his hand and nodded, pulling away slowly.

I drew a deep breath, forcing the heaviness of the moment to leave me. *They've made their choice,* I reminded myself.

Their goodbyes finished, each member of my company turned to me expectantly. Even Narek, though he stood apart from us with his arms crossed, waited for my word.

I pressed my fist to my heart and nodded to Marke and Kam, to Laydin and Avalee, to Dalen and Fia, to Loae and Keriv. "I will do all in my power to ensure your loved ones' safety and to bring them home to you," I promised. "I will not take their service to my kingdom and my family lightly or disregard what you are giving today for your people. Thank you."

They saluted me back, wiped tears from their eyes, and lifted their faces high.

"Let's go," I said, forcing my voice to ring out strong and clear.

The atmosphere was still and solemn again as we proceeded down the street. Men, women, and children watched from every corner and every window we passed, gazing mutely or offering their salutes. No one called out to bid us farewell, perhaps because fear had descended on them again, or they felt the best tribute they could offer was respectful silence as my companions and I left our home behind.

With the rising sun warm on my back, I kept my chin high and my gaze forward. Somewhere to the northwest lay Evren and home, where Rev was perhaps just now opening his books to begin the day's work and Lyanna was likely cleaning before sitting down to sew. A lump formed in my throat that I couldn't quite swallow away.

And Avrik… I tried to brush aside the memory of my last vision of him, but I could still see his eyes flashing with anger and pain as he spoke to his imprisoned father.

I set my jaw. *But we will not be passing through Evren. We'll keep too far south for that.* I didn't know if that thought was comforting or painful.

We spent a great portion of the day in the rolling countryside beyond the capital's gates, taking the inland path along dirt roads. We passed occasional carriages occupied by farmers riding into the city, but otherwise the roads were empty.

I watched my breath rise toward the sky, where a deceptively bright sun, now sinking toward the horizon, offered no warmth. Skirting around a patch of ice, I pulled my cloak tighter around my body and found myself longing for the warmth of Lyanna's kitchen, even if it meant being inside cooking rather than traveling somewhere new.

"It seems our princess longs for the comfort of her carriage," Narek said.

I jerked my head up at the sound of his voice to see him walking alongside me. Just ahead, Layk shot him a scowl over his shoulder.

Brushing a few strands of hair from my eyes, I matched Narek's level gaze. "With an attitude like that, it seems you long for the comfort of your cell. Shall we return you to it?"

Narek merely smirked. "You wanted me to accompany you."

Gare approached Narek from behind. "You are here because the princess thinks you *might* be helpful," he growled. "The rest of us are simply waiting for an excuse to end your wretched life. I wouldn't be so cocky." He turned to me. "I think we should disarm him. I know you think it's wrong for him to be unarmed in the forest, but he's a threat and deserves death anyway."

Narek's eyes flashed, betraying his tumultuous emotions for an instant. "If you want to survive in Toryn, I suggest you don't kill the man who lived there."

Jennah, who had been walking ahead with Layk, slowed her pace to fall into step beside me. She raised an eyebrow at Narek. "You—the Captain of the *Misrothian* Royal Guard—are from Toryn?"

Questions flooded my mind, but I waited, wondering what other information Narek might supply on his own.

But he didn't answer. Instead, he glanced up, blinking against the setting sun's rays and nodding toward the forest looming ahead. My heart quickened; I hadn't looked up recently to study the landscape and see how close we already were to Evren Forest.

"We should stop for the night," he said. "We'll be safer outside of the forest once the light fades." He spared a look in my direction. "It's best not to spend more nights within it than we have to."

Trust me, I know, I thought, but I didn't respond. Instead, with a quick nod, I signaled my agreement and the others turned off the road to set up camp under the forest's shadow. I followed and slipped off my pack, letting it thud to the earth and sighing with relief.

While Jennah and Gare unpacked our provisions, Layk ventured into the forest to do some hunting. I turned to Narek, my eyes narrow. "Come, leave your weapon here and follow me. We need firewood."

I could feel Jennah's eyes on me, wary, as I led Narek beneath the canopy of trees. Perhaps she thought me a fool, but I wanted Narek to know I was not dependent on my friends to protect me from him. The shadowy air was cool and crisp, but the scent of dirt and decaying leaves and wood was warm and familiar. And a little bit discomforting. It hadn't been that long ago when Kyrin had left me for dead in these woods, or when I'd spent a long night fighting a sedwa alone.

Narek crouched to gather kindling from the forest floor without a word of protest, following my lead when I stepped deeper amongst the trees to add to my own pile. I was sullen and cautious, listening for every movement he made even when my eyes weren't on him, my muscles constantly taut and ready to drop my burden and draw my bow.

"You're from Toryn," I said at last, accusingly. Though I had known not to trust him from the beginning, the fact that he had withheld this information still left me whirling with anger and suspicion. With Misroth's borders closed to Alrenor and Toryn, I had never met anyone from either of those kingdoms and had difficulty imagining how or why Narek could be here now.

Narek paused, the picture of a trained guard as he stared into the forest like a sentry on watch. Then he shifted his arms to redistribute his firewood and knelt to grasp another stick.

His silence only further incited my anger. "You said before you hoped to earn your freedom from me, but perhaps what you truly want is to return to Toryn. Are you only waiting for your chance to escape?" I shot him a glare. "Because, as I said, you are a prisoner and will be treated as such, so do not set your hopes on escape."

Narek chuckled. "Why would I want to return to Toryn and its nightmares? I told you, this prisoner has not relinquished his hopes for freedom. I pledged my allegiance to you when I killed your father."

I did not respond to his comment. "You were young when my father promoted you to captain of the guard," I said instead. "How long did you live in Toryn? How well do you remember it?"

Narek's jaw went taut, but he flung a nonchalant glance in my direction. "I was sixteen when I came to Misroth, and when your father chose me as his captain. It happened quickly, but I suppose he saw potential in me." He flashed me a crooked grin. "I had a lot of experience in combat from my time in Toryn…more than most of his guards had."

"He probably saw someone young and naïve enough to manipulate easily," I scoffed. "No wonder the guards all hated you." I clutched my pile of kindling close to my chest, measuring it with my eyes to weigh whether I needed more. All the while, my mind continued to process everything Narek was sharing. In Misroth, we calculated age beginning at one's day of birth, but Toryn went by the closest estimate they could make of someone's day of conception. "Sixteen by Misroth's standards, or Toryn's?"

He chuckled, but the laughter held no mirth. "Toryn's," he said. "I've had to acknowledge a false age here as well as a false allegiance. It is just another reminder of how little Misroth values life."

I clenched a fist around a piece of kindling, splinters pricking my palm. "That sounds truly noble, coming from the man who tried to murder me when I was a child."

"Your ropes came undone," he said.

I blinked, taken aback for a moment as I remembered the night I'd almost drowned. I'd struggled for what felt like ages until the bonds around my ankles had slipped free, allowing me to kick toward the surface. But Narek had still thrown me into the sea, not knowing whether loose bonds would truly save my life or not. He'd still burned Jennah and Marke's home, still imprisoned my friends and me, still tortured and killed countless people in my father's name. Even if he had killed my father in the end.

Where did his true allegiance lie?

False allegiance—his words echoed in my mind. It was clear from his bitter tone that he hated Misroth. Then why come here at all? Why serve the king and shed innocent blood only to kill him later? My head pounded from all the questions, all my distrust and confusion swirling together.

I let my rage flood through my veins once more. "That changes nothing," I said.

Narek nodded. "It does not. Besides, you're not a child now. I think we can both agree that if either of us fails to serve the other's purposes, we will kill one another without regret." He turned his steely eyes on me, and I clamped down my unease.

I squared my shoulders and began to lead the way back toward our camp. "I'm not like you or my father," I said evenly. "I think I'll always feel remorse for any life I take." I tossed him a look over my shoulder. "But if you ever endanger my kingdom or my people, I wouldn't hesitate to kill you."

Narek smiled coldly. "Perhaps you are more like your father than you think."

I stiffed at his words, but despite the chill that ran down my back, I couldn't let him know how they'd affected me. Tossing a glare over my shoulder, I led the way back to camp without another word.

When we returned, Layk was coming back to the camp as well, a rabbit clutched in each hand. His eyes caught mine and despite my best efforts, read the fear on my face. Tensing, he flicked his gaze from Narek and back to me. "Did he threaten you?" His grasp on the rabbits tightened until his knuckles turned white. "Do I need to kill him?"

Gare stood hastily to his feet. "Just say the word, princess."

I rolled my eyes and set my kindling on the ground. "I can handle him," I said, perhaps more confidently than I felt. "Please don't kill our guide."

Narek deposited his pile of kindling at Jennah's feet. She gave him a scornful smile. "Perhaps you can make yourself useful, *captain*, and start the fire."

I moved to stand near Jennah, taking comfort in the fearless aura she always possessed. Narek's words still echoed in my head. Did he know how much they had shaken me?

While Gare began to skin the rabbits and Narek set to work starting a fire, Layk joined Jennah and I, tossing us each an apple before biting into his own.

"I'll take the first watch tonight," he said, glancing pointedly in Narek's direction.

Sitting back on his heels as flames began to lick at the wood, Narek cast Layk an impervious look. "We'll all want to sleep with our weapons within arm's reach," he said.

Layk laughed. "And they called *me* the pessimist of the group." He settled onto the grass beside the fire.

Gare shot him a grin. "You are."

As the sun set and a cold breeze rustled the grass, we all gathered near the fire while Gare roasted the rabbit. The trees cast long shadows over us, settling our camp into gloom even after the stars appeared. Whether it was our recent goodbyes to our loved ones or the eerie atmosphere of the forest, quiet fell over us as we ate and then settled down for the night.

I lay my bow and quiver close to my bedroll and then burrowed within it, keeping my cloak on for extra warmth. As I stared up at the stars, trying to soak in the warmth of the fire even as it began to burn low, I heard Jennah shift nearby me and sigh.

"Right now, I would be tucking Laydin and Avalee in," she whispered. I turned my head to see her studying the night sky, her gaze wistful. "When Marke was home we would all say a prayer together and then he and I would take turns telling them bedtime stories: the tales of the warrior Shyla and how she slew the dragon Vehgar, or legends of long-ago princesses I think my mother made up to tell me when I was young." She smiled.

From his post near the fire, Layk fidgeted. His gaze remained fastened on the deepening shadows of the woods and his voice was low. "I told Dalen and Fia stories before bed too." He wiped his face and to my surprise, I saw his eyes were glittering with tears. "The last hours we spent together, on my leave from the castle a couple days ago, they said they needed a great story for all the weeks or months I would not be there to say goodnight. So they asked for a story about me on this adventure." He laughed. "They made up most of it. At one point they had me wrestling a bear."

Everyone laughed. Even Narek, in his bedroll on the far side of our camp, cracked a smile.

"Ah," Gare said softly, "it's been a long time since my son was young enough to tuck in, but he still likes my stories." He winked at Layk. "Maybe when I return I'll tell him a story about *me* wrestling a bear."

Layk raised an eyebrow at him. "I won't be surprised if that story becomes true by the end of this journey." He paused, a smile slowly spreading across his face. "No, I would be," he amended. "Any bear would be too terrified of you to get near enough to wrestle."

We spent some more time laughing and enjoying one another's company, but just like my companions, I couldn't shake the memories of those I was leaving behind either. As quiet fell over us again, I thought of nights by the fire with Lyanna and Rev, reading a book while they talked or undertaking my favorite activity, knitting. I grinned at that memory and realized that I'd even return to an evening of knitting if I could spend one more with Lyanna and Rev before I entered Toryn and unknown dangers. If I could just say goodbye…

No matter how hard I tried to keep them at bay, memories of Avrik also flickered through my mind. I remembered fireside conversations we'd had or visits to Wanderer's Rest. I recalled the way he laughed or how his smile revealed a dimple in one cheek and made most girls in

Evren swoon. To them, he was a handsome face and a charming personality, but to me he had been a loyal friend, a confidant, a boy I'd trusted until he'd abandoned me. A friend I'd kept my true identity from for four years.

I cringed with guilt and rolled over. My armband dug into my skin when I pressed my weight on my arm, and new images came to mind. My mother's shocked face, the light dying from her eyes. Her final words left unspoken. Blinking, I felt something wet trickle down my cheek and realized it was a tear. I swiped it away and shoved the pain and confusion away with it.

Closing my eyes tightly against the night, I willed myself to sleep.

Rest, so you have the strength to face the forest again tomorrow. Rest, so you can find Gillen. Before it's too late.

CHAPTER FIVE

THEY CAME LIKE WRAITHS, SURE-FOOTED forms shrouded in darkness. The moonlight glinted off their black armor, but beneath it, their forms were indiscernible, their faces hidden within their helmets. Slipping from shadow to shadow, they were silent but for the harsh, guttural sounds echoing throughout the city ruins: they were speaking in their language, surrounding their prey and taunting it as they went.

Leaning against the wall of a half-collapsed building, Gillen swept a hand across his sweaty brow and gulped down a great lungful of air as silently as he could. He clutched his sword hilt with both hands and glanced around, catching the eyes of his two companions from where they hid behind crumbling walls on either side of him.

"*Iyg kurik vouren… Iyg kurik vouren…*" The hissing voices repeated the phrase all around him.

Trembling, he closed his eyes, steeling himself, and approached the corner of the building to peer out into the street. A light flared in the blackness and he blinked against it, trying to see beyond the growing flames and smoke. The fire's acrid tang saturated the air as it climbed one of the nearby husks of a building, crackling through timber in mere moments and sending blazing light along the empty street. He covered his mouth and nose with his shirt to stifle his cough and avoid giving away his location.

The forms appeared within the fiery building, even as splintered boards sparked and snapped around them: huge, hulking figures ringed in smoke and fire that didn't faze them. And they were coming for him, coming to burn his body to ash, to envelope him in fury and pain and darkness…

I awoke panting and sweating, as if I truly had been standing beside Gillen, close to a raging fire. With shaky arms, I pushed myself to a sitting position and took in the starry sky above me, gloriously free of clouds and as bright and beautiful as I'd ever seen it. I could clearly trace Vehgar's form sprawled across the darkness, snarling in defiance at Shyra, the warrior constellation across from it.

A blade hissed nearby as someone drew it from its sheath. I turned back to study our camp, where Jennah and Layk were each stirring from their bedrolls and Gare and Narek were standing with weapons drawn.

"Get up!" Gare urged, and I realized it was his voice that had first yanked me from sleep. Hours must have passed if it was his watch now.

Bleary eyed, I stumbled to my feet while Jennah and Layk sprang from their bedrolls. In one swift move I grasped my bow and quiver and joined Gare and Narek near the edge of our camp, where they were peering into the forest. I nocked an arrow to my bow and grasped the string, preparing to shoot as soon as I could pick out the golden eyes I was sure were staring back at us.

Coming up behind me with his own bow in hand, Layk whispered, "What is it?"

Narek lifted a hand to motion for silence. Jennah drew two curved daggers and tossed him a narrow glance. "If you and Gare sense we are in danger," she murmured, "I think we should know what it is you've—"

The shadow leapt toward us and charged for Narek and Gare, at the front of our band. Narek fell into a fighting stance, his blade a blur as he lifted it for a strike. Layk and I released our arrows at the same time, but the sedwa was too swift. My arrow bounced harmlessly off the creature's scaly back and Layk's deflected off its side. Snarling, the sedwa pounced toward Narek, who swung his sword in time to meet the predator in the air and sent it sprawling backward. It rolled to its feet and crouched low, its eyes gleaming with hate and its fangs dripping saliva.

I shot another arrow, but the sedwa was already moving by the time I pulled the string. Darting in, it slashed its claws at Narek's leg and sprang away before he could even parry. With a grunt of pain, he staggered back just as Gare lunged forward. He sliced his blade along the sedwa's neck, but the steel clanged harmlessly away. Growling, the sedwa snapped at Gare's side, forcing him back.

This time, with the sedwa distracted by its own bloodlust, my arrow struck true, burying deep in its eye. The sedwa unleashed a bloodcurdling cry and turned on me as I strung another arrow. It launched itself forward, running low to the ground and impossibly fast.

Layk and Jennah jumped between it and me.

"Move!" I cried. "Let me face it!"

My words were out too late, my friends already moving in to strike. Layk had his sword out and slammed its blunt side straight between the sedwa's eyes, dazing it. But only for a moment. Before Layk could attack again, it buried its fangs into his arm. Jennah dove forward and plunged a dagger into one of the sedwa's paws and I followed her, trying to press in close enough for a clean shot.

Narek took advantage of so many of us crowding around and distracting the sedwa. He threw himself onto the grass and rolled beneath the monster, driving his sword so deeply into its belly its point pierced through to its back. Black blood streamed from the wound and onto Narek's face. The sedwa screamed and thrashed, still clawing and snapping at us even as it died. Narek rolled away and it collapsed.

The world fell eerily still again as Jennah, Layk, Gare, and I stared at the sedwa's still form and Narek. He stood slowly, favoring his injured leg and wiping at the blood on his face. Limping toward the sedwa's carcass, he stood over it for a quiet moment before he wrenched his sword from its body and wiped the blade clean in the grass.

Jennah was already scanning the forest's undergrowth again, expecting another sedwa to leap from the shadows. "I thought they only attacked travelers *within* the forest or on the mountains."

"Not anymore," I spat out. Anger swelling, my eyes fell on the bloody gashes in Narek's leg before I met his gaze. As usual, his eyes were dark and unreadable, but his face was pale and drawn with pain. *Justice,* I thought smugly.

I turned toward Layk, but Gare was already inspecting his wound. "It could have been much worse," he said.

"Yes, I could have lost it," Layk said between gritted teeth.

Gare looked over his shoulder. "Jennah, gather the medical supplies so I can clean and bind it."

She nodded in Narek's direction. "What about *him?*"

Narek had already forced himself to his feet and was hobbling toward his own pack. He wrenched it open and dug around inside, not bothering to spare Jennah a glance. "I can care for myself."

We fell silent as Gare cleaned and bound Layk's wound and Narek tended to his own. Jennah stalked toward the fallen sedwa to inspect it more closely and I approached the forest's edge to peer into its depths. There were no eyes staring back at me, yet the woods were still eerily quiet, as if another creature were preparing to attack us. I spun on my heel and strode back to where Narek was sitting and grimacing as he dressed his leg.

"Do they ever hunt in packs?"

Narek leveled inscrutable eyes on me. "No," he said. He turned back to his leg, but I stepped nearer, compelling him to look up once more.

I gestured over my shoulder. "Then why is the forest so silent?"

With narrowed eyes, he stared into the woods again. "Just because they don't hunt in packs doesn't mean another could not be nearby." He finished wrapping his leg and glanced back up at me. "Or something else could be disturbing the wildlife."

"Anything is better than another sedwa," I said.

Narek watched me for a minute, the dark shadow I'd seen before passing over his face again. "In Misroth, I'll agree with you."

Jennah approached, her brow furrowed with disgust. "If there are more of those creatures possibly watching us this very moment, then there will be no more rest for us tonight." She gestured toward the forest with one of her daggers. "We could continue traveling."

I glanced back toward Gare and Layk, who were both studying us and the forest by turns.

"That means entering the woods at night rather than waiting for the dawn," Gare mused. He turned to me, and it was in that moment that I realized everyone was watching me expectantly, waiting for me to make the decision.

I cast another look toward Evren Forest. If the sedwa had become bold enough to attack beyond the wood's boundaries, then waiting for daylight hardly guaranteed our safety. We could just as easily be attacked again in our camp as we could within the forest. However, the woods were thick and dark; it would be difficult to see far ahead and harder to defend ourselves once within it.

"Let's keep going," I murmured, and walked away to gather my supplies before I could change my mind. "I'd prefer to be awake when the next sedwa attacks."

It only took us a few moments to pack up camp and approach the forest. When we stepped into its shadows its darkness seemed to consume us. I stole a glance toward Narek, who was just ahead of me, limping slightly. Without hesitation, he had taken the lead and we fell into step behind him. He studied our surroundings with a practiced eye, his gait sure even with his injury and his hand never straying far from his sword hilt.

"And those are some of the creatures our king is facing?" Layk murmured beside me.

I tossed him a surprised glance. I'd been so caught up in searching the forest, so lost in listening for any sound over our own footsteps and breathing, I'd unconsciously caught my breath. Our companions started at the sound of his voice as much as I did—all except for Narek, who didn't even acknowledge his words.

"Among others," I said, refusing to look at him. Though the decision to join me had been their own, I still couldn't shake the guilt wriggling in my chest. One encounter with a sedwa and we already had two injuries, and my visions were promising far worse.

"If it's true you see visions…what *have* you seen?"

I turned to Layk then, in time to see him cringe and offer a quick salute. "Forgive me, princess," he said. "That was impertinent."

Swallowing, I forced myself to hold Layk's gaze, even though it felt like his bright eyes were burning me. Echoes of my visions returned: fire and shadows, annihilating everything in their path. What if I survived and my companions did not? What if I had to return and look into Layk's brother's and sister's pale, horrified faces as I told them their brother had perished?

Narek halted abruptly, turning his piercing eyes on me and forcing the rest of us to stop as well. "Yes, what exactly have you seen?"

I narrowed my eyes at him. "You do not seem surprised to hear of my…gift." I hesitated over the word, hardly feeling that the nightmarish visions and perils that always seemed to surround me now could be called a gift.

"One of the servants in attendance when you accused your father thought perhaps you had one of the fabled gifts of the Alrenian god. He shared his theories before…" He gave a careless gesture with his hand, pretending to sever his neck.

I turned away. "I've seen visions of Gillen near the swamp and in the ruins of a city," I said. "In both, he and his companions are being hunted or killed off by…by things I've never quite seen clearly in the visions."

A heavy silence fell over us, and Narek stared at me for several beats. "That is to be expected," he muttered at last.

"Will you tell us more? What these creatures are and how to survive them?"

"When the time comes." Narek turned on his heel and pressed onward, and to my surprise, the fear hanging over the rest of us kept us from protesting and demanding more answers. Perhaps none of us truly wanted to know. Not yet, when turning back would still be all too easy.

We followed Narek wordlessly. With nothing but the oppressive quiet of the forest and the memories of my visions to fill my ears, I shoved away branches groping for me like hands and watched my breath be carried on the wind. For a while we struggled through the thick undergrowth and skeletal forms of barren trees before the wood thinned out a bit, giving way to a stand of great pines that stretched to the sky. The ground began to slope downward until we found ourselves in a narrow ravine with the trees towering over us on either side, nearly blocking out our view of the sky. I tried not to imagine golden eyes peering down at us from above, but I couldn't shake the feeling of being watched as we trudged through the snow.

My companions felt it too, for they all kept their hands close to their weapons. Layk and I both unstrapped our bows from our backs while Narek continuously swept the area with his eyes. At last, we climbed from the ravine and reentered the thick of the forest. As the night wore on, the wind gradually picked up and stirred the boughs above us, like spectators craning for a better view of the five small figures trekking through their wood. The air bit at my face and fingers no matter how low I pulled my hood or how much I tucked my gloved hands into my cloak, and I longed for the comfort of our campfire. The silence gradually gave way to the soft stirrings of nocturnal creatures around us: the occasional hoot of an owl or flutter of wings made me wary. I hid my uneasiness. What sort of leader would I be if I inspired fear rather than courage in my companions?

At last the dark sky melted to a soft gray hue, the stars snuffed out, and the first glimmer of dawn sparked. It took time for the sun's rays to reach us, but once they did, they made the snow glitter gold and the air seem less frigid. I knew this was only a temporary reprieve.

With the threat gone, I finally noticed how stiff my legs had become. Though the arrival of sunlight had given me a jolt of energy, I felt unfocused as sleepiness stole over me. My legs grew heavy and my feet moved clumsily through the snow until I began to stumble.

"Perhaps we should stop now," Gare said gruffly when we entered a small glade. He paused beside me, compelling the rest of us to stop with him. I noticed how pale Layk's and Narek's complexions had become and wondered how much pain they were in, though both refused to indicate it. "We have injuries to tend to, and we all need the rest."

Assenting, we lay down our packs and set up camp. After we ate a hasty meal and Narek and Layk each tended to their wounds, Gare volunteered to take the first watch. Near enough to relish the heat from the fire, I curled up in my bedroll and pulled my hood low to block out the daylight.

"We needn't rest for long," I announced. "We should start again before sunset, in order to avoid…in order to leave the forest as soon as possible."

"The mountains will probably be just as perilous," Narek said.

"When we stop in Kelwed to restock our supplies, we'll have a chance to restock our courage too," Gare rejoined.

We fell into silence once more, drifting close to sleep. I closed my eyes and tried to prevent my mind from racing, though I couldn't help but wonder if my visions would return in my sleep. Were they all of past events, or did my visions ever show me the present? Where was Gillen at this very moment, and was he safe?

My heart ached with worry, but my exhaustion gradually consumed me anyway. Lulled by the sound of crackling logs and the comfortable warmth surrounding me, I fell into a heavy sleep.

Hours later, I woke, shivering, to find that the fire had burned low and daylight was fading fast. Night's chill air was already creeping through the forest, enclosing the world in heavier frost and ice. Everyone else was still asleep but for Jennah and Layk, who were building the fire back up and conversing in muted tones.

"Do you regret your decision?" Layk asked as the fire sparked back to life, the flames flickering higher until light danced across his face.

Watching him across the fire, Jennah's gaze did not waver. With a quick lift of her chin she responded without missing a beat. "Do you?"

Layk's gaze drifted to some distant point in the forest and the muscles in his jaw went taut. He ruffled a hand through his blond hair, making it all stand on end in a quirk that suddenly, painfully, reminded me of Rev. Then his eyes snapped back to Jennah, his shoulders squared, and his expression settled into a guard's customary impassive look. He was Layk again. "I only want to know Dalen and Fia will be safe and happy. I've risked my life for that, and I will risk it again. My only regret will be if I cannot be there for them."

Jennah nodded slowly. "I feel the same," she said, "but I know Marke and my mother are there for my girls."

Layk ran a hand wearily across his face. "I already miss them so much," he admitted. "I miss Dalen's smile, Fia's laugh…" His voice trailed off.

Jennah's eyes softened. "I think about my family all the time too. But know this: every moment you think of them, they are thinking of you too," Jennah said. "Trust me." She hesitated, then added, "And I know my mother and husband will do everything in their power to ensure they are safe and happy…if we never return."

Layk bowed his head in acknowledgment, but said no more. Gare and Narek were stirring. Following their lead, I sat up and flung the covers off, letting the cold air wash over me.

"How is your arm?" Gare asked Layk by way of greeting, strolling immediately toward the campfire.

I joined them, brushing snow off a log for a seat and then turning my face toward the flames. The heat flowed toward me in welcome waves and I sighed in relief.

Layk raised his arm, letting Gare pull back the bandages to inspect the wound. "We'll apply more salve to it, but we shouldn't have to worry about infection," Gare said. He turned to Narek, who was taking more time to pull himself to his feet. "What about you?"

Narek limped to the fire and plopped down on one of the logs before it, stretching his fingers over the flames to warm them. "I'm fine," he grunted, though his pale face said otherwise.

Gare merely shrugged his shoulders and turned away to dig the salve from his pack. As soon as Gare had tended to his injury, Layk showed us the squirrels and rabbits he'd shot during his watch and set to skinning them. I was already longing for the familiar seafood I ate in Misroth City or the lamb and beef in Evren, but as soon as the meat began roasting over the flames, my stomach rumbled.

Narek redressed his wound and Jennah and I packed up camp while Layk prepared our meal and Gare watched our surroundings warily. By the time we finished eating, kicked snow over the fire, and hefted our packs onto our sore shoulders, the sun was already low on the western horizon, its rays barely piercing through the rows of trees stretching before us. Our great shadows like ghosts following on our heels, we set off through the snow once more.

As soon as darkness settled around us, the oppressive feeling struck me again: the sensation that perhaps we were being watched, being hunted. Dread hung so thickly in the air I could feel it tingle on my tongue, creep down my throat, and descend toward my pounding heart. With every step, I scanned the gathering shadows for golden eyes and kept my bow in hand, even when the air grew so cold that my fingers felt numb trying to keep their grasp on the weapon. We were all quiet as we walked, all too intent on listening for possible danger to carry a conversation.

After several long, anxious hours, Narek stopped, his body going rigid as he peered intently into the forest. Layk drew an arrow while Gare studied the area warily. Jennah seemed as lost as I was. *Did you hear something?* I longed to voice the question pulsing through my head, but I was afraid to make a sound.

Layk had already fitted an arrow to his bowstring when Narek drew his sword from its sheath. Gare stiffened and unsheathed his own blade and Jennah drew her daggers. As I plucked an arrow from my quiver, I cast an uneasy glance toward Jennah, but she tossed her head, a few ringlets falling defiantly from her knot of hair. Her heritage shone true as ever. If Alrenians ever felt fear, they never seemed to show it.

A shadow leapt from the underbrush, flying straight toward us. Layk had already released his arrow, but his hasty shot went awry. The sedwa collided with Gare, who flung it back with a well-timed kick to its jaw. Snarling, it rolled in the snow twice before springing back up and snapping at Narek. He sliced his blade at its legs, but the creature anticipated his intent and darted away.

Panting, its great eyes studying us raptly, the sedwa began circling us. Layk and I both shot at it, yet each time the sedwa was faster. It seemed to know our attack maneuvers before we executed them.

Snatches of a vision fluttered through my brain: the sedwa stalking a form through the woods, watching its movements and learning. The sedwa attacking one night and leaving the man—Marke—wounded and bleeding. The sedwa had learned from its last encounter with a human. The vision faded, and I looked up. Another form lurked in the darkness...

"There's another one," Layk hissed, nodding toward the blackness behind us.

A second pair of eyes launched itself from the shadows. This time the pair attacked in tandem and our defense fell into chaos. The creatures were too swift to stop with our shots, and even the arrows that struck the sedwa glanced off their scales or simply grazed them, scarcely drawing blood. We clumped into a tight circle, back to back, and sliced, swung, shot, and kicked wildly. It seemed like fangs and scales and claws and golden eyes were everywhere. There were more than two sedwa now, more than I could count while fending off constant attacks.

I shot again and again toward pairs of eyes that flashed in the blackness. One of my companions cried out—Gare? Layk?—and I heard Jennah grunt. A creature jumped straight toward me and I knelt in the snow and aimed for its underbelly. The sedwa collapsed into a heap, glaring at me until its body shuddered and fell still. Shaking from cold and adrenaline, I stood and aimed at another sedwa. The creatures were all around us now and closing in.

The world grew unnaturally quiet around us, as if everything had frozen while the sedwa stared at us and we stared back at them. I counted four in my view and imagined at least that many behind me, facing the companions at my back.

This is not how we die, I thought, and shot one of the beast's eyes.

Behind me, Narek spoke. "Prepare for them to all leap at once."

"Because they never hunt in packs," I muttered, but he ignored me. But I knew what he meant. The sedwa learned from their encounters with humans, and these ones had learned enough to adapt their hunting style.

Perhaps the sedwa were waiting in order to relish the panic on our faces. I fully believed they were intelligent enough to do that. With shaking fingers, I strung another arrow. Something rustled in the underbrush ahead. My chest tightened. More sedwa? An arrow whirred through the air and struck one of the sedwa from behind, bouncing off its scales but enraging it. Whirling around with a low growl, it turned to face its new attacker. Nothing but the shadowy forest awaited it.

I didn't have time to wonder, because that was when all the sedwa attacked. I struck one in its open maw, temporarily driving it to retreat. Then the rest were upon us. Hundreds of pounds of muscle and fangs plowed me to the earth.

Thoughts that had come to me before in moments like this, the ones that seemed to come from something outside of me, filled my head again. *Keep fighting! You can do this…* I felt the same jolt of determination I'd felt years ago when I'd nearly drowned in the Alrenian, the same courage when I'd been on the chopping block on my father's orders.

Two sedwa snapped at my legs and I barely had time to squirm back through the snow, narrowly avoiding their fangs. I still had a tight hold on my bow, but it took extra effort to extend my arm and grasp another arrow. Desperate, I kicked at the sedwa's heads, forcing them back. They were hardly dazed by my efforts, but I continued to thrash and cry out, anything to keep them from leaping on top of me and sinking their claws into my chest. Fangs pierced my boot and cut through the leather, sinking toward my leg, puncturing the skin. Hot pain lanced through my ankle.

Jennah tossed one of her daggers toward me. With another grunt of pain, I embedded it deep in the sedwa's mouth. It released its hold and, bleeding and groaning, sank to the ground, leaving a scarlet trail in the snow. I slashed across the soft patch of skin beneath the second sedwa's eye the same instant an arrow landed in its other eye. It collapsed instantly, and I spun toward the forest, from which the arrow had come.

A figure followed the arrow. It slipped out from the trees with ease, so silent and graceful it nearly blended with the shadows. Its black cloak and hood shrouded the figure so that I couldn't determine if it were a man or woman. It nocked an arrow to its bow and shot at another of the sedwa, striking it first in one eye and then the other with stunning speed and accuracy. Before the figure had fully emerged into the clearing, the sedwa was sprawled out dead on the ground with the others we'd killed.

Jennah's hand was on my shoulder and she was saying something, perhaps urging me to my feet, but I felt trapped in place. My ankle throbbed, my pulse raced, and I was mesmerized by the stranger's movements—so practiced, so confident, so *familiar*.

Nearby, Narek sliced a sedwa's head clean off, spraying black blood over his shirt and face. He swiped at his cheek and spun on his heel to face the last of the creatures, but Gare made short work of it. Jennah yanked me to my feet, offering her arm for support. My eyes snapped to the stranger once more, just as the form threw back its hood and met my gaze.

Avrik.

CHAPTER SIX

I STOOD MOTIONLESS AS THE breeze fluttered through my hair and pushed tendrils into my eyes. My tongue fastened to the roof of my mouth; my heart beat out an erratic rhythm against my ribcage.

Avrik stood stiffly while his dark eyes traveled over my face, my unusual garb, and back again. There was no sign of his familiar grin or the light in his eyes that, until now, I hadn't realized had comforted me so much. Stubble bristled along his jaw and his clothing, the usual brown trousers and shirt of hunters, appeared tattered and dirty, like he'd been in the forest for days. His complexion was pale and smudged with something black—dirt, or sedwa blood?

Before I could speak, Jennah stepped forward. "Who are you?"

Gare shot her a sidelong glance. "Thank you for your help," he cut in.

Avrik's eyes never left my face. "Perhaps you should ask her," he said in a low voice, nodding to me.

Layk glanced at me. "You know this boy, my lady?" His voice was dark with suspicion and he studied Avrik warily.

Boy? You two are nearly the same age. Biting back my retort, I nodded and swallowed, trying to bring moisture to my mouth. "He is my…" I cleared my throat. "This is Avrik of Evren. He is a…hunter." My eyes snapped back to Avrik, who still hadn't moved, though he was now studying my companions.

I drew a deep breath and dared to approach him. "What are you doing here?"

He pressed his lips together, and for as long as he'd watched me, I was surprised when he turned away to avoid my gaze. "I could ask you the same question." Recalling himself, he hastily pressed his fist to his breast. "My lady."

Narek swept toward me, sheathing his blade in one fluid motion. "*My lady*," he said, and the sarcasm was so heavy in his tone that even Avrik frowned and watched him through narrow eyes. "We must be on our way." He flung a careless glance in Avrik's direction. "Thank you for your help, though I think it'd be wise if you returned to Evren and abandoned your hunt. Unless your intent is to anger the creatures." His gaze turned suddenly piercing.

I turned back to Avrik in time to see him flush. "That was not my intent at all," he protested. He hesitated, shaking his head. "I was a fool, thinking I could make a difference. But I guess if my foolishness helped you in the end, it was not completely ill-fated."

"You can say that when you've made it safely home," Narek muttered, turning away from him to press toward the edge of the clearing.

"Wait," Jennah snapped. "Halia was hurt. We can't leave yet."

But she hesitated, for I couldn't stop staring at Avrik in surprise and confusion. A thousand words hung between us, things too heavy to say, yet also far too heavy to hold inside. They swirled inside me like frantic caged birds catching a glimpse of freedom just before that door closed to them forever. I wanted to ask how Lyanna and Rev were, how our friends fared, how *he* was. But I supposed I already knew the answer. Memories of my vision of him visiting his father Kyrin replayed before my eyes: the hurt and anger on his face, the contempt in his tone when he spoke my name.

You shouldn't be out here. You should be safe in Evren. But I couldn't say those words either, because I knew the furtive glances and whispered words that awaited him there. The association he held with a man who had endangered the entire town must have made him an outcast overnight, perhaps even to some of our old friends. And where was his home? An empty log cabin set near the woods, full of memories of parents he would never have again?

Though I couldn't feel guilty for revealing the truth and speaking out to help save Evren, I also couldn't shake the horrible knowledge that it was I, as surely as anyone, who had sentenced Kyrin to death. Avrik was grieving and angry—this blood-spattered, pale version of himself with darkness in his eyes—because of me.

"Sit," Jennah demanded at last, and I obeyed wordlessly. "It isn't too bad," she murmured once she'd removed my damaged boot and stocking. An ugly cut ran along my outer ankle, but it was shallow and thankfully hadn't done more than pierce some skin. Jennah's hands worked quickly, cleaning the wound, applying ointment to keep infection away, and wrapping it in clean cloth. She helped me find a clean stocking in my pack and pull my boot over my foot.

"Let's be off," Narek repeated, shifting on his feet impatiently.

Jennah shot him a glare as she helped me up. But a little pain and Narek's edginess couldn't keep me from turning back to Avrik again.

He dared to meet my stare, then nodded toward Narek with a grim expression. "Who is he?"

There were too many complicated answers to that question, too many things I hadn't yet sorted out myself. Ally? Enemy? The man I would condemn to death if I ever returned to Misroth? "My guide," I responded. I turned and gestured to my companions. "And these are my friends." My voice nearly failed me on the word *friends*, jumping up a few pitches almost of its own accord. I looked back to Avrik, but his expression showed no sign he had taken notice.

"And guards," Layk added in a low voice.

Gare stepped forward. "I hate to admit it," he said, the frown creasing his brow a confirmation of the sentiment, "but Narek is right, princess. The woods are still dangerous. It is best to be on the move…to leave this place." He cast a glance at the sedwa carcasses littering the glade.

I studied Avrik's face, wondering what I wanted more: for him to disappear or for him to stay. After weeks of longing to see him again, of feeling abandoned and rejected, of wishing I could comfort him, my emotions swirled in a confusing mass I couldn't begin to sort through now. "You'd be safer traveling with us than staying alone in this forest tonight." I hesitated for a moment before adding, "Come with us."

The muscles in his jaw tensed. "Is that an order…princess?"

Frowning, I watched his brow furrow as I slowly shook my head. "No," I murmured, turning to walk back to my companions, "but it is wise advice."

My companions and I began to file out of the clearing quietly, our boots crunching in the snow as we went. The pain in my ankle was slight, more of an annoyance than anything, much less problematic than the hole torn through my boot that let the cold and snow in with every step I took.

Behind us, Avrik hesitated for an instant before following. I couldn't tell if the breath I released was due to relief or frustration, but I ignored my feelings and concentrated on surveying my surroundings and ducking around clawing branches.

After a long while, when we'd seen no sign of more sedwa stalking us and our sense of foreboding weighed less heavily on our hearts, Jennah spoke. Except for the moments when the underbrush grew too close for two to walk side by side, she had kept pace with me this entire time, now and then stealing glances at me. I had the uncanny feeling that she was reading my feelings and thoughts all too easily, and no matter how I tried to set my jaw and lift my chin with a nonchalant air, I knew I couldn't fully mask my discomfort about Avrik. Perhaps Alrenians could also detect a person's fear and the trait had carried through the generations to her.

"Princess, are you going to tell Avrik where we are going?" she asked, as if Avrik, who walked behind us, couldn't overhear.

"He's under no obligation to accompany us there," I muttered. "We can part ways as soon as we leave the forest."

"A wise idea," Narek, in the lead as usual, cut in. "You hardly need further distractions."

The way he said the word, even with his back turned, made my cheeks heat. *Distractions.* As if anything could delay or dissuade me from my purpose. If Avrik hadn't been able to keep me from joining the rebellion in the capital, he certainly would never keep me from saving my cousin.

"The only distraction here is you," Layk cut in. "You are just as likely to embrace the freedom offered to you now and flee as lead us anywhere near our king. Are you truly a helper, or only a hindrance?"

Walking behind him, Gare set a steadying hand on Layk's shoulder, a gentle reminder for him to hold his anger at bay.

Narek spun on his heel to watch Layk. "I killed your king, yet you doubt my allegiance?" A smile played about his lips, seeming to contradict everything he said. His eyes glittered in the darkness.

"Yes," Layk snarled back, "and I—and most of my comrades here— have the scars to prove my doubts."

Narek's lips were still twisted in a grin when he turned his back on Layk and pressed onward into the night. "Have you considered that perhaps I want to return to Misroth? That I may even want a new monarch on the throne, since I killed the last?"

I watched Layk's body tense as his hands formed into fists, but he said nothing.

"You're traveling to Toryn to find the crown prin—the new king?" Avrik's voice sounded soft behind me after Layk's angry outburst.

Without turning, I said, "We are going to find my cousin and put him on his throne."

"The word in Kelwed was that the people wanted to make you queen…princess…whether Gillen was alive or not." Again, Avrik's voice betrayed no emotion and I was tempted to turn around, to see if the old light was back in his eyes and my friend had returned to me. I resisted and continued to put one foot in front of the other.

"The throne is not mine to take," I said firmly.

"Not according to the people," Avrik muttered. "My lady," he added quickly, his voice stumbling awkwardly over the unfamiliar address. I hated how it sounded but didn't dare correct him.

I closed my eyes to extinguish the memories of my visions, blood and darkness and death and Gillen's pale, hunted face. "Gillen is not dead. I will not take the throne from him."

The rest of the night was blessedly uneventful, with our company keeping mostly quiet as we looked and listened for more sedwa. Now and then my companions cast curious looks at Avrik, but we were all too tense and exhausted to speak much, so they held their questions. As the sky began to soften to grey, we found another short clearing to set up camp and ate a meal of jerky, apples, bread, and leftover rabbit meat Avrik had stored in his pack. The first rays of dawn were peeking through the branches of the trees when I settled on my bedroll, watching Avrik recline just a few feet away. Narek, Gare, and Layk had already retired and Jennah, who had first watch, stood at the edge of the clearing, silently watching the sunrise with a pensive expression.

I considered lying down and ignoring Avrik, but somehow, despite my anger and hurt, I couldn't tear my eyes away. "Why *were* you in the forest?" I asked, wondering if I truly wanted to hear the answer.

He paused, sitting cross-legged on his bedroll and watching me intently. Unbuckling his belt and laying his hunting knife by his side, he ran his fingers along the leather sheath absent-mindedly. "I think you know the answer to that."

I bowed my head to avoid his gaze. "I'm sorry."

When I dared to look up again, his eyes seemed softer, though the light was still painfully missing. "He's dead."

The air felt thick between us as I considered the pain and betrayal and despair and bitterness packed into those two words. Was he relieved?

Grieving? Confused? My brain groped for the memory of my father's death, already seeming so distant, but I still felt numb. Instead, I returned to my mother's final moments, her last attempt to speak as her lifeblood spilled out onto me. Without thinking, I slid my fingers over my armband, the cool leather a cruel reminder of losses carved into my soul long before my mother's passing. I'd grieved her loss long ago, but somehow that hadn't made her death any easier.

Avrik fidgeted with his knife, unsheathing it and tossing it from hand to hand as he watched the firelight reflected on its blade. His voice was surprisingly even as he continued. "I suppose that is what you wanted."

"Avrik, I—" But my voice died before I could protest. That *was* what I'd wanted, wasn't it? When I'd left Evren, I had hoped for justice—justice for Evren, justice for all of Misroth. I'd wanted to know my people could live in safety without people like my father and Kyrin throwing them into danger. But after longing for justice for years, I'd found that it had an ugly side I wasn't sure I could face. When I blinked, I could see the executioner's axe falling and my father's loyalists die in a mess of blood the Misrothians had welcomed. I sighed, guilt slithering through my heart like a poison. "I wanted to know the people were safe."

Avrik slammed the knife into the snow, releasing it to stand on its own. He glanced back up at me. His face was still calm, almost thoughtful, but he couldn't hide his churning emotions from me. I could see the storm lurking in the depths of his eyes. "I did too," he admitted, his tone surprisingly soft. "That's why I am in Evren Forest. I was a fool, thinking I could hunt the sedwa to extinction and redeem my father's actions." He ran a weary hand across his face. "No, I wasn't truly thinking. And now I've probably only enraged them more with each one I have killed."

Speechless, I studied the pain etched across his face and wondered if he was angrier at me or his father. Or himself. "You can't stay in this forest," I said at last. "You'll get yourself killed."

"I can't go back, El—princess." He drew a deep breath. "They don't...no one looks at me the same. Some even suspect I was involved.

I…I can't stand the suspicion or the pity."

"I understand." I shifted my gaze to glance at the rising sun, wishing I could feel its warmth instead of only the bitter cold enclosing me. "Perhaps you can go with us to Kelwed and start fresh there."

Avrik released a slow breath, wrenched his knife from the snow, and wiped it across his trouser leg. "The past isn't that easy to leave behind."

I closed my eyes. *I know,* I thought.

"You should sleep," he said gruffly. "I…goodnight." Sheathing his knife, he slipped off his cloak and burrowed into his bedroll without another word.

I lay down as well. My attempts at sleep failed for a long while, even when sounds of steady breathing informed me my companions were swiftly falling asleep. Rolling over, I caught Jennah's gaze as she leaned against a tree. The knowing expression on her face told me everything: she remembered our long-ago conversation with her daughter about love and knew exactly who Avrik had been to me. But who was he to me now?

Ignoring her look, I forced my eyes shut and slipped into uneasy dreams, where Kyrin was hung before a crowd in Evren and Lyanna and Rev turned with disapproving eyes to ask why I had sentenced an innocent man to death. Then the dream shifted, and it was my mother dying in my arms again, except this time she managed to breathe out her last words to me: "Perhaps you are more like your father than you think."

Jennah woke me only a few hours later. Startled, I jerked away from her hands. "No," I mumbled, still more ensnared by my nightmares than awake to the real world.

Jennah sat back on her heels. She glanced over her shoulder at the others, who were all either stirring from their bedrolls or already sitting beside the fire. "Do you want to keep going? Or do you need to rest a while longer, princess?" she teased.

I sat up quickly, rubbing my eyes, and glared at her. "No, I was only dreaming. I'm fine." As if I could shake the dreams out of my brain, I shook my head.

As I joined the others around the fire, my eyes snagged on Avrik and I felt my heart twinge in response. I averted my gaze.

"Will you go with us to Kelwed?" Gare was asking Avrik.

His shoulders hunched uncomfortably, Avrik was quiet a moment as he warmed himself by the fire. "I suppose. I sort of…lost my way in the forest."

Layk studied Avrik as if he had a thousand questions, but again, no one pressed him for more information. Yet.

We ate breakfast and tended to our wounds hastily. My foot was uncomfortable but manageable, and I refused to linger when my friends suggested it. We left our camp while the sun was still high in the sky, just discernable above the tangled, twisted boughs overhead.

With the woods bathed in light, our hearts were light and our footsteps free as we walked. Gare began to share old tales he'd learned during his days in the military, stories of the great battles won and lost in Misroth's quest to break free of the Alrenian Empire. Some were common knowledge throughout Misroth and others were new to all of us. He even told us accounts of Eldon and Tamelle, laughing aloud as he described some of Eldon's feats against the former empress of Alrenor, and all but Narek broke into a smile at his accounts.

"My favorite is the tale of when Eldon first wore the insignia Tamelle made for him in battle: the constellation Vehgar across his chest," Gare finished after we'd requested many stories from him. "They say Empress Ilett's face turned scarlet at the sight of a dragon on her opponent's armor, especially knowing the Misrothian tale about Vehgar and Shyla…" He chuckled. "A dragon that is *slain* by a Misrothian warrior? That was the height of insult and rebellion. But if that was bad, the stories say that the empress screamed loudly enough to be heard all the way across the Great Sea when he approached her own dragon and it submitted to him before her very eyes. But that is one I know you all have heard countless times, so I will spare you from hearing it again." He chuckled and flashed Jennah a knowing smile. "The Alrenians may be known for their fearless strength, but may it always be known that we Misrothians have spunk and fire to match theirs."

Jennah winked at her friend. "That is why I cling to the best traits of my heritage, yet pledge my allegiance to Misroth."

Even Layk's usually somber expression relaxed into a grin, giving him a boyish look at odds with the aura of the hardened guard he often radiated. "If only dragons lived in Misroth as well as Alrenor. Imagine what it would be like to ride a dragon." His face shone with excitement.

"We do not need dragons!" Gare cried. "Alrenians are the Dragon Tamers, but *we* are the Dragon-Hearted," he boasted.

Curious, Avrik's expression brightened for the first time since he'd joined us. "They wouldn't need their dragons for war anymore, unless they've moved on to conquer the kingdoms across the Great Sea," he said, pushing a branch aside and matching his pace with Narek's. "This morning, Layk told me you are from Toryn. Have you had many associations with the Alrenians? Do they still train and ride dragons for sport?"

Not breaking his stride, Narek scowled. "I haven't been in Toryn for years."

"Then what a joyous homecoming this will be for you," Layk said, his voice heavy with sarcasm.

Narek shot him a mirthless smile, and silence fell over our group.

To our relief, we left Evren Forest before nightfall and walked several more hours into the open countryside before we made camp. With the snow fully melted now, the grass was blissfully clear and my feet were finally both dry. After journeying with minimal rest, we spoke little until after dinner was over. I retreated early to my bedroll and Narek kept his distance from everyone, but my friends remained gathered around the fire.

When I lay back on my bedroll and found I could at last study the stars clearly once more, I felt a small portion of my tensions sink away. Out of habit I found Vehgar, taking comfort in the familiar reminder of some of the traits my kingdom held dear: strength, beauty, and light. I grinned to myself. Not because the dragon was considered strong or beautiful or full of light, but because a kingdom of people who could conquer such a beast possessed all those qualities and more. The more I thought about Tamelle's rebellious spirit in choosing to stitch such an insignia on the new Misrothian flag, the more I thought I would have liked to meet her.

When I rolled onto my side, I could see Narek seated a few yards away, avoiding the conversation around the campfire and polishing his sword religiously. His brow furrowed in concentration and his eyes dark as ever, he studied the blade carefully, watching the way the night sky reflected along its glossy surface.

Perhaps you are more like your father than you think. His words made me wonder why, if he'd slain my father and believed I bore his resemblance, he hadn't yet killed me.

The conversation from my friends at the fire reached my ears and I lay still to watch and listen. It seemed they were finally at ease enough to ask Avrik about himself.

"So," Layk said softly, poking aimlessly at the fire with a stick. "What was an Evren hunter doing so deep within the forest? I didn't think anyone ventured that far into the monster-infested woods these days."

Avrik shifted uncomfortably on the rock he was seated on and stared down at his hands. "I was leaving Evren." He cleared his throat. "My friends are few these days."

"I'm sorry to hear about your friends. Though knowing you were leaving Evren is a relief to hear." Gare chuckled a little, as if trying to lighten the mood. "I was about to ask if the people of Evren made a habit of hunting sedwa in their spare time."

Avrik smiled wanly. "Not unless they want a death sentence."

"Are you a criminal then?" Layk pressed.

This time, Avrik was a little taken aback. He titled his head to one side, as if considering.

Jennah sat down beside Layk. "Come now! He's traveled this far without killing us in our sleep," she jested, nudging his shoulder. "I think you can trust anyone Halia vouches for."

Layk shrugged. "I was just…"

Narek had set aside his sword and was fidgeting with an instrument I was unfamiliar with, an intricately carved piece that resembled a flute. "Practicing your interrogation skills?" he asked from his seat on the other side of the fire. His eyes flicked to Layk's arms, where some of the burns he'd inflicted on him were hidden beneath Layk's sleeves. "Maybe you should fetch your matches."

Layk glared and jerked to his feet. His hand was on his sword hilt in an instant. "Do you *want* to die, you filthy bas—"

"Stop!" Jennah snatched his arms to hold him back.

For a moment I gaped at the scene, for I'd always thought of Layk as the perfect image of discipline and self-restraint. I'd never seen him lose his temper like this. Remembering myself, I stood, wondering if I would need to spring between him and Narek and remind Layk of my authority. Gare was also standing, his hand resting on his sword hilt and his gaze flashing between Layk and Narek, as if unsure where he was truly needed. Avrik remained seated, watching the scene warily. Perhaps he was questioning the wisdom in traveling with our group, after all.

But Narek had not moved and his sword still lay untouched at his side. He laid down his instrument and quirked an eyebrow at Layk. "I know you hated Zarev, but I thought you would be more grateful, considering I killed him for you."

"You idiot," Layk spat. His face was more controlled and he no longer struggled against Jennah's grasp, but his eyes burned like blue fire. His voice trembled. Slowly, Jennah released him and he dropped his hands to his sides. "Why would I be grateful to the man who tortured my friends and me?" He rolled up his shirtsleeve to reveal the angry red flesh marking one of the places he'd been burned during his captivity in the castle dungeons. "To the one who almost murdered my friend's mother and children?" Behind him, Jennah pressed her lips into a firm line, as if she were questioning her choice to hold her friend back from hurting Narek. "To the one who served the man who murdered my parents?"

There was no trace of a smile on Narek's lips this time. For an instant, I thought I saw the color drain from his cheeks, then wondered if it was merely a trick of the firelight casting shadows on his face. He swallowed. "We each of us have done what we must."

"Why *did* you kill the regent?" Gare demanded. "It seems you only pledge service to whomever can offer you what you want, when you want it." He glanced in my direction. "If you expect mercy from her, if you thought you could wheedle your way into her graces because you slew her father and helped end her rebellion when Zarev was losing ground, you are a fool. Her gift will help her see through your lies and her friends will be more than happy to kill you if you lay a hand on her. Ever."

Narek shook his head. "I'm not here to make friends. You don't have to remind me you all hate me." He offered me a mock salute. "Goodnight." He began to unpack his bedroll, but I could not help but think that for once, he had been shaken by my friends' words.

My throat felt tight as I approached the fire and turned to Layk, who was finally sitting back down. Beside him, Jennah patted his shoulder consolingly. Gare joined them, his eyes full of sympathy. "My father killed your parents?" I asked. I had known Layk and his siblings were orphans, that he had cared for them ever since their parents had died, but I'd never heard the story of how or when they'd died. Even though I already knew my father had committed countless atrocities, against myself and my people, it struck a painful chord within me to hear this evil he had committed against my friend. As if I were partially responsible. Maybe I was. *If I had returned to the city and spoken out about him sooner...*

Layk stared into the fire, his expression once again stoic. "They were members of the rebellion, almost from its infancy. They tried to be secretive about it, to keep me uninvolved, but I was already training to be in the guard and thought I could be useful by gathering information for them." He shrugged. "I was fourteen, so they finally agreed to let me join some of their meetings. I sat in on their last one."

Gare's and Jennah's faces were taut with sadness. It made sense. As fellow members of the rebellion, they would have known Layk's parents. They'd probably endured countless losses long before I'd even known a rebellion existed, when I was still hiding in Evren and playing the role of a country girl. My stomach churned with guilt.

I hovered near the fire but felt too uncomfortable to sit or even look my friend in the eye. He had been fourteen when he'd attended his first rebel meeting, while I'd once used my youth as an excuse for my cowardice.

"My father was a professor of mathematics at Vaerda University, and frequently used his position to speak out against Zarev and recruit rebels. My mother did much the same as a midwife, although occasionally she tended to noblewomen or Councilor's family members, and then she acted more as a spy to gather information on what the king was planning next." Layk picked up the stick he'd been using earlier and broke it in half. "The next morning, after our meeting, they left for work and never came back. We heard the news later that they'd been taken by the Royal Guard on suspicion of treasonous actions. That was before the king regent began public executions, so it was not until a few weeks later that we received word they'd been drowned in the Alrenian." His expression hardened. "I joined the rebellion after that. My parents had been wrong about me being too young. I had siblings to care for and a cause to pursue. I was hired into the city guard not long afterward and began using my position just as my parents had used theirs before me."

For a while, I stood in stunned silence. What could I say? It was Avrik who broke the stillness.

"Are we a band of orphans then?" he asked. He smirked, even though I knew his pain was still raw, his lighthearted demeanor a farce. His eyes drifted toward me and then quickly away.

Jennah shook her head. "My mother still lives."

Gare shrugged. "And my parents are happy and healthy, last I heard, living in Argelon, my home. Or what was my home until we were told we were at war for the first time in two hundred years and I was stationed in Misroth City to train and prepare for…" He shook his head and laughed. "The imaginary war."

I clamped down the emotions of sadness and guilt that threatened me and turned to Layk. My voice was steady and clear. "I'm sorry about your parents, Layk. Please accept my condolences."

"It's not your fault, my lady."

Rather than responding, I bid my friends goodnight and returned to my bedroll.

Gare, Jennah, Layk, and Avrik remained close to the fire, soon dispersing the heaviness that had settled over us all by talking and laughing so freely it was as if Avrik had known them all his life. Apparently Layk's suspicions melted away as he learned more about Avrik, because he stopped trying to interrogate him. I heard snatches of what Avrik shared: descriptions of hunting and trading trips he'd taken with his father years ago, though he managed to avoid talking much about his father. His manners were easy around them, full of his natural charm, and the storm in his eyes all but disappeared when he smiled at my friends. He looked like the Avrik I remembered when he was with them, not the new, haunted Avrik he was around me. I tried to ignore the way this knowledge cut, but I couldn't.

"We practiced tracking and hunting in Argelon, but I can't say any of our soldiers would come close to your skill," Gare said with a smile. "From what I saw of your shooting the other night, you would make a fine soldier yourself."

Avrik waved his compliment away. "In a small town like Evren, there is a lot more time to dedicate to archery or hunting practice. Although," he added with a frown, "it's rightfully considered a dangerous occupation, especially now. My father—well, when I was young I would stay near the edges of the forest to track game, and now, with the sedwa having attacked some townspeople, no one really hunts at all." He frowned. "I…thought I could help Evren by trying to kill all the sedwa, but I was a fool and I've probably done more harm than good."

Catching Avrik's dark expression, Jennah turned to Gare. "How about another tale of one of the great battles in the Misrothian Rebellion?"

With a grin, Gare launched into another of his old war tales, and Avrik sat as enraptured as Layk and Jennah were. Biting back a sigh, I rolled over to face away from them and squeezed my eyes shut. It took a long time, but eventually I fell asleep to the sound of their distant voices and laughter.

The next morning's trek through the countryside toward the port city of Kelwed was an easy one, especially after the enclosed, eerie atmosphere of Evren Forest. It took only a short while for us to discover the old dirt road winding toward the city. It had once been a route that passed all the way through the wood, but it was now rarely traveled this far east. Still, it connected Kelwed to various nearby villages—including Evren—and therefore wasn't fully overgrown with disuse.

After the cold nights within the forest, the morning sun offered a comforting warmth as it burned unhindered on our backs. There were few clouds overhead and the sky was such a bright blue one could almost imagine winter was already long past. A few birds twittered as they darted through the air overhead, making me wonder if they already sensed the approach of spring.

Before long Jennah was entertaining us with old Alrenian songs, sung in her rich alto tones, and even my burdens felt eased. Strolling along beside me with her head held high, her curls flying free of her knot, and her dark skin glowing gold beneath the sun, she looked too joyful to be walking into the nightmares I'd seen waiting for us. Yet at the same time, clothed in the black leggings and tunic the royal seamstress had fashioned for her, with her curved daggers strapped to her belt, she looked too imposing to be singing love songs on a mild winter's day.

When she sang of the Life-Giver my mind went back to calm mornings in Evren's garden and I drew comfort from the memory. I imagined Lyanna and Rev beside me and Avrik near, still a loyal friend, and I could almost forget the armband of mourning tight on my arm, the visions of Gillen, the guilt of all I hadn't done. All I might now be attempting to do far too late.

Gradually, the countryside around us began to show signs of population. We came across grazing cattle, sheep, and goats picking their way through the rolling fields. The road began to widen until we found we weren't the only travelers on it anymore; smaller paths began to intersect the road and occasional horses and wagons came into view, their riders most often turned westward, toward Kelwed. I saw brick cottages creeping with ivy and moss and roughly hewn log cabins nestled against the hillsides, and then the sprawling mass of Kelwed showed on the horizon: a city perhaps half the size of the capital, but looking quite imposing even from the distance. Far beyond the city, I could even make out the vague shapes of the Vorvinian Mountains stretching toward the sky.

Finally, we found a bubbling stream winding between the hills and rushing past the roadside. It was too small to be found on the maps of Misroth I'd studied, so I didn't even know its name, but its presence was comforting. We paused to replenish our dwindling water supply and wash our grimy faces. The water was cool and refreshing, a welcome relief even in the chilly air after days without bathing.

Eventually the stream turned, and where it intersected with the road a small wooden bridge had been built. As soon as we crossed it I realized how near we had drawn to Kelwed. Its gates already loomed before us, and the road was growing thick with traffic bustling to and from the city. Though Kelwed's gates were much smaller than those of the capital, they were still impressive, set within a great stone wall erected less to keep invaders out of the city than to keep questionable foreigners from the harbor within and cut off from the rest of the kingdom.

The gates were flung wide for the afternoon traffic, and the guards posted on either side as well as along the ramparts appeared about as idle and lazy as guards standing stiff and solemn at their posts could. Despite the clothing we wore, marking all but Avrik and Narek like we were members of the Guard, we passed through unnoticed, blending into the crowds as if we were merely another group coming to trade goods or spend an afternoon shopping.

Once within, the crowds reminded me of the throngs within the capital, except there were almost no noblemen or noblewomen to be seen, only common villagers and citizens dressed in unassuming attire in drab brown, white, and grey or muted green and black. However, the city itself seemed just as large as Misroth City, a great maze of cobblestone streets winding past rows of towering buildings made of timber from Evren Forest and the Vorvinian Mountains. Here, even more than in Misroth City, I noticed the roar of the Alrenian, like a constant undercurrent ever blending with the chatter of crowds, the click of horse hooves, the rumble and creak of carriages, the tolling of bells, and the cries of gulls overhead. Unlike the capital full of its squares and open markets, we passed only one small city square, adorned with a simple stone fountain now dried up for the winter and full of melting snow. There were no outdoor stalls or vendors crying out to the passersby about their wares. Instead there were only closed-up shops with narrow windows offering brief glimpses of their interiors. Most of the people I saw, especially the patrolling guards, wore suspicious expressions, as if they expected a foreign invasion to begin within their harbor at any moment, despite nearly two hundred years of peace within our kingdom.

As we drew nearer to the harbor I could make out the shapes of great sails billowing over the rooftops ahead, while the steady ringing of hammers filled the air as ships were repaired. Sailors' shouts or snatches of songs floated toward us on the wind, which seemed even brinier than the air of the capital. The scent settled in the back of my throat, burning as it went down and calling up reminders of the night I'd nearly drowned in the Alrenian. I willed the memory away.

As we drew further into the city, Layk turned to me. "Avrik mentioned an inn he's stayed at before, if you would like him to lead the way there, my lady."

I nodded. "Lead the way, Avrik."

We followed him silently as he turned off onto a quieter, narrower street. We passed a fabric shop, its windows full of its most expensive, colorful rolls of material, and a bakery, where the scent of bread hung so thickly that my stomach began to growl. Avrik stopped before an inn with a weatherworn sign over the door that read *The Rusty Anchor*.

He pulled open the door and we filed inside. The inn was larger than Wanderer's Rest in Evren, though the great wooden support beams lining the ceiling and the huge hearth at the opposite end of the room lent it a familiar atmosphere. The room was open and spacious, with sunlight pouring in through windows nearly as large as the walls they occupied. The windows to the left offered a view of the street outside, while the windows on the right provided a view of a quiet edge of the harbor, away from the bustle and noise of the docks.

At this early hour, only a few patrons sat at the fireside, and they cast us curious glances as we entered. I felt uncomfortable for the first time in the outfit the royal seamstress had provided. What if citizens in Kelwed recognized me and demanded to know more of the rebellion in the capital and my current plans? Few were likely to recognize me on sight outside of the capital, not when I'd spent so much of life all but unknown, but I didn't want to take the chance. While my companions threw back their hoods, I kept mine pulled low.

An elderly man shuffled forward from a room deeper within the inn. "Greetings! What may I do for you?"

Layk glanced at me for confirmation before he spoke. I gave him a nod, and he turned back to the innkeeper. "We need accommodations, just for tonight," he said.

While Layk paid the innkeeper, I turned to Avrik, who was studying our surroundings quietly, his face a mask that almost hid his emotions but for the dimness in his eyes. Was he imagining a time he'd stayed here with his father, years ago?

The innkeeper called on another man to guide us to our rooms, and soon Jennah and I were settling into our own space. We took turns soaking in the tub in our private washroom, which a maid filled with steaming buckets of water upon request. Once we were dressed in fresh clothes, Jennah tended to my ankle again. We left the inn briefly to visit a cobbler down the street, where I purchased a new pair of thick leather boots. Then we returned to the dining room of The Rusty Anchor, where Layk, Avrik, Gare, and Narek joined us. Their faces were scrubbed of filth, their clothes were fresh, and Layk and Narek had new bandages after requesting the services of a local healer.

We settled into a table near a window overlooking the harbor just before the evening crowds began to arrive and ordered bowls of hearty venison stew, eating to our content and enjoying the fire's warmth. After two servings and a mug of soothing tea, I began to feel drowsy. Narek left us to sit by the fireside, drink ale, and swap stories with the locals who didn't recognize him; I watched him in puzzlement for a while before I turned away. I'd never seen him appear so sociable or…friendly. He was a mystery I wouldn't solve easily. Saying he wanted to watch Narek, Layk soon joined him.

Gare stretched, finished his drink, and announced that he was going to get some rest to prepare for an early departure the next morning. Despite my exhaustion, I wasn't ready to retire just yet. I watched Gare leave and then glanced toward Avrik, who was silently stirring his spoon around in his stew and watching the other patrons with unseeing eyes.

I sighed and turned away when Jennah caught my eye. "I'm going to sleep too," she said with a pointed look.

As soon as she left, I shifted uncomfortably in my seat, but Avrik startled me by breaking the silence.

"I'm going with you to Toryn."

For several beats I merely stared at him, too dumbfounded to speak. I shook my head to clear it and folded my arms over the tabletop. "Why?"

"Nothing I can do here on my own will stop the sedwa from attacking Misrothian villages, and everything my father and I already did has only put the people in further danger." He drew a deep breath, his eyes drifting away from me and out the window, toward the sea. "If returning the true king to the throne means our people will finally have someone who will protect them, I want to help see it done."

There was no arguing with that, but my thoughts were an endless whirlpool nonetheless. What if he were killed—could I live with myself? Could I rely on him this time, or would he turn back if our cause ever looked hopeless? Was this a chance for us to reconcile, or was he determined to avoid me even while traveling at my side?

He plucked me from my reverie with his sharp tone. "Are you going to order me to stay behind?" he asked darkly.

Frowning, I shook my head. "Never," I snapped. "You are free to make your own decisions, whether you think them through or not."

Avrik narrowed his eyes at me, but did not respond, apparently satisfied that I wasn't going to challenge his choice. Looking down at his bowl of stew, he drummed his fingers on the table as if anxious to leave. With the way we had avoided one another these past days, he probably was.

I took another sip of tea and steeled my courage. "Avrik," I said, my voice ringing out louder and firmer than I'd intended, forcing him to look up, "I need to know how Lyanna and Rev are."

He watched me for a moment before answering bluntly: "They're devastated."

My stomach dropped, though the news didn't surprise me. "Do they—do they hate me too?"

Slowly, he shook his head. "They are worried and miss you."

I bowed my head and closed my eyes, pressing the grief out of my heart and mind. Finally, I opened them, letting my gaze search his. "If you come with us to Toryn, can I count on you?" I asked in a low voice.

Avrik's drumming fingers stilled. "What do you mean?" his voice was a little uneven, giving away his rising anger.

"When things get hard, will you stand by my companions and me, or will you turn back?" This time, I couldn't keep the edge out of my voice as the familiar pain and anger of the betrayal erupted.

Avrik held his hands out helplessly. "He was my *father*, Elen...princess." He turned away and shook his head. "Can you blame me? How do you think *I* felt when I found out you weren't even who I thought you were? When his life was in danger?" When he looked back, I could see the hint of sadness in the lines on his brow, in the subtle dip of one side of his mouth.

I held his gaze without wavering before finally looking away. What was there to say? My mouth felt like sandpaper. A thousand excuses had always rippled through my brain for my actions ever since Avrik and I had parted, but seeing his pleading, accusatory eyes made them feel weak. I'd been far too consumed with my sense of betrayal to give much consideration to his, but he had every reason to feel as betrayed as I did— perhaps more so. Did he see his father die every time he looked at my face? Did he feel like Elena, the friend who would have comforted and stood by him in his grief, was lost forever—or had never even existed?

"I wanted to be Elena," I whispered.

His mouth was a firm line, his voice raw with pain. "You couldn't trust your closest friend?" He reached for me across the table, almost like an unconscious reflex out of habit, or maybe a final plea for us to find a way to set things right. His hand was warm and reassuring over mine.

"I…" The words would not come, failing me at this crucial moment. None of my reasons seemed good enough now. Nothing I could say could undo the past; there was only the future, and the future involved me accepting my place as royalty, whether or not either of us wanted that.

As suddenly as he'd reached for me, Avrik pulled away and averted his gaze. "I'm going to get some rest," he said, and was gone before I could even react.

Stunned, I sat with my head in my hands for a long while before a loud burst of laughter nearby recalled me to my surroundings. Jolting upright, I scanned the room until my gaze fell upon Layk and Narek still gathered near the fireside with a handful of other men. Layk looked surprisingly comfortable, his face brightened with a rare smile, and even Narek emanated an almost carefree aura. As if feeling the weight of my stare, Narek turned to me and shot me a half-smile that made me turn away with a grimace. If my pain was amusing to him, I wondered how long he would deem me useful before he tried to end my life as he had ended my father's.

CHAPTER SEVEN

I DREAMED OF MY MOTHER, of her dark, shimmering hair catching the light of the chandeliers adorning the castle ballroom ceiling, of the endless folds of her ivory gown sweeping across the vast black marble floor. In my dream we were attending one of King Reylon's grand balls, hosted perhaps in celebration of a birthday or in remembrance of a historic event or holy day. Whatever the occasion, the events were all similar: grand affairs that filled the castle with dozens upon dozens of lavishly arrayed guests swathed in silk and lace. Each time, my parents forced me to smile and dance with countless boys who could someday become potential suitors.

Amidst the delighted babble of the crowds, the elegant notes of the orchestra, and the rustle of gowns, I walked away from my mother to take everything in. I watched couples on the dance floor, clusters of noblemen and noblewomen on the sidelines observe and gossip together, and servants approach guests to offer them trays laden with golden agma juice, countless wines and liquors, aged cheeses, crusty bread, smoked fish, or chocolate delicacies imported all the way from Teramyl. My father strode into view, his usually stern face slightly softened from the wine he'd consumed. When his gaze lighted on me, his smile almost reached his eyes.

I clasped my hands and bowed my head, mentally reviewing if I'd done anything wrong at the ball: if I had said the wrong words to a nobleman's son, made a misstep during a dance, or forgotten to smile or laugh while pretending to listen to the older noblewomen's prattle. *How can he be so charming and hospitable with others, but so stern and demanding with me?* I thought fretfully. I'd dearly hoped to please Father and Mother at this ball, as I had at every other important occasion we had ever attended together.

But when I glanced up, I realized he wasn't looking at me at all anymore, but at something over my shoulder. When I turned, I saw my mother standing behind me, poised and graceful. Her eyes sparkled and her soft lips curved in the sort of smile she rarely shared with anyone, at least, not in my presence. She nodded once toward me—a gentle nod of approval, perhaps even pride, that made my heart warm—and then gazed up at Father. In two strides he was beside her, pulling her out onto the dance floor.

Looking more carefree than they usually permitted themselves to be, they stepped and spun as if no one else were in the room. I watched the candlelight flicker across their faces, their feet move rapidly, agilely, in beautiful movements that left the entire gathering captivated.

Then the dream changed: my parents aged before my eyes, their hair growing streaks of white and grey and wrinkles forming about their eyes and mouths. My mother's eyes held the same haunted, faded appearance they had possessed on the last day of her life. As I stared at the scene before me, I realized that the crowd had changed too: most of the people had become skeletal forms with pale, gaunt faces and blackened eyes. Rows of pikes, topped with severed heads, lined the ballroom walls while puddles of blood pooled across the marble floor.

My breath snagged in my chest. Once again, my father plunged a dagger into my mother's back, even as he continued to embrace her. But no—the dream changed again, and it was *me*. I held my mother in my arms; I thrusted the blade into her flesh. Her blood spilled onto my hands, my chest, my face, but I continued to hold her close. When I lifted my head to stare over her shoulder, my father's grey eyes were watching me, full of something I had never seen in them before: approval.

I lurched awake with a gasp, instinctively running my fingers along my arms and face to feel for blood and finding I was in a cold sweat.

Jennah was already awake and dressed, her curls tied tightly at her neck and her daggers strapped to her sides. She spun away from where she'd been hovering over the hearth. "Are you all right?"

"Another dream," I rasped, pushing myself upright. "I'll be fine."

She watched me a few moments longer before giving up and looking away.

"We need to replenish our supplies and leave as soon as we're able," I said, tumbling out of bed and pushing stray locks of hair from my eyes. I was anxious to leave the comfort of the inn, where warm bathwater and luxurious beds and plentiful food provided far more than Gillen had likely seen in months.

Jennah nodded silently.

I approached the sole window in our quarters and gazed out at the view of the city, its winding streets already brimming with people. Grey clouds had gathered on the far horizon, where gulls swooped low and called to one another and the early rays of dawn were painting the sky a faint gold hue. In the distance beyond the city rooftops, I could make out the vague outlines of the Vorvinian Mountains, their snowcapped peaks stained with the morning rays. Somewhere beyond the mountains, in the unknown reaches of a hostile kingdom that haunted my visions, my cousin was fighting to survive.

And he is *alive,* I reassured myself, despite the misgivings my visions had given me, despite the doubts all my companions clearly carried. *I know he is.*

"We are not taking horses into Toryn," Narek said firmly from his position at the table. I glanced up into his dark eyes and for just an instant, felt like I could read traces of his past there. "They will only cause trouble. The walk to Landari Pass will be easy and swift."

Leaning back in his chair, Gare crossed his arms over his chest and scowled. "Who made you leader of this journey?" he demanded.

Mouth twitching, Narek turned to me. I stared at him for a moment before saying evenly, "We do what he says."

Avrik's eyes flicked from the map spread across the table to me so suddenly my breath caught involuntarily, but his gaze was difficult for me to read. I longed for the days when we were close, and our thoughts had been easy to share. But no, I had kept so many secrets, that bond had been broken. I looked away first.

"If all is settled then," Jennah said in a low voice, "we should be on our way."

Her face was grave now, but hers was not the only one. A sense of solemnity had fallen over our group this morning. We had already finished purchasing provisions, including restocking our supply of arrows, bandages, and medicines, and eaten a hasty breakfast. Now we lingered at our table only long enough to study the map Layk had procured and discuss plans one last time. Though Narek had protested he did not need a map, and I still had a clear picture of all the places I'd been forced to pore over for years under my royal tutor, there was something reassuring about having the locations displayed in black and white.

"Is the map of Toryn even accurate anymore?" I asked Narek as Layk rolled it up and stored it in his pack.

For a long moment, Narek said nothing. Then: "How can I say, Your Majesty? I haven't been in Toryn for years; your visions probably tell you more than I could describe."

I cringed at his address, but let it go as I chewed on his words. "You don't know what we will find."

Narek's eyes flickered with an emotion I couldn't quite place, something dark and mirthless. "Oh, I have my ideas."

Without another word, I stood with my companions to shoulder my pack and file from the inn. It was a one-day journey to the foot of the mountains, our final stretch before pressing through the Landari Pass and leaving Misroth behind. We took the road stretching out from Kelwed's gates through the rolling plains as the sun was beginning to climb higher in the eastern sky.

Our stay in Kelwed had done much for us: we all felt refreshed, and Layk's arm seemed almost recovered thanks to the healer's help. Narek didn't limp anymore. Even the air, though still chilly, grew mild under a bright sun unimpeded by a single cloud. Despite all this, our company remained quiet and grim. We had already faced dangers and knew many more awaited us.

We stopped for the night in a stretch of open grass nestled close to the base of the mountains, their peaks looming like dark and ominous shadows against the western sky, blazing with the vivid orange and red hues of sunset. Grasping his bow, Avrik vanished into the pines that ascended the mountains, Layk and Gare built up the fire, and Jennah began furiously sharpening and polishing her daggers. I watched Narek slip out of our camp and disappear amongst the trees before any of the others noticed. Frowning, I plucked my bow from my back and ducked into the forest after him, not waiting to signal to the others or hear their disapproval.

The air was thick with the sweet scent of pine needles and cool within the shadows of the towering trees. It was dark enough, with only patches of evening light shimmering through holes in the forest ceiling, that it was difficult to see my surroundings clearly, especially when my eyes had not yet adjusted. Despite knowing it was only dusk, too early for the sedwa to hunt, my pulse pattered wildly, and I started when a squirrel rustled through some branches overhead.

I couldn't help but anticipate an attack from Narek; I plucked an arrow from my quiver and strung it softly to my bow.

"Your judgment seems a little hasty." His voice came from the shadows, and I had to catch myself before I jumped in surprise.

"What am I to expect but desertion or betrayal when you sneak off like this?" I growled, refusing to remove my hand from my bowstring.

Narek stepped into the sunlight so I could see his face. I wasn't surprised to find he was smirking at me, but his hands were held out to show they were empty and his sword was still sheathed at his side. "I am surprised you came in here alone. You have guards to risk their lives for you, you know."

"I am *not* my father," I said, hoping my voice was as low and firm as I wanted it to be. "I don't want to risk anyone's life."

A thoughtful expression crossed Narek's face as he tilted his head to one side and dropped his hands, but he made no response.

"What are you doing in here?"

"Oh," Narek said, his eyes lighting with comprehension, "you were worried I'd harm Avrik."

I ignored his comment, my fingers still grasping the bowstring. "I expected an escape attempt in Kelwed, not in the mountains."

"Escape attempt?" Narek breathed out a soft laugh and took a step closer. "We both want to go to the same place. I was only taking a walk, hoping for some privacy to think."

Narrowing my eyes at him, I lowered my bow but didn't remove the arrow. "You are not a free man."

Narek's face grew solemn. "Trust me, I know that better than you do, princess."

"And if you *do* ever harm Avrik," I snarled, "I'll make my father seem tame."

He smiled. "So you *do* have your father's blood in your veins." He waved a hand through the air. "Harming him won't bring us to Toryn any faster, so it's hardly worth the trouble."

I sighed, returning my arrow to my quiver and strapping my bow on my back. "Now that we are this near Toryn, I would like to know more about what we will face."

"Not yet. I need to make sure you still have enough reason to keep *me* alive," he said.

"*Tell me.*"

Narek watched me with an easy smile. "No. You can wait for your information…unless you would like to torture it out of me," he added as he strode back toward camp.

Swallowing back my anger, I followed silently.

Jennah, Gare, and Layk looked up in surprise to see us return together. "You should have sent us to retrieve him, princess," Layk said, his fury written across his face and flashing in his blue eyes. "*You*," he added, spinning on Narek, "you I have a mind to skewer now. We can find the king ourselves and spare the inconvenience of your unpleasant company."

I held up a hand as Layk reached for his sword hilt. "Enough," I said, interjecting as much authority in my voice as I could. "He wasn't trying to escape or harm me, and I am capable of defending myself." I shot Layk a pointed look. "Let's not waste time and energy arguing. There are sedwa in the mountains and far more enemies once we arrive in Toryn, so I think we should focus on that."

Releasing his sword hilt, Layk stepped back, displeasure etched in his furrowed brow. He gave a slight nod of obedience and stalked back toward the fire, where Jennah was seated with her daggers, watching the proceeding. I was surprised when she didn't add her own thoughts on the subject, but she merely pressed her lips together and returned her eyes to the blade she was currently polishing.

Gare shuffled close and lowered his voice. "If you ever need anything, princess, do not hesitate to call on me."

"Thank you, Gare," I murmured.

He smiled softly and returned to the fire to plop down on the log beside Jennah. I joined them, resting my chin in my hands as I willed my visions to reveal more about Narek and his dealings with my father. But the truth had never come to me when I wanted it, so I wasn't surprised when nothing happened.

"Jennah, could you tell me more about Marke's gift?" I asked after a long silence.

She raised her eyebrows at me. "I believe I've already told you all there is to share, but if you wish it, yes." She shrugged. "What I do know of all the gifts is that they can appear at any time in someone's life, and that was true for Marke. He didn't discover his gift for discernment until after we were married. At first, I thought he was overconfident in his judgement of character, and I admit I was skeptical about his claims that it was a gift. Then one day he insisted one of our regular clients was untrustworthy, so I decided to keep a closer watch on him whenever he entered our shop. About a week later, I saw him pocketing some of our merchandise. That's when I realized that perhaps Marke *was* gifted with discernment about people. After that we relied heavily on his gift for the rebellion movement; it was one of the few reliable resources we had in those desperate times."

"And what do you know about other gifts?"

Jennah shook her head. "Not much. There are many unique gifts— so many that I am not sure they are all even recorded in Alrenian history or stories. Some are not as obvious as yours or Marke's, either. It is rumored that King Eldon was gifted in protection, which would explain his abilities—at least as told in books and legends—to lead armies into battle that rarely received more than a few casualties. But a gift of that power, on such a great scale…" Her voice drifted off. "Well, I have my doubts."

I shifted in my seat, still longing for answers about my gift, still longing for a way to control it so I could call upon visions of Gillen or other truths whenever I wanted. What was the purpose of being gifted in the truth if I remained ignorant of the truth so often?

Jennah lowered her eyes and her voice before casting a sideways glance toward me. "I believe that I too have a gift. Actually, I believe most people do. For some it may be the gift of charisma and charm, others the gift of persuasion. Some possess love in such abundance I think they are actually gifted in it." Her eyes had a faraway look to them. "There are such tales told of great deeds done with the power the Life-Giver grants…"

I watched her curiously and she turned back to me, as if suddenly returning to herself. "And your gift?" I asked.

She seemed almost embarrassed, an expression that looked foreign on her. When she moved her head, a frizzy curl drifted across her brow and dangled in front of her brown and gold eyes. "Courage," she said simply, sweeping back her hair. "The ability to push aside fear when I need to and to inspire courage in others." A gentle smile curved her lips.

I grinned back. "You do inspire courage, but I always assumed that was an Alrenian trait. All the stories I've heard about Alrenian warriors being fearless *and* fearsome made me think you just took after your ancestors."

Her laugh was light, carefree. "You are gifted with the truth, my lady, but you also possess skills and characteristics such as intelligence, bravery, love, and even self-sacrifice when needed." At her praise, I averted my eyes. "But your visions and ability to see the truths around you are especially strong and unusual, and something that you weren't born with, correct?"

I nodded slowly.

"It was not something you learned, but something you were gifted with. You can learn about and grow in your gift now that you have it, yet you could not attain it in your own power. I believe that is the difference. My gift came to me suddenly, allowing me to bolster the hearts of the rebellion and giving me bravery when I thought I should shudder in fear. The Alrenians value fearlessness to the point of recklessness and raise their children to face their fears, to be conquerors. They learn their courage, and they do not lend it to others."

My eyes darted toward Narek, who was pretending to watch the fire while I suspected he was truly listening to us. In fact, I realized in that instant that quiet had fallen over our entire group and Jennah's and my conversation had become something of interest to our entire party.

"Do you instill courage in everyone around you?" I asked, studying Jennah's face. "Or are you able to…choose?"

She offered me an understanding grin. "No, I do not give courage to my enemies. I am not entirely sure how it works yet, but it seems that in times of fear, my courage will rise, and so does that of every friend around me."

I glanced around again at our group, imagining how much we might need courage on our journey. Wondering what other gifts the people I knew might have, gifts they might not have even realized they possessed. Wondering if and to what extent the gifts could be controlled and perfected.

"It's growing late," Layk said after another quiet moment. "I would expect Avrik to have returned already." His eyes were on the sky, where twilight was slowly fading to night. The first few stars were already twinkling over the mountain peaks and the pine forest was murky, a vast expanse of shadows and looming danger as the light vanished. An uneasy feeling slithered through my heart.

But before we could worry any more, Avrik's form appeared at the edge of the forest. He clutched a rabbit in each hand as he entered our circle of firelight, nodding quietly in Gare and Jennah's direction. To my surprise, he sat beside me. As he set to work skinning his kills, I turned resolutely toward the fire in a vain hope that I could ignore him, but I could feel his presence as surely as I could feel the fire's heat.

"See?" Gare's laugh seemed easy and light at first, but it ended with a peculiar weight attached to it, like a happy moment cut short. "Avrik is fine. It is too soon for us to be worrying about…not returning."

After a long moment, Layk spoke. "Yes, too soon," he murmured, staring into the flames. "But…not too distant now either. The closer we draw to Toryn, the more I think about the chance that none of us will return. But perhaps some of us will and…we could give messages to the family of those who do not. I keep wondering: what would you want your loved ones to know, if you did not make it?" He lifted his eyes and peered at Jennah, then Gare and Avrik, and last of all, me. I looked down.

Gare's face was grim, his eyes set toward the mountain peaks without a hint of fear in their depths, but perhaps some regret. He ran a hand through his thick beard before responding. "I already said my goodbye. If I die, I can only hope I die a soldier's death. I would want my wife to know I died honorably."

Jennah shuffled one of her daggers from hand to hand and raised her chin to watch Layk unflinchingly. "I want my family to know I did not want to leave them, but I chose what I believed was best for them. I will do anything to ensure Laydin and Avalee can live in safety and peace, and though I do not want them to live without their mother, I would die a thousand deaths before trading their wellbeing for my own comfort."

"Well spoken," Layk murmured. He glanced up at Narek, almost as if just remembering his presence. "Everything for you lies in Toryn and not Misroth," he said, sounding accusatory.

Narek crossed his arms over his chest and glanced away. "No, there is nothing for me anywhere." For a moment, I was certain I saw something unfamiliar flicker across his features—regret? sorrow?—but then it was gone just as quickly.

"What about you, Layk?" Gare asked.

Layk tapped out a rhythm with his fingertips on the log he sat on. "Like you, I told my siblings everything I could think to share before I left." He hung his head in his hands. "But it'll never feel like it was enough—not if I don't return." Slowly, he lifted his head and shifted to look at me. "And you, princess?"

A dozen regrets swirled through my mind as I thought of Lyanna and Rev, of all the things I had never said. I pressed my lips together and stared down at my hands, folded tightly in my lap. "Halia," I corrected him, even though I knew he would still refuse to call me by name. "And…I don't want to talk about it."

Layk nodded slowly, silently. He turned his eyes on Avrik.

Avrik refused to look up as he fixed his freshly skinned meat on a spit and held it over the fire. The muscles in his jaw tightened before he finally answered. "There is no one to tell."

Guilt singed the back of my throat and I swallowed thickly. When I blinked, I could see Kyrin's face: a noose around his neck, his eyes dark and angry, his expression pale and haggard. Nothing I said to Avrik would ever undo that. I squeezed my hands into fists and drew a deep breath.

Our company fell quiet, sinking into our own despondent thoughts as the smell of roasting meat enveloped us. We ate our meal in silence, picking at pieces of meat with our fingers and wiping our mouths on our sleeves like ruffians, as Lyanna would have said, and I could not help but feel a thrill at how far I'd come from the dreary dining hall experiences at the castle only a few days before. There were no comforts of home there, only aching reminders of a past I could never retrieve.

Drawing a deep breath, I let the thoughts fall away.

Finally, Gare raised his voice. "Enough of this dreariness! What will we do *when* we return home?" He smiled around at us all. "Now that is the question we should be asking. I know I, for one, promised my son I would be there to officially bless him and his pretty young girl at his marriage ceremony. If they are waiting all this time until I return, I'm sure the instant I set foot in the city again they'll rush me into the sanctuary." He chuckled.

Jennah smiled softly. "I don't think I will let my family out of my sight, not for a long while."

Layk nodded in agreement. "I'll be happy to continue to serve as a guard, whether for the king, if he asks, or the people of Misroth. And…" He shrugged a little shyly. "I'll paint. Maybe some scenes of the adventures and things we see, things I can show Dalen and Fia to bring my stories for them to life."

Gare grinned. "You never told us you liked to paint."

Layk reached for a chain about his neck, giving us a glimpse of a plain locket hanging from its end. "I made portraits of my siblings to carry with me."

Jennah turned to me. "What will you do when you've brought your cousin back to his throne?"

I stared at the ground for a long moment. "I'll want to help him in any way I can. I owe so much to Misroth. But..." I hesitated. "As soon as I can, I want to return to Evren, at least to visit."

"Anyone else?" Gare asked brightly, trying to keep our moods light.

But Avrik was sullen, and Narek had already walked away from our gathering around the campfire.

Not to be dissuaded, Gare launched into a discussion with Jennah about knife fighting techniques, which quickly turned into a challenge. They began a friendly sparring match in the open grass. Layk settled down to watch, laughing and shouting out advice, encouragement, and taunts to both sides.

Across camp, Narek removed his instrument from his pack. When he held it to his lips, it did not sound like any pipe or flute I'd ever heard before. The tones held a low quality that seemed to shudder through the air and whisper amongst the gathering shadows like it belonged in dark, hidden places. The song sent a chill up and down my arms.

Avrik and I kept a careful distance between us as we each watched our friends spar. Gare defeated Jennah and Layk took her place. A few calculated moves won him the match, and then Jennah paired up against him.

"Don't look so solemn," Jennah teased as Layk swung at her and she ducked. "Unless you're practicing how to slay your enemies with your glower."

To my surprise, Layk shrugged a bit sheepishly, a movement that gave Jennah an in. She struck swiftly and put him back on the offensive. She was hasty but fierce; his movements were graceful and precise, marked with his years of training as a guard.

In a few more swift moves, Layk disarmed Jennah and succeeded in knocking her to the ground, where she lay laughing good-naturedly up at him. "A few more years of training under you and Gare and perhaps I'll be more of a match," she said as he helped her up.

My mind flashed back to our days in Misroth City, attending secret meetings, spreading news for the rebellion, and training in the unused basement beneath a sympathetic priest's sanctuary. Layk had shown his skill then, but not like this.

I crossed my arms and called out to him. "Layk! All those sparring matches and training sessions in Misroth City and I do believe you were going easy on me."

To my surprise, Layk flushed a little. "W-well, you looked like a country girl, not…" His eyes flicked to Jennah. "Not intimidating like Jennah."

Jennah laughed lightly. "I've heard I do give an intimidating first impression sometimes."

Gare nudged her arm. "Ah, is that right? Was that Marke's first impression of you also?"

She smirked. "He may have been a little nervous the first time he ever approached me. Of course," she added with a wink, "I helped him out by giving him some encouragement."

Gare gestured toward Avrik and me. "Would either of you two like to join us?"

"Actually…" Avrik hesitated a moment. "I wanted a word with you," he said, his eyes darting to me. "If that's all right."

Set in his pale face and framed by dark circles, his eyes seemed hollow, and I knew I was a fool to feel hopeful.

I nodded once. My tongue felt trapped to the roof of my mouth.

I thought of days back in Evren when we were exchanging easy conversations even in my mute state, silently sharing a joke at school or considering what it would be like to explore the lands beyond Misroth. I felt a sudden urge to reach out and brush a wayward strand of hair from his brow or touch his shoulder, just to assure myself that my old friend was truly there.

But he wasn't there, not really. The memories pinched my heart, so I blinked them away.

The Avrik I knew now, the one with hollow eyes, fidgeted uncomfortably, even as he watched me earnestly. "Walk with me?" he asked, uncertainty slipping into his tone—something the old Avrik had rarely shown. He stood and offered me his hand, and I could not refuse him. I let him help me to my feet and guide me away from the campfire and through the grassy field beyond, where the cool air embraced us.

Watching my breath rise toward the starry sky, I waited for Avrik to speak. "I suppose conversations are supposed to begin on a princess's terms, and not mine," he said after a long while. "I meant no disrespect, my lady."

"Please stop calling me that." I hated the way he shuffled his feet uncomfortably, the way his eyes flitted almost anxiously to my face, and the way he dropped his gaze to the ground. This was not the confident, easygoing, cheerful Avrik I knew, not the one who treated me as an equal. As a friend.

Just like that, the discomfort was gone, only to be replaced by anger. Avrik stopped mid-step and spun toward me, his eyes bright in the darkness. "Then what would you have me call you? *Elena?*"

I cringed and turned away.

Sucking in a deep breath, he stared off toward the forest as he let himself cool. "My father was not a good man, but he did love me, which I know is more than you can say of yours." He hesitated, his eyes flitting back toward me. "I could not stay in Evren after his hanging. As much as I hate everything he did, I *miss* him, Elena, and I can't help wondering what sort of person that makes me."

I ran my fingers along my leather armband. I started at that familiar name, even if it was only used by mistake, nothing but the result of an old habit.

"Every time I see you, I'm reminded of…everything. Of who he was and who I thought he was. Of who I thought you were." He scratched his neck, almost in a timid gesture. "But you are our leader and heir to the throne, at least until we find your cousin. And I owe you my allegiance."

Wearily, I swiped a hand across my forehead. I couldn't help the bitterness that leaked into my voice. "Is your allegiance to Elena or Halia?"

Avrik stared at me for a long moment, his expression giving away nothing. "I may not trust Halia and your secrets, but I trusted Elena and I trust your cause. You know I am loyal to whatever I believe in." I thought of his passion over the years as he defended his father and me from any unkind words or town suspicion in Evren. Of his passion when he left me to ensure his father was safe.

I nodded slowly. "Then I accept."

He watched me with a sad curve to his mouth, a shadowed look in his eyes. "Elena truly is gone, then."

My head snapped up. "What do you mean?" I asked, more sharply than I meant to.

"Your manner is different…the way you act, the way you carry yourself." He gestured at me vaguely. "Did…did she ever even exist? Was it all an act?" The timidity and pain in his voice wrenched at my heart.

It felt like a piece of my world was being torn away from me, dismantled before my eyes. I desperately longed for the Evren countryside, for the homey scent of dried lavender filling my bedroom and the feel of scratchy, warm wool to keep out the winter cold. For the feel of dirt beneath my fingernails and wind in my hair. For the sounds of Lyanna's laughter, Rev's easy tones, and Avrik's playful jibes. Elena was who I'd longed to be when I was afraid, when I'd wanted to forget my past. All at once I was homesick and lost. "No," I protested, shaking my head.

But Avrik didn't see what he wanted to in my eyes. He turned away with a sigh. "I don't know Halia, but I will serve her. From a distance."

He lifted his gaze to meet mine and his meaning was clear: our friendship, at least as it was, was over. And with the loss of our friendship, the hope I'd once cherished of becoming something more to him vanished too. He meant to keep his distance from me, to treat me as a stranger. Because I was Halia, not Elena. Pain rattled through my every breath, but I stood firm and didn't look away.

With a silent salute, Avrik turned away and melted into the blackness, leaving me to stand alone, listening to the night wind whisper through the forest and rustle the grass around me. It slithered around my cloak and left me feeling robbed of warmth, of breath, and of something else I couldn't quite place. A headache throbbed dully in my temple and I sought the cool surface of my armband again, the motion feeling so natural that I couldn't ignore the fact that I had been reaching for it often lately.

Narek was at my side so suddenly it took me a moment to register his presence and still another moment to realize his music playing had fallen silent some time ago. Had he been listening to Avrik's and my entire conversation?

"I thought your cousin and aunt were all you had left," Narek said, "but it seems you have at least one other…friend."

I refused to give him the satisfaction of turning around and letting him see the surprise on my face. "What does it matter to you?"

"The less one has, the more one is willing to sacrifice for their people."

"I died for my people," I said, turning to him at last. Arms crossed, he was watching me with a level gaze, his eyes unreadable in the shadows. "What other proof does anyone need of what I am willing to sacrifice?"

Narek's lips twisted in a slow smile. "I'll spare you the question, but I wonder just how much you really are willing to lose to save your kingdom."

"And what does *that* matter to you?" I snapped.

He watched me for one long, terrible moment. "I killed your father because he was full of unfulfilled promises. Don't give me a reason to do the same to you."

I squeezed my fists together so tightly my nails dug into my palms. "You cannot hold anything over my head. I owe you nothing; you are *my* prisoner. Remember?"

Narek didn't answer.

"I am tired of your secrets. You owe me *some* answers. What promises did my father make to you?" I demanded, heat rising in my cheeks. I was surprised at how quickly the anger possessed me, leaving me breathless.

"Promises of freedom," Narek murmured into the wind, so softly I almost did not hear, and then he was gone.

CHAPTER EIGHT

THE ATMOSPHERE OF THE MOUNTAINS was not any less ominous for its lack of visible danger during the first day and night. Our trek into the pass was quiet and uneventful: a long, gradual climb up the rocky slopes of the forest until the trees thinned out and we began a winding path toward the mountains' snowy summits. By evening we were high enough that the air felt thin and great snowflakes were littering the ground around us, adding to the drifts of fluffy snow we had spent hours trampling through. We found a shallow cave to provide warm shelter for the night and ate a cheerless dinner.

No matter our attempts to share lighthearted stories or cheer ourselves with laughter and song, we couldn't shake the knowledge that we were about to pass over the border into unfamiliar, deadly territory. As night enclosed about us, I listened to the wind build until it howled outside like a living thing, a lonely, fretful creature far from the comfort of our small fire. I imagined the sedwa stalking through these mountains. With the deep of night smothering us and a snowy, wailing wind for company, it was too easy to imagine golden orbs watching us from somewhere outside the cave, waiting until our senses dulled and we dozed off.

I took the first watch, passing several uneasy hours perched in the cave's mouth with my cloak wrapped tightly about me. Hugging my knees,

I searched the darkness for any sign of a black shape or gold eyes. My mind was full of tumbling, restless thoughts.

Over and over, my mother's face flashed before my mind's eye, the green eyes we both shared staring back at me with the sort of maternal softness I'd spent more time longing for than basking in during her lifetime. Her voice was melodic, more like a half-remembered song or the sweet notes of a violin than actual words. I blinked, forcing the image away, but another rose up just as swiftly to replace it: my mother dying. Her own blood gurgled in her throat as she fought to share a message she would never finish. *"I...I..."*

What was she about to say, and why did my brain so persistently agonize over this moment? *I'm sorry. I love you. I believe you. I'm proud of you.* What difference would the words have made for me now, even if she'd spoken them? A final apology could not undo years of pain.

I squeezed my hands into fists. *Nothing you can say will change what happened,* I thought vehemently, as if I could somehow send my message across the unseen universe to wherever my mother's spirit dwelt. I tried to imagine her in an afterlife, radiant and *happy* in a way she had never been in life, but every vision I conjured up was hazy, based upon vague descriptions I'd been offered by priests. They only made her feel even more distant, more unreachable. I was alone, twice abandoned by the one I'd once thought loved me most in this world.

A numb sensation settled in my bones as I realized it was only in my spoken words that I was limited to the truth: I could lie to *myself.* What difference would my mother's words have made for me? The truth was a whisper I couldn't run from. *They could have changed everything.*

Jennah rose softly from where she'd been slumbering before I even attempted to wake her. Maybe she had never been asleep at all.

"You should sleep, my lady," she murmured as she settled herself beside me, leaning against the wall of the cave.

Sleep felt impossibly distant, so I shook my head. "You can go back to sleep; I'm not tired. I'll keep watch a little longer."

Jennah tilted her head. "I can't sleep either, so if you don't mind, I'll keep you company."

Allowing myself a smile, I nodded.

We sat silently for a few moments, each lost in our own thoughts as we stared out into the night. The wind swept the falling snowflakes into strange imagined shapes, wraiths haunting the mountainside beneath a moon all but lost behind the heavy clouds.

"You should not feel guilty for the choices others have made," Jennah said at last.

I pulled uncomfortably on the edge of my cloak, sliding the rough fabric through my fingers.

"Not even King Eldon saved the Misrothians on his own," Jennah continued. "You need us, yet you never ordered us to come. We made our own choices fully aware of the risk."

I hated the uncertainty that plagued me, longing to tuck it away from everyone, including myself.

Her voice continued, gaining strength. Without protest from me, she allowed herself to sound firm. "Your father's choices are not yours."

"I know," I said softly, still staring out into the night. I could feel Jennah's gaze on me, but I couldn't meet her eyes.

"If you ever want…I am here for you…to talk," she went on. "Zarev took something from all of us, but he took most from you."

I nodded, my throat too tight to form words, if I'd even known what to say.

"We will find him," Jennah added. She reached out to touch my knee, a reassuring gesture more befitting an elder sister than someone in my service, and I was relieved at the comfort and familiarity in it. "I believe you are *meant* to have those powerful visions of your cousin, to lead us to him. To tell us he is alive."

I squeezed my eyes closed. "I hope you're right. Thank you," I said.

Several long moments of silence passed before I spoke again.

"Could you…teach me the Alrenian language?"

Jennah smiled slowly. "Are you asking to begin now?"

"As long as neither of us can sleep, I thought it would be something useful for me to learn. Something we could do to pass the time, to distract ourselves when we are gloomy."

With a light laugh, she launched straight into teaching me a few Alrenian phrases. She made me repeat *dieni*, the word for hello, about a dozen times until she said my accent was acceptable.

At last, I began to blink sleepily from exhaustion and she encouraged me to try to sleep. With a short nod, I left her to watch at the cave's opening and settled onto my bedroll, close to the warmth of our campfire's low-burning embers, and waited for sleep to overtake me. My body felt weary, but my mind would not quiet. Attempting to force the memories and visions far away, I lay staring at the cavern wall, studying its bumps and grooves and the way the shadows played along its rough surface, until at last, warm and comfortable, I slipped into sleep.

Another day of slow, difficult trudging through the snowy pass and a night of taking turns watching the still, dark night came and went without event. On the third day in the mountains, the heavy snow clouds that had darkened the sky for the past two days dissipated, leaving the air feeling open and impossibly blue above a world of white. By noon we came to the lonely fortress guarding the edge of Misroth's border, where shocked guards came out to greet us.

"Princess Halia?" one man stammered, his eyes widening when they landed on me. He and several men behind him dropped to their knees. "We received a shipment of supplies only a few days ago and heard the news. We didn't expect to see you so soon. Your Majesty," he stammered out quickly.

As the men ushered us inside, offering us rest before a cozy fire and the first hot meal we'd had in days, it became clear that the news of my father's death was welcome. They were nervous about my decision to enter Toryn, and even offered to send a few more men with me, but I refused. I didn't want to risk any more men, and I was sure a smaller party would draw less attention from the Toryn monsters.

Instead, the men filled our bags with additional food supplies, saying they had more than enough to last until the next party of guards made the dangerous trek up the mountains to replenish theirs.

"Do you ever…hear or see anything beyond the border?" I asked. "Has anyone…or anything…tried to cross?"

The captain of the small band shook his head. "It's a lonely job up here. The only threat we have here, aside from the cold and blizzards, is the sedwa, and those attacks are rare."

Early in the afternoon, not wanting to waste more time, we bid the guards farewell. Soon after leaving the fortress, we came to a high ridge that afforded us a view down the sloping mountainside, beyond the drifts of snow to the tree line, and further down, barely visible from this height, a vast smudge of green and brown, the details of the land indistinct from this elevation.

"That is Toryn," Layk said, voicing what we all knew in an awe-filled voice.

As we stared, the wind grew in strength, fluttering about our cloaks and brushing tendrils of hair into my eyes. Perhaps I should have made a habit of pulling it back into a knot each morning as Jennah did; but that felt too restricting, too like my hours in attendance at my uncle's court or under my royal tutor's scrutiny, too distant from the freedom of the Evren countryside I was homesick for. I tucked the wayward strands behind my ear and drew a deep breath to steady myself. Here we were. The beginning of the descent out of Landari Pass marked the place where Misroth's border officially ended and Toryn's began: the far side of the Vorvinian range was Toryn.

Before I had time to consider, I turned to Avrik, whose eyes caught mine. The eager expression on his face mirrored my feelings. *We're leaving*

Misroth, our looks said silently, and for one moment we shared the excitement of a dream fulfilled, of a distant promise we'd made together coming to pass.

I turned away and took a resolute step forward. My fears threatened to claw their way out of the hidden depths of my heart, but I ignored them and set my shoulders. "Then this is where we bid Misroth farewell," I said firmly.

We pressed on through the snow without further hesitation. Gare and Layk led the way, while I brought up the rear. Silently, Narek fell into step beside me, and I studied him warily in my peripheral. His posture said everything he did not; even without looking at me, his message was like a shout in my ear: *There can be no doubt or turning back now, Your Majesty.* I refused to turn to him and acknowledge his lofty attitude or his warning.

And then, just like that, without any other sign or perceptible change, the ground sloped downward in a gradual descent and I left my homeland to enter a hostile kingdom. It felt surreal: without crossing a single wall or gate, with no sign of a Toryn fortress or guard in sight, I had left everything familiar behind and entered a different world. Yet at the same time, everything was the same. The wind still breathed against my face in a steady, cool stream, the sky was still a perfect blue, and the world about us was still quiet.

"How will we know if we've passed through a barrier?" Avrik asked at long last, his voice low.

The same question seemed to be flitting through everyone's brain, along with a breathless fear. Were we easy prey as soon as we entered Toryn? Everyone was on edge as we trudged forward; fingers brushed against sword hilts and eyes darted about warily.

Before anyone responded, something *did* change. I felt a dull thrumming run through my body, as if the air itself had acquired a pulse that beat all around me. The hairs on my arms prickled and my legs shook until I stumbled and nearly lost my footing. My friends paused in concern; apparently they had not sensed the change like I had.

"Halia!" Layk cried out. He and the others surged toward me.

Catching myself before I tumbled into the snow, I felt a rush of blazing anger. I ignored my friends and spun toward Narek, who had fallen behind me.

"*Narek*," I growled, stalking forward with all the confidence I could muster. "Does this barrier keep ou—"

I was three yards away from him when I slammed into something solid yet invisible. The barrier.

Though I'd always known it was a possibility, the stark reality of the fact made my entire body feel like it had turned to ice. The barrier hadn't been created to keep only Toryn's monsters out of Misroth; it kept people out of Misroth too.

With a sharp intake of breath, I reeled back and pressed a hand to my temple, where the pain was already becoming a steady ache. Narek was laughing, passing through the barrier to approach me with long, easy strides.

"You *knew*," I spat.

The words were scarcely out of my mouth when my friends were on him. Gare and Layk snatched his arms and shoved them behind his back, Jennah slipped in close and pressed a dagger to his neck, and Avrik pointed an arrow at his heart.

"I knew you were desperately depending upon my honesty," Narek said, his voice dripping with irony.

It was true that I'd never believed him, but I'd never placed much faith in the myths either.

"Tell me, would it have made any difference?" Narek's eyes were piercing, his gaze unpleasantly searching as he stared unflinchingly back at me.

The most maddening fact of all was that he was perfectly unfazed by the multiple threats of death. Gare's face was firm, a soldier prepared to follow orders, and Jennah's was ruthless, a descendant of a long line of warriors. But it was the young men on either side of Narek who appeared the most intimidating in that moment. Layk's eyes were ice; Avrik's were fire.

"No," I said at last, refusing to look away from Narek. He wouldn't glance away either, so we were at an impasse, staring each other down as my friends waited for my word to kill our prisoner.

"You knew the risk," Narek continued.

"Yes, but if you lied about the barrier, you could lie about anything." I took a step forward, my heart hammering in my ears. "And if you lie about *anything* regarding Gillen's location or how to survive Toryn, you outlive your usefulness."

Narek looked unfazed. "I never lied outright. Do you really want to kill me and throw away help from the only member of your party who has ever been in Toryn, or fought its monsters?"

"I have my visions," I said evenly.

"We await your word, my lady," Layk announced, tightening his grip on Narek's arm. There was an unfamiliar gleam in his eyes that made me uncomfortable. Bloodlust.

Narek's smile never wavered. *Perhaps you are more like your father than you think.*

I relaxed my stance, unclenching my fingers so my hands hung loosely by my sides. "He has done nothing I didn't expect him to do," I said at last. "This changes nothing. Release him."

Layk watched me for a long moment before, slowly, reluctantly, he and the others stood down. He and Gare dropped Narek's arms, Jennah sheathed her dagger, and Avrik lowered his bow, though he didn't return it to his back.

For a breathless moment, no one moved. I stared at Narek, Narek stared at Avrik, Avrik stared at Layk, and Layk stared at me. It took me several instants to realize that Gare and Jennah were also studying me, rather than watching Narek as I would have expected.

This changes nothing, I thought again, but that wasn't entirely true. It was not Narek's deception that had shaken me; it was my own foolish confidence in my belief that the barrier couldn't exist. In my head I had considered every possible eventuality, yet in my heart I had always been sure. I hadn't believed I could have been raised in the castle and be so ignorant of my kingdom's history, of my own ancestor's actions. My tutor had never talked about it and it hadn't been mentioned in any history books I'd been made to read while under her tutelage. Was the border a secret only the ruling monarchs had access to? It wasn't simply a forbidden action to cross the borders; it was an irrevocable choice.

My eyes darted over my companions, trying to imagine all they were thinking. They were trapped in a foreign kingdom, far from their families, and it was my doing. Despair crushed so heavily down on us all that it was nearly palpable in the air itself, like an unwelcome, shadowy presence standing behind us, breathing against our necks.

Then my focus snagged on Narek again, who had turned back to me.

"How could I never know about a barrier surrounding my own kingdom?" I fumed, running a weary hand across my forehead.

"It doesn't surround Misroth," Narek said. "The barrier envelopes the borders of Toryn, Alrenor, and the Wastelands, permitting humans and creatures to enter those lands but never to leave. This is why Misrothians can carry on trade and welcome consuls from the Lesser Kingdoms but none from Alrenor or Toryn have entered your land for two hundred years."

"But you are *Toryn*," I protested, still dumbfounded that I could have been so easily duped. "How is this possible? How could you have entered Misroth when the barrier is real?"

He stared at me for a long moment, letting the quiet settle around us once more before responding. "Heirs of Eldon have the ability to pass back through the barrier and leave Toryn, and to bring others through it with them," he said gruffly. "That is what your father learned and proved to be true. He came to Toryn, years ago, in search of vylae, a poisonous plant native to our kingdom—the one he used to kill your uncle. When he returned, I entered Misroth with him."

"How did he walk through the barrier?" I demanded.

"I don't know," Narek said.

My fingers curled at my sides, and I struggled to control my anger. "I don't believe you." I drew a deep breath. "How did Eldon create this barrier?"

"Do you think anyone from Toryn understands it? The story passed among our generations says that Eldon was gifted in protection, a skill that not only won him the war but created this mysterious barrier. One day our people found we were trapped within our own borders with the monsters that were threatening our kingdom. We'd already all but fractured from the Alrenian Empire ourselves, not due to Misroth's help so much as Alrenor's fear of the dangers our land held. Toryn abandoned the Alrenian language for the common merchant tongue, the New Language as you call it. Our leaders sought help from Eldon and the newly free Misothian kingdom when the monsters continued to plague us, and instead of an answer, we found a barrier. The rumor has always been that an heir of Eldon would be the only one with the power to break it." He watched me steadily.

"And my father never shared how he passed through it?" I repeated firmly.

Narek shrugged. "As far as I could tell, the barrier never blocked him. It was as if it didn't work on him. I'm not sure why it does for you."

I frowned, dissatisfied with his answer.

A threat still shimmering in his eyes, Layk stepped toward Narek. "Shall I force the truth from him, my lady?"

I stared at Narek for a long moment, searching for I knew not what. His dark eyes never wavered, the gleam within them seeming only to taunt me.

I am not my father. My eyes darted to my companions, catching on the ragged scar marring Jennah's face and Gare's missing finger. Layk's burns were covered, but I could clearly recall the angry markings that hid beneath his shirt. I turned away to avoid everyone's gazes and stared at my boots. "No," I murmured. "We are better than him." I hesitated for another moment, then asked Narek, "Now what?"

"The plan doesn't change," he said easily. "We continue through Toryn, journeying toward Calidar because it will offer us the best protection, and if Gillen is somehow alive, we will likely encounter him on the way or find he has taken refuge there."

"Then let's go."

Striding forward, I kept my chin lifted high to mask my doubt. Slowly, quietly, the others began to trudge behind me, Gare and Layk hemming Narek in on either side as they walked. The weight of my friends' glances nearly crushed me; their unspoken thoughts were suffocating. I wasn't sure if I was having another revelation or simply imagining it all, but either way, it was almost more than I could bear. When I closed my eyes, I could see the nightmarish creatures from my visions again. We were trapped in a land as gruesome as any tale about the underworld I'd ever heard, and I had led my friends here.

"Halia." Avrik's voice shocked me out of my reverie, though not quite as much as his use of my true name. He hadn't slipped and called me Elena, yet hadn't used a formal title either. I refused to slow my pace, but he easily swung into step beside me and awaited my response. When I turned toward him, I could read the concern and intensity in his eyes.

"Yes?" I dared at last.

"Choosing to remove a threat to your life does not make you like your father." His voice was earnest, all but pleading. For an instant, I forgot my anger and guilt, and simply let the comforting knowledge that he cared wash over me. Then the feeling vanished.

"You do not know what we are facing," I said, my voice nearly dropping to a whisper.

He was silent for several beats, our footsteps thudding in harmony along the rocky ground. "Then tell me." A bitter edge crept into his tone as a shadow flickered across his face. "Stop keeping secrets."

"I've seen…creatures attacking Gillen and his men from the sky," I said softly. "And…others in armor who don't seem affected by fire. I don't know much else," I finished, "but I know who can tell us more."

I looked over my shoulder at Narek. "Tell us about the creatures of Toryn. No more holding back."

Narek shrugged. "Perhaps I was afraid the tales would scare you away before we arrived."

"You mean before we were trapped here," I snapped. "You will also tell us *why* you wanted to return to Toryn, if it is as terrifying as you say it is."

Narek popped his neck. "Well, since you asked so kindly." He lifted his face to stare at the sky and his voice turned grim. "The first beasts we will have to concern ourselves with will be the ichgor."

Gare frowned at him. "The ichgor? I've never heard of such a creature, not in any of the myths I've heard regarding the Wastelands."

"You Misrothians didn't even know this barrier was anything more than myth," Narek growled. His eyes flashed, dark as a midnight sky dusted with distant, blazing stars. "Who are you to doubt me now?"

Gare's frown didn't vanish, but he turned away and said no more.

For several long moments, our company fell silent as we took in the changing landscape around us. Underfoot, the ground was becoming less rocky, the snow giving way to mud and grass, fed by a leaping stream that curved its way past an outcropping to our right until it wound its way past us. It gurgled down the final slope of the mountain and fed a vast ocean of green before us: great grasslands that stretched onward as far as my eyes could see. Under the white sheet of clouds that cloaked the sky, after the endless snow of the mountain pass, the grasslands were such a vivid green the sight almost hurt. I blinked as I tried to trace the stream's path, but quickly lost it amidst the waves of grass.

At last, impatient for more information, I tossed a glance over my shoulder and leveled my gaze at Narek. "Tell us of the ichgor."

Narek drew a deep breath, and for the first time, to my own dismay, I sensed his growing fear. For all his bluster and arrogance, even Narek was afraid to return to his homeland. His voice was soft, heavy with an emotion that might have been grief. "They come at night, from the sky. They're so dark they are all but invisible, swooping down on great wings to devour their victims."

I repressed a shudder as memories of my visions flashed through my brain. Would the men's screams ever stop echoing in my ears?

"They are bat-like, hunting their prey not with their sight but with their ability to detect shapes and forms in the landscape with their cries. And they can *smell* you." Narek's gaze had a faraway look, his eyes reflecting past horrors I could imagine all too well.

"Then you must tell us how to survive them," I said.

Narek was silent for a long moment, leaving us to watch him. Brow furrowed, Layk was scanning the sky as if he expected an ichgor to materialize at any moment. Gare kept his eyes trained on Narek, his fingers hovering close to his sword hilt.

"Surviving Toryn will not be easy," Narek said.

"But you wanted to return," I snapped. "You must know *something*, or you wouldn't have been so determined to come back."

"Toryn is my *home*. Do I need another reason to return? To refuse to abandon it?" He cast me a cool glance. "But the danger is still great. There is never a guarantee of survival, no matter your strength or skill or wit. There is only the day you are conceived and the day you die, and all else is a series of moments you either embrace or endure." His fingers drifted to his sword hilt and his expression grew dark. "I've seen far greater warriors than me slain on the battlefield in an instant."

"Your vague speeches will not save us," I said impatiently.

He grinned, but the expression was mirthless. "Then let's hope you really are good with a bow."

"And what else?" Layk interjected. "What else is there?"

Narek grew solemn again. "We won't have to worry about them for a while longer, I hope."

"What are they?" Layk pressed.

"The nestrae. Fire demons and Nesrelle worshippers, they serve the Dark Goddess with sacrifices of terror and flame."

I closed my eyes as flashes of my latest vision returned, and I could see Gillen hiding in the ruined city again, his unseen enemies taunting him in their chilling language. "By *sacrifices*, you mean victims they choose to become their sacrifices." It wasn't a question, because I knew the answer.

Narek nodded. "Their goddess thrives off the fear and pain they inflict on their victims. They've ransacked, scorched, and eradicated entire cities." A muscle in his jaw twitched. "The best way to survive them is to evade them."

Gare set his shoulders. "Then we take cover at night to avoid your demons from the sky, and we cling to darkness to hide from your demons of fire."

"That is far more difficult to do than you imagine," Narek said. "We will travel at night, so we're awake when the ichgor hunt, but that will be the most we can do for a while." He nodded to the flat, open landscape stretching before us. There were few trees, no hills, and no houses or towns to be seen. "After all, how much cover do you see for us?"

Our group fell silent and solemn.

I have cursed us to death.

Closing my eyes, I tried to block out the images, tried to push away the echoes of the screams. My mind swirled with doubt. Even if Gillen was alive, what if I never found a way to cross the barrier and return to Misroth? Instead of accepting the throne in Gillen's stead, I had left my people leaderless. What if I had abandoned my kingdom for a hopeless cause?

As we moved forward, as I felt their gazes on me, I didn't dare meet my companion's eyes. I wondered if they were asking themselves the same question I was asking myself.

Had I doomed us all?

CHAPTER NINE

DARKNESS DESCENDED ALL TOO SOON, finding us still traversing through the shadow of the mountains. We were deep within a sea of grass, the stalks reaching to my waist and rustling in the soft evening breeze. If the screams and sensation of splattered blood against my cheeks hadn't lingered, I would have found the landscape beautiful, even peaceful. As it was, it held a looming threat.

"If we aren't sleeping tonight, I think we should stop to rest and save our strength," Jennah said, casting a sidelong glance my way.

I forced a smile to my face and tried to shove away all concerns of what she thought of me and my mission. "Yes," I said simply. I glanced away.

As we stopped to set up camp near the only cluster of trees we could see for miles, I quietly busied myself with restringing my bow, away from the others. Uncertainty plagued me. I was feeling small again, a young girl in my uncle's court, desperate for my father's approval and love.

"It's not your fault."

Jennah's voice made me start and stayed my trembling hands where they had been fumbling with my string. Slowly, I lifted my face to meet her eyes: warm, golden brown, and comforting in a way that vaguely reminded me of Lyanna. I cut that thought from my mind before a familiar ache touched my heart.

"We *chose* to come, understanding the risks."

I drew a deep breath, but I couldn't banish my worry that I'd see my visions come to life again, this time with my friends as the victims.

"And you have your gift for the truth," Jennah continued. "A vision could show you how an heir of Eldon may pass through the barrier and take us all home."

"I've never been able to call upon my visions at will—or to control what I learn in them."

Jennah's gaze did not waver. Confidence seeped into me as I watched her, and I dared to hope again.

"Do not believe in fear. The Life-Giver won't forsake you now, not after he saved your life and restored Misroth for its true king. We will find Gillen. And we *will* make it home."

My heart thudded uncomfortably against my chest. Her words made sense and I wanted to believe them, but I couldn't completely dismiss the misgivings that followed me everywhere, growing stronger with each vision I had.

As I walked back with Jennah to rejoin the others, I studied their faces. Layk was intent on building a fire with the few branches he could gather from beneath the trees, but Avrik watched me quietly, as if to say, *It's all right.* Gare stepped forward as we approached and clapped a hand on my shoulder.

"Do not trouble yourself, my lady. We will find your cousin and return to Misroth. If your father found a way, you most certainly will too, to set things right."

I nodded.

"What are you doing?" Narek snapped, storming toward Layk and his growing fire. "I told you, the ichgor hunt primarily through their senses of smell and hearing." He stomped at the flames fluttering about the kindling Layk had gathered.

"We need to eat," Layk protested.

Narek stared unflinchingly back at him. "There will be berries and nuts we can scavenge on the way. With those to help, we'll have to make the supplies we can eat cold last until Calidar."

Jennah began unpacking some of the jerky, dried fruits, rolls, and cheeses we had left amongst our belongings and we all sat for an uneasy meal. No one spoke much, our eyes darting frequently to the sky as it melted to a shade of deep blue and the first stars began to appear.

Narek's sword slid from its sheath, startling us all. He laid it in the grass before him, where it gleamed like a torch in the night, reflecting the stars along its blade. Quietly, we all followed his lead, drawing swords and daggers or unstrapping our bows from our backs.

Gare glanced around at our solemn faces and flashed us a grin. "What about a story to pass the time?" he said.

I nodded. As night darkened about us, we sat studying the sky, our weapons in our hands, while Gare's words weaved a tale of adventure and courage about us. As he spoke, the story came to life in my mind, springing up before me in vivid colors almost like I was having another vision, and I could, even for a short while, block out my surroundings and worries. Comfort settled in my heart, a strange emotion when mixed with the rising sense that *something* was about to happen, that this night would not end without another test of our strength and skill.

"Before Eldon met the Misrothian seamstress Tamelle, when he was still merely another Alrenian nobleman in the empress's court," Gare began, "Empress Ilett took notice of him and tried to win his affections. Eldon was a handsome man, son of a wealthy and well-respected man and woman of the court. At the Festival of the Empire, when Alrenor celebrated its might and power in a week of parties, balls, feasts, and displays of its finery and strength, he wore an exquisitely crafted sword that caught the eyes of many. Though the piece was not Alrenian, nor even made by one of Alrenor's conquests, Eldon believed it was a testament to Alrenor's might that his family could trade with Brevinn and acquire such a fine piece."

The wind stirred a little louder in my ears this time and the clouds slipped over the rising moon, enveloping us in shadows for a moment. I caught my breath. For a beat, Gare was silent as we all assessed our surroundings, unsure if the rustle of the breeze had carried with it another sound, or if it was merely our imagination. After several moments, when we heard nothing more, I let my muscles relax ever so slightly. Gare cracked his knuckles and continued.

"Because he was from a lesser family among the nobility, Empress Ilett had not noticed Eldon before. But so many gathered within the crowds to see who wore such an exquisite sword that he drew her notice that day. She saw him walking along the capital's streets, standing tall with the sunlight setting the gold flecks in his blue eyes on fire. He made a tall and impressive figure: even with hundreds of elaborately attired men and women around him, he stood out with his flashing smile and bright eyes. And so Ilett approached him, because she was empress and accustomed to having whatever caught her fancy. She complimented him on his sword, but her intent quickly became clear to Eldon. Now Eldon was loyal to the empire and his empress, but he had no interest in Ilett or sharing her throne. His polite disinterest frustrated Ilett, a golden-haired beauty who had captured the attention of many suitors over the years."

Gare leaned back and smiled up at the sky, as if in defiance of whatever may come against us. "Time passed, and Eldon continued to spurn Ilett's advances. No one could understand why he did such a thing, not even his mother and father, and they encouraged him to accept her. But Eldon saw beyond the empress's appearance into the greed, selfishness, and coldness of her heart. Her parents had begun the practice of taking members of the Forwyn people as slaves, since Forwyn was the first kingdom to strongly resist Alrenian conquest, and the only one that had not fallen into abject submission upon losing their kingdom to the empire. Empress Ilett embraced this custom and especially treated her slaves ill, so that they cowered before her presence and trembled whenever she spoke. She also hired free servants, though they were little better than slaves themselves. Even before he met Tamelle and learned of the empire's cruelty, he knew the empress could never win his heart.

"The empress began to send Eldon fine gifts—exquisite clothes of the best materials fashioned by her skilled seamstress, fruits and chocolates from around the world, a Brev dagger wrought with gold and jewels. No matter how much she sent or how often she invited him and his family to feasts and balls and celebrations, he would politely refuse her advances. She'd request he join her on afternoon walks through her gardens and he would smile and bow and listen to her chatter, yet always with a distant look in his eye.

"Ilett grew more and more frustrated. She knew she could demand or threaten him into marriage, but she hoped for his heart, for his true affection. So she turned to her seamstress and demanded still more—more gifts for Eldon, more fine gowns for her to wear and display her beauty.

"Now her head seamstress was named Tamelle, a lovely young woman whose skill far surpassed any of the other seamstresses in Ilett's employ. However, Ilett had worked her to exhaustion, and day and night Tamelle rushed to finish the long lists of demands Ilett continuously sent. At last Tamelle did the unthinkable—she made a mistake.

"When Ilett delivered a beautiful cloak to Eldon, she found a small patch where the seam ran crooked. Her cheeks flushed red with anger. 'Send this back to my seamstress!' she cried to the slave attending her, tossing it into his arms. 'Tell her this is unacceptable. She will fix it immediately and receive no pay for today. If she fails…well,' –and her eyes were dark— 'she must not fail again.'

"'Wait!' Eldon said, raising his hand, and the slave hesitated at his command. For even then Eldon had a presence about him, a calm and clear authority that bid all around to listen. His voice was kind and his words full of wisdom. 'I will take the cloak back to your seamstress myself. Since it is mine, I will ensure it is repaired to my standards.'

"Ilett hesitated. She hated to let another order any slave or servant of hers, yet she longed to please Eldon. Therefore, after a long moment, she agreed, and her slave returned the cloak to him.

"So Eldon set out that day to the palace, where two guards escorted him deep, deep down into underground chambers where many of Ilett's servants lived and worked. They brought him to Tamelle's small, dimly lit workroom, where she labored over her special assignments from Ilett apart from the other seamstresses and tailors.

"The guards waited in the hallway and Eldon stepped into the room. Even there, in plain, worn clothes surrounded by shadows, Tamelle's beauty was evident. Her hair lay long and dark about her shoulders, her olive skin was smooth, and her eyes were bright.

"Eldon lay the cloak on the table before her, and her nimble fingers set aside her work to examine it. 'Forgive me,' she said. Her voice was rich with a Teramese accent. 'I will correct this immediately.'

"Eldon laughed lightly, startling Tamelle into a frown.

"'I don't want it,' he said. 'But I heard Ilett will cut your wages for the mistake. She tarnishes the glory of the Alrenian Empire with her childish and cruel ways.' He reached into his pocket and set two dremas on the table.

"Tamelle's pride shimmered in her eyes. 'I do not accept charity,' she said.

"'Then make a fine new cloak for me—one I can be proud to wear. One that is not from Ilett, but from you, the most talented seamstress in the empire.'

"Tamelle sighed, staring at the money. Little did Eldon know then how much she struggled, that what he'd set before her was enough to feed her young siblings and father for a month.

"'Very well,' she said.

"Eldon's smile was warm and bright when she met his eyes. 'I will come to check on your progress again tomorrow.'

"'It will be ready tonight.'

"'Then I will see you again tonight,' he said, and for the first time he left the palace with a smile."

Gare's lips quirked in a smile of his own.

"Tell us about when Eldon tricked the empress," Avrik urged eagerly, his eyes bright.

Gare cleared his throat. "Patience," he said, and continued, skipping a little ahead in the story. "After Eldon and Tamelle had fallen in love, she began to open his eyes to the Alrenian Empire's cruelty. She explained how her father was a Misrothian merchant who had fallen in love with a Teramese woman, and once they were married, they'd settled together in his home in Misroth, despite her misgivings that it was within the empire.

"However, times grew hard and the empire's taxes were steep. Tamelle's mother taught her children Teramese to spite the empire's laws, refusing to stifle her heritage from her children. In fact, their home did not speak Alrenian at all, only Teramese and the New Language that was growing popular in the rebellious pockets of the Misrothian kingdom.

"Eventually, when Tamelle was nearly full grown, Alrenian soldiers discovered this rebellion. Tamelle's mother was taken away to be imprisoned and Tamelle never saw her again.

"At seventeen, she convinced her father to move their family to Alrenor where she could put her talent of clothes making to use for noble families. The steep Alrenian taxes had impoverished them and her father had grown ill, too ill to travel as a merchant any longer. When Tamelle's family arrived in the capital, Ilett soon discovered her and brought her to the palace, where she lived and worked. Once a month she was able to leave and visit her family, and in the meantime, she sent her meager earnings to her father to help feed and care for him and her young sister and brother.

"Tamelle took Eldon to meet her family and others in similar situations. It soon became clear to him that anyone who was not Alrenian-born was suffering. They had little money to feed and clothe themselves, and anyone who could not afford the heavy Alrenian taxes was imprisoned. Any defiance or protest of Alrenian's strict laws, making anything but Alrenian culture, customs, and beliefs illegal, could draw a death sentence.

"This was when Eldon began to conspire. He began by befriending many of Ilett's palace servants and slaves and familiarizing himself with the grounds. He continued to tolerate Ilett's advances, but now with the hope that her good graces would help him find her weaknesses.

"One day, when Ilett had grown especially desperate to impress Eldon, she led him from her garden to her menagerie, where she kept wonderful and beautiful animals from all over the world.

"'Is this the best of all the empire possesses?' he asked.

"So she led him through her stables and showed him her fastest stallions. She rode with him through the grounds on her fastest steed and then set it at a gallop. When they returned to the stables and dismounted, Eldon asked, 'Is this the best of all the empire possesses?'

"So she took him through the palace and showed him her vast library, where old scrolls and new books from all over the world in every subject anyone had ever written about resided. Shelves stretched from the floor all the way to the ornate ceiling in aisles that seemed to go on endlessly.

"'Is this the best of all the empire possesses?' Eldon asked again.

"So she walked him through her halls of artwork and statues, of historical relics and treasures, of impressive weapons and armor from every corner of the empire and even from the free kingdoms across the Great Sea.

"'Is this the best of all the empire possesses?' Eldon asked yet again.

"And so she led him up, up, to the cliff overlooking the Alrenian Sea where her dragons were housed. She made her Dragon Keepers ride for him, circling about the cliffside and diving and racing one another, all to display their skill.

"'But is this the best of all the empire possesses?' Eldon asked once more.

"Ilett led him into the Dragon Keep, where the dragons were housed and fed and cared for within great caverns dug deep into the rock. She brought him to the place where her own dragon was kept. He was a magnificent beast with vivid scarlet scales, the biggest and strongest and fastest of all the dragons. 'This is Raklov. He is familiar with only me, and only to me will he answer,' she said proudly. 'Only I have tamed him and only I can ride him.'

"So she rode for Eldon, showing off her dragon's speed and her own talent. And when she landed, for the first time Eldon let his wonder and astonishment appear on his face, a fact which greatly pleased her.

"For days afterward, she brought him to the Dragon Keep so he could watch the Keepers ride, but he always asked to see Raklov and watch her ride. Ilett was too proud to see the way Eldon plotted, how he keenly watched the way the Keepers tamed their dragons to their will and held themselves during flight.

"'One who is permitted to visit and care for your dragon must be a trusted and honored person indeed,' Eldon said one day as he watched one of Ilett's servants lead Raklov away into the Keep.

"Ilett's smile turned flirtatious. 'Do you wish for the job?'

"'I would be honored,' Eldon said with a bow, careful to set his countenance to look surprised.

"Ilett waved her hand toward him with a flourish. 'Then it is yours.'

"And so that was how Eldon tricked Ilett into allowing him to slowly gain Raklov's favor until the dragon responded to Eldon's commands. It is the moment we now mark as the beginning of the Misrothian rebellion and Eldon's choice to set his loyalty toward the Alrenian Empire completely aside."

After Gare's story ended, quiet settled around our company once more. I drew a deep breath, then said, "I think we have rested long enough."

Gare gave a quick nod. "What good does it do to sit here and await danger? If it is coming anyway, let's go out and meet it bravely."

Strapping his bow on his back and rolling his shoulders, Layk frowned back at Gare. "I thought a soldier was ever cautious, not eager for danger."

Jennah smiled and laid a hand on Gare's shoulder. "You know our friend," she told Layk. "He is one for action. And I agree: I will go mad if we sit here and wait any longer. Besides, maybe we will find better cover further in," she finished uncertainly.

"There will be no better cover until after we cross through Irevek Swamp," Narek said. His eyes never left the sky as he spoke, but the rest of us shared uneasy glances. Then Jennah pressed her lips together in a determined line, Gare threw me a reassuring look, Layk settled his hand on his sword hilt, and Avrik lifted his chin and plastered on the easy, confident grin I knew so well. Only tonight, I could see that it was a façade, probably more to buoy his own courage than to fool us.

We all took one last swig from our canteens, swung our packs on our backs, and ensured our weapons were in easy reach. When everyone paused and I realized that they were awaiting me, I straightened my back and stood tall. I squinted into the night sky, wishing for the moonlight to return but thankful I couldn't detect any movement among the clouds. I drew a deep breath. "Let's go," I said, and we set out into the darkness.

The sky was fading to grey when we at last began to breathe easily, knowing we had made it through our first night without incident. Narek, however, remained grim. "We are still close to the barrier," he muttered. "The deeper we venture into Toryn, the more dangerous it will become."

We set up camp as the sun began to rise, eating a hasty meal and then wearily curling up in our bedrolls. Layk took the first watch, so I was soon lost in dreams. It seemed as if I had only slept a few minutes when Jennah was shaking me. As soon as I rose, she tumbled into her bedroll and fell asleep.

Huddling inside my cloak for warmth against the cool breeze, perched on a rock high above the long stalks of grass surrounding me, I wondered if Jennah was dreaming of her family. My heart pinched to think she might never see them again.

Life-Giver, please… I begged, but felt at a loss for words. He may have spared my life, but my questions about my gift and my purpose still felt endless and I couldn't shake the sensation of having been abandoned. In the wilderness of Toryn, left to rely on my enemy, I felt lost and desperate.

Drawing a deep breath, I tried to find peace in my surroundings as I scanned the horizon, watching the sun sink low. It turned the sky a vivid orange-gold, so bright and beautiful in this vast expanse of green that it took my breath away. If only sunset didn't also herald another dangerous night for us all. I turned away from the western sky, only for my gaze to fall upon a figure approaching from the north. I squinted against the evening glow, but the form was indistinct before the hulking shapes of the mountains.

I rose from my seat and fixed an arrow to my bow in one fluid motion. I concentrated on holding my breathing steady. The figure approached slowly, without any show of menace of visible weapons, but I couldn't imagine who else would be traveling the Toryn wilderness, and alone, no less.

Just as I opened my mouth to cry out, recognition swept through me and my heart jolted with an entirely different sort of fear. The man at last drew near enough that I could see his face even beneath the hood of his cloak, his familiar smile sending hope coursing through my veins. Like the first time I'd met him in Evren Forest, power emanated from his very aura. My body and mind knew, instinctually, that this was a man who would be obeyed, and who could be deadly if he so desired. Knees quaking, I withdrew my arrow from the string and dropped my weapon to the ground. I couldn't move my gaze from his warm brown eyes or that smile that spoke of affection and pride in a way my own father's never had.

Breathless, uncertain, I took a wavering step forward, then another. I didn't know if I was afraid to approach or if I longed to feel his embrace again, whether I was angry it had been weeks since our last encounter or relieved that he was here at last, in this desolate land. An indescribable emotion overwhelmed me: all at once it was like reuniting with Rev and Lyanna, like reconciling with Avrik, like having my parents restored to me, as if they had never wronged my family. It went against everything I'd ever been taught about the gods and goddesses of the earth—and yet here I was, approaching the Life-Giver, the one who held life and death in his hands, as if he were of my own blood.

"You came," I choked out, and I realized, half embarrassed, that my voice had come out nearly in a sob. Uncomfortable, I drew back, but he beckoned me closer. I cast a quick glance about the camp, but my companions slept on undisturbed.

"You are afraid you have already failed," he said as I stepped forward.

Nodding, I bowed my head and stared down at the grass while it rustled against my cloak and tunic. There was no use denying the truth, even if my gift would have permitted me to lie. "I'm not even sure what I'm supposed to be doing." My throat felt tight, my chest constricted.

"Why do you doubt yourself?" His eyes were piercing, searching.

I blinked and averted my gaze once more. "I…I cannot control my gift. How can I help my comrades when I don't know how to help myself? I was not trained to lead—but to follow. To follow my cousin, the heir to the throne, and to serve my kingdom. He is Misroth's protector and defender, and I am his. But I am no soldier, no queen. I am an heir of Eldon, but I am not Eldon. I know nothing of this barrier or this land, or how to save Gillen or my kingdom."

"Do you think Eldon knew who he would become or everything he would do? Did he meet Tamelle knowing that she would one day inspire him to fight against his empress, against an empire?"

Slowly, I shook my head.

"Have you failed the mission that brought you to Toryn?"

"Not if Gillen is still alive," I whispered. "But how—how will we ever return?"

His gaze was softer now, yet no less discerning. I felt vulnerable and exposed before him, but his intimate knowledge of my feelings and thoughts was strangely comforting as well.

"You place too much weight upon yourself because you are a member of the royal family and you have a gift, or because I spared your life when you thought you should die." The words were gentle but humbling, and I felt my cheeks turn pink. "Halia, you are not the only one with a gift. Do not imagine the fate of your kingdom rests entirely on you." He paused, placing a hand lightly on my shoulder. "Your emotions both hinder and help you."

I opened my mouth, wanting to ask for more, but his face turned grim. "The sun has set, Halia. Danger is upon you."

CHAPTER TEN

NO SOONER HAD HE SPOKEN the words than an inhuman cry rent the air. My body remembered what it was like to be locked in battle and sprang into action. I turned my face toward the sky, searching the clouds for a form, for wings, for even the dimmest shadow in the night. Nothing. When I glanced back toward the Life-Giver, he was gone. Cold fear turned my muscles rigid.

"Danger!" I screamed, but my companions—trained guards, soldier, hunter, and mother—were already stirring at the noise. The air was heavy with a threat, even when that threat was invisible and had gone silent. Dashing forward, I retrieved my bow and arrow from where I'd left them in the grass and joined my company.

As one, we crouched low, lifted our weapons, and scanned the sky.

"Use the grass as your cover," Narek said, sinking so low the stalks nearly concealed his entire body. His face was a mask, and I wondered how many horrifying memories he was reliving in this moment.

I shrank down against the earth until the grass wavered over my head, but the cover was little comfort. All I could remember was my vision of Gillen and his men desperately trying to hide in the grass, and how so many of them had still been devoured by their invisible foe. *Protect us, Life-Giver*, I pleaded, though I wished he had remained to fight by our sides.

The screeching pierced the night again, sending my heart into a wild gallop and stifling my breath. Heavy wings beat at the air, thudding in my ears and chest. The sounds were everywhere but I couldn't see their source. I pulled back my bowstring and aimed for the sky, praying I would see a form in the darkness before the ichgor came upon us.

"To the left!" Gare's voice rang out clearly, even as the ichgor's screams clamored against our ears.

A strong hand pushed between my shoulder blades and shoved me flat to the ground; then a body pressed against me, covering me. I heard Avrik breathing and felt his warm breath in my ear. Another scream tore the air as fury exploded inside me. I wasn't afraid—I was angry. My companions were prepared to risk their lives to protect me at all costs, simply because Eldon's blood ran in my veins. Because I was an heir to a throne I didn't want. They could die tonight… for me.

Squirming against Avrik, I shouted, "Let me go! That's an order!"

"An order he, as a loyal Misrothian citizen, can disobey, my lady," Layk said from somewhere close on my left. They had flanked me, pressing me in on either side with their bows pointed to the sky. But, despite Layk's words, Avrik pulled back to release me. He hovered near, the warmth of his body reassuring me.

I lifted my head to see a huge black shape swoop down toward us, its wingbeats pulsing through the air like thunder. Wind whipped my hair into a swirling mass about my face until curls tumbled in my eyes and I was blinded. Pushing the strands away, I stared at the creature landing in the grass ahead. The sight took my breath away.

Its black, leathery wings stretched at least as wide as the Misrothian castle entrance and ended in sharp claws. Beady red eyes gleamed back at me, but the cloudy film obscuring them reminded me that it was not with its eyes that the beast watched me. Raising its head to the sky, the ichgor opened elongated jaws and screamed, its yellow fangs trailing saliva. Still shrieking, it veered its head this way and that, twitching its bat-like ears as it detected its own cries echoing off our bodies and revealing our position.

With a grunt, Avrik released two arrows at once, aiming straight for the ichgor's head. It snatched the arrows in its jaws as if they were only flies.

"We still outnumber it!" Gare shouted.

"For now," Narek said. He rose from the grass, brandishing his sword with the finesse of a highly trained Royal Guard. "Distract it with your arrows! Gare, Jennah, help me attack it from behind." He shot a look at Gare, then Jennah, who each nodded in turn and fell in line behind him as he began advancing toward the beast.

I shot my arrow, sending it flying toward the ichgor's eye. Once again it devoured the weapon in a single bite. It advanced on us, clawing its way through the dirt.

Under one of the ichgor's massive wings, Narek ducked low and Jennah and Gare followed his lead. Layk shot at the ichgor's wing, piercing its leathery skin and halting it for the briefest of instants. Snarling, it clawed forward. Its great wings rose and fell and nearly smashed into my companions. Narek, Gare, and Jennah dropped just in time. They charged beneath its wings, rose to their full heights, and lifted their blades to strike.

I crouched lower in the grass and reached for another arrow. *Imagine you are back in Evren,* I commanded myself. *You are competing with Avrik and Bren and Shilam. There is nothing around you but your bow, your arrow, and your target.* Sucking in a deep breath, I focused on the feel of my bowstring as I pulled it taut. With my eyes I traced the path I wanted my arrow to follow and released. My arrow sank deep within the ichgor's chest.

Enraged, the ichgor screamed and staggered back. My friends leapt backward to get out of its way, then continued to move into position, surrounding the beast in a semicircle. Jennah's form was tall and lithe, a picture of determination and fearlessness. Gare stood strong and solid, an unwavering soldier awaiting orders from the former Captain of the Guard, who was a shadow crouched in the darkness, his flashing blade the only bright thing about him. On either side of me, Layk and Avrik shot toward the ichgor's underbelly as it began to advance once more.

I snatched another arrow from my quiver. Wind rustled my hair across my face, but my gaze never wavered from the creature. Seeking out one of the ichgor's eyes, I drew my arrow back.

Then everything vanished. It was as if something in my vision snapped: one instant the ichgor and my companions surrounded me, and the next the scene had changed. Moonlight, tinged a sickly yellow, filtered through wispy grey clouds on another night in the grasslands, and this time there were countless ichgor spread out as far as I could see. Some swooped down from the sky, so low the wind from their wing beats rushed over me and the sound pounded against my ears. The rest had landed within a small town. Shrieks pierced the air, both the inhuman ichgors' as well as human cries of fear. People flooded down the town's streets and poured out into the endless grass, trying in vain to hide within the stalks before ichgor seized them with long, knife-like fangs. Blood stained large patches of the grass deep scarlet. Archers and men and women wielding swords and axes tried to fend the monsters off, but they were gravely outnumbered and the ichgor seemed to pick them off effortlessly while suffering few casualties themselves. Everywhere there were people running, people screaming, people dying.

Clinging to a huge sword, a girl not much younger than myself sprinted toward me, dark strands of her long hair streaming behind her like a banner. Flashing in the darkness, her eyes were striking, deep black flecked with grey shimmering like silver. Two ichgor swooped low, looming close, their persistent screams and twitching ears pursuing her. There was nowhere to hide.

My breath caught in my chest. I glanced about for my bow and arrow only to find that I'd dropped them in the grass. In my concern for the girl's life, I forgot I was trapped in a vision and there was nothing I could do to help.

"Reylinn!" a voice tore through the air. I turned to see a boy close to the girl's age dashing toward her, calling out desperately as he clung to a tarnished, war-beaten sword.

Reylinn slowed to crouch before a body, torn and bloodied almost beyond recognition. She breathed a silent prayer and spun to face the charging ichgor. Her stance was poised and prepared, a highly trained warrior facing her enemies.

White-faced, the boy staggered to a stop beside her, panting and clinging to his own blade with an unsteady hand. He was bleeding. I could see him clearly now. Recognition flashed through my brain and I gasped in surprise. Narek. "Reylinn," he said. "You can run; I'll hold them back. It's over. We've lost."

The girl turned to him, scowling. "Shut up, you idiot. I'm not running like some coward and leaving you to die alone."

Reylinn lifted her chin toward her enemies in defiance. "Let's put our years of training to use!"

And then the ichgor were upon them.

A jolt of pain shocked me back from my vision. Blinking, I found myself sprawled face down in the grass with the taste of blood filling my mouth. A weight pressed down on me, making it hard to breathe.

"Stay down!" Layk shouted. I could feel his arms digging into my back. When had I stood? I cringed when I realized how deeply immersed I must have been in my vision.

Groaning, I lifted my head to look at my surroundings. The ichgor had taken once more to the air, screeching and attacking with fangs and claws as it dove low. Narek swung his sword with ferocity and grace, forcing the ichgor back each time it drew near. A claw swiped for his head. He ducked and drove his blade into the ichor's foot. My friends wasted no time, moving in tandem with Narek. Jennah hurled one of her daggers at the ichgor's belly and Gare slashed a hole in its wing. With a snarl the beast jerked back, its wings pounding wildly against the air.

A figure darted out from behind me, straight toward the ichgor. My heart jolted sharply in my chest. The ichgor dove for him, but Avrik stood tall and confident. Head high, he lifted his bow and nocked an arrow to the string. He never wavered as he took aim and drew the string back to his jaw.

Shoot now, my mind pleaded, wishing Avrik would move faster. *Before it reaches you.*

"Get off me," I growled at Layk, who still pinned me to the earth.

"I can't do that, my lady," he said. "You can't help—"

"I died for Misroth!" I cried. "Don't make me watch him die!"

My words had their desired effect and Layk slid off me. I sprinted toward Avrik, Layk on my heels. The world felt darker, the wind colder. A ringing filled my ears until every sound seemed muffled, like I was separated by a great distance from the battlefield.

The ichgor extended its claws, stretching toward Avrik. I was too far away, and Layk wasn't any closer. A hundred yards of grass rippled between Avrik and me. I wouldn't make it to him before the ichgor did.

I launched myself forward as the ichgor slashed at Avrik. He threw himself down, twisting in the air so he landed in the grass with his bow still pointed up. Miraculously, the beast clawed at air and Avrik shot it in its underbelly.

The ichgor shuddered forward a few more beats and then pulled up, looping around to strike again. When it dove for her, Jennah was ready. With one clean swipe she sliced off its toe and then bounded away. But the ichgor was faster. It snapped at her, catching her arm with one of its fangs and knocking her down. She lay bleeding and dazed in the grass, her dagger out of reach.

The ichgor lunged for her again, but Gare leapt between them. He stabbed for the beast's eye and it jerked away with frightening speed. It landed before him, fangs clashing and tongue flicking from its jowls as if it could taste him already. Its ears twitched as it listened to his every movement, every breath.

The sight of Gare battling the ichgor was almost graceful, if grace could be found in the vicious, wild movements of a fight. Gare wielded his blade with power and assurance, every plunge and strike of his weapon precise. He deflected the ichgor's attacks effortlessly. Whenever the creature bit at him, Gare pressed near and countered with his own attack. He took one of the ichgor's eyes and left a gleaming red wound across its neck.

Layk, Avrik, and I unleashed arrows on the ichgor that helped distract it and leave it vulnerable for Gare's onslaught. Coming from its blind side, Narek leapt onto the ichgor, caught a fistful of its fur, and climbed up its back. He poised his blade over the creature and plunged it deep into its back until it unleashed an inhuman scream that rattled the air around us. It threw Narek from its back. He dropped his sword and hit the ground rolling.

The ichgor flung itself upon Gare with the raw desperation of a dying animal. It snapped its jaws at him repeatedly, forcing him to stumble backward and deflect blow after blow. Then it struck with its claws. Its movement took Gare by surprise and he didn't have time to block. The claws smacked into him and sent him sprawling to the ground, where he lay motionless.

"Gare!" Jennah screamed, still scrambling to find her dagger. Blood coursed down her arm.

I shot at the ichgor again, piercing its soft side. It howled and dipped toward Gare to finish its kill. Jennah grasped her dagger at last. Before the ichgor could sink its fangs into her friend, she flung it with her good arm straight into the beast's open maw. The ichgor's scream turned into a gurgle; it retreated, swaying and flapping its wings to take to the air. Avrik shot it in its good eye and it crashed to the earth. The ground shook with the impact and nearly knocked me off my feet.

We all hesitated for one breathless moment, staring first at the felled creature and then at Gare's form. Then we flew into action: Narek strode toward the ichgor, and the rest of us raced to Gare's side.

Jennah reached him first. Kneeling beside him, she reached with shaking hands and called out his name. No answer. I felt dread stab my heart at the sight. Blood soaked the earth around Gare, who lay face down in the grass and hadn't so much as moved in response to Jennah's touch. She brushed his shoulder, her voice choking on tears as she spoke again. "Gare, answer me!" Gently, she nudged his shoulder again, then gave a fierce push with both hands, straining and groaning at the use of her injured arm.

"Jennah…" Layk began. I turned to see him standing beside me, his face pale and his eyes full of a look I knew too well. It was the look of a hundred pitying well-wishers and hopeless healers, telling my family and me that my uncle would never sit on his throne again.

My stomach dropped. Jennah's anguished cries sounded distant in my ears and Layk's voice was lost amidst a rushing noise, like waves tumbling, like a vast cold sea opening wide to swallow me. A hand rested on my shoulder, buoying me up, but that sensation felt far away too, an insignificant fact in the face of this one horrible truth. Gare was dead. My friend had died on *my* mission, under *my* orders. Somewhere back home, Gare's family waited in vain for their soldier.

"He died a soldier's death." It was Narek's voice, breaking through the rushing in my ears, which, as suddenly as it had begun, was receding.

I stared at the ground. Despite Layk's words, Jennah had rolled Gare onto his back, revealing the gaping wounds marring his chest. His sightless eyes stared up at stars he would never see again. I yanked my gaze away.

"I do not want words from you, *garash*," Jennah spat. Tears streamed down her cheeks, yet her eyes shone bright and fierce in the night, more gold than brown in her anger and grief.

"We need to tend to your wound," Narek continued, stepping toward Jennah.

Jennah sprang to her feet and stepped back, her eyes flashing and her stance tense, like a cat ready to pounce. "Stay away from me."

"Narek is right," Layk said. "Jennah, we have to stop the bleeding."

"I won't let him touch me," she choked out.

Layk was by her side before she could dissolve into sadness once more. She wiped at glistening tears with her good arm while he pulled dressings from his pack and bound her wound. "You will be all right," he said softly, but Jennah shook her head.

"His wife is…she's waiting for him," she whispered. "His s-son."

Layk nodded slowly, and as his eyes met hers I could see the painful understanding that passed between them. It was not merely a friend they grieved, or the sad news we would bear to his family, but the knowledge that their own families awaited them, possibly in vain also. Gare's fate could easily be their own. They too had made promises to return that they might break.

A breeze whispered through the grass and brought me back to the present. I turned to the ichgor's dead body, strewn across the ground like an ugly deformity in the landscape. Narek had beheaded it, tossing the severed head several yards away from the body and leaving a gory mess that I cringed away from. There was blood everywhere—the ichgor's blood, Jennah's blood, Gare's blood.

I turned to my companions. Jennah was pale, her hair a tangled mess falling from the knot at her neck and hanging in damp ringlets around her face. Layk was solemn and quiet, his eyes surveying the aftermath with an emotion I couldn't quite read, and Avrik was watching everyone with the wide eyes of an empathetic outsider. He hadn't known Gare as well as the rest of us, but he felt our pain and fear clearly enough. I glanced at Narek, covered in the ichgor's blood and staring at me with an expression the closest to terror I'd ever seen on his face.

"We cannot linger," he said. "More will come. Others will have heard this fight for miles around."

I looked back at Gare's body. I could still see him fending off the ichgor with powerful strokes, unyielding when it came to defending his friends and kingdom. I could see him laughing and gesturing with his arms as he brought a tale of Misrothian history to life for us. I could see the courage in his eyes as he pledged to follow me, despite the risks, despite the possible sacrifice. But stronger than any other memory was the one of him closely holding his wife before we'd left the capital, murmuring words of comfort. *I will be thinking of you every day, every moment.*

I squeezed my eyes shut, unable to believe that my friend, so full of life and strength, could be gone. There had been no chance to even try to save him or to say goodbye. How could we rush off into the night and leave his body behind? Animals would devour his remains until he was nothing but bones picked clean and left to scatter and decay.

"You must think of the living," Narek said sternly. "Gare gave his life to defend us. Would you throw that away?"

Around me, my friends lifted their heads at Narek's words and turned to me, awaiting my order. My choice.

Gare's words echoed in my head. *We are the Dragon-Hearted.*

How could I act like a coward and leave him behind, without offering him due respect, when he had given everything for our safety? But how could I risk my friends' lives?

I let my eyes meet Jennah and Layk's gazes. They were watching me with determination in their eyes; despite our loss, despite our fear, there was only courage and strength etched on their faces. At my side, Avrik nodded at me, as if he could already read my thoughts. Perhaps he could.

"We will burn his body and offer it to the Life-Giver to take to the afterlife." My voice rang out strong and unyielding. "He deserves this from us, at least."

Narek's jaw muscles tightened, sharpening the lines of his face, yet he did not protest. Turning his face to the sky, he gave a brief nod. "Follow your Misrothian customs, but be quick, or you'll be offering the rest of us to Nesrelle. She is the only deity who rules in Toryn."

He moved away, back to the ichgor, where he began plucking arrows from its body and laying out the unbroken ones for Avrik, Layk, and I to collect later.

My other companions and I set to work preparing Gare's body. We swallowed back our emotion and stripped him of his sword and the gold circular pendant he wore around his neck.

"From his wife," Jennah whispered, as if we needed to be reminded of our Misrothian wedding custom. She slipped the chain over her neck, where it hung beside her own pendant, a diamond-studded silver rendering of the constellation Shyla.

Together we placed Gare's arms at his sides to honor his status as a soldier always ready to defend his kingdom. Misroth's emblem, where it was stitched on his tunic across his chest, gleamed in the starlight, and I could almost ignore the tears below it that revealed the bloody gashes running across his body. Layk doused Gare's body in some of the precious oil he carried and we all stood still for a silent moment to pay our own respects to our friend.

I drew a deep breath and lifted my eyes to the sky, where grey clouds shifted endlessly, concealing and then revealing the starlight in a constant battle between shadow and light. Even as I spoke the words, I could hear my father speaking them over my uncle four years ago, "Giver of Life, we ask that you take him into the afterlife with you, freely offering him a new life greater than this one, greater than we can imagine."

Then Layk set the fire.

"We must go *now*," Narek said. "There are too many monsters roaming the night for us to stand by this beacon and create so much noise."

Pushing back my pain, I nodded. "He's right. We have to go."

With heavy hearts, we shoved the arrows into our quivers and shouldered our packs, but kept our weapons in our hands. We left our friend behind and pressed further into the night.

CHAPTER ELEVEN

THE NIGHT WAS A BLUR of snarled emotions. Cold wind bit at my face, whipped through the grasses, and made my ears ring as I stumbled after Narek, walking endlessly into blackness that seemed alive with all my guilt, sorrow, and fear. I kept my head low and tried to ignore Layk and Jennah as they trod behind me, silent and solemn, as if in a daze. Next to me, Avrik tried to catch my eye more than once throughout the night, but I refused to acknowledge him. I couldn't face my friends, couldn't face the pain or the knowledge of just how much this expedition could cost us.

As the grey of dawn bled into the eastern horizon, a vast swampland sprawled ahead. Draped in moss, the barren limbs of old gnarled trees created slashes of black against the mist curling up from the muddy waters. With a backward glance to urge us on, Narek plunged in, sinking nearly to his thighs. I followed, shuddering as the cold water lapped against my legs. The mist shifted and thickened, sometimes blocking Narek from my sight, other times shrouding him until he was nothing but a shadowy figure, like a lonely specter left to haunt the Toryn wilderness alone.

Our walk through the swamp felt endless, a miserable journey set in the middle of a nightmare. The muddy depths of the swamp clung to my boots and made it difficult to keep my footing. More than once I stumbled and caught myself in a panic, splashing water and mud until I was completely soaked, dirty, and shivering.

At last a mound of land rose over the swamp, like an island amidst the shifting shadows and fog. Vast trees extended toward the sky, so tall they looked like they could pierce the clouds, while tangles of moss draped from their boughs hid whatever lay beyond them. His legs coated in layers of brown slime, Narek climbed onto the muddy bank and peered into the dimness, seeking a safe place behind the cover of the mossy veil for us to camp. Looking over his shoulder, he waved us onward.

I glanced up: already the stars had dimmed and the eastern sky was tinged with hues of gold. My heart lightened for an instant with the knowledge that daytime meant safety, but pain stabbed it again when I remembered that safety had come too late for Gare. I swiped at the mud crusted on my face in vain and crawled after Narek onto the solid earth.

"We are safe, for now," Narek muttered as we all gathered, sinking to sit and rest our weary legs. "I will take the first watch."

No one responded. We didn't have the energy to protest or even distrust his motives now. There were tear trails left in the mud splattered across Jennah's cheeks, and Layk's bright eyes were dim with pain and exhaustion. Layk redressed Jennah's wound with fresh bandages quickly and quietly, noting that the injury was not severe and should heal soon. Avrik was uncharacteristically mute as he lay his bow down and curled up on the ground, not even bothering to unpack his bedroll. In a daze, I leaned against a tree trunk and shut my eyes, wishing I could block out reality. Wishing I could fall asleep.

I glanced over to Narek, who had already crept to the edge of our makeshift campsite, gazing out over the swampland stretching ahead under the first rays of dawn. His shoulders were hunched, his posture tense. Flashes of my vision returned, and I wondered what memories he was reliving now. How many times had he watched the ichgor kill his people and destroy entire towns and cities? Whose deaths haunted him every waking hour and visited him in his dreams?

I dozed fitfully—for how long, I couldn't be sure—before I gave up. The mist had grown thick and heavy, a clammy embrace that made my teeth chatter no matter how I tried to wrap my cloak or blankets about me. Standing, I crept away from the sleeping forms of my friends and Narek's vague shadow to the water's edge and peered into the swamp. Somewhere overhead, beyond the shifting fog and murky, skeletal trees, beyond the shroud of grey clouds I imagined still covered the sky, the sun was burning, warm and golden. But that light was far beyond me here.

Seating myself in the grass, I stared out as far as I could into the fog and let my mind wander. Over and over, it brought up memories of Gare: I could see his smile, feel his comforting hand on my shoulder, and hear his deep, throaty laugh, so contagious. At last I clamped down on my thoughts and forced myself onto a new topic.

Our party would never survive this vast wilderness for long unless Toryn's capital could provide us with real shelter, something Narek seemed convinced of. But how much more devastation had occurred since he had last been within the borders of his kingdom? Even if Calidar could offer us a haven, our only lasting hope lay in finding a way across the border—whether we found Gillen or not.

I had to learn the barrier's secret. I had to become master of my visions.

Squeezing my eyes shut, I tried to remember the Life-Giver's advice. *If only his help was clearer,* I thought in frustration.

My thoughts and feelings weren't easy to focus: they consumed me and tormented me; they were a writhing mass enveloping me as thickly as the mist. I tried to concentrate all my energy on the barrier and imagining a vision that could bring a solution.

I knew the instant reality was snuffed out like a candle and my vision began. My mind's image of the barrier faded and was replaced by a comforting hearth, its fire so large I could feel its warmth on my cheeks, even from several feet away.

"Are you sure going on this mission is wise?" a woman spoke tremulously behind me.

Turning, I saw Gare and his wife resting on a settee, staring into the flames together. Loae was curled up close to her husband, her head resting in his lap. Gare leaned back, his broad shoulders slightly slumped, his face grave as he turned his eyes from the fire to gaze into his wife's face.

My heart ached. This scene from the past felt too intimate for me to intrude upon, even if I couldn't force it to melt away, not for all my longing or my attempts to concentrate on something else. I stared at Loae, this woman who was looking so comfortable and safe beside her husband in the past, yet was waiting in vain for him now. He would never return to her. This woman was a widow at this very moment because her husband had chosen to accompany me on this wild mission.

Gare ran a hand through his wife's golden curls. "It's what is right. For so many years, I've trained for battles that never came. Now our fight is almost over. Our kingdom has been restored to its true king—and it is my responsibility to my king to ensure he returns safely, and to my kingdom to ensure we are not left leaderless. Or worse—subjects to a new tyrant who might claim Gillen's throne in his absence."

"I know," she whispered. "I know this is what you have to do. I only…I only keep wishing that it was not." She closed her eyes for a long moment, and I wondered if she was fighting back tears. "The rumors you have spoken of—the things the princess claims live in Toryn and threaten the king now—I cannot stop the nightmares. Every night I see you fighting strange monsters in my dreams." She reached up and brushed his cheek. "I just want to know that you will be safe. That you will come back to me."

My vision ended, evaporating as abruptly as it had begun. I didn't want to cry, didn't want to feel the guilt and sorrow gnaw at me. *Emotions are weakness,* my father's voice spoke in my head, so I turned back toward our camp.

By sunset, the mist had melted and the clouds had dispersed enough to bring a bright evening that felt almost insulting to the grief overshadowing our company. I could hardly choke down a meal, but knew without it my strength would fade too soon.

As the others finished packing, I stood huddled in my cloak and hood beside Layk, gazing out at the dreary swamp. I could feel the weight of his stare as soon as he turned his eyes on me.

"You have not lost our loyalty," Layk said after several long moments.

I blinked, not sure if I wanted to look him in the face, not sure if I even wanted to speak at all. The only thing I could see was Gare's wife, her eyes filled with worry and longing, love and doubt, all mingling together until her eyes glimmered with unshed tears. If I was on this mission for my kingdom, how could I return and tell her, one of my people, that she had sacrificed for it? Perhaps I could still save Gillen, but at what cost to Misroth?

Layk set a gentle hand on my arm, startling me from my thoughts. "We all know what this may take from us, but we also know that the loved ones we left behind are worth any price."

Finally, I turned and met his piercing gaze. Brow knotted, jaw set firm, he searched my face earnestly. "You cannot waver. The battles we face may seem impossible, the price too steep, but, through it all, you must remember why we fight. Don't lose focus."

I nodded, even though I was unsure if I could ever find comfort in his words.

Narek stepped beside us and cast a cool glance toward me. I wondered what he saw in me now: haunted eyes and a pale face? A ragged, lost girl burdened with fear and guilt? Or the daughter of Zarev, determined to achieve her purpose even if it meant harming others along the way? Whatever he saw, I was grateful there was no sign of condescension or mockery in his eyes this time when he looked at me. He waited as I drew a breath, stretched my muscles, and shifted the pack on my shoulders.

"Lead the way," I said.

We survived another long, yet thankfully uneventful night trekking through the swamp and another restless, uncomfortable day camped on a small, muddy mound. By nightfall I was weary of the muck, wet, and cold and the eerie mist that clung to our skin. The only relief was that the cooler air meant there were no flies or mosquitos to make our journey even more miserable.

It wasn't long before the clouds that had hovered over us for days unleashed a cold flood that soaked through my clothes. Only a few stars were visible occasionally, when the thick clouds shifted and our path was illuminated by their light, turning the world black, grey, and silver.

"Should we find shelter?" Layk shouted to Narek over the rush of rain in our ears.

Narek paused only long enough to turn so his words could be heard. "No. This is the safest we will be traveling through Toryn; the ichgor will not be hunting tonight."

Without protest, we traveled onward, clutching our dripping cloaks about us as if they could keep out the water and cold. The night was so dark, so wet, that it was nearly impossible to see more than a few feet ahead even when the starlight filtered down. Now and then, beyond the hunched forms of my companions, I caught glimpses of shadowy trees, their trails of moss hanging like long, limp sashes. The rain splattered into the swamp until its muddy waters began to rise around us. An irrational panic clamored inside me, telling me that perhaps it would never stop rising and we would drown.

At last the swamp ended, giving way to blessedly solid ground. The rain-drenched grass was slick beneath our feet.

Without warning, Narek halted and I nearly collided with him. Before I could ask what had happened, he lifted a hand and pointed into the dimness. At first my eyes couldn't discern anything at all. It felt like staring into unending blackness, broken only by slashes of silver rain in the night. Then I saw the first shape and a flash of movement, and my heart shuddered within my chest. *Ichgor.* As I continued to stare, I was able to see more: the outline of trees rising toward the sky, the mass of black wings folded across a huge body, and the shadows of more and more ichgor hanging upside down from branches. The sight seemed to stretch on endlessly until all I could see were the trees and the resting ichgor. I didn't dare move, didn't dare speak. I could sense my friends' stillness behind me and wondered if they were close enough to see what I could. How could we even travel around the ichgor when the night was so deep we could barely see? The creatures appeared to be resting, but I didn't doubt they would snatch at us in an instant if we ventured near.

"This way," Narek said, gesturing to the right.

"We could kill some," Avrik said in a low voice. The intensity of his tone surprised me enough that I glanced back at him. His fingers hovered close to the fletching of an arrow, prepared to draw it from his quiver.

Narek stared back at him for a long moment, as if considering. "They can still fly in this downpour if we provoke them. We can't strike when we are outnumbered like this." But before he turned away, I sensed his bitterness—in the tone of his voice, in the slump of his shoulders, in the remorse and anger gleaming dark in his eyes. Ignoring this chance at revenge was not an easy choice for him.

Avrik's hand dropped to his side, though his eyes remained fastened on the visible ichgor a long while more.

"Besides," Narek added, "this is the beginning of the Woods."

Layk drew nearer, his wary eyes never leaving the ichgor's forms as he spoke. "The what?"

"It's a large, wild forest—it was wild and unknown even before creatures like the ichgor invaded Toryn. Now it is infested with sedwa, and, as you can see, also a haven for the ichgor. We would not find any shelter under these trees and would waste time venturing through it, anyway. We need to bear further west." He gestured to our right. "Let's go."

The rain had turned to a drizzle by the time dawn lightened the sky, and we found shelter beneath a cluster of trees apart from the forest. All our belongings were soaked, so we huddled under the trees and struggled to make a meal out of what food was salvageable in our packs. After a damp, unsatisfying meal of dried fruit and jerky, we passed a long, restless day camped there.

At last the rain ended and we could lay out our belongings to dry, but it took hours for me to even begin to feel warm. We dozed until the sun drew low in the west.

The night was already settling around us when we packed up. Though the comfort the rain had brought by keeping the ichgor from hunting was gone, the clouds were too, which meant we had far more light to travel by. A waning, golden moon hung low in the sky and set the landscape alight with a yellow glow, and the open skies were piercingly beautiful, full of glistening constellations and planets suspended in blackness rich as velvet. All I could think of as I scanned the sky were long-ago nights when Gillen and I snuck to the castle towers and studied the stars—nights that felt like they could have occurred to someone else, lifetimes ago.

Please be safe, I thought.

As the days and nights passed, the landscape began to change further. The forest still rose up, dark and thick on our left, but we also began to pass over hills and through copses of trees that were sparser and, according to

Narek, safer than the forest. Occasionally we dared to venture a few yards into the forest to scavenge for types of roots, berries, nuts, and mushrooms that could be found in Toryn this close to springtime. Much of it was food I'd never seen before. There were tart red fruits that grew from slender trees and sweet silver berries we plucked from shrubbery clustered on hillsides; crunchy round nuts we plucked from swaying, leafless branches and buttery ones we found in bushes that were otherwise still bare.

One night we spotted a shadowy form far on the horizon, but for all our tense watching and weapon brandishing, it never came our direction. Another night a creature soared toward us and Layk, Avrik, and I managed to shoot it down before it could attack. Its body slammed into the earth, shuddering, and we paused for a few breathless instants, staring at our unexpected victory and gathering back our undamaged arrows, before pressing on into the darkness.

The next was more eventful. Not long after night had fallen, ichgor shrieks shattered the quiet air. I glanced around for cover, but the land was still open and flat, with grass that only came to our ankles and no trees to be seen. Ichgor silhouettes swept across the sky: one, two—six forms at least. Cold fear shuddered through me. There was no way our small party could fend them all off, not without heavy casualties.

My bow was already in my hand when I turned to Narek. "What do we do?" I demanded.

His face was pale and grim. "Run. We have to find cover."

The ichgor barreled toward us as we charged through the grass, following Narek's lead. All around, the world felt surreal and too-bright, like a silver-soaked nightmare emerging from a shadowland. I didn't dare look back, but I could hear the ichgors' pursuit in the thunder of their wings and their hideous cries. My friends' feet pounded the ground beside and behind me, our breaths ragged and panicked. Everything else was still and empty, as if the ichgor and us were the only living things in the whole kingdom.

They closed in swiftly. I hazarded a glance over my shoulder when one shrieked just overhead. It dove for me and I threw myself to the ground, palms against the cold earth, grass tickling my face. My pulse roared in my ears. I knew the grass was a flimsy cover from the creature's strong jowls and grasping claws.

Just as I expected to feel pain lance into my back, the ichgor screamed and pulled up and away. Two arrows had pierced its eye. Several feet away, Avrik lowered his bow. I leapt to my feet and continued my race after Narek.

Off to my right, Layk shot one ichgor from the sky; it crumpled mid-air and landed several yards away, making the earth quake. I nearly lost my footing but caught myself before I stumbled into Jennah. The downed ichgor snarled and began crawling after us, leaving a trail of blood smeared across the grass behind it.

Two more ichgor dropped from the sky, hurtling toward us with open maws and claws extended. There was no outrunning them now, so we turned and faced them. I shot three arrows in quick succession, one lodging itself in an ichgor's chest. Layk's arrow snagged the other ichgor in the mouth while Avrik pierced its snout. But the wounds didn't faze them. The first snapped at Jennah, encircling her with its claws. It started to rise with its prey still ensnared and struggling, despite Avrik's and my frantic shots landing across its body and making it hiss and shriek in pain. Jennah squirmed and shoved both of her daggers deep into the beast's leg. It dropped her. She twisted midair, landing lightly on her feet. Still clutching her bloody weapons, she tossed an easy smile in our direction to show us she was unharmed.

The other ichgor circled around toward Narek, who crouched to avoid its snapping fangs. Before the creature pulled back, he plunged his blade up into its neck. Blood spurted across the grass and the ichgor gave an unearthly, strangled cry. Enraged, it beat at the air and the force of its wind knocked Narek backward. Before he could recover, it descended toward him.

I sprang forward and shot the ichgor in the neck, the mouth, the chest… Narek stood and thrust his sword into the ichgor's eye—deep, deep, until it collapsed.

When I looked up, countless more ichgor were swarming toward us.

"Run!" Narek shouted again, even though they were tearing through the sky at an impossibly swift speed.

The grounded ichgor lunged at us, but we stumbled away. As we raced through the grass I saw the distant point Narek was making for: a hill rising over the grasslands, its summit crowned with trees. But could the trees provide us with enough shelter?

Another ichgor slammed into the earth ahead of us, barring our path. We scattered, moving around the ichgor like the sea parting around a rock. Just ahead of me, Layk deflected a snap from the creature's jaws. On its opposite side, Avrik ducked under its wing and shot it in the side. We all managed to circle around it, but the ichgor was angry, and now that it could detect us all fleeing in one direction, it moved quickly. It lunged after us at a speed we couldn't outpace, not until we reached the hill. And the others in the sky were closing in. Sweat slithered down the back of my neck. I couldn't lose anyone else to this mission.

"Keep going!" Layk shouted. "I'll hold them back and distract them to give you time."

"No!" Jennah sounded terrified, and that sent another wave of panic through me.

But Layk had already stopped and lifted his bow at the oncoming ichgor: two on the ground, dozens in the air. "Here! Come have a taste of these arrows!" he cried, waving his free arm and leaping so they would focus on his movements and noise.

Jennah halted, standing stubbornly at his side, and I turned to join them, but Narek clutched my arm. His fingers were hard as steel and unrelenting against my struggles.

"Keep her alive, for Misroth," Layk said, nodding toward me as he shoved Jennah away, hard.

"Run now, or we'll all die." Narek's voice held a vicious edge.

We sprinted for the hill, Narek's fingers never leaving my arm. Horror stabbed at my heart, trying to grapple with what had happened, what would become of Layk. Yet my mind could hardly process anything beyond what my body felt: cold wind rippling through my hair and snapping at my cloak, lungs aching, blood pulsing, head throbbing.

Narek led us straight to the foot of the hill, where a boulder nearly concealed the narrow opening of a tunnel. The closer we drew the larger it looked, like an abandoned cave burrowed into the side of the hill, or the burrow of some giant animal. We ducked inside, where our breath echoed loudly in our ears. Soft starlight filtered through the opening, revealing the dirt walls and floor for a few feet until the space was consumed in shadow. The darkness was so deep that I couldn't tell how far into the hill the tunnel went.

"We can't leave him," Jennah said, her voice raw and broken.

Face pale and drawn, Avrik looked from her to me, uncertain.

Narek's hand was still on my arm, refusing to let me go. I kicked him in the shin, my unexpected assault loosening his grip enough for me to break free and bolt for the entrance. As I peered out I strung an arrow to my bow and—

Layk barreled into me, sending us both tumbling back onto the tunnel floor. My bow landed at Narek's feet and my arm smacked Jennah's leg. Arrows spilled from my quiver. Layk sprang up to get off me so quickly it looked like he'd been burned. "Forgive me, my lady..." he spluttered, extending his hand. "I..."

I burst into a smile and then blinked when I realized how foreign a smile felt on my face these days.

"Thank the Life-Giver!" Jennah cried, embracing him. "Are you hurt?"

Layk shook his head.

"You risked your life to save us, and now you're apologizing?" I asked.

Outside, the ichgor continued to scream. Even in our refuge I could hear the heavy beats of their wings as several passed over us. My smile faded.

"What is this place?" Avrik asked, turning to Narek.

"A temporary haven. A place of refuge where there are no others." Narek sat and leaned against the wall, saying no more. Wiping his brow wearily, he laid his sword on the ground beside him and closed his eyes. "We will wait for daylight, when we can hope to travel far enough that we can find another refuge before night falls again. I suspect we won't pass another quiet night for a while."

So we rested and waited, sleeping fitfully until the ichgor left, the darkness outside dissipated at last, and the safety of morning came. We left the tunnel warily, ensuring that the only ichgor bodies outside were carcasses. The injured had either fled or perished in the night. Once again, we scavenged for any unbroken arrows. Our supply was dwindling, and I hated to think of venturing through Toryn without any.

We spent a solemn, weary day passing through the Toryn countryside. The landscape grew even hillier. A brook gave us a place to pause and rest, refilling our water supplies and scrubbing our faces, arms, and legs as clean as we could.

As the sun drew low in the western sky, we came across the first sign that this had once been a kingdom filled with towns and cities and life. A few crumbling, half-scorched houses nestled in a dip between two large hills, all that remained of a town that once could have held a population similar in size to Evren. Charred, rotting logs and great patches of grey ash in spaces where no grass or plants grew was all that remained of the other houses and buildings that had once lined the dirt road, now overgrown with weeds.

Narek led us to the sturdiest of the houses to find that the door was surprisingly still intact, closed fast against the elements. He turned the knob and it swung inward with a creak, revealing floorboards almost black with dust and a family's home frozen in time. As we walked inside, none of us spoke, too overcome with our own dismal thoughts. A few empty dishes lay on the table, as if waiting for a family to return to the meal they'd never finished. Once a wife had kneaded dough in the kitchen, cheerily looking out through the window, much as Lyanna did in Evren. Once she and her husband and their children had curled up on that settee and those armchairs near the hearth and read the books lining the shelves set nearby. Once they'd dreamed and loved and grieved here. And now there was only silence and emptiness.

The place reminded me so much of Lyanna and Rev's that it hurt. It felt like coming home only to find everything was wrong. The heaviness stealing through my bones was greater even than the pain I'd felt when I'd returned to the castle.

Avrik's eyes strayed to mine and for one instant I knew we were thinking and feeling the same things. We would give anything to be back in Evren with Lyanna and Rev and to know they would always be safe from horrors like this.

"We can stay here tonight," Narek said.

As if we'd all come to an unspoken agreement, we lay our bedrolls in the main living room, where the empty hearth and the cobweb-coated, dusty kitchen were open to each other. Venturing into either of the bedrooms felt like intruding too far and none of us wanted to be alone. That night we lay still for a long while, listening to the wind whistle and the ichgor swoop and shriek outside, searching for prey that had managed to evade them one more time. At last I fell into a fitful sleep.

The next day we passed through more villages, occasionally finding another home that had survived.

"I think," Narek said at last, when we had come upon the third destroyed village that day and our moods, if possible, had become even more somber, "that we have gone too far east." His face was taut, full of lines of sorrow he couldn't hide. "Although, much could have changed even in a few years…" he finished uncertainly. He shook his head as if to clear away the painful thoughts. "This way," he announced, leading us southward.

A few more days melted into one another, all full of vigilance and caution, all full of weariness and the wild and empty countryside of Toryn, until it became difficult to track them in my mind. Some nights we found shelter in empty caves or the remains of another home or shop. In some of the homes and shops, we found arrows still strong and useable, and replenished our supplies. Most food had been consumed by insects and scavengers long ago, though we did find some canned vegetables and fruit still sealed and safe to eat.

Other nights we walked warily through the countryside, our eyes forever scanning the clouds. Sometimes we heard the ichgor screaming in the distance or flying toward us and ducked for cover amongst a cluster of trees or against a hill, waiting motionless and breathless until the creature passed into the distance. The days felt like an eternity, every step marked by grief and fear. The deeper we drew into the kingdom, the more uneasy Narek seemed to grow. Our food supplies quickly dwindled, and nothing we collected ever seemed to be quite enough, always leaving my stomach hollow. I began to wonder how long it would take for hunger to overpower fear and we gave into lighting a fire.

Finally, near the end of another long night, when my legs were weary from walking, a dark shape grew ahead. At first it jutted up from the earth like a cliff, but as we approached and it became clearer, I was able to see the features of a crumbling stone wall. Set against the hillside, the remains were mostly huge slabs of grey stones toppling over into a surrounding pile of rubble. Beyond the wall, climbing up the hill, were more forms: the hollowed-out, broken remnants of a city stretching on and on, over the hill and far beyond my range of vision.

We paused beside the ruins for one breathless moment, silently taking it all in, and then Narek strode purposefully onward, directing us around the hill. He led us alongside the wall, where huge holes or complete gaps in places offered us glances into the lonely city within. Eventually we arrived at what had once been the city gates: an open archway revealing nothing more than a gaping hole where the gates once had stood.

The early morning sun glinted off spaces where the stone still looked polished and new, and I could imagine what this city had once been. Spiraling upward on the grassy slope, even its ruins were vast and tall, seeming to reach the heavens and making me feel small. When I studied the wall more closely, I realized they were covered in engravings. I saw horses and dragons, soldiers and priests and priestesses, landscapes of mountains and valleys, and likenesses of Toryn gods and goddesses. The carvings ran all the way up the wall and within what was left of the old archway, which was suspended precariously in the air, one half of the wall it was anchored to having been destroyed.

"Delgoth was once a majestic city," Narek said, his voice low, his eyes never leaving the ruins.

"I've never seen Delgoth on a map," Layk interjected, his brow crinkled in confusion.

Narek turned his sharp gaze on the guard. "Toryn has been cut off from you for two centuries. Entire kingdoms rise and fall in less time than that. Did you expect our kingdom to never change?"

Layk's protests fell silent at that.

"When ichgor, sedwa, and nestrae destroyed surrounding towns and cities," Narek continued, "many Toryn fled to Delgoth seeking safety. Defended by a great stone wall, no one ever expected it to collapse into ruin. But one night a particularly brutal ichgor attack destroyed a portion of Delgoth's wall. After that, it was only a matter of time before the nestrae overwhelmed the city with fire. They tore the city apart, leaving any survivors with nothing but ruins. No protection from the ichgor, the sedwa. Nothing but this mockery of a once-great city."

My mouth was dry, my knees weak. Delgoth's remains reminded me of the vision I'd had of Gillen and his men hiding from an enemy that walked through flame and smoke. What chance of survival did we have against an enemy that could wreak this level of destruction?

Narek spun toward me. His eyes were like dark pools concealing mysteries I couldn't yet begin to fathom. "This is the fate Misroth abandoned us to. We are always wary, always waiting for the next onslaught from enemies who outnumber us severely, whose power overwhelms our own. Always living in anticipation of death, or the deaths of all we hold dear."

Avrik stepped forward to stand beside me and gaze up at the crumbling buildings marching up the slope. "What a way to die."

Grim-faced, Narek looked at him before his eyes flitted back to me. "What a way to live."

We marched quietly behind him into the city, letting the shadow cast by the wall swallow us. For a long while we climbed the winding, dusty cobblestone road up the hillside as the golden sunrise reflected on broken, empty buildings, disintegrating timber, abandoned courtyards and fountains, and more carved archways poised over the streets. The sky was soft blue and cloudless, an endless, beautiful pool reminiscent of serene places I might never see again: of Evren's garden filled with vibrant flowers and heavy with their fragrance, of Evren's countryside filled with rows of crops and hillsides speckled with grazing livestock. With Avrik close by my side, I could almost imagine away the ruins of Delgoth around us and pretend we were back home, traversing the town's streets or headed back to Rev and Lyanna's cabin. But Avrik was stern and silent, with lines of weariness marring his face and his bow clutched in his hand, always uneasy, always restless.

When we crested the hill, the unexpected sight took my breath away. Instead of rising to a peak, the hill dipped downward like a basin to reveal a glistening lake, its waters tinged such a bright gold from the sun that I almost couldn't look at it. Encircling the lake, I could see Delgoth's cobblestone street stretching onward and its toppling buildings and statues gleaming in the daylight, a beautiful sight even in their decay. A gentle breeze drifted across the waters, whispering of footsteps that had echoed along this path once yet would walk it no longer, of destruction and pain, fear and sorrow.

Turning away, Narek led us to the left, where the shell of a stone building stood. It was still whole, but blackened from smoke, with glassless windows that looked like empty eyes staring back at us. Some of the panes lay shattered on the street below, each splinter of glass capturing the light so perfectly that they looked like piles of blue and gold jewels. The interior of the building was both wondrous and dreary: an expansive domed ceiling stretched far overhead, supported by stone pillars, and silver brackets inlaid with gems and still bearing torches lined the walls. But most impressive of all was the opposite end of the room, which contained an empty pool basin that encircled a towering white fountain, blackened and empty. The wall behind the fountain, even stained by smoke and smeared with ash, still bore all the vivid colors of a gorgeous painting depicting a Toryn goddess with smooth brown skin, piercing violet eyes, and dark hair spilling all the way to the water flowing at her bare feet. It was clear that this building had once been a temple, pristine and extravagant, but left to stand tarnished and abandoned while all about it the rest of the city toppled and decayed.

"Delmae, goddess of water and tranquility," Narek said in a low voice, still studying the painting. After a long moment, he tore his eyes away from the wall to meet mine. "We'll stop here. But no fire."

I didn't protest. Numb with exhaustion, I readily set to work unpacking my bedroll and helping Avrik gather what remained of our food supply to form a bland meal. Chewing my portion of jerky and nuts made my jaw ache. Our supply had dwindled so much that our meager rations did little to abate our hunger.

"We will have to hunt and build a fire soon, or starve," Layk muttered, but Narek did not respond.

Quietly, Jennah took the first watch while everyone else settled into bedrolls. It seemed I had only just fallen asleep when I woke to Narek shaking me.

I sat up and peered around at our dim surroundings, momentarily confused to see darkness had crept into the corners of the temple and high overhead, within the vast reaches of its ceiling. Turning, I gazed outside to see that a stretch of clouds had tumbled across the sky, muting the sun and leaving us in a sanctuary of shadows. My companions were all motionless in their bedrolls, their rhythmic breathing signaling that they slept undisturbed.

"It's silent," I said. "Maybe we should all sleep and save our energy for the night, when the threat is greatest."

"The threat is always great. We need to always keep watch."

Narek's tone made me look up sharply to study him. His chiseled features were dark in the dim light, and his face was impassive as ever, but I recognized the glint of pain in his eyes. I was not sure how I recognized it so easily. Perhaps it was in the tight line of his jaw. Or maybe those who carried their own heartaches were more adept at seeing it in others. Whatever the reason, I couldn't help but blink in surprise. I was startled by this side of Narek, yet even more than that, I was startled to realize that I felt a twinge of sympathy for him, my longtime enemy.

Slowly, I rose from my bedroll and reached for my cloak, where I'd laid it in a bundle at my side. Tossing it over my shoulders, I crept to the nearest window to study our surroundings. The air was pleasantly warm, carrying the scent of spring and coming rains. Beyond the empty street, the lake lay still and smooth as silk. Delgoth was quiet and peaceful as ever, but I knew how easily peace could be broken.

When I heard Narek's footsteps stop just behind me, I didn't bother to turn.

"You'd do well to keep your bow near."

I brushed my fingertips along the windowsill, dislodging a layer of ash and dust. "You haven't been sleeping. How can you stand guard or keep your strength when you don't rest?"

"My people do not know rest. Not anymore."

I turned to peer into his face, reading the same sorrow in it as before. Memories flickered in my mind of my vision of a Toryn village's destruction and Narek and his friend Reylinn facing the ichgor. Who was she and where was she now? What horrors had this man witnessed? Hesitantly, I opened my mouth, trying to form the words to ask him about his past and about the destruction of his home, but before I could form a sentence in my head, the world around me blinked out and a new one sprang up in its place.

Once again, I was out in the fields of Toryn, wind rushing about me and rippling the tall grass like endless waves on an angry sea. People were running, screaming. I glanced up and watched a shadow pass over the large, brilliant moon. *Ichgor.* My throat closed up.

"Stand and fight!" came a girl's voice. I turned to see Reylinn and Narek poised much as they had been in my last vision. The rushing air of an approaching ichgor whipped Reylinn's raven hair into a whirlwind about her face and looked nearly powerful enough to thrust her and Narek off their feet, yet they held their ground. Eyes wild with desperation, they met their enemy head on.

Landing, the ichgor snapped at them; they danced back and then leapt forward to attack at the same moment, their blades gleaming in the silver light. They wielded double-handed swords with the ease of warriors who'd trained for years, despite their youth. I watched the battle unfold in growing amazement of their skill. But then another ichgor swooped low, clawing at Reylinn from behind and sending her sprawling on the ground. She shrieked and clutched at her arm and then her side, where ugly scratches oozed blood. Her wounds looked worse than the ones Narek bore, but they both looked weakened and worried.

Narek raced forward, grasping her hand and helping her to her feet as both ichgor pressed in to attack from either side. Hemmed in, the two faced their enemies back to back, Reylinn leaning her weight on Narek for support.

"You'll be all right," Narek said. "I've got you."

Reylinn's face looked dangerously white. When she swung her blade to deflect the ichgor clawing at her, she was unsteady on her feet. Then more wing beats reverberated through the air and another ichgor struck.

"You're right. We have to run," Reylinn gasped. "We can't win."

A look of panic shot across Narek's face and then vanished. "All right," he said steadily, his voice even, his face set firm. He slid his hand in hers and with one final glance exchanged between them, one final moment that conveyed a thousand meanings that words could not, they fled as one. Reylinn stumbled and panted, yet Narek caught her each time, nearly pulling her along to ensure she kept pace with him.

But their speed and determination were in vain. In moments, the first of the ichgor had descended upon them again, snatching Reylinn in its claws and ripping her away from Narek.

"Reylinn!" Narek screamed, making a mad dash back toward her as the ichgor took flight, its prey swinging and fighting within its clutch. "Reylinn!" He stood staring up at the sky, his hands tightly fisted in fury, in fear, in absolute hopelessness.

Another ichgor dove toward the first to snatch Reylinn from its claws, snapping eagerly with its fangs and tearing her away. With a fierce shriek, the first ichgor snapped back and the two fought over her in a grotesque battle. Her screams, mingled with Narek's, were still ringing in my ears when the vision fell away from me.

Shaking, stomach heaving, I stumbled backward and hit the wall behind me. "You—you—" I choked out, my voice tremulous.

Narek's face mirrored my own horror, as if he knew what I had seen, as if he had been reliving it in that very moment himself. Maybe he had been. Maybe he always was.

"I'm sorry," I whispered hoarsely. "I'm so sorry." Sweat slithered down the back of my neck and I shivered in the breeze that only seconds before had been warm and comforting.

Narek watched me carefully. "You see what we have suffered all these years, no thanks to your ancestor."

Somehow, amid my horror, a realization rose up inside me, perhaps connected to my vision and my gift. I turned away again to stare out unseeing at the lake. "Your deal with my father. It wasn't asking for a Misrothian army to cross the barrier and help, was it?" It wasn't really a question. With terrible certainty, I knew what he wanted from me. I knew what I could but couldn't do.

"Do you think an army—and not only an army, but simply the promise of one—would be enough?" There was a hard edge to Narek's tone. "We have been cut off from everything for two centuries, our kingdom left to decay in isolation and hopelessness, our people left to slowly die off. You can carry on trade and build alliances; we cannot even escape the confines of our own nightmarish land."

I spun on my heel to meet his gaze and found him unexpectedly close. His eyes searched mine, his face full of more emotions than I'd ever seen in it before: anger, horror, sorrow…hope. Not ungently, he grasped my chin in his calloused hand and lifted my face to his until our foreheads nearly touched.

"You would do anything to protect those you care about, even at the gravest of costs. I've seen it. So you know what I too would do for my people. Misroth forsook us, yet we have held on to survival all these years when all hope vanished. You are Eldon's heir, and you know what should be done. What must be done. The barrier must come down."

I wanted to back away, but one step back and I would tumble out the window or slam into the wall. His breath was warm on my face and I cringed, remembering everything about him that I hated. Yet his eyes were pleading, speaking volumes about his concern for his kingdom, even if he was brutal and cold in his tactics to save it.

Enemy. Killer. Liar. Untrustworthy. My mind spun through a list of warnings against him, of all that he was and all he had done.

"That is not true," I insisted, shoving his hand off my face. He let it drop to his side. "Your argument is flawed. You know I would do anything for my people; therefore, you know I could never take down the barrier and watch my kingdom fall too. Even if I knew how to bring the barrier down, which I *don't*. Is one kingdom worth the price of another?"

Narek's face turned grim. "That is what your forefather thought. He chose Misroth's safety at the cost of Toryn's. Perhaps risking Misroth to right past wrongs would be your kingdom's retribution."

"My people owe you nothing," I snapped. "It was my ancestor who forsook you, not me. Not Gillen. Not my people."

"You will change your mind," he said darkly.

I lifted my chin and narrowed my eyes at him. "I would think not."

"The Toryn people should be free to cross their own borders and seek refuge or assistance from other kingdoms. Misrothian troops cannot guarantee a victory, but a world without barriers would ensure that your kingdom would be just as desperate for victory against the creatures of the Wastelands as my people are. We need more than meager assistance, and even more than a sanctuary. We need a kingdom that wants our safety as much as we do." He leaned forward, his eyes boring into mine. "I had no use for your father when he refused to help me. You cannot trust that your companions won't outlive their usefulness as well. You are the only one I need to destroy the barrier and help my kingdom."

I tried to push down my fear, but my old childish nightmares of him coursed through my mind. My breath hitched and I grappled for a threatening response. Something, anything. He called me the Queen of Misroth and I called him my prisoner, and yet all my earlier threats crumbled away now.

"Step away from her." Avrik's voice cut through our tense silence and my eyes snapped over Narek's shoulder to the corner where Avrik had been sleeping. He was on his feet, his bow already in his hand. There was a weight to his words I'd never heard before. I knew instantly that my friend wouldn't hesitate to kill Narek, no matter how he had once shuddered at the memory of killing a man in Evren.

A cold smile playing on his lips, Narek turned to face him. "The queen has her friends fight her battles for her now," he sneered.

Avrik lunged, dropped his bow to shove Narek back against the wall and draw his hunting knife. He pressed the blade against Narek's neck and stared into his eyes, his expression so fierce and hard I could barely recognize my old friend.

Narek merely laughed. "Do you think I would kill *her* when she is the only hope my people have?" His eyes gleamed cold in the afternoon light, and I glowered back at him. Who could say what he would do, this man who had once nearly drowned me on my father's orders?

He kneed Avrik in the stomach, knocking the breath from him. Gasping, Avrik doubled over and dropped the knife, letting it clatter to the stone floor. Then they were both lost in a tangle of legs and arms, swinging punches and slamming one another into the wall and then onto the ground. Avrik kicked Narek back and then shoved him through the gaping window, sending him sprawling onto the cobblestones outside. He leapt after him just as Narek jumped back to his feet.

I swung over the windowsill and chased after them as they began wrestling by the edge of the lake. Pinning Avrik down, Narek pushed Avrik's head underwater and held him there. Thrashing, Avrik reached his arms blindly for Narek's own neck, but with Narek's entire body pressing him down, he was helpless.

The world spun as horror ripped through me. Memories of a cold sea closing in were suspended in the back of my mind, an ever-present nightmare. Dashing toward the lake, I screamed at Narek to stop.

He drew back abruptly, leaving Avrik to pull himself up coughing and spluttering. He staggered to his feet and water ran in rivulets down his face. It splattered into the lake encircling his legs, the water glittering and beautiful and dangerous.

I leveled an angry stare at Narek. "Are the creatures that invaded your land the true monsters," I demanded, "or are *you?*"

Layk and Jennah were behind me, awakened by the noise Avrik and Narek's fight had caused.

"We should kill him and be done with it," Layk snarled. Jennah gave a short nod, her nostrils flaring.

I sucked in a breath, trying to think clearly. Could I risk losing Narek's help to find Gillen? If we made it to Calidar alive, would the Toryn people accept us without hostility if we didn't have one of their own with us?

"Did you really think I would kill him here?" Narek's eyes never left mine. "You and your friends best serve my purposes alive, for now. Enemies or allies, Halia, we need each other."

I hesitated, my eyes flitting between Avrik and Narek. "He's right," I murmured, lowering my eyes to the ground. "For now." I hated to admit it, but it was true. I couldn't risk what might happen without him, and I could feel his desperation to save his people. As little as I trusted him, I believed he would pose no threat to my friends or me—yet.

Layk shifted uncomfortably on his feet, a dissatisfied frown sliding across his features, though he didn't protest my decision. Avrik watched me for one long, painful moment before he turned away to stare out across the lake. Something like disappointment had appeared on his face and vanished just as fast, and I wondered what he was thinking. He had been willing to make a stand for me, but what had I done for him? Did he feel like he had been betrayed once again? I looked away and refused to allow myself to dwell on it.

"We need to go," I said, glancing at the western sky, where the sun was already beginning to hang low. "There's no need to waste time if we are all awake."

Before anyone had a chance to respond, something in the street, near the lake's edge, caught my eye. Something gold and glistening. I stepped forward, kneeling on the ground to lift the gold chain and study the pendant hanging from it. My breath felt trapped in my lungs. It was a rendering of Vehgar, wrought in white and yellow gold and set with tiny diamonds that mimicked the stars forming the constellation. It was a royal piece once belonging to my uncle, King Reylon, to commemorate his marriage to my aunt, and something that Gillen had inherited upon his father's death.

Gillen was here. The cold echoes of my vision fluttered before my eyes: Gillen trapped within the flaming ruins of a city, hunted by dark, whispering creatures. Gillen had been here, but was he still alive? Was this necklace something he'd lost in a fight, or a sign that he hadn't survived the battle? Fear crept up my throat. What if we were too late?

Jennah approached me silently. "What is it?" she asked softly.

"Gillen was here," I whispered. "This is his. It—it belonged to his father."

"Then he could be near." Her eyes caught mine, a glint of hope shimmering in her stare.

Or dead, I thought, but didn't dare speak the words. Determination crystalized inside me. This was no time to waver. I had to find my cousin. Securing the chain about my neck, I let the pendant rest against my collarbone, beside the diamond star I wore for my mother, and stood to face my companions. I set my face to hide my growing misgivings and the disturbing images haunting the edges of my vision, and looked at Narek.

"Lead us onward," I commanded.

CHAPTER TWELVE

T HEIR ATTACK CAME WITHOUT WARNING. One instant we were descending the opposite slope of the hill, tracing the winding roads of Delgoth, and the next arrows were raining down on us from an invisible enemy.

"This way!" Narek shouted, diving toward a narrow alley on the left.

We charged after him, arrows clattering on the stones around us, ricocheting off buildings, and whistling past our ears. I heard someone cry out in the chaos, but there was no time to stop, no time to think as we sped for cover.

Narek led us on a haphazard path through alleys and crumbling buildings in the opposite direction of the attack until at last, panting, he spun on his heel and held up his hand for us to stop. The air had fallen quiet once more, our enemies ceasing their shots now that we were out of sight. But where was the pursuit? My heart rattled against my ribs as I pulled my bow from my back and drew an arrow.

"Who is that?" Layk demanded. "Do we run or stand and fight?"

"Nestrae," Narek whispered. "And we are surrounded, so we don't have much choice in what we do. We must flee. *Don't* pull it out," he added, his eyes snapping to Avrik.

Face white and drawn, Avrik was leaning against the closest building, one hand clasped around an arrow staff protruding from his left arm.

Blood bubbled around the wound and he cringed, snapping the shaft to shorten it.

Jennah held both of her curved daggers as she studied our surroundings. Every shadowy corner of the alley, every empty home and shop held the threat of the unknown now. "How do you know we're surrounded?"

Narek's face was solemn. "It's how they always attack."

"If you know their tactics, then what's next?" Layk said. "What do we do?"

"We'll be outnumbered. We can try to hide, try to slip past them and out of the city, but we haven't much time. They'll set Delgoth ablaze and force us out."

I hesitated. "And you said…the fire does not harm them?"

"Fire is their weapon."

My hand strayed to the pendants at my neck. "Run," I said hoarsely. "If there is no way to stand and fight them off, show us the fastest path out of here and we will take our chances trying to get past their forces." I set my jaw. "We will not die cornered and cowering in the ruins of a dead city."

Avrik, Jennah, and Layk nodded back at me, pressing their hands to their hearts.

"I know of a way, if we can find it quickly enough," Narek said, and he pressed forward, his drawn blade glittering while he ran.

We dashed through shadowy alleys and across ruined courtyards; we skirted around collapsed buildings and cut through shops, some still filled with decaying goods or moth-eaten bolts of cloth; we leapt across sullied statues sprawled over our path and splintering timber, charred remnants of the fire. The streets swept on and on, curving downhill and then rushing alongside a burbling stream that wound a dizzying route through the city. Sometimes we raced beside it and other times we crossed stone bridges stretching across its length. Soon the moon rose in the night sky, its light glancing off the stream.

Our footsteps beat out a heavy rhythm I was sure our enemies could hear for miles, but caution did not matter anymore. Louder still was my pulse clamoring in my ears, threatening to muffle every other sound as I tumbled after Narek, my friends flanking me as closely as possible. My tunic fluttered about my legs, my hair flew across my face, and sweat collected along my neck. As my bow slipped in my clammy palm, I feared I'd drop it, so I squeezed my fist until the roughly hewn wood dug splinters into my fingers.

Behind me, Avrik's steps grew clumsy and more than once I heard him stumble. I reached back and clasped his arm, pulling him along with me. His face was drawn tight with pain and his wound was still dripping blood, leaving a scarlet trail our enemies could track easily. What if he collapsed before we ever had the chance to escape? *Don't let go,* I thought frantically. *Don't ever let go.*

We ran so long without any sound or sign of pursuit that a new concern curdled in my stomach. Perhaps they knew, even without having set fire to the city, that they were drawing us out. Maybe the shooters had been part of a trap meant to lead us into an ambush of even greater numbers waiting on the other side of Delgoth, ready to cut us down. I knew our hope at escape was desperate at best, yet I'd been clinging to the thought that our small numbers might be able to become invisible and slink past them. Not if they were already waiting for us.

When we approached the last bridge, we found it more damaged than the others. Blackened and crumbling, with huge blocks removed from its floor to reveal the dark swirling water below, it resembled a dragon arching over the stream. We started charging across when I saw what lay before us: there was a rift cutting the bridge in half.

Narek ran and leapt across, landing neatly on the opposite side and tossing a look over his shoulder to urge us onward. Hesitating, I watched the bridge and the water below it shudder—rising and falling, swaying and heaving—before my eyes. I felt dizzy and disoriented, like the entire stream was swirling about me and consuming everything, including me. I gestured to Layk and Jennah, waving them ahead. They paused for an instant, and then Avrik, still beside me, was resting a warm, reassuring hand on my shoulder.

"Go," he told them, and they dashed forward to make the jump.

Avrik's hand tightened on me. His wound was still bleeding lightly.

"Are you strong enough?" I couldn't hide the fear wheedling through my entire being, lending scratchiness to my voice.

A smile burst across his face like a glimpse into the past at my old friend, the boy who was still confident and unafraid. He winked and grasped my hand again.

"We'll do this together, Elena," he said, and suddenly I felt grounded, if even for the briefest of moments. We were back in Evren about to race through the fields and over the hills together. We were preparing for distant battles and adventures as we sparred with practice swords or competed during target practice. Our fears and pain were a part of us, but they were in the past, pushed to the back of our minds in the comfort of friendship, of safety, of home. I was the mysterious mute with the tragic past, he was the son of a disliked, brooding man, yet no one in Evren could trouble us with their gossip. Together, we were unstoppable.

The night wind whistled in my ears as our steps pounded in accord along the bridge. Hand in hand, we made the running leap across the gap. I landed hard on the other side, my boots skidding across stone until I lost my balance and slammed into the ground. Avrik stood over me, gasping for breath and shaking his head as if he could dismiss his pain and heal his injury that easily.

"Up, no time to waste," Narek said gruffly.

As I scrambled to my feet, light bloomed on the horizon and flashed across my comrades' startled faces. Smoke curled into the air, slithering over stars and blotting out the rising moon. Flames roared high and greedy in the distance.

"Hurry," Narek repeated, as if we needed further urging.

We scurried down the bridge and along the street, which traced a path beside the stream. With every step I could imagine my visions coming to life: the flicker of flames, the acrid tang of smoke, the hissing voices of inhuman soldiers taunting as they encircled their prey. *Iyg kurik vouren…*

Panic stabbed through my mind when I realized that the words were no longer echoing through my mind from my memories, but being spoken into the night, whispering through the shadow, glancing off the walls about us, and settling in our hearts as heavily as our fear. "*Iyg kurik vouren. Iyg kurik nestryk.*" Even without knowing the nestrae's meaning, terror skittered through my being and made my eyes scour the darkness, trying to find the speakers. In the distance, the flames crackled, leaping ever higher and ever closer, filling the air overhead with a black cloud that glided toward us. And yet the nestrae's voices could be heard over the roar of the fire, over the splitting noise of timber breaking and falling as it was consumed.

"Where are you?" Layk growled, lifting his bow and turning in a full circle as he walked to survey our surroundings. "Give us a real battle. Come out and face us."

Narek flung a dark glance at him. "Quiet," he hissed. "Our hope is to sneak through."

Is that possible if we are surrounded? I clung more tightly to my own bow. Avrik walked closely beside me, his body tense and alert, prepared to spring despite his wound.

We walked in the shadows of two towering stone buildings stretching toward the sky, so tall they almost reminded me of Misroth's castle. Our footsteps resonated around us, thudding dully in our ears beneath the steady rush of the oncoming fire and the ongoing whispers of the creatures closing in. They seemed to come from every direction, even above and below us, bouncing off every wall in the city in a maddening way that transformed fear into panic. I wanted to scream at Narek to run, but he seemed intent on creeping through the narrow passage between these buildings, clinging close to one wall so we were concealed in blackness and harder to spot. As much as I longed to flee, I knew that hiding was likely our only chance at survival. The nestrae's taunts were making it harder to think clearly. Harder to breathe.

We turned the corner and encountered another crumbling courtyard, but this time the fire blazed clearly ahead, flickering through a cluster of wooden buildings across from us. Smoke billowed high into the sky and spilled into the surrounding streets, rushing into the courtyard like waves in high tide until our world was black and hazy. Coughing, I ducked low and pulled the corner of my hood over my mouth and nose, but the burning, sickly sweet scent was everywhere. Squinting against the smoke, my eyes blurred, and my companions became vague forms shrouded in a thick cloud.

Something smashed into me from the side, sending me careening onto the cobblestones below. I hardly had time to catch my breath before I saw a hulking form standing over me, dressed in black armor and ringed in smoke. I caught the barest glimpse of its eyes through the visor of its helmet: they were unnaturally large and endlessly black, like its eyes were all pupil, with no irises or lids. I looked at the creature's body again and realized it was not dressed in armor at all—its skin was dark and armor-like, a hard shell encasing and protecting its body like an insect. Its long, thin fingers ended in wickedly curved claws. The nestred clung to an axe bearing a black blade larger than my head. Dazed, I tried to sidle away, but the nestred was quick. In one smooth motion it lifted its weapon and swung. But Avrik's arrow was faster yet. It pierced the narrow space between the nestred's shoulder and helmet, finding soft flesh and dropping the creature in an instant. Its axe clanged against stone and its body twitched and shuddered before falling still.

Avrik and Jennah were at my side, pulling me to my feet and dragging me away as the smoke closed in on us and concealed the nestred's body entirely. Fire flared in the smoke around us: flaming arrows rained down, oil spilled, and flames blossomed everywhere. One of the arrows struck Layk's cloak and set it alight. He tore it off and left it burning on the ground as we continued our race through the courtyard. Through the haze I could see more figures enveloped in fire, demons of the goddess Nesrelle intent on making our misery their sacrifice and dragging us into the afterlife. With a start I realized that the nestrae weren't standing near the flames; they were setting themselves on fire, stalking toward us with their weapons glittering and deadly in the flames, their armored bodies shining, their steps smooth and deliberate, not revealing a hint of pain or terror in their movements. Instead of screaming in pain or choking on the smoke or falling in flaming heaps, they continued their march forward, never wavering, never perishing from the fire.

My heartbeat was erratic, my head pounding from the polluted air and my own adrenaline. I could scarcely get air to my lungs as I pressed my hood to my face and gasped for breath. Everywhere I looked there were flames and burning forms, smoke and ash, yet I kept pounding forward, trying to follow Narek's path as best as I could when sometimes he disappeared completely before the cloud of smoke shifted and I found him again.

The hissing voices continued, a constant accompaniment to the roar and crackle of the fire. They taunted, they chanted, they whispered, and still they came toward us with the slow, maddening pace of those who knew their victory was sure. Layk, Avrik, and I lifted our bows and began shooting a flurry of arrows into the nestrae's ranks as we ran, but our arrows flew wildly in our hurry and our struggle to see the enemy clearly. They drew ever closer, their boots stomping on the stone as they swung black axes, maces, and swords or scraped their blades together in a grating, bone-shuddering screech. The nestrae's flaming arrows continued to fly, sparking as they glanced off the cobblestones and walls or sliced through the air nearby.

Then they were all but upon us, their forms leering tall and straight on every side. I strung another arrow to my bow and aimed at the enemy, trying in vain to pick out a weak point on their bodies as I squinted against their light. One of the closer forms lurched forward, reaching a flaming arm toward Jennah, who darted away with a cry.

"Stand and fight!" Narek shouted, his voice ragged and wild, the tone of a desperate man filled with the fervor of vengeance. His eyes were scanning the cobblestones at his feet, searching frantically for I knew not what. Gripping his sword in one hand, he knelt and brushed his fingers carefully along one of the stones. "Hold them back."

Layk and Jennah stopped beside him. Gasping through the smoke, I joined them, with Avrik on my heels. His hand brushed my arm and I turned to look at him, watching the firelight flicker across his face and in his eyes, still warm but lacking the old carefree light that had once been so familiar. They spoke of desperation and regret now, of words we couldn't speak, perhaps not even if we had the time.

"We are the Dragon-Hearted," he whispered, pulling away to raise his bow.

My thoughts, like words whispered to me from someone else, also rang with encouragement, but not as strongly as they had in times past. *You can do it...you ca—don't give up...* I frowned, but shook my head to clear it from this puzzle. There was no room for distraction.

Nodding at Avrik, I aimed my own weapon at the approaching throng. White-hot and furious, the flames clung to them long after any oil they were using should have burned away, yet they never scorched the nestrae. In the light of the fire, their eyes were more clearly visible: huge orbs like abysses, cold and soulless, with only the reflection of flames to lend them any light.

I set my aim on the neck of one of the nestrae, said one breathless prayer as I pulled back my string, and let the arrow fly. My shot landed true, felling one enemy in an oncoming swarm of enemies, one in a regiment, perhaps an entire army. Swathed in fire and smoke, their numbers seemed endless, either because they were or because it was impossible to see far beyond the first rows of flickering forms.

A hand grasped my leg and I cried out. Spinning, I turned to confront my enemy only to see Narek gesturing toward a hole in the courtyard floor. "Go," he said urgently.

With a backward glance at my friends still fending off the nestrae, I stepped toward the hole, hesitating. Before I could argue, Narek shoved me in. Blackness enveloped me as my hands and knees hit hard earth. From above, the clamor of flame and arrow, marching and shrieking, steel dragging across steel, and my companions' anxious shouts hammered dully in my ears. As I scrambled to my feet, I saw Avrik through the tunnel entrance, his form a silhouette against an orange, smoky sky, as he leapt down after me. Layk and Jennah followed quickly, with Narek bringing up the rear, climbing down a rickety ladder I hadn't noticed earlier and slamming the door of the tunnel shut, immersing us in the darkness.

A match flared, and Narek's eyes stared back at me. "Run," he said.

CHAPTER THIRTEEN

O UR RAGGED BREATHS BOUNCED OFF the enclosed walls about us as wildly as the torchlight glanced off dirt and rock. I could hear the tumult of our enemies behind us and knew it was only a matter of time before they dove into the underground space after us and filled the tunnel with smoke. The walls felt stifling, constricting us and making us easy targets for our enemies if we did not outrun them.

Narek led us on a winding path, charging through narrow spaces and coming to new tunnels that branched off the first one and delved deeper into the earth or sloped upward toward the world above. I couldn't tell if the tang of smoke I tasted on my tongue was old or fresh. Up and down and round and round the tunnels led us, until the sounds of the nestrae grew dim and I dared to hope we had lost them, for now.

At last the tunnel widened and we splashed across a shallow stream cutting through our path. Two side tunnels branched off at the water, one mostly filled with the stream, leading downward, and another carving a winding path to our right. Ahead, the torch continued to cast eerie shadows along the walls.

"I'm not sure which way to take," Narek admitted, studying each path carefully.

"Where do these tunnels lead?" Avrik asked, his tone guarded. Though he was trying to appear strong, he was hunched against the nearest wall and I could see the beads of sweat and lines of pain marring his brow. His wound no longer oozed blood, but I wondered just how much he had lost and how much farther he could go on.

Narek opened his mouth to speak and then froze, his body tensing. Pounding footsteps were coming from the tunnel on our right, and I couldn't tell if the scent of smoke came only from Narek's light or something else. As one we readied our weapons.

Dark figures charged toward us from the tunnel's mouth, metal flashing. I shot at the first figure's head, but it deflected my arrow with a swift sweep of its blade. Narek roared and leapt for it. Their swords clanged together for a moment, long enough to still the frenzy of battle, and everyone hesitated.

These were not nestrae, but two men, armed with blades and bows and dressed in dark leather armor. My hand froze on my bowstring.

"Haed?" Narek asked, his eyes wide, lowering his blade.

The first stranger took a step back from Narek, studying him with an incredulous expression, and he too lowered his sword. His eyes, rich brown and ringed in black, darted from him to the rest of us, lingering on the Misrothian insignias stitched on our sleeves. A suspicious shadow passed over his face. "Narek," he said. "I thought you were dead with the rest of the Zare'forith. And who are they?"

A suspicious tone edged into his voice, and concern throbbed in my chest. If the people of Toryn chose not to trust Narek, they certainly would never trust the foreigners traveling with him.

I watched the strangers cautiously. Their hair and eyes were dark like Narek's, but their skin was unnaturally pale, nearly translucent, making the blue of their veins in their necks and hands show in startling contrast. Haed appeared young, close to Narek's age, but the man behind him, holding a torch aloft, was middle-aged. His beard was black and grey, and wrinkles edged his eyes, but I could see the resemblance between him and Haed.

"Not your enemies," Narek responded firmly. "But we don't have time to explain now. The nestrae pursue us."

"We thought we heard them," the older man said grimly. "I suppose our trip was for nothing."

"Forgive me, Captain Luiken," Narek said, bowing his head in deference.

Captain Luiken shook his head. "Never mind that."

Haed's eyes flashed angrily. "The tunnels have been compromised. Narek, how could you—"

"We were trapped."

Captain Luiken cut in. "Now is not the time. We must turn back."

But I couldn't postpone my burning question another moment. "Wait." Stepping forward, I drew the Toryn men's searching glances toward me. "Have you encountered any other Misrothians recently?"

Captain Luiken shook his head. "You're the only ones."

Lowering my head, I tried to conceal the disappointment overwhelming me. They knew nothing of Gillen.

"We can't tarry here," Captain Luiken continued urgently. "We'll speak in Calidar."

Without another word we plunged deeper into the tunnel, back the way Captain Luiken and Haed had come. My weary legs ached in protest; it felt like we had been running for hours, both through the streets of Delgoth and along this underground path, but I couldn't complain when I thought of Avrik's injury. Eventually the ground began to slope upward, and then, abruptly, we were stepping out into grass and moonlight. The sky seemed infinitely vaster after our time underground, though I was surprised after what had felt like ages of traveling that dawn hadn't already come and gone. Stars twinkled, deceptively peaceful in a deep blue sky, and wind rustled through the grasses all about us, mild and warm with the promise of spring.

"Two hours till sunrise," Avrik said beside me, and I wondered if it was for my benefit or his.

"Hold on," I murmured. He didn't respond.

Glittering like a long silver snake ahead was a river. The map I'd attempted to follow in my head was muddled after traversing a city I'd never known existed, but my best guess was that this was the Elhalin River. We would have to cross it to reach Calidar, somewhere beyond its far bank.

Haed and Captain Luiken traced an unwavering path through the long grasses and toward the Elhalin's edge. They unstrapped their bows from their backs and scanned the skies with the same watchful gaze Narek possessed. It was only now, in the silvery light around us, that I clearly saw the men's weapons: their bows were curiously crafted, forged with metals I didn't recognize that looked sturdy yet flexible, and their swords were huge, curving blades with two-handed hilts strapped to their backs. Stalking quiet and nearly invisible through the night, these men made powerful allies and formidable enemies, and I breathed a silent prayer that we could keep them on our side.

We cut a wandering route alongside the river without any sign or sound of pursuit. Despite exhaustion and hunger, we traveled through the gathering light of dawn, and even long after the sun had risen and we felt safe enough to put our weapons away. The Elhalin was our constant companion, coursing slowly with a steady murmur of sound, a soft backdrop against the unusual quiet of the day. A gentle warm breeze soothed our cheeks and rustled our cloaks. Despite the pleasantness of the day and the lack of immediate threat, I couldn't shake my feelings of unease and discomfort. My stomach was painfully empty, my feet were sore, and my legs ached from countless miles. Avrik, contrary to his usual grace, was stumbling and looking weaker by the hour. I tried to think of encouraging words for him, but my brain felt hazy and nothing I could think of sounded reassuring.

At last, we paused beneath a copse of trees at Captain Luiken's signal. He and Haed stood side by side, staring silently across the river while my companions eased into sitting positions within the shade. Avrik collapsed against a trunk, closing his eyes and sitting motionless for a long while.

Pushing back my worry, I strode to Narek's side. "How far are we from Calidar?" I demanded, breaking the long silence that had fallen over our group. My gaze slid back to Avrik.

Narek merely shook his head and nodded toward Captain Luiken and Haed, who had pulled small shards of glass from their packs and were using them to catch the sunlight. I watched, fascinated, as they signaled to the opposite side of the Elhalin and then three flashes of light were returned from across the water. I could hardly discern the form of whoever stood across from us, responding to Captain Luiken and Haed's signal.

The Toryn men returned the glass to their packs and seated themselves on the riverbank. "Now we wait," Haed said.

The minutes slipped by agonizingly slowly. I seated myself next to Avrik and watched the river, searching for any sign of the form I'd seen on the other embankment. The air grew warmer and made me drowsier. Sunlight danced along the water, dazzling my eyes until I had to turn away to stop the headache beginning in my temples. I leaned back against the trunk and closed my own eyes, wishing Toryn away, wishing myself back in Evren with Lyanna and Rev. My whole being ached at the memory of them, at the feelings of safety and love I'd had in their presence and at the reminder of how I'd left them: without a goodbye or an explanation. Without any idea of whom I truly was.

"Finally." Layk's voice cut through the sleepy fog filling my mind and I jolted upright, blinking and disoriented. I glanced back at the river to see several long canoes gliding across its surface. It was hard to distinguish the features of the men rowing them toward us, since they were still some distance away. Slowly, I eased to my feet and, flanked by Jennah and Layk, watched the strangers approach.

By the time their canoes slid into shallow waters, the men were easily recognizable as Toryn by their dark hair and eyes, unusually white skin, and colorful clothing, always shifting and changing in the sun. They leapt easily from the canoes and waded through the edge of the river, pulling the canoes ashore with them.

"Welcome home, Captain Luiken, Haed," they murmured in turn, each bowing their heads in respect. Their eyes flitted to us, lingering on the Misrothian insignias on our clothes, but they asked no questions.

"It's good to be back," Captain Luiken said simply, not offering any answers. "We have an injured man with us." He nodded back toward the tree where Avrik rested, and two men approached him to help him to his feet. Avrik tried to gather his pride and wave away their assistance, but as soon as he took his first step he stumbled and was forced to lean on the men for balance.

We climbed into the canoes, Narek staying with Captain Luiken and Haed while I followed Avrik into his. Though my stomach lurched when one of the Toryn men shoved our canoe into the water, I concentrated on our approach to Calidar and the fact that Avrik would soon have help. Though I wanted to sit beside him and offer him comfort, I still felt the rift between us, so I contented myself with sitting across from him.

As we drew near Elhalin's far shore, I occupied myself with studying my surroundings. At first the landscape appeared similar to the grassy country we had left behind, but then I noticed the difference in the hills. They were rockier, more unkempt and severe against the mild sky than the rolling ones we'd seen before. Even the trees seemed different: taller, older, rougher. I looked in vain for the docks from which the canoes had come, or for any sign of Calidar. In fact, there was no sign of any civilization at all. Everywhere I looked there were only trees and hills, no homes, no distant city gates, no grazing sheep or fields of grain or farms. It was a vast and wild land, looking like no human had set foot within it for many years.

Before I could wonder much more, our canoe turned toward a hill rising along the river, its rocky side tangled with vines and tree roots, and with a start I realized that what I at first thought to be a shadow was the mouth of a cavern. The river flowed straight into it, disappearing into its black depths and echoing dully. One of the canoes ahead of ours vanished inside and we followed closely, leaving the bright open sky for the damp closeness of the cave. Within, every sound seemed magnified a hundredfold: each splash of the oars, each breath of the men around me, each beat of my heart.

It took several long moments for my eyes to adjust, but when they did, I was surprised to realize that the cave was not completely dark. Growing along its rough walls and ceiling, fungi, moss, and long-stemmed plants I'd never seen before cast their own radiant glow in dozens of colors: red, green, blue, violet, gold, silver…everywhere I looked were endless, ever-changing colors, like an infinite night sky full of foreign stars. My breath caught from the beauty of it all and for an instant I forgot all my concerns about the people of Calidar not accepting us, about the ichgor and nestrae, about Gillen, about Avrik, and about the loved ones I'd left back in Misroth and the possibility of never seeing them again. Here I was, just as Avrik and I had once dreamed when we were safe in Evren, exploring a new land and seeing new sights I had never even imagined.

The docks I had been looking for earlier were set along one of the walls, near the rocky shore that led deeper into the cave. Toryn sentries, dressed in leather armor like Haed and Captain Luiken, patrolled nearby, smoking pipes that breathed colorful smoke or leaning lazily against the wall. They snapped to attention as soon as Captain Luiken and Haed's canoe drew near, bowing their heads and calling out greetings. Men leapt from our canoes to pull us into the docks while the sentries approached and assessed our numbers.

One of the men tugged on his pipe, blowing tufts of blue-grey smoke about his bearded face as he quirked an eyebrow at Captain Luiken. "It is good to see you," he said, "but who are these strangers?" He had a grin plastered to his face, but his uncertain tone betrayed his unease.

"They are here as my visitors," Captain Luiken responded firmly as another sentry assisted him out of the canoe. "At least, for now." His eyes roved over us, glinting with unmasked suspicion. I dipped my eyes downward so I wouldn't reveal my concern.

Two men helped me and then Avrik climb out.

Once we all stepped onto the cavern's uneven floor, Jennah and Layk joined Avrik and me while Narek stayed close to Captain Luiken's side. The other Toryn men flanked Haed and Captain Luiken, clearly separating my group from them as we marched deeper into the tunnel.

Cool, clammy air pressed in on all sides and water dripped from stalactites. If not for the beautifully eerie light of the fungi and vines sprouting from the walls and ceiling, the cavern's shadows would have consumed us. Our path was a winding one, following numerous tunnels that branched off the main one, always leading further in and further down. The slope was gradual in most places, though there were a few areas where the floor dropped off suddenly like steps in a jagged staircase. Occasionally we set foot in wider tunnels whose walls were striped with sparkling veins of metal, some shimmering in colors that made me guess they were copper, silver, and gold.

As we drew deeper into the cave, we began to encounter other guards patrolling the tunnels and even a few unarmed Toryn who bowed low when they saw their leaders and kept their eyes downcast, refusing to stare. I wondered if they'd caught sight of the strangers entering their midst and what they thought. We passed through tunnels that led into rooms for the guards: I caught glimpses of some barracks and training rooms as we wound our way ever deeper into the cave, until I felt lost in an endless maze.

At last we paused before the entrance to another cavernous room. This one was protected by two guards posted on either side. They saw Captain Luiken and immediately bowed their heads, allowing us all to pass.

The sight beyond the entrance made my breath catch. We stepped into a vast room, gleaming with the vibrant lights of plants swaying gently in a cool draft fluttering in from adjoining tunnels. There were long, rough-hewn tables and benches spread across one end of the room, all occupied with countless Toryn, and an open space on the other side that led toward more entrances to other rooms and tunnels. Overhead, the ceiling was so high it was merely a shadowy space like an overcast night sky, dotted with glowing flowers, twisting vines, and hanging moss. Beneath the glowing ceiling, the Toryn people themselves shone like distant starlight: their colorful garb emitted shimmers, each person's clothing shifting in different colors. One man wore a shirt and trousers that changed from red to gold as he moved, while a nearby woman's clothes transformed from green to blue to silver. The effect of so many dressed that way, under the multi-colored iridescent plants overhead, was mesmerizing.

Captain Luiken turned to one of his men. "Take him to the infirmary," he said, nodding toward Avrik. As the man led Avrik away, Captain Luiken glanced at another Toryn man. "Have the meal sent to the council room. We will speak with our visitors there."

Despite his people's curious or outright livid stares and murmurings, he led us across the vast room and down one of the connecting tunnels until we reached another, much smaller room. This one had a low-hanging ceiling, connected to the floor in one spot by one great rocky column, and was sparsely lit with blue fungi and silvery moss. Another table sat in the middle of the room, covered in parchments, books, and maps. Every wall was lined with weapons of every sort imaginable: ancient-looking blades, heavy maces, Alrenian gold-hilted daggers, black-bladed axes, wood and metal bows, and quiversful of arrows.

Several men posted themselves as guards about the room while Captain Luiken sat on a bench at one end of the table and gestured for us to sit opposite him. Haed hovered near his father's side, refusing to sit. I drew a deep breath as I settled myself onto the bench next to Jennah and tried to steel my nerves. Every part of me longed for a hot bath, a hearty meal, and a real bed, but seeing the inside of a prison seemed more likely.

Captain Luiken folded his hands in front of him and gazed at Narek, then the rest of us, for several long seconds. The silence was uncomfortably heavy with questions and doubts. "Tell me," he said, finally settling his stare on Narek, "who your companions are and how you are here." His lips were a grim line. "It has been years since you disappeared, Narek. We assumed you were dead. Now, in the company of these Misrothians, *especially* after compromising Delgoth's tunnel system, you have a lot of explaining to do."

Narek ran a hand along the stubble lining his jaw, a deceptively casual gesture. "I spent years in Misroth, thanks to its former king and his promises to help Toryn if I served him. I admit, I spent a lot of time pursuing that fruitless hope and I have...regrets. But it was not all in vain." He glanced at me and I refused to meet his eyes, staring instead at Captain Luiken. "This is Princess Halia, daughter of the deceased king regent of Misroth and cousin of the missing heir to the throne. Her cousin Gillen was sent into Toryn by her father. She's here to find him."

Though he tried to conceal it, I could see the surprise on Captain Luiken's face, written clearly in the slight widening of his eyes. He shifted in his seat and leveled a more intent look at me. "Will she inherit the throne if...if Crown Prince Gillen isn't found?"

"Yes," Narek said, that single word cutting the air like a knife. *How dare you talk about Gil's death so carelessly,* I thought heatedly.

"She is an heir of Eldon?" Captain Luiken continued, his voice low.

Narek gave a short nod.

Haed paced behind his father, his eyes flitting from me to Jennah to Layk and back again. "If the stories are true, she could set us all free." For the first time, I truly looked at him, taking in his youthful yet hardened face, the taut lines around his eyes and across his brow, the steely glint to his eyes.

Captain Luiken fidgeted with one of the maps scattered across the table. I studied its torn edges, sketches of wild terrain, and scrawling penmanship before noting the title jotted in its lower right corner: *Forsaken Kingdom.* His voice was thoughtful and unexpectedly soft. "Does she know how?"

"Not yet," Narek responded, shooting me a pointed look. "But she has a way to learn—a sort of gift for knowledge, if you will."

I'd had enough. "You speak as if I'm not here in your presence," I said, forcing myself to keep my voice level. I studied first Captain Luiken, then Haed. "I assume you two are the leaders of Toryn, or what is left of it?"

Haed halted in his tracks. "You can address my father with respect," he snapped, but Captain Luiken raised a hand to silence him.

"I am, until death passes the title of captain to my son," he said easily.

"Then I thank you for saving us." I dipped my head briefly in the way I'd seen other Toryn show respect. "And now, I would appreciate it if you addressed your comments regarding Misroth and myself toward *me*."

"Forgive us, princess," Captain Luiken said. "You must understand that we in Toryn are not quick to trust foreigners." His eyes darted to my companions and back to me. "Not that we encounter them frequently."

"You are not quick to trust your own either, it seems," I said, glancing toward Narek, who shifted in his seat and stared down at the maps on the table.

Captain Luiken hesitated, clearing his throat. "I'm sure by now you are no stranger to the trials our land has faced, without assistance from your kingdom."

I raised my chin. "Toryn's sufferings are not my fault."

"But you *do* have the power to end them."

I watched him carefully, weighing my answer.

At that moment bells began to toll throughout the underground city of Calidar, echoing along the cavern walls. I counted eighteen tolls, marking the eighteenth hour, and my stomach growled as I thought of dinner. As if on cue, a man and woman entered the room, each bearing trays laden with food. They passed out tin plates filled with thick slices of bread, leafy greens that resembled some of the plants I'd seen growing from the cave walls, and a dish made from chopped mushrooms and various unknown spices that tickled my nose.

"We'll resume after we've eaten," Captain Luiken said.

Without further preamble, he and Haed stopped our conversation and began plucking food from their plates with their hands and eating, and Narek soon followed. My stomach growled with hunger, and even though the food was foreign to me and Lyanna would have been appalled to see me eating with my hands, I began shoveling the dishes into my mouth as fast as I could.

When my stomach finally felt satisfied for the first time in days, Captain Luiken slid his plate to the side and faced me again. He waited as the man and woman gathered the plates and exited the room, then drew a deep breath.

"My people have long resented Misroth for forsaking us to face the creatures of the Wastelands alone," he said, resuming our conversation where he had left it as if we'd never stopped speaking. "Our history records that our kingdom tried to forge an alliance with the newly free Misroth, attempting to secure our own freedom from the Alrenian Empire. *And* safety from the monsters slipping into our borders. Eldon answered with silence and this cursed barrier. For generations we have prayed for a way to destroy the barrier and call upon Misroth's aid." He glanced down at the map before him, sighing as he idly traced the line of the Elhalin with his finger. "And now it seems we each have something the other wants."

My breath felt trapped in my throat, unable to fill my lungs and unable to leave my mouth. I settled my face into a firm, unreadable expression. When I spoke, my voice was measured, so much the voice of a diplomat that I could not deny the value of my royal tutelage. "I thought you said you hadn't seen any other Misrothians. Are you saying that somehow you *do* know where Gillen is?"

"No," Captain Luiken said, crushing my hope with a single word. The breath rushed painfully back into my lungs. *Show no weakness,* came my father's voice, still echoing through my brain from years ago, and so I resolved to show the Toryn people none. I stamped the pain from my heart and focused on the solid table beneath my fingers, the glowing light reflecting off Captain Luiken and Haed's faces, and the cave's thick scent of dirt and damp.

"But we could help you find him," Captain Luiken continued. "And in the meantime, we can offer you and your friends the refuge in this gods-forsaken land that you desperately need to survive."

"This is madness. You want me to remove the barrier and risk the lives of everyone in my kingdom for the *possibility* that you can help me find Gillen and will actually offer us protection?"

"Whether you trust us or not, you are dependent on us for shelter from the nestrae, ichgor, sedwa…all the creatures I'm sure you've encountered throughout Toryn by now," Haed responded darkly.

"What good does overrunning Misroth with your enemies do for you?" I demanded. "Is this truly about your safety, or *revenge?*"

"It is about survival," Captain Luiken said firmly. "Why would you send an army to us? Why would we trust your word—the word of a kingdom who abandoned us long ago? And even if we pushed our enemies from our land, how do you expect our kingdom to do more than simply survive when we are forever cut off from the rest of the world?"

The words froze on my tongue. Nothing I could say or promise would be enough for them. What would the Toryn do to my friends when I denied them what they wanted?

"Besides," Captain Luiken added, his voice gentler, "you would never send an entire army to our aid with the risk that they might never return through that barrier."

My head was beginning to pound. The walls felt as if they were closing in around me; the ceiling seemed ready to cave in. *We are in a prison,* I thought.

"Everything you know about the barrier is based on rumors and stories," I protested. "I don't even know how to bring it down, or *if* your belief that I can do so is even true."

Narek turned his piercing gaze on me. "We already have proof an heir of Eldon has power over the barrier, since your father was able to take me across it."

My stare was as unyielding as his. "That is not proof I could destroy it."

"Perhaps a stay in the prisons would help her figure it out," Haed growled, stopping behind his father to glare down at me. I looked back into his face without flinching.

Captain Luiken's face was stern. "No, we need an alliance."

Haed scratched his ear and studied the wall, a thoughtful expression on his face. "A marriage alliance may bind Misroth's interests to ours, if their king is found and returns to his throne while *she* remains with us." His eyes darted to mine.

Icy waves rolled over my skin at his words, and this time, I avoided Haed's stare. Rallying my determination, I stood. In my peripheral I noticed several guards reaching for their sword hilts in response to my sudden movement, but I ignored them. "I did *not* come to negotiate a marriage alliance." I forced my frustration in check, keeping my voice firm but even. "I came to save my kingdom, not subject it to more destruction. You can threaten me as much as you want, but I am not afraid. And I *will* find my cousin with or without your help."

"You will abandon us again." Haed's hands were curled into fists at his sides.

"I was not the one who chose to abandon you before." I narrowed my eyes at him and slowly lowered myself back onto the bench.

Captain Luiken sighed and gestured at the walls around us. "You see how we are forced to hide, to eke out an existence without the sun while our enemies overrun our kingdom. I *know* the Misrothian army could help us push these creatures back into the Wastelands and reclaim Toryn for its true people."

I sat still for several long moments. Though I'd spoken boldly, I knew I was in a precarious position. Here the Toryn people vastly outnumbered us, and their desperation to save their kingdom at least matched my own. They might attempt to bargain and persuade now, but I knew if I continued to refuse that they could do far more than threaten. They wanted Misroth to help willingly, but if pressed, they could try to force me to yield instead. Though they couldn't risk my safety while the barrier existed, they could harm my friends.

The damp air felt even colder now; the dim lighting was much more unnerving than before. Here were a desperate people, stripped long ago of hope and filled with deep resentment. Worry consumed me. *We are not safe here.*

"I need time to consider," I said.

For a sickening minute, neither Captain Luiken nor Haed spoke as they watched me. I could almost hear their thoughts as they assessed me: *Stubborn. Foolish. Scared. Weak.* They thought they could win. They thought they knew me, but they were wrong.

"All right," Captain Luiken agreed with a short nod. "That is only natural." He turned to his son as he said, "For now they are our guests. I will expect everyone to treat them as such."

Haed bowed his head.

Rising, Captain Luiken gestured for us to follow his movement. With one accord, like obedient servants, the three of us stood. "You will follow me to the Common Room, where you will be introduced, and then you will be shown to your own rooms."

I felt the weight of Layk's and Jennah's eyes on me, yet I avoided them as Captain Luiken and Haed, accompanied by Narek and several of the guards, led us back to the large room we'd first entered. As soon as the people at the far end saw us enter, their conversations hushed until a discomforting quiet settled over everyone. I could sense more than I saw the people's animosity toward us, since I did my best to hold my head high and stare beyond them all to the opposite wall.

Show no weakness, I thought again.

On either side of me, Layk and Jennah each laid a supporting hand on my shoulders.

"People of Toryn," Captain Luiken began, his voice echoing about the chamber and resonating in my chest, in my bones. "We have important guests with us this day. Please welcome representatives of Misroth, here to form an alliance with us!"

I pressed my lips together to hold back my protest as the startled crowd began a smattering of applause that grew into an uproar.

"Hope is restored!" a man shouted, and soon others took up the cry. "Hope, hope, hope!" the people chanted, lifting their arms, clapping their hands, stomping their feet.

I felt Jennah's and Layk's grips on me tighten and recognized their tension in the way they stood and sucked in deep breaths. Their fear was growing with mine.

This announcement had all but sealed our fate with the Toryn people: either we cooperate, or we make fierce enemies of an entire city.

CHAPTER FOURTEEN

TWO GUARDS LED US DOWN one of the adjoining halls, where rows of entrances, covered by curtains to form makeshift doors, lined the walls. They gestured to a room for Jennah first, showed Layk to his next, and finally, near the end of the hall, brought me to mine. Pulling back the curtain, I slipped inside, thankful for some privacy. Like the rest of the cave, the air was cool and damp, the room dimly lit by blue and green fungi and vines. A few leaves draped so low from the ceiling they brushed the top of my head as I walked beneath them. To add to the lighting, two torches were set in sconces on the walls. Rather than lending a homey feel to the space, they made it look even more foreign and uncanny as they set shadows dancing in the corners.

A simple metal-framed bed rested in one corner while a small table and two chairs sat in another. There was a single rug on the floor, woven from the same colorful thread that made the Toryn people's clothes, but it hardly added the warmth or softness it had been designed to create. Another curtain covered the entrance to a private washroom, complete with a tub I was surprised to find already full of lukewarm water. A pile of thin towels lay on the dressing table beside it, along with a fresh, plain white nightgown and an outfit that changed from blue to green to violet when I shifted it beneath the light of the single candle flickering on the washroom wall.

As much as I longed to soak in the hot water and relish the feeling of being clean for the first time in days, or to relax my aching, weary muscles, I bathed quickly. Even with my bow and arrow resting beside the tub, it felt too far away after traveling in a land where I could never feel safe, never fully let my guard down. How long would Captain Luiken and his son let us keep our weapons, anyway? This underground city and its people left me feeling on edge, wondering how long I could stall a final decision regarding an alliance or renegotiate its terms when they would never trust my word. How long would their hospitality last, before my friends and I were at their mercy? The desire for revenge blazed strongly in their veins, maybe as strongly as their will to survive.

Unwilling to surrender my Misrothian tunic and leggings to a people who would more likely burn than clean them, I dipped my soiled clothes in the cooling tub water and scrubbed them with the bar of soap, rinsing them as best as I could. I lay them across the dressing table to dry, and then slipped into the Toryn nightgown.

Turning back to the dressing table, I searched its drawers until I found a comb and small looking glass. It took ages to unsnarl my hair, tangled from weeks of travel across the windswept countryside of Toryn, and that gave me far more time than I liked to study my reflection. The change in me since the last time I'd looked at myself, back in Kelwed, was a little startling. Days of rationed food and exertion had left their mark and my features seemed sharper: my jawline was harsher and my cheekbones more prominent. Grief and exhaustion had shadowed my eyes with dark circles, and my skin looked paler than ever, glowing a blue-green sheen in the cavern lighting. But worse than all that was the painful reminder of my heritage written in every familiar line and curve of my face, every sweep of my hair, and every expression that flitted through my eyes.

Even when the very idea of my father's blood flowing through my veins haunted me and made me want to claw at my skin, I couldn't forget the lessons he had engrained in my heart for so many years. I couldn't stop hearing his voice telling me to be strong and to not give in to what others wanted. My fierce will to stand against the Toryn people and remain firm in my beliefs—that obstinacy had been inherited from and molded by him.

And now a man was dead because of me. Guilt pounded on the gates of my heart again, but I refused to let it consume me. Was I that much like my father?

Narek is wrong, I told myself. *He must be.* I slid my fingertips along my armband, tracing the etched lines of sythrel.

Despite the comfort of sleeping in a bed at last, sheltered from the ichgor and nestrae, I slept fitfully that night. I listened to the bells marking the hours throughout the night. The sounds echoed uncannily throughout the tunnels, the sound soft enough that the Calidans must have found them to be safe, but still loud enough to be heard by their entire city. It was disconcerting enough to be within monster-infested Toryn, trapped in a cave like a cornered animal. Worse were my fears that my friends and I weren't any safer here than we had been aboveground.

Had we merely traded one set of enemies for another?

I woke that morning with nothing to do, so I returned to the washroom to comb through my hair and check on my Misrothian clothes. It was no surprise to find them still damp in the dank cavern air, but I was still disappointed. With a sigh I slipped into the Toryn outfit. It was more comfortable than I expected, and warmer too, like enveloping myself in a blanket to ward off the damp, chill air. The tunic was longer and looser than the Misrothian style, with a sash to tie across the waist. No matter what Layk or Jennah might say about it, I also reattached my armband as soon as I'd dressed. Both Gillen's and Mother's pendants had never left my neck.

A knock echoed from the entrance of my room. Stepping from the washroom, I approached the curtain and cautiously tugged back the fabric a few inches. It flashed silver and blue in the light as it moved, and I blinked against its brightness. Standing outside the entrance was a girl about my age, clothed in a long dress that trailed along the floor behind her and looked white at first, but glittered gold and violet when she moved. Despite the cool air, she wore thin slippers made of a material that matched the changing shades of her dress. A sash was tied loosely about her slender waist, almost as an afterthought. Her black hair flowed long and straight down her back and her eyes were large and blue, a vibrant contrast to her translucent skin. She reminded me of the paintings of Toryn goddesses I'd seen, as if she were not quite earthly, an ironic thought since she was trapped belowground.

"You are Princess Halia of Misroth," she said, a statement rather than a question. "I wasn't sure if I would find you awake at this early hour. I am Iyleth, daughter of Captain Luiken." Her eyes flitted over my shoulder, then back to me. "He sent me to speak with you. May I come in?"

I blinked, taken by surprise. Did I really have a choice in the matter? Stepping back to give her room to enter, I nodded again.

Iyleth strode in and settled into one of the chairs in the room without further preamble. She made a sweeping gesture to the one sitting across from it, so I plopped down and continued to study her curiously. Her manner was relaxed and easy, nothing like the suspicious attitude her father and brother had possessed. She leaned back in the chair and draped one of her legs over the other, letting the skirt of her dress flow out around her, and then she threw one arm over the back of the chair and drummed her fingers against it. I repressed a frown, for I had never seen manners like this in any woman I'd ever met before, royalty or otherwise.

"You're quiet," she said, chewing on her lip as she assessed me. "I didn't expect that in a princess. Possibly even the new queen, they said, if you don't find your cousin. Are you close with him, or are royal families too reserved and formal to show affection toward one another?"

I quirked an eyebrow at her and crossed my arms. "Tell me why you're here."

"Straight to the point? I like that. No nonsense." She grinned. "But maybe not very diplomatic. And that is why I am here: diplomacy. My father hopes to build an alliance with you, to give my people a better chance to not simply survive, but to reclaim our kingdom and…*live*. Not hide in caves." She rolled her eyes and waved her hand in the air at the rocks about us in general, and then focused her large eyes back on me. "But alliances aren't built on fear and intimidation; they need mutual trust and understanding. Perhaps—dare I say it?—friendship. I want to get to know you, Halia, and I want you to get to know me. I want you and your friends to see my people and see how we live here in Calidar, or what has become our new version of our capital. I want us to be friends."

I narrowed my eyes at her. "How can I build a friendship with a girl who wants me to endanger the lives of my people?"

"Haed said you had a way with words." Iyleth flashed me another grin and then just as quickly, it faded. "I don't want you to endanger your people, either," she said, her eyes wide and serious and her voice low. "My father and brother may want you to take that risk to save us, but I understand your fear. I've seen the pain and loss my people have experienced, and I have suffered alongside them. I would never wish this upon another kingdom, even if it gave hope to mine. It's not worth that cost, not to me."

"I don't believe you."

She tossed her hair over her shoulder, repressing a laugh. "I can hardly blame you. But hopefully you will see that I am on your side, in time. If we can build trust between us, we can have a true alliance, one in which perhaps you will find a way to help my people and, in the meantime, we can help you by providing you with shelter in Calidar and assistance in your search for your cousin."

I watched her silently, weighing my words. "Perhaps," I said at last.

Iyleth swung her legs to the floor and stood, gracing me with a tight-lipped smile. "Well, I won't trouble you more now." The bells began to toll the seventh hour, and she shrugged. "I'm sure you'll want some breakfast and some time with your friends."

"And Avrik," I cut in, before Iyleth could leave. She turned back, raising her eyebrows at me. "The injured member of my party you have in the infirmary," I clarified. "I would like it if you could show me to him, so I can see how he's faring."

Her smile was more earnest this time. "Of course! I'll be back here this evening to show you the way."

After Iyleth left, I peered out beyond my door curtain to find two guards on either side of my entrance. Even though I'd already known we were all but prisoners in Calidar, the sight made me cringe inwardly. I stepped out, hoping not only to return to the Common Room for breakfast but also to measure the guards' reactions at my coming and going from my quarters.

To my relief, they watched me warily but never moved to follow me. I passed several more guards stationed near my friends' rooms as I wound my way down the tunnel and back into the Common Room, where a simple meal of bread and sausage and cheese had been laid out at a side table. A few people milled about, serving themselves or conversing comfortably with one another. I saw Jennah and Layk seated together at the far corner of one of the tables, leaning close to speak in low voices. The Calidans were giving them a wide berth and shooting dark glances their way.

As soon as I entered the room, a tense quiet fell. Some of the women murmured to each other as I passed, and a few men glared at me openly. Although not all the Toryn faces were unfriendly, it was clear that last night's welcome had mainly been a show out of respect for Captain Luiken. Most of the Calidan people held no fond feelings for me.

One of the men said in a tone loud enough for me to hear: "Eldon was nothing but a coward. Any heir of his deserves all the wrath of the monsters we've faced and all the guilt of the innocent blood that has been spilled for two hundred years."

Working my jaw, I gathered my food wordlessly and sat down with my friends. Jennah was in a Toryn tunic that shifted in colors of shimmering green and gold, while Layk wore a Toryn shirt and trousers changing from silver to a shade of blue that complemented his bright eyes.

"They hate us," Layk muttered. "So much for their cheerful greeting last night."

Jennah held her head high, flashing her smile at anyone who dared to glare in her direction. "Tell us something we don't already know. This is no surprise: they've had time to doubt Captain Luiken's enthusiasm and remember all their old reasons for hating us. And for that matter," she added, shifting in her seat to lean toward him, "try being Misrothian with obvious Alrenian heritage and see how much more they hate you, their constant reminder of both kingdoms they despise."

I bit back a smile. "You seem to handle it well."

Jennah's golden brown eyes shone in the iridescent glow surrounding us. Her fingers played with the two pendants dangling from her neck—Gare's and her own. "I will endure anything for my people. Besides," she said with a grin, "if there is one thing about my heritage I take pride in, it is that Alrenians do not believe in fear."

"I know we'd be fools to leave, but I don't like this," Layk said, his eyes darting about the room as he ate, like he was constantly assessing the space for threats. "I don't trust them. And..." He glanced at me, hesitating over his next words. He kept his voice low. "You aren't considering their offer of an alliance, are you?"

I followed his lead, leaning forward and whispering to avoid being overheard. "To break the barrier and doom our kingdom?" I scoffed. "They're fools if they think I'd sell Misroth for their help."

Jennah watched me levelly. "So you're stalling them."

I poked at the sausage on my plate with my fork. "Time can change circumstances," I said, a little uncertainly. "I might be able to convince them to accept terms for Misrothian help that don't involve destroying the barrier. We might build trust during our stay and find ways to mutually benefit our kingdoms." I shrugged. "Or I could have a vision that can lead us to Gillen without their help. Maybe one to even show me the way back through the barrier."

"So, for now, we wait," Jennah said.

I nodded. "And hope they will let us travel aboveground now and then. But time will be our friend." I glanced at Layk, a playful smile curving my lips. "So please try to be agreeable with strangers for once. We *would* like an alliance, just with different terms."

"I can be agreeable with strangers!" Layk protested.

Jennah laughed, her eyes twinkling with mischief as she nudged Layk on the shoulder. "Oh yes, we'll rely on your charm to persuade them to trust us and agree to our terms. *That* will be the new plan."

Smirking, I added, "I remember when I first met you. Your hospitality was legendary."

As Jennah and I dissolved into giggles, Layk tried to resist laughing along with us, and failed.

We spent the rest of the day in my room, reciting Alrenian phrases Jennah taught us both. When the noon bell struck, we left to gather lunch and then brought it back with us to avoid the angry stares and words. Layk brought out a deck of cards he'd found in his room earlier and we played games for the rest of the afternoon.

At last, another knock came at my entrance. When Layk pulled back the curtain, Iyleth grinned up at him. "I'm here to take the princess to Avrik," she announced.

At the mention of Avrik's name, Jennah gave me a teasing smile that I tried to ignore. Even Layk gave me a friendly nod, silent encouragement. I wanted to tell them there was nothing to tease about, but with Iyleth there, I said nothing.

When I joined her in the tunnel, Iyleth looked at me brightly, like we were friends about to go on a walk together. "You seem close with your group," she said.

I refused to be baited by her friendly attitude. "That tends to happen after you've faced death a few times."

She kept quiet after that, leading me on a winding path past the Common Room and through countless more tunnels. Two guards trailed us, ones that I assumed were part of her personal guard, or maybe just assigned to her while strangers lived among the Calidan people.

Along the way, we walked past entrances opening into rooms: a dim library, devoid of people; a large space even larger than the Common Room with an underground river, where men and women were gathered, washing laundry; others where a few small animals, like goats and pigs, could be raised; and a room full of men and women working diligently at a forge, the air thick with smoke from its limited ventilation. The underground city seemed limitless, full of as much life as the Toryn people could manage given their dark circumstances.

At last Iyleth paused before another entrance, this one opening into a long, low-ceilinged room lined with cots. Its walls were covered in shelves filled with countless jars of ointments, liquids, and herbs, bandages, and surgical tools. A large vine twisting across the length of the ceiling emanated a dim red glow, tinting the entire room in an unpleasant light that made both the healers walking about the room and the injured occupying the cots look otherworldly.

Iyleth turned to me. "You'll hear the bells ring the seventeenth hour when it's time to return to the Common Room. Everyone but the sick is expected to gather at the same time for every dinner. If you need help finding your way back, you can ask for help." She gestured to one of the healers standing close to the entrance: a young woman with wispy hair and wide, dark eyes.

"Thank you," I murmured as I stepped within the room and began to search the cots for Avrik.

"I'll…leave you alone," Iyleth finished, and left quickly.

"Your friend is over there." The healer Iyleth had gestured to came forward and pointed to the last cot at the far end of the room. I thanked her and headed toward it.

The room was heavy with the murmuring of healers all clothed in shimmering red and silver tunics, the sick, and a handful of other visitors. Now and then a cot creaked with the weight of its occupant as he or she shifted and groaned.

Avrik was sitting up in his cot and drinking a bowl of broth. Though his face was still drawn with weariness, his eyes were already bright with renewed life.

"They seem to work wonders here," I said.

He turned in surprise at the sound of my voice before looking down again at his bowl, idly sloshing its contents around. "I didn't expect to see you here...princess."

Uncomfortable, I glanced away as well. "I want to ensure all members of my party are well cared for. How are you?"

Avrik touched his arm gingerly where the healers had bound it with thick bandages. "Mostly weak from blood loss." He turned curious eyes on me and lowered his voice. "They seem hospitable enough?" The question was clear in his voice.

"They hope to form an alliance," I whispered back, "but I don't trust them."

Avrik frowned down at his bowl. "Maybe we need to leave. My lady," he added quickly.

I shook my head. "We're safe here, for now." Reaching up, I wound a strand of hair around and around my finger, trying to ignore the awkward tension between Avrik and myself, the way the walls and ceiling felt as if they were crushing in around me, and the weight of the decisions enveloping me. *I'm glad you are all right,* I longed to say, but the words would not come, sitting painfully unsaid on my tongue. "You must regret entering Toryn," I finished lamely. "I'm...sorry."

Avrik stared at me for a long, uncomfortable moment. "Since when does royalty apologize to their subjects when their subjects do what is expected of them? I am here for my kingdom. Not for you. There is no need for personal guilt on your part."

I dipped my head in assent, mostly to hide the blood warming my cheeks. "Right." It was bad enough that his words made me feel like a fool; I especially did not want him to know how much they stung. Of course he wasn't here for me. I'd known that all along…so why did this cold statement hurt so much?

I dropped my gaze to my feet and muttered, "Keep resting, Avrik," and turned to leave before he could respond, before he could say something else that would further bruise my heart.

Rather than ask for directions, I risked wandering the tunnels outside to explore the city, taking a winding, haphazard path. My footsteps led me down a narrow, dim tunnel, where the vegetation thinned out until it disappeared entirely, leaving everything in complete darkness and silence but for the sputtering torchlight along the walls. The air grew clammier and thicker, as if the blackness itself had substance that pressed heavily about me. I had to stop once or twice to shut my eyes against the panic that threatened at the edges of my mind, taking me back to a time in my past when the cold dark sea had swallowed me. With tons of rock above and around me, I longed more than ever for the open skies of Evren. I even wished to be back in Lyanna's warm kitchen, working long hours kneading dough for supper or failing miserably at knitting while I sat by the cozy fireside.

I miss you, I thought, swallowing to try to ease the tightness in my throat at all the memories of Lyanna and Rev greeting me.

I'd begun to wonder if I'd wandered into an uninhabited portion of Calidar's underground maze when a huge entrance yawned before me. Golden light filtered out into the tunnel from the opening, making my heart twist with joy. How much I already missed the natural light of the world above. Had I found an exit?

Stepping forward, I peered into the room, my mouth dropping open before I noticed and clamped it shut. It was even larger than the Common Room, filled with rows upon rows of tilled earth being prepared for planting season. The walls were lined with additional openings, perhaps leading to even more space for growing vegetation. None of the luminescent plants grew here, leaving the cavern ceiling and walls barren of all but its natural rock formations and salt crystals. As startlingly large as this room was, what was most awe-inspiring of all was the fact that there was a hole in the ceiling, guarded by a huge metal grate, but otherwise open to the distant blue sky. Peering upward, I could see rock walls rising on either side, as if the hole in the ceiling were at the bottom of a high wall, or a dry well.

I glanced around, but I didn't see anyone in the room. Walking into the sunlight, I relished its warmth on my skin. The scent of fresh air filtered through the room, sweet and comforting and such a keen reminder of springtime in Evren I felt my eyes begin to water despite my earlier resistance to my emotions. Stirred by a gentle breeze, the air felt lighter here, less constricting and clammy.

"Already missing the world aboveground, I see." Narek's voice rang out behind me and jolted me out of my moment of peace.

Spinning on my heel, I shot him a frown. "What are you doing here?"

"I expect the same thing as you." He strolled forward, his hands in his pockets. It was so unusual to see him off his guard that I couldn't keep myself from staring. "Enjoying the sunshine." His eyes met mine and for a few beats we said nothing.

The customary tension between us seemed to melt in the daylight, falling away like forgotten nightmares after waking to sunrise. At last I felt as if I understood Narek, and with my understanding, my fear of him had diminished.

"How can they have…this?" I asked, gesturing up at the open grate. "Isn't this dangerous?"

Narek smiled, but it did not reach his eyes. "The grates can close, and they only open them for short periods of time, always under watch." He nodded to several guards hovering in the shadows along the walls. They clung so close to the darkness and stood so still and quiet, I hadn't even noticed them. "We're also beneath Old Calidar. This grate is in the middle of its ruins, cleverly hidden away at the bottom of an empty well or fountain. Or so I am told. There are others in the rooms beyond these, as well as in the kitchens, smithy, and…their barn, as they call it. For the animals. Besides," he added, "they say the nestrae rarely visit Calidar now."

"But they found us in the ruins of Delgoth."

"It's believed Delgoth is close to a fortress of theirs," Narek said grimly, "and it's also home to a lot of necessary plants the healers use. The Calidan send scouts there regularly enough that the nestrae have learned to stalk Delgoth often."

I noticed how Narek spoke of his people as if he was set apart from them, as if already he felt like a foreigner from his years away. But I said nothing, choosing instead to turn my face toward the sun again, closing my eyes to relish its warmth.

"We're not that different, you and me," Narek said. I opened my eyes and watched him reach out a hand, studying the way the light played across his fingers.

I said nothing, simply watching the way the beams of light shone in his hair, gleaming wet like he had stepped out of a tub mere moments ago. His Toryn clothing, woven to shimmer red and gold in the dark, was a subdued grey in the light and suited him well.

Maybe he was right. Once he had dearly loved someone and lost her; once he had risked traveling to a foreign land and trusting a stranger to help him save his kingdom. Whether or not he had any family or loved ones left alive in Toryn, he still cared deeply about the fate of his people and was willing to do anything for them.

"The only difference is that you hate my people," he finished.

"I do not hate your people," I said softly, averting my gaze as he turned toward me.

Narek raised his eyebrows, an amused look flitting across his face. "Well then. Only me."

"Besides, you cannot claim that you don't hate mine." I quirked an eyebrow at him. "Suspicion and hatred are not the same thing, although considering you once nearly killed me, they may be, in your case." I resisted the urge to narrow my eyes at him and continued. Perhaps if he could be civil, then so could I. "I'm beginning to understand you, which means I think you must understand me too. When you say we are alike, you must also have realized that we are both obstinate. I care about my people as much as you care about yours, and I will *not* risk mine, as much as I am sorry for the fate of yours."

Narek crossed his arms. "I wonder if it came down to a choice between Gillen and Misroth, which you would choose."

My blood ran cold and, almost unconsciously, my fingers slipped to Gillen's necklace hanging from my neck. *Is that a threat?* But before I could open my lips, the bells began to ring the seventeenth hour.

He shrugged. "They'll be gathering in the Common Room for dinner." Without waiting to see if I would follow, he turned and disappeared back into the tunnel.

Vowing to continue to be wary, I trailed after him.

When we arrived, the Common Room was once more bustling with people standing and chatting in the open, sitting and conversing together at the tables, and scurrying back and forth carrying trays laden with large dishes. Layk, Jennah, and Avrik were already sitting together at one of the tables, looking starkly out of place. Layk's blonde hair shone like a small sun in the sea of dark hair around him, while Jennah's brown, gold-tinted skin tone attracted constant stares, most being less than friendly. Noting the empty spot beside them, I abandoned Narek and hurried to my friends.

"You're here," I stammered to Avrik, immediately regretting my words and repressing a grimace. *I sound like a fool.*

"I explained the only way I would regain my strength would be if I could have a real meal with my friends," he said, though I noticed the way his tone wavered slightly on the last word and his eyes flicked away. "That broth…" He sighed and shook his head.

"You've recovered quickly," I said in some surprise.

He smiled faintly. "Mostly."

I seated myself between Layk and Jennah. "Avrik looks well," Jennah murmured in my ear. "Perhaps you want to sit next to him?"

Shaking my head, I glanced away to hide the blush rising to my cheeks. She of all people had to know that nothing between Avrik and me was that simple.

At that moment, a hush fell over the crowd and heads turned to look at the other end of the Common Room, at the entrance from which Captain Luiken and Haed were now emerging, their guards at their sides. They paused and Captain Luiken lifted his hands in supplication. He raised his voice until it bounced off the walls around us and thudded in my ears.

"People of Calidar, let us take this moment to thank the gods for their provisions." Around me, people lifted their eyes heavenward and stretched their arms above them, reaching as one toward their gods. My friends and I sat politely still and hushed, watching with interest. "To Wynla, we thank you for the safe haven you have provided us to keep the remnant of our people alive and well."

"To Wynla!" the people shouted.

"To Delmae," Captain Luiken continued, "for giving us tranquility during our grief, hardship, and fear."

"To Delmae!" the Toryn echoed.

"To Thyred, for giving us food even in this barren underground city."

The list went on for several more minutes, until at last Captain Luiken bid us to "Eat and rejoice in the moments we have left!"

The dishes were endless: various types of bread were passed from person to person at our long table. Next came bowls of mushroom soup, plates of fish, potatoes, and canned vegetables. We filled our mugs from pitchers of water and pots of steaming tea with a spicy sweet flavor I'd never tasted before.

Though we ate our fill without trouble, most of the Toryn people avoided talking to us or snarled rude words in our direction. One thin, middle-aged man set me on edge when he refused to stop staring at us from across the table. At last, Avrik leaned forward. "Do you find me irresistibly handsome?" he asked, shooting him a cheeky grin.

The man scowled and glared down at his plate without a word, but he did not stare at us again.

Others were not so easily put off. "You may be under Captain Luiken's protection," a burly man down the table called, "but you should still watch your backs, strangers!" Men and women around him chuckled or clanked their mugs together in agreement.

"We will change Captain Luiken's mind about them," a woman said. "I heard how they refuse to make an alliance with us."

Another added, "If they're not our allies, they're our enemies. Anyone who refuses to help us wishes us harm. They don't deserve our protection."

I kept my gaze low and tried to avoid making eye contact. As soon as I'd finished eating, I stood to leave and found myself face to face with Iyleth.

Grasping hold of my arm, she pulled me away, murmuring in my ear, "Don't listen to them."

I pulled back and she released her grip.

"Forgive me, princess—" she started, but the expression on my face must have cut her off.

Rubbing my arm where she'd touched me, I swept away from the Common Room, leaving her standing speechless amongst her hateful people.

They arrived in the night, or what I assumed was still night in the endless dark that reigned within this underground city. Wrenching me from restless dreams, a raucous crowd of men and women shoved me out of my room and into the purple and green tinted hall. Disoriented, I blinked and struggled fiercely to push them away, but one of the men kicked me in the leg in response, knocking me off balance. I grunted with pain and crashed against the cold, damp floor, grit and pebbles cutting into my palms.

"Get her up," a woman snarled in the darkness, and rough hands hauled me back to my feet.

With two men grasping my arms and others marching before and behind me, they guided me down the hall. I glanced around, searching for the guards who had been stationed at my doorway only a few hours earlier, only to find them both crumpled against the wall, unconscious. A deep uneasiness shivered down my spine. This mob was not afraid to attack their own in order to hurt the strangers among them.

We passed more unconscious guards along the hall, but others seemed to have simply disappeared from their posts. The crowd led me away from the Common Room, down more tunnels that seemed mostly empty and unused by the Calidan people. Some were lit with differently colored plant life that reflected macabrely on the crowd's faces, and some contained glittering veins of silver in the walls or breathtaking formations of rock.

Stones scraped my bare feet and the cool air whispering through the thin shift I wore made me shiver. My limbs felt weak and my brain was still hazy with sleep, but I made an effort at bravado. "Only cowards drag a girl from her bed and avoid a fair fight," I growled.

Walking just ahead, the woman who had spoken earlier laughed coldly. "This isn't a fight; this is an execution." Red light reflected in her black eyes and glowed against her pale complexion as she bared her teeth in an ugly grin.

Smatterings of visions sparked to life: the Toryn gathered in dark recesses of their vast underground cave where only torchlight flickered across their faces; Captain Luiken's dispassionate gaze as he recited lists of crimes; and shackled prisoners being flung into a shadowy pit where their screams ran on, endlessly until I thought my ears would burst. Sweat collected on my brow as I blinked the images away. Where were Captain Luiken and Haed? Surely they wouldn't toss aside their chance at an alliance so quickly and kill their only hope of breaking the barrier.

The Toryn crowd shoved me into a larger room lit by torches, just like the place in my vision. Others already awaited us, surrounding Layk, Jennah, and Avrik, who were each restrained by at least two men. Avrik was fully dressed and had a blackened eye, and Layk, with his split lip, looked like he'd also been in a scuffle. Barefoot Jennah had an angry welt on her forehead and bruises on her arms. My friends had clearly been more alert when torn from sleep than I had been.

A Toryn woman stood tall near the edge of the gathering, lifting high a green banner bearing the purple silhouette of a bird. Toryn's insignia. The men holding me shoved me toward my friends, their grips tightening like vices on my shoulders as I stood beside Layk. I could feel his eyes on me, but I refused to remove my stare from the woman who had spoken to me earlier, the apparent leader of this gathering, who had now taken a position beside the woman holding the Toryn flag. Tunic fluttering about her ankles in flashes of red, pink, and violet under the torchlight, she stepped up onto a boulder and raised her arms for silence.

"Do you know how we execute Calidan criminals?" she demanded, her eyes boring into mine as her words rang gruffly off the stones around us. A few wrinkles traced her brow and her dark hair was streaked with grey, though she moved with the strength and grace of a young woman.

Fear is weakness, my father's voice murmured in my ear. *Never let them see you weak.* I held my head high in defiance, gritting my teeth against the cool air whispering along my skin. I didn't want the men holding me to feel me tremble and have reason to gloat.

"Off in these far reaches of our cavern lurk even more monsters, the invaders from the Wastelands that Misroth abandoned us to." Her eyes flashed with rage. "They live in the depths of pits burrowed deep within this rock and lined with loose dirt and gravel that make it impossible to climb back out once you have fallen in. And unlike the sedwa or even the ichgor, a vilspen won't eat you quickly. It will devour you slowly, bit by bit, sucking the lifeblood from you until at last you perish."

The screams from my vision crowded my ears, and I struggled to push them away and focus on my surroundings.

"Captain Luiken is a fool for putting you under his protection," the woman snarled, "and we, the people of Calidar, have made our choice. You are not welcome among us, to take from our provisions and our protection, all the things we have fought so hard for since your kingdom left us to fall. We find you guilty of countless Toryn deaths and the destruction of our cities and our way of life."

"It was not our hands that swung the weapons or set the fires," Jennah said, her voice low and steady, her eyes focused narrowly on the woman across from us.

Descending from her perch, the Toryn woman stalked toward Jennah. "Do you think I'm ignorant about what is happening? Or regarding who *she* is?" She stabbed a finger in my direction, making me glower back at her.

"Then you're a fool if you plan to kill her," Avrik spat.

The woman's face split in another unnerving smile. "Oh no," she said, "she's here to watch." She gestured to the men holding my friends back and they began to surge forward, jostling them toward the pit.

"Stop!" My screams rent the air in vain as I wrestled against the Toryn men's grips. *Bargain with them,* I thought frantically. *Agree to destroy the barrier.* But the thought alone conjured up imagined sights of nestrae and ichgor attacking Lyanna and Rev, Velaire and the councilors, and Jaren, Shilam, and Bren. Mouth dry, I found myself despising my gift once again and longing for the ability to lie, just this once to gain time, to save my friends' lives. *Yes, I'll destroy the barrier!*

"I'll never agree to your terms if you kill them!" I shouted.

Still smirking, the woman turned back to raise her eyebrows at me, unfazed. "I am not hoping for an alliance. This is beyond your choice now. You *will* destroy the barrier for us. We will kill your allies, drag you to the barrier, and force you to break it, if we have to torture you until every ounce of your will has been broken," she snarled.

Fury and fear churned through me as I watched Layk, Jennah, and Avrik shoved to the pit's edge, hovering dangerously near.

"After centuries of suffering, this is our victory!" the woman shouted, and all around, the crowd took up her cry.

"Victory, victory!" they chanted, the word pounding mercilessly against my skull.

"Which one will go first?" the woman continued, a mad look shimmering in her eyes as she stepped closer.

I spat at her.

Chuckling, she wiped the saliva from her cheek and turned her head, her eyes drifting over the forms of my friends as she assessed each one. "He stands firm," she said, nodding toward Layk. The men holding him pushed him forward so that he was leaning over the edge, staring down into the abyss below him, but he didn't make a sound. Her eyes darted back toward me, studying, studying.

I glared. "If you harm a single one of them, I swear to you, no matter what you do to me, I will *never...*"

She waved her hand dismissively. "Proud, bold words from a privileged royal who has never truly tasted of death and despair." She spun back toward my companions. "Not him," she ordered her men, who pulled Layk back toward them. "Not yet." Slowly, her lips curled into a smile. "Perhaps it is the handsome young man here you care for most?" She gestured toward Avrik.

The men pulled him forward, so close that the rocks beneath his feet skittered into the pit. Something far below moved in the darkness, shifting gravel and sand.

I narrowed my eyes and stared unwaveringly back at the woman, but my heart pounded wildly, desperately. "This is madness. Captain Luiken will execute you too when he finds out what barbarism you have committed—"

The woman smirked. "Oh, but whatever happens to me won't matter much to you once your friends are already dead," she whispered.

"Victory! Victory!" the people were still chanting, their collective voice rising stronger and more passionate.

Dread and fury swirled through me like a rising storm, so thick I could taste the hatred I had for these Toryn on my tongue. "If this is what your people are, you deserve this fate," I snarled.

"Which one do we start with first, Avela?" a man in the crowd asked the woman.

She smirked back at me before nodding toward Avrik. "That one."

And without ceremony, Avela strode forward and shoved Avrik from the men's grasp, sending him teetering into the abyss.

CHAPTER FIFTEEN

N O!" I SCREAMED, TRYING TO tear myself from the men holding me back.

Avela turned back to me, a satisfied smile crossing her face. She turned toward Jennah next, stepping forward to throw her in…

The shouting around us wavered before abruptly halting altogether. An uncomfortable silence fell over the crowd, and Avela paused, turning toward the entrance to see what had upset the mob. I looked too, though there were too many people blocking my view.

Hope bloomed in my chest. *Captain Luiken? Would he remain true to his word and put an end to this madness?*

But it was not the leader. As the crowd moved aside, I saw half a dozen guards escorting Narek as he strode toward the pit, and beside him, dwarfed by all around her, walked Iyleth. Her slippers trod elegantly over the slippery rocks lining her path, as if she were not confined to a cavern but was a noblewoman at court. Poised and slender, she looked unintimidating, yet her face was so grim that all who watched her went deathly still. The torchlight danced in her raven hair and in the depths of her eyes until she looked like she was lit from within, all fire and confidence and strength. The Toryn watched her in awe. And that was the moment when I wondered: was it truly Captain Luiken and his son who ruled the people, or his daughter?

"What is this?" Iyleth said, her face still harsh, though her voice was calm. Her eyes found the crowd's leader and fastened on her. "Avela."

"I…" Avela bowed her head, staring at her feet before she jerked her gaze upward again and twisted her mouth in defiance. "Perhaps I have disobeyed Captain Luiken's commands, but I did so to help our people survive. We have struggled so long, suffered and despaired… This is our hope. Our chance to reclaim Toryn and live in the sunshine again." Her brow creased with pain.

Iyleth watched her with soft eyes, her lips frowning in sympathy. "I know," she said.

"Please!" I cried out. The men gripping Layk, Jennah, and I released us, and I tore through the crowds toward Iyleth. "They threw Avrik in the pit. Give me a weapon—something…"

Iyleth's face paled. "I'm sorry…" she stammered.

Narek stepped forward. "Take this," he said, his voice gruff as he shoved his sword hilt into my palm. He unslung a coil of rope from where it rested over his shoulder. For an instant I stared at him, shocked that not only had he come prepared, but also that he was willing to help at all. Perhaps he wanted me to die down there.

His motivation didn't matter. Nothing would stop me now. I didn't pause another moment to wonder why he was helping me, didn't stop to listen to Iyleth's frantic cries of "It's suicide!" contrasting sharply with the breathless silence of the people around us. Layk and Jennah's worried faces loomed close as Narek and I slid to a stop at the pit's edge, but I ignored their words and attempts to stop me.

"Your Majesty—"

"Don't do this—"

"It's too late—"

"I'm so sorry—"

Narek looped the rope about my waist, tying it taut. "I'll pull you out when you get to him," he was saying, but I wasn't waiting, wasn't stopping. I charged into the pit.

The rope tugged painfully around my hips as I stumbled down the pit, running until the decline and loose sand beneath my bare feet made me tumble forward. Falling, I rolled the remainder of the way into darkness, dropping onto soft sand at the bottom. Overhead I could see the cavern plant life along the ceiling and walls, its eerie glow failing to reach the bottom of this hole. My ragged breath was loud in my ears, but I could hear movement nearby. I staggered to my feet, holding the blade out before me, willing my eyes to adjust to the blackness.

"Avrik!" I shouted.

I heard him grunt, heard him fall. "Elena!" His voice was terrified. Not for himself. For me. "You weren't supposed to—" He gave a cry of pain and I charged forward, not caring that I couldn't see.

Something lashed out in the darkness, a solid force slamming into my body and hurling me backward. I swung my sword blindly, angrily. Striking something solid, I heard a squeal and could almost see the shape of *something* skittering away from me.

"Elena!" Avrik's voice was right beside me, his warm hand grasping mine and pulling me up. I could just see him in the dark now, his bright eyes watching me in concern, his breath warm on my face. There was a flash of metal as he turned back toward our unseen foe, his hunting knife poised at the ready, but now was not the time to ask how he was armed.

"Hurry, we need to get out of here!" I said, grasping his hand tightly. "Hold onto me!"

Avrik's eyes darted to the rope around my waist. He stepped forward, sliding his arms around my lower back, and for just an instant, I was lost in a surge of warmth at his closeness. When he pulled me nearer, he was tall enough that his chin rested on the top of my head. He smelled of soap and earth, and his hands were warm through my shift.

I drew a breath to clear my head and reached up, tugging on the rope to signal Narek. In response, the rope went taut as it started tugging us up.

But the vilspen was faster.

Moving from the shadows, crawling on huge, spindly legs plated in an armor-like shell, it reached forward with pincers that gleamed like blades. Suspended in the air, Avrik and I ducked. The pincers snapped in the air above us, severing the rope. We dropped, smashing to the ground and rolling away. Dirt clouded the air and burned my eyes.

"Get up, run!" Avrik shouted. Clasping hands, we pulled each other up and dashed away as the vilspen drew nearer. It stretched forward, but we were faster, faster… But the severed end of the rope dragged in the dirt behind me, and panic was taking hold.

Maybe Avrik sensed my fear somehow, or maybe he was trying to reassure himself too. "We can do this," he said firmly, squeezing my hand.

Together, we turned back toward the vilspen, its long legs stretching, searching every curve of the pit for its victims. Now that I could see even more clearly in the shadows, I could discern the endless eyes covering the creature's head and the great fangs hanging from its mouth. There were claws at the end of every one of its legs, sharp and long as sword blades. I released Avrik's hand and grasped Narek's sword with both of mine. It was heavy in my grip, not made for me, but it was a weapon.

"We can do this," I echoed back to Avrik, who stood at the ready with his knife.

The vilspen stabbed at us with one of its legs, scattering us in two different directions. Though the force of the creature's strike nearly knocked me from my feet, I stumbled forward before it pulled back and slashed out with my sword. The blade bounced harmlessly off the vilspen's shell, just as I'd feared, but it still recoiled and squealed again in rage. Multiple legs thrust out all at once, slamming into sand and stirring up thick clouds of it. The force shook the ground and knocked me down. Another leg struck next to me, and, coughing and blinking away sand, I rolled away, praying I wasn't rolling into the path of another. I tightened my fist, only to realize it was empty. I'd dropped the sword.

Somewhere, Avrik was shouting for me, but my world had been reduced to endless sand and noise, the grit digging into my face as I moved, the sound of the vilspen's pommeling legs thundering in my ears. Pincers snapped overhead, like blades clashing together again and again.

Then the creature squealed and its legs stopped. I pushed myself up and scrambled back into the shadows, blinking sand from my eyes. *Where is my sword?* I thought frantically, scanning the ground. A glint far to my right caught my eye.

"Come here, you monster!" Avrik taunted from somewhere on the opposite side of the pit. The vilspen spun away from me and darted toward his voice.

Setting my shoulders, I charged forward. My hand snatched the sword up on my way and the weight of the blade nearly slowed my steps. I longed for my bow.

Ahead, I could see Avrik dodging the vilspen's blows, darting as close as he could beneath the monster's legs whenever he had the chance and swinging his knife. It was the perfect distraction.

I slowed my steps as I neared, keeping each footfall soft and light in the sand. The earth shuddered beneath me which each of the vilspen's strikes, but I kept my feet as I edged up on it. My eyes sought out the creature's underbelly, where one pale patch appeared softer than the rest of its body. I darted forward, the sword's heavy weight now reassuring in my hand.

With another leap forward, I threw myself beneath the monster and plunged my sword upward. It pierced deep into its body, and the vilspen gave one final, hideous squeal, shuddering on the sword's point. I summoned my strength and shoved the blade still further into the vilspen until it trembled, stretching out viciously with legs and pincers to attack Avrik, and finally stilled. Then the full weight of it began to collapse.

"Watch out!" Avrik charged and shoved me forward, out from beneath the creature.

As the vilspen collapsed in the sand, we tumbled away. Narek's sword was tight in my hand and Avrik still grasped his knife when we sat up, panting, and stared at one another. Sand swirled around us, coated our faces, and dusted our hair and clothes. Avrik's chestnut hair had grown long enough to stand up wildly on end and the bandages wrapping the wound on his arm were bleeding again; but his face…his face was alight with victory, with happiness, with that familiar expression I was used to seeing cross his face whenever he looked at me.

We dropped our weapons and laughed, wrapping each other in a fierce embrace.

"We did it!" I cried.

I pulled away, just a little, to see him grinning back at me. In that moment, I thought I could watch him smile like that forever. I never wanted this moment to end, never wanted him to let go.

"Of course." He reached out, running his fingers through the tangles in my hair and dislodging some of the sand. "We're survivors. We can do anything."

His face was so close, I could have reached out and brushed my hand through his hair too. Or kissed him. Or I could have told him how sorry I was and how much I cared, how much I longed for everything to be set right between us. The moment felt natural and right. Maybe we *could* forget the hurt between us. Maybe he really did feel the same way I did…

"I'm just glad you're alive," I said softly.

"Thanks to you," he murmured. Then he caught himself and added, "My lady."

It was amazing how those two simple words could immediately recall every problem between us—the way I'd concealed my identity from him for years, the way he'd left me when I'd needed him most—making discomfort and pain and doubt wash over us again. We broke apart.

We are not in Evren, I reminded myself, *and I am not Elena.*

As we stood and gathered our weapons again, my relief quickly descended into fury. "We have to get back up there," I said, looking up to where I could still, just barely, make out the forms of Narek and my friends leaning over the pit. I realized that though we could see them, the light was too bright up there for them to see us. The sliced rope and sudden silence down below had to have them all on edge. "We have to return to those *murderers* and let them know their alliance is broken."

Avrik was quiet beside me, anger written clearly across his face. He bent down to slide his knife into his boot, and I cast him a curious glance.

"They didn't check you for weapons before they pulled you out of bed, did they?" he smirked. "I was restless and couldn't sleep, so I put on my boots and grabbed my knife to try to sneak out for a walk when they arrived." He frowned. "I wish I'd had my bow, but that would have been too obvious."

"Me too." I stormed toward the edge. "Narek!"

After several long moments, another rope was tossed down into the pit. I tucked Narek's sword into the rope still tied around my waist and began to climb, Avrik following. As soon as I reached the top, where Narek, Layk, and Jennah held the other end of the rope, the crowd's silence broke.

Men and women erupted into startled conversation everywhere, gesturing wildly, some looking relieved and others furious.

Before they could finish asking if I was all right, I pushed past Layk and Jennah and stormed toward Iyleth. "The alliance has been broken. Your people tried to kill my friends!"

All around us, the mob dissolved into heated shouts and cries for "Justice!" I sensed Avrik close behind me, tension rising off him.

"What?" Iyleth's eyes widened. "No, you know that my father did not condone—" She stopped herself, taking in my ragged appearance and warily eyeing the bloody sword I held aloft. "I'm sorry," she continued, "and we will return Avrik to the infirmary immediately, but what Avela started here is *not* condoned by the Toryn leadership." She spun to face the angry crowd behind her and lifted her voice. "Quiet!" she shouted, gesturing with her hands for them to cease.

The people stopped, staring at her as she turned to study each section of the crowd in turn. "Return to your beds. Leave this place."

Her people hesitated, murmuring to one another and blinking in confusion and fear. "Now!" she shouted, and her guards began to usher the people toward the entrance.

They dispersed rapidly. Some cast hateful looks over their shoulders at my friends and me as they shuffled out. Avela leveled me a glare full of unspoken threats.

I studied Iyleth suspiciously. Narek stood beside her with his arms crossed, watching the Calidan people leave. I still did not know what to make of his help.

Iyleth turned to me, and for the first time I read uncertainty in her gaze. "Take me to your father," I demanded, my voice cold.

"Tomorrow I will need to speak again with the people," Captain Luiken said, pacing the length of the room he'd first met with us in. As before, guards lined the walls, studying my every movement while I stood across the table with my friends and Narek. Avrik had refused to return to the infirmary, insisting a healer could check on him in his room later. Iyleth kept close to her father's side.

"The alliance you promised us has been broken," I said firmly. "Another speech is not enough."

Captain Luiken turned back to me, his expression set with determination equal to my own. "We can rebuild it."

"How can we trust you if you cannot even protect us from your own people? Your guards failed us—some, I believe, even joined the mob or at least let the people take us."

"Forgive me," Captain Luiken said, "but I did not expect this level of…insubordination. Or incompetency. You can trust that the appropriate punishments will be given, both to the people and the guards."

"Even I know you can't execute or imprison an entire mob. You'll only divide your people even more."

"What do you plan to do without our protection? Traversing the Toryn countryside, as you well know, is far more dangerous than the threat of mobs I know we can control. We have too much to offer for you to just leave—"

"And I have too much to offer you to ever risk the safety of my companions again," I interrupted, staring straight into his eyes. "You ensure they stay alive and well, or I swear to you, your people will never receive Misrothian aid."

"We can punish the leaders in a show of force," Captain Luiken insisted. "And we will set new guards outside your rooms—I will personally ensure they are loyal and prepared for any eventuality." He paused. "And *you* will choose the leaders' punishment."

I blinked. "What?"

Captain Luiken stretched out a hand toward me. "This is my show of trust in you, my gesture to forge our alliance stronger than before. You will not simply take my word that these men and women will be punished. You will be a part of the process to ensure you and your friends are safe as long as you stay with us."

Slowly, I nodded.

"At first light, I'll summon you. I'll have the mob leaders already imprisoned and we will determine their fates."

Some of Captain Luiken's personal guard led us back to our rooms. In the tunnels, I tried to catch Avrik's eye, but he kept his head lowered.

We are strangers now, I reminded myself. *Companions with a shared desire to save Misroth and survive, that is all.*

I glanced at Narek, who was beside me. He was silent, his face impassive.

"You saved us from that mob," I said, keeping my voice low. "How? And...why?"

He cast a quick glance at me before looking away again. "The how is simple. The noise outside my rooms woke me, and it was easy to guess what that crowd was planning. I grabbed that rope and found Iyleth and her guards. As for why…" He smirked. "How will you save my people if you are dead?"

"You know that is why they wouldn't dare kill me. Only my friends." I paused. "You could have let them die. They wanted me desperate and frightened, to force me to submit to them. Isn't that what you have wanted all along?"

Narek raised his eyebrows. "Do I look like a fool?"

Just ahead, Layk let out a short laugh. Apparently our conversation had not gone unheard.

I chewed the inside of my lip. "You may be a free man amongst your people, but I can tell they don't trust you either. That is perhaps the only thing that the Toryn and I have in common."

"I haven't asked you to trust me," Narek said, a bemused smile flitting across his lips, "but your friends *would* be dead without me."

"And someday they could still be threatened with death *from* you," I snapped. "Don't think we'll let our guard down around you because of one good deed. You still tortured my friends and tried to kill *children* while in my father's service."

Narek stopped to enter his room while the rest of us continued onward. His voice drifted after me. "Your ropes came undone," he said, repeating his words from our conversation long ago. "And Jennah's children were not at home."

Jennah looked back sharply, then flicked her eyes toward me. I stared back at her and pressed my lips together firmly.

"It's a trick," she growled under her breath.

But I brushed into my room with my thoughts whirling. Narek was the type of man to withhold the truth when it suited him, not lie outright. And so many of the things I'd thought I'd known about him before this journey had proven false.

Enemy or ally?

The next morning Iyleth and her guards arrived at my doorway to lead me to the Calidan prison cells. With the threat to my friends still fresh in my mind, no place felt safe in this underground city and my manner with Iyleth was even stiffer than before.

"Avela was the primary leader in the move against you," Iyleth explained as we descended further into the bowels of the earth, wending our way down a dank, cramped tunnel. "But we captured a few others we believe played roles in starting the mob."

A fourth of your city was in the mob, I thought, but I bit back my words.

As the ground evened out beneath our feet, I noticed the barred gate blocking the path ahead. Flanked by two guards, Captain Luiken stood waiting before it. Light from vines on the ceiling painted his face a silvery sheen.

"Come," he said, nodding to one of his men, who plucked a set of keys from his belt and unlocked the gate.

It was unsettling to follow the Toryn leader into their prison, knowing only a shaky alliance prevented me from becoming a captive here. Both sides of the path were lined with cells, most unoccupied, all lit by the silver vines tracing patterns along the ceiling and walls. The air smelled dank and stale and made me shiver.

We didn't have to travel far before we arrived at the first occupied cell. I peered in as Captain Luiken gestured for his guard to unlock the door. Avela perched on a thin mat near the back wall, her eyes narrow and fierce, her face hard, and her mouth a thin, sharp line. There was no penitence in her expression.

"Avela," Captain Luiken said, his gravelly voice echoing in the confined space as he entered the cell. Warily, I followed, with Iyleth close behind.

Avela gave a short nod of acknowledgment at her leader's entrance, but otherwise didn't so much as shift in her seat. "Captain Luiken."

"My men told me you were cooperative when they questioned you, so I'm hoping you will not make this difficult for us."

If possible, her eyes narrowed still further. "Our people are dying, and you are concerned about what is *difficult?*"

"I hope," Captain Luiken said, raising his voice, "you realize that every decision I make is with our people in mind. Our alliance with Princess Halia can bring hope and life to our kingdom, and you have sought to destroy it."

Avela sneered. "This girl will never break the barrier without…*motivation.*"

I met her gaze unflinchingly, but said nothing.

"You disobeyed my direct orders and committed treason," Captain Luiken continued, ignoring Avela's claim. "Those crimes are punishable by death. Are you prepared to die for your cause?"

She crossed her arms and stared into his eyes. "I held my son, a mere child, as he drew his last breath. I watched my husband lay down his life trying to defend his land against the nestrae. I fought to survive as countless enemies decimated my kingdom and laid waste to my home. I have walked among the charred bodies of my neighbors and friends, searching among the dead for just one who might still live. I have little left, and if I must die for my cause, then I will."

Captain Luiken's tone was low, barely keeping a tremor in check as he spoke. "We share the same cause. Only different methods." He turned over his shoulder to look at me. "What will her punishment be?"

My pulse hammered through my body until I thought I could burst. All I could see was blood bursting across my vision as the men who had tried to assassinate me in Misroth were beheaded. All I could hear were this woman's words reverberating through my mind.

Slowly, I shook my head. "My companions and I will not sentence your people to death. If you hope to build an alliance with Misroth, we can't bring further division between us. Your people will hate Misroth even more if you throw your own to the vilspen on my orders."

Captain Luiken studied me for a long, silent moment. Avela blinked up at me, too astonished to conceal her widening eyes, her parted lips.

"Consider the danger to your friends…" Captain Luiken began. He shook his head and for the first time I noticed his own discomfort. There were dark circles under his eyes and his shoulders stooped as if bowing beneath a great weight. "If they perish at the hands of one of these prisoners, if my guards fail to protect you, you cannot accuse me—"

"My companions and I know the risks we face by choosing to stay in Calidar," I cut in. "But I will not have Toryn blood on my hands."

"Misroth already does," Avela snarled. "And you'll continue to if you do not destroy the barrier."

Captain Luiken glared at her. "It would be wise for you to keep your mouth shut for a long while."

She bit her lip and bowed her head low, finally showing some humility.

"You will speak to your people," I told Captain Luiken. "You will remind them of our alliance and the protection you offer us, and you will explain that we have chosen to show Avela and her companions mercy. You will continue to post guards at my friends' rooms at all hours and you will allow us to bear our weapons anywhere we venture in Calidar."

"Agreed." Captain Luiken offered his hand. I shook it firmly. "Except on one point." He nodded toward Iyleth. "The people adore my daughter. Perhaps they will listen to the warm reminder of someone they love more than another threat from me. She can give them a message of hope, something to cling to when they need to remember that this alliance is in their best interests."

That evening before dinner, my friends and I stood once again with

Captain Luiken and Haed. Guards led Avela and three men from their cells and unbound their hands in front of the Calidans' eyes. As the people sat hushed in their seats, uncertain what sort of public display they were about to witness, Iyleth stepped forward and lifted her hands. She gestured in vain, for the stillness was so heavy I could easily hear the rustle of her skirts as she moved. Every eye in the room followed her, most shimmering with reverence.

"Last night I witnessed treason from friends and neighbors," she said. "They dragged their own guests from their beds and tried to feed them to the vilspen." A few murmurs rippled through the crowd. Men and women bowed their heads in fear and shame. "They disobeyed my father's orders and threatened the alliance we are striving to build with Misroth, an alliance that could bring new hope to our people, the likes of which we have not seen in far, far too long.

"I know we have been fighting just to survive. But vengeance is not what will bring us victory or secure our hope." She drew a deep breath. "And I *know* your pain. Gods, I know it. I know you miss lost loved ones, but this will not bring them back. We have survived dark days, and we will continue to do so, but it will not be because we are furious or vengeful or hateful. It will be because we have held on.

"I know that many of us have lost so much hope that we hardly dare seek it anymore, hardly dare to trust Fayla herself to hear our pleas for it." Frowning, she scanned the faces of her people, meeting countless pairs of eyes with an unwavering ferocity in her expression. "But we *will* be heard. The gods *will* grant us our request. And when hope returns to us, it will be with a passion and power to match every ounce of this crushing despair and pain, every fiery shred of determination that carried us when hope failed." Iyleth lifted her face defiantly, the sharp line of her chin unyielding. "It will claim us with a courage that will make the goddess herself quake and doubt herself."

Her words were bold, her voice tremulous with emotion, and I could see it spark faith in her people as they listened. Their eyes lit up, some even smiling. Their fear and shame vanished into enthusiasm. Captain Luiken was right. The Toryn loved Iyleth and accepted the words she offered them like starving wolves falling upon a carcass.

"My father wanted to remind you that our alliance with Misroth still stands strong, because we have not given up this chance at hope," Iyleth said. "Our faithful guards will protect our guests as long as they are with us."

She turned to me, stretching her arms out toward me as if we were close friends. Her face burst into a wide smile. I forced a tight-lipped one in response. "And in a gesture of mercy and a demonstration of our newfound friendship, the Misrothians have chosen to forfeit their opportunity for justice. The leaders of all who threatened them last night will not be put to death, but set free." Iyleth grasped my hand, thrusting our joined hands over our heads and shouting, "This is our alliance! This is our hope!"

All around us, the people responded. With a roar, they stood to their feet, threw back their heads, and lifted their arms to the sky, some calling out to their goddess of hope while others shouted words like "Hope!" or "Allies!" The sound echoed through the room, thundering in my chest until even I almost felt the enthusiasm that coursed through the people.

When the noise at last began to die, Iyleth dropped our hands and gestured toward my companions and me. "We will not find our hope in the same destruction that drives the enemies plaguing our land. We will accept our visitors' mercy, and in return show them our generosity and protection. We will build a true alliance with Misroth, one that will save our people."

I woke late the next morning, almost too late for the first meal. Rolling from bed, I ignored the Toryn clothes laid out for me the night before and dressed in one of my Misrothian tunics. For a moment I brushed my fingertips along my bowstring, considering, but decided not to make a show of force at the breakfast table. Let the Toryn think I felt confident and secure.

In the tunnel, I passed the entrance to Avrik's room. Almost unconsciously I slowed my steps. The curtain stirred and Avrik emerged, startling me enough that I halted mid-step.

"Good morning," I said quickly, catching myself.

Avrik bowed his head. "Good morning." He fell into step beside me. "I wanted to speak with you, actually."

I cocked my head. "Yes?"

He kept his eyes on the ground before him, kicking up stray pebbles as he walked. "I…wanted to thank you for helping me fight the vilspen."

My answer came so hastily it sounded angry. "Did you think I wouldn't help a member of my party when his life was endangered? That I wouldn't aid someone who had pledged service to my kingdom, to my cousin?"

Eyes wide, Avrik pressed a fist to his heart. "Forgive me. Of course not."

I suppressed an urge to grimace. While Iyleth wove her words into something beautiful, I forged mine into weapons. But it was too late to take them back. We were at the end of the tunnel, Iyleth awaiting us with a soft smile. Her eyes strayed unabashedly over Avrik's face and her grin grew wider.

"Good morning, Avrik." She glanced at me. "Princess Halia."

"Good morning," Avrik replied with a grin.

"I thought if I could have breakfast with some of you, I could work on strengthening the…bond between Toryn and Misroth," Iyleth explained. Her eyes were still on Avrik, and red flooded her cheeks.

I stiffened uncomfortably and kept silent, but neither of them seemed to notice. Not for the first time, I wished Avrik wasn't always so charming to everyone.

"Of course," he said, grinning until his dimple showed. "I know that's important."

Pushing my way past them, I approached a side table where food had been laid out for latecomers. I filled a dish with an assortment of cheeses, dried meats, and bread with honey. The meat and cheese were special enough in Calidar, where few animals could be sustained for long and hunting excursions were rare, but the latter was an especially unexpected treat.

Iyleth strode up behind me, laughing lightly at something Avrik had just said. "Try our honey," she said eagerly. "We've stored it for generations and only bring out some of the supply on special occasions. This is to celebrate our alliance." Though she spoke to Avrik, her eyes darted hopefully toward me.

Ignoring her, I found a seat at one of the mostly empty tables and began to eat. An elderly woman several chairs down from me cast me a curious glance, her eyes narrowed with suspicion, but I merely stared back at her until she looked away. Avrik and Iyleth sat together across from me, talking and laughing as if I weren't there.

"What brought you on this mission? Are you a Misrothian soldier?" Iyleth was asking.

Avrik shook his head. "A hunter."

Her eyes widened, and she set down the bread and honey she'd been about to bite into. "So you spent a lot of time outside," she said, almost in awe. "Can you…can you tell me what it's like?"

"You've never been aboveground?"

Wistfulness in her gaze, Iyleth shook her head. Avrik launched into a vivid description of the Evren countryside, making me homesick.

"Is the sun as beautiful as others say?" Iyleth whispered. "You know…to see it up there. Not the little light that comes down here," she finished bitterly.

"Yes. Sometimes it's gold and bright, and other times, at sunset or sunrise, it's red or orange and paints the sky a thousand different colors."

Iyleth stared into her eyes, and when she murmured, "Wow," I wasn't sure if she meant his description or the way his brown eyes shined under the colorful Common Room lights. Feeling like I could be sick, I turned away, staring sullenly down at my plate. Hoping neither of them had noticed me or my dark mood, hoping I could slip away without being missed.

As I took my last sip of tea and stood, I couldn't help but overhear Iyleth. "Oh—you have some—here—"

It was like I couldn't help myself. I both wanted to turn away and couldn't stop looking over at them. Cheeks flushed even brighter than before, Iyleth was giggling and wiping her napkin over a spot of honey stuck to Avrik's cheek.

Looking a little embarrassed himself, Avrik joined in her laughter. "Hunter, remember?" He shrugged lightly. "I guess I wasn't raised with the elegant manners of a royal—or captain's daughter…"

Scowling, I stalked out of the Common Room, back to my own room where I could try to forget the image of them laughing together, of Iyleth blushing and flirting and reaching out to touch him.

Jennah waited for me there, perched on my bed as if she owned the place. As soon as I entered, she sprang from the bed and threw me a smile.

"As long as we are trapped down here, I can teach you more Alrenian to pass the time."

I lifted an eyebrow at her.

"I saw you in the Common Room," she added quickly by way of explanation. "I saw…" Her voice faded away. "Well, I finished eating before you and thought you might want a distraction. Layk will be along soon too."

My shoulders dropped in relief. "Thank you," I sighed.

The three of us spent hours that way, taking breaks from practicing Alrenian to play cards or listen to Layk tell some of the bedtime stories he'd used to tell Dalen and Fia.

"Why are we spending so much time learning Alrenian, anyway?"

Layk asked a long while later, after we'd taken our lunches back to my room again.

"Because Halia wanted to," Jennah said. "But also because it is part of our heritage, whether we like it or not. Misrothians may despise Alrenian because it reminds us of our period of enslavement, but our very names are rooted in it." She waved toward me. "Halia means 'of the light.' Her mother's name, Ryn, is the Alrenian word for love."

I clenched my jaw. "Ironic," I managed.

Jennah ran a hand through her hair, already falling from her knot in wild ringlets that framed her face. "I'm sorry."

Shrugging, I looked away and dared to let my thoughts stray toward Evren and Lyanna and Rev, even if for one brief, painful instant. "I found love in other places."

Layk quirked an eyebrow. "With Avrik?"

Jennah shot him a warning glance. He must have missed the moment Iyleth had started to flirt with Avrik.

My cheeks heated. "I told you we are—were—only friends. Whatever I feel…felt…" I swallowed and tried again. "I never spoke to him about it and it's…the chance is gone now. We've both changed. And now there's Iyleth…" I shrugged helplessly, bitterness flooding my tone despite my best efforts.

"Perhaps," Jennah said thoughtfully. "Or you're both just stubborn."

Days passed in a monotonous rhythm. Iyleth and Captain Luiken had forced their people to accept us, some hopefully and others grudgingly. Gradually, more and more warmed to the idea of building an alliance, while others seemed curious. After being cut off from their neighboring kingdoms for so long, focused only on survival, they knew little about the outside world. I found myself accosted with questions at breakfast, lunch, and dinner until I started to dread the thought of wandering beyond my rooms into the crowds of strangers.

Occasionally the people would be summoned to the Common Room, not for a meal but for a send-off. Small groups of men dressed in leather armor would bid goodbye to their people, who bestowed the blessings of their gods on them, and then the band would depart for aboveground. They would return in the evenings with goods such as plants and herbs that wouldn't grow in the limited sunlight, bundles of wood, or fresh game. Sometimes they would come back injured or missing members of their parties, and the people of Calidan would quietly mourn. Every time I watched another group leave, I longed to be going with them, searching for Gillen, but Captain Luiken refused. "Not yet," he'd say, or give some other vague, dissatisfying response.

While the Toryn worked during the day, I spent long hours within their underground library, filled with musty books and weathered parchments the Toryn had managed to save from the destruction aboveground, yet rarely used by the Toryn themselves. While they were going about their daily chores in communal rooms--men and women sewing and preparing meals together, delving deep into the cave to mine metals, concocting herbal remedies, washing laundry, or countless other ways they provided for the remnant of their kingdom—I scoured their bookshelves. Unwilling to ask Captain Luiken, Haed, or Iyleth for anything, I searched the library daily until at last, on the fifth day, I found it: a rough map like the one Captain Luiken had, the one labeled *Forsaken Kingdom*.

The parchment paper crinkled as I spread it out across a small, rickety table and studied it beneath the fluttering torchlight. Fragile and stained from the cavern's incessant damp, the map was hard to read, with landmarks and cities labeled in a faded, scrawling hand. My finger traced a path across Irevek Swamp and the great fields beyond until I found Delgoth resting atop its hill, though the city's name had been crossed out. Beside it, in a different, cramped handwriting, was written, Fallen.

Beyond Delgoth, I found Calidar and its notation: *In hiding.* I scanned the surrounding countryside, the labeled cities and landmarks, most marked as in ruins or in hiding, committing the map to memory.

My desperation grew greater with each passing day, and the same visions of Gillen pursued by nestrae haunted me, waking and sleeping. *Where are you, Gil?* I closed my eyes and clutched his pendant in my fingers, trying to find solace in its smooth, familiar surface.

"What do you look for?" Iyleth's voice cut through my thoughts and jolted me straighter in the chair.

Frowning, I glanced away.

"I've helped ensure your friends are safe with us and they are grateful, but you're still wary." Iyleth leaned against a nearby set of shelves, watching me with a curious tilt of her head.

"We are all still wary. Everything you do is for your people's benefit, not ours." I folded my hands tightly in my lap, refusing to meet her gaze directly.

"I could say the same of you."

"Then we have every reason to be wary of each other." Pulling at the edges of the map, I rolled the parchment up and stood to replace it on its shelf. "We will each put our own people first." Finally, I turned to face her. "I know what you want. You can come to me daily trying to build friendship, trying to earn trust, but I am no fool."

Iyleth did not respond. Instead, she turned to fidget with the books behind her, wiping layers of dust and grime off their worn spines. "Do you know where your cousin might be?"

"I was hoping you could help me." I narrowed my eyes. "But I suppose I'm trapped down here, unable to look for him, unless I bargain with you."

Iyleth folded her arms against her chest and bit her lip pensively. "I will speak to my father."

"He will never agree to let us go," I argued.

A light danced in Iyleth's eyes. "You underestimate me."

I raised my eyebrows in mild surprise, remembering the sway she held over her people with her words.

Iyleth flashed me a smile. "Some of Toryn's most powerful deities are goddesses. Father may be Captain and Haed may be the one to someday take his place, but they will always listen to me, their Intercessor." And with that, she slipped from the library, leaving me with the first sense of hope I'd felt since arriving in Calidar.

That evening when I entered the Common Room for dinner, it was different. The dim light of the tunnel gave way to countless torches filling the walls, far more than I'd ever seen in this room before, combining with the glow of the plants curling overhead to give a surreal, pulsing atmosphere of light and color. Anticipation tingled in the air as people murmured together, eying the space that Captain Luiken, Haed, Iyleth, and a small cluster of guards and musicians occupied. Already the men and women were at their instruments, tuning and preparing, only awaiting a signal from Captain Luiken to begin.

Jennah and I exchanged a glance and slipped into the room with a group of stragglers. At the table, Layk stood from his seat beside Avrik and waved at us. My gaze slid past him to my former friend, but he was watching Iyleth and the other Toryn. As accustomed as I was to reading his expressions, I detected the anxiety lurking in this eyes immediately. Was something amiss?

Jennah and I took our seats near Layk and I noticed Narek sitting across from us, his manner somber and detached. He didn't speak to those around him and they seemed content to ignore him as well.

Captain Luiken led their daily prayer and then gestured toward the musicians, who began to play a light, cheerful tune. As the food was brought out and everyone began to eat, I tried to capture Avrik's attention. But no matter how many times I leaned forward and caught his gaze, he always turned away.

At last, as the meal had almost ended, I had my answer. Captain Luiken stood and returned to his place in front of the musicians, who ended their song. With hands uplifted to call for silence, he raised his booming voice until it echoed throughout the cavern chamber.

"My good people of Calidar," he began, "as you are aware, my beloved daughter Iyleth, the Intercessor for our people, chosen by the gods themselves, is of age to choose the suitors who will compete for her affections." He glanced toward my companions and me. "For the benefit of our guests, let me explain: Iyleth is dear to all of our hearts because it is she who goes daily before the gods and goddesses and beseeches them for mercy and blessings on our entire kingdom's behalf. We have found that only one of every generation of Toryn people will be born with the sign marking them as a chosen Intercessor." He nodded toward his daughter, his smile warm and affectionate. "She is the only blue-eyed one among us, just as her mother was before her." His voice wobbled slightly with emotion. "She is gifted in words and carries the hope of our people. She walks in grace and light and the favor of the gods and her people.

"And this," he continued, his tone rising in strength, "is why we will only accept the best men as her suitors. Some have already been chosen, but tonight, my daughter has decided to name another, whom I have approved."

Applause followed this statement. As realization struck, I felt my stomach clench. Captain Luiken nodded to his daughter, who rose from her seat and strode forward to the continuing cheers of her people.

"Citizens of Calidar!" she cried. "Let this choice tonight, and the competition of my suitors in the days to come, be a symbol of our resilience in these dark days. Despite what we face, we continue not only to survive, but to prosper and find ways to celebrate life. Tonight, let's celebrate life and a new offering of friendship and hope, in a beautiful alliance! I name Avrik of Misroth my newest suitor."

For a moment, the cheers faltered. Men and women glanced at one another, clapping softly and uncertainly. A few murmurs rippled through the crowd.

"This is a gesture to strengthen our bond with our neighboring kingdom. To lay aside old prejudices and past hurt and embrace a new future we can all enter together. He has been deemed fit to compete with our own men of Toryn by myself and my family." Her eyes sparkled as she sought out Avrik in the crowd. "Avrik, do you accept this challenge and agree to step forward tonight and prove your worth to my people?"

The crowd was still, all eyes turned toward Avrik. It hurt to look at him, to watch the quick, familiar way he rose and tossed first Iyleth, then all around him his confident grin. Any uncertainty I'd seen in him fell away, his aura of assurance so strong it made me question whether I'd ever seen doubt in his face at all. He grasped his bow and quiver from where they leaned against the bench beside him. I hadn't thought anything of it before, used to his quirk of carrying it everywhere, but now I understood that tonight the action had been deliberate.

As he stood before the people of Toryn, cheers broke out again. He hadn't even begun to shoot or show off his skill, and already the people were warming to him. Because they loved Iyleth, whose admiration was clear. Because Avrik's charm had never been lost on anyone. Because he'd accepted Iyleth's challenge and was willing to partake in Toryn custom, the strongest sign, aside from my earlier choice of mercy, that we were friends, not foes.

Several Toryn scurried out with a target, placing it on the far wall from Avrik. Iyleth, her family, and their guards stepped back to watch Avrik as he slung the quiver over his shoulder and then drew an arrow. Everyone was quiet, leaning forward in anticipation. He released three arrows in quick succession, each one hitting the target's center every time. He had always been talented, but perhaps he had improved since our days of friendly competition in Evren. Who knew how many sedwa he'd killed since then?

The people burst into applause, some standing and shouting their approval. With the same smile that had drawn the admiration of countless

Evren schoolgirls, Avrik bowed playfully to the crowd. I slid from my seat and pushed my way to the tunnel entrance, back toward my room. Narek stood in the shadows, leaning against a wall, and I almost backed away at the sight of him. In the noise and surge of standing and applauding people, I hadn't noticed him leave the table earlier.

I frowned at him. "This is a tradition your own people celebrate, and you are choosing not to watch?"

He pushed off the wall to step closer. With a scoff he waved his hand over my shoulder, toward the Toryn still laughing, gasping, and clapping, their earlier silence broken for their new festive mood. Avrik was clearly still showing off. "I'm as restless with this foolishness as you are. Will we be attending the wedding to unite Misroth and Toryn next?" I flinched. "None of this is saving my people. We will all rot beneath the earth—you and your companions with us—if we continue to linger in this hiding place and do nothing."

I couldn't hold back my smile, his words echoing my own feelings so well. "You are not in agreement with your people. They don't seem to be in a hurry to let us go anywhere."

Narek shrugged. "If they let you out of their sight, you could abandon the alliance and forget them. Captain Luiken and Iyleth will want to take their time building trust and friendship. A wedding would be perfectly suited to their needs. If they don't win you to their side, they can gradually win your companions until they no longer side with you."

"Impossible," I growled.

"Captain Luiken is stubborn."

I studied him thoughtfully as he leaned back against the wall, arms crossed. The red glow that dimly illuminated him matched his Calidan-made clothes. Face once again impassive, he peered into the Common Room from his place in the darkness, watching his people as if they were foreign to him.

"You're an outsider here."

He turned his head at my words, surprise flickering in his eyes before he could conceal it.

Unafraid, I leaned against the wall beside him, turning my eyes back toward the tables of people eating and chattering merrily. Some were standing and clapping; others dancing and swaying to the music that had started up again. Fathers held children on their shoulders. Mothers bounced babies on their laps. To them, this was an opportunity for a better life for their sons and daughters. A chance to renew their kingdom's strength and glory. From this angle, I thankfully couldn't see Avrik and Iyleth.

"It's true," Narek conceded slowly, just when I'd almost forgotten the words I'd spoken to him, too wrapped up in the event occurring just beyond us. "When your father arrived, I was one of Calidar's best swordsmen, having trained in Toryn's most skilled regiment, the Zare'forith." His smile was bitter. "Why do you think your father chose me as his new Captain of the Guard at such a young age? His other guards were fiercely jealous, but they couldn't match me in a fight and didn't dare question your father's choice to his face." He sighed. "But I disappeared from Toryn for years, after all my comrades died, and I served the Misrothian king by my own admission. Even though I've returned now with *you*, heir of Eldon, the Toryn are suspicious. Captain Luiken is building an alliance on his terms and is openly sharing his belief that it is in his people's best interests. But they aren't convinced that my— Misrothian ties—were made only for Toryn's benefit."

I raised my eyebrows. "So they think *we* are friends?"

"I helped save Avrik. I want the same thing you do: to leave Calidar and continue your journey. Captain Luiken placed me in a room under close watch, just like the rest of you, and told me he wanted to see that my allegiance was still with Toryn. Do not mistake that the guards are only there to protect you; they are there to defend the Toryn from *you* as well."

"I know," I said, studying him thoughtfully. Perhaps he was willing to help my companions and me now, but could I trust him more than

Captain Luiken or Iyleth? Would he just as soon slit my friends' throats as save them from the vilspen, if the former proved to be the best option for saving his kingdom?

"If this is a show for Misroth's alliance with Toryn, you should probably rejoin them," Narek continued, nodding toward the Common Room.

I bit my lip, saying nothing and refusing to move. I could still see the way Iyleth smiled when she looked at Avrik, or the way his face lit up when he grinned. My heart ached, even though it had no right to. I'd missed my chance. Avrik and I could exchange a hundred apologies and still I wasn't sure they could undo the damage we had inflicted.

"You know he couldn't exactly refuse," Narek added, as if reading my thoughts. "How could he feel like he had a choice when publicly rejecting Iyleth would look like he was making a mockery of Calidar's favorite daughter? What would that do to the alliance?"

I ignored his words and pushed past him to stride deeper into the tunnel. "They haven't even noticed my absence," I protested, and returned to my room.

CHAPTER SIXTEEN

AFTER THIS, THE DAYS PASSED differently. The Calidan people began to embrace us with an enthusiasm they hadn't possessed before, and Captain Luiken requested that we begin to work alongside them. Even then, he separated my companions and I from each other, clearly still wary of us spending too much time together. Jennah was sent to work in the laundry rooms, Layk was made to help patrol the outer reaches of the Calidan cave with other guards, and I helped in the planting rooms, a fact that lightened my mood considerably. If Avrik was given a task outside of courting Iyleth and preparing for the suitors' competitions, I did not know or ask.

Whenever I saw Narek, whose tasks seemed to alternate between working as a guard and helping in the smithy, he always kept to himself, never speaking much to his people, and his people never much acknowledging his presence either. Some cast him doubtful glances or watched him warily. It seemed that whatever friends or family he once had in Toryn either didn't trust him anymore, had found shelter elsewhere, or were long dead.

Iyleth and Avrik spent increasing amounts of time together, often sitting together at meals and ignoring the dark glances cast their way by other young Toryn men, those I could only assume were Iyleth's other, all but forgotten suitors.

I tried to ignore it all, tried to remind myself that my only concern was for Gillen and the Misrothian people. There was no room for love when all I could focus on was survival.

It almost worked.

I was sitting beside Jennah at dinner in the Common Room one night when Iyleth slipped into the empty space beside me. She offered a warm smile, as if we were old friends, fellow conspirators. "My father will send men with your party to search aboveground two days from now," she announced.

Blinking in surprise, I let out a soft breath of relief at the news.

Iyleth nudged my arm with hers and winked at me. "Maybe we are not so awful after all."

Overhearing our conversation, Jennah turned, her brow arched in a question. "Aboveground?" At her words, Layk and Avrik, seated next to each other, leaned forward to listen. Their gazes were wide-eyed, curious.

"You don't have to go," I said. "It's not—"

Jennah waved my words away. "Don't be absurd, Halia."

Layk gave a short nod. "We're going. We came with you this far; we're not going to hide underground now."

Avrik cracked his knuckles. A light shone in his eyes, easing my heart to see. He looked more like himself than ever, even though we had been trapped within a cave for days and among people who had threatened us with death. He was filled with his old energy and restlessness. Our eyes met briefly and, unbidden, a smile swept across my face until I realized what I was doing. Cheeks heating, I dropped my eyes to my plate, but not before I noticed the half smile he'd given me in response.

"All right." I lifted a crusty roll from my plate, studying it a little too intently. "We will all go aboveground. First thing in the morning, two days from now," I added, glancing at Iyleth.

She nodded. "Our men will be ready," she said. Her eyes flicked to Avrik briefly, offering him a warm smile and mouthing "Good luck." Then she left to eat with her family.

Layk, Jennah, and I cast curious glances Avrik's way, but he shook his head and offered no explanation. I decided she was probably just wishing him well in advance for tomorrow's journey.

I ate with more ease that night, ignoring the frequent glances from a young woman across from me, who watched me with equal amounts of curiosity and distrust. Soon I could leave this underground space, if even for a short while. I could look for Gillen again, even if it was unlikely I would find anything helpful in just one day. It was a step toward convincing the Toryn to help me more.

As we ended our dinner, Captain Luiken, Iyleth, and Haed approached the open space along the far wall. Three chairs awaited them there. Several men laid out various swords before them. While Iyleth and Haed sat, Captain Luiken stood and lifted his voice for his people to hear.

"Good men and women of Calidar," he said, "tonight we witness the first round of competition amongst Iyleth's suitors: Devron, Jabek, Torrilev, and Avrik!"

Applause followed his statement. The Toryn around me set down their silverware and leaned forward in anticipation. I folded my hands in my lap and avoided looking over at Avrik.

"Tonight, in the first competition, we will watch her suitors display one of our most basic and necessary skills: ability in combat. Each will face another in swordplay, fighting until one is defeated. This is *not* a fight to injure one another, but a friendly match. When one suitor is victorious over his opponent, he will face another, until only one suitor remains and is declared the winner of this first round."

More cheers and applause echoed Captain Luiken's words as he stepped back and seated himself beside Haed.

Tonight, there were no musicians.

"First," Iyleth cried, rising from her seat, "we welcome Devron and

Avrik to take their places before us and begin their first match! May the gods bless each of your efforts, and may the most suitable man win tonight!" She reseated herself, smoothing the folds of her green and violet dress. Arrayed in her kingdom's colors, she was a sight to behold, a beloved daughter that countless men hoped to win.

I studied her curiously. Once I had thought nothing of being betrothed one day to a man of my parents' choosing for my kingdom's welfare. I had neither anticipated or dreaded it. It simply was customary, my expected future. Amongst Misrothian nobility, love was often a matter of convenience and advantage, of securing alliances and furthering family prosperity and glory. Here, love was a game.

Now I couldn't imagine an arranged marriage with anything but dread. Was Iyleth content with the thought that her favorite suitor might not win?

Avrik stood from the table and stepped forward, confidently choosing a weapon from the selection laid before him. He walked out into the middle of the open space reserved for the match, idly swinging his sword in the air. As he waited, another man stood from a bench. Broad shoulders pulled back, Devron strode with the lazy assurance of someone accustomed to victory. He didn't smile, his mouth a firm line and his dark eyes focused and intent. He plucked a sword from the ground and squared off in front of Avrik.

Devron stared at his opponent as if measuring him with his eyes. Muscles rippled along his arms as he grasped his sword hilt. Avrik smirked.

"Let the first match begin!" Captain Luiken called.

Immediately Devron barreled into Avrik with a series of vicious strikes. His size made Avrik look small beside him, but Avrik didn't shrink away. He met each heavy strike from Devron with grace and precision, moving with confidence and speed. Whenever Devron swung, Avrik was prepared, already moving to evade or parry and counter with an attack of his own.

It was clear Devron thought his size would overwhelm his opponent, that he'd underestimated Avrik's abilities. But even I could predict each move Devron made before he struck; I could see the way his body tensed, the way his eyes darted about and then hesitated a little too long on whichever portion of Avrik's body he attempted to strike next. Avrik was quick, never faltering, never stumbling or losing ground when Devron unleashed a full-fledged assault. He waited patiently for Devron's weaknesses to show and then used them against him.

Devron eyed Avrik's legs, and before he could swing low, Avrik leapt into the air and slashed downward. Steel on steel clanged together and Devron's arm shuddered a little from the blow. He blinked and staggered back, but Avrik was already chasing him. He swiped his leg behind Devron and dug his heel into the back of his knee. Devron crumpled but didn't fall. He swung his fist wildly at Avrik's face, but Avrik had already ducked and kneed Devron in the crotch. With a groan, Avrik's opponent fell to his knees. Avrik easily knocked the blade from his hand and caught it. Both swords held aloft, he spun toward Captain Luiken and his children with a grin.

The people burst into applause.

As Devron slunk away in embarrassment and Iyleth stepped forward to announce the next match, Layk leaned toward me, eyebrow raised. "How did an Evren hunter learn so much about swordplay?" he murmured.

I laughed lightly. "Avrik spent all his free time reading every book about swords and combat his father would allow him to have. His father traveled around Misroth and acquired many things from all over the kingdom..." My voice wavered a little. "He and I would practice for hours. Hadn't you wondered where I'd learned to use a sword?"

Layk smiled. "This skeptic..." –he grinned and corrected himself– "...*former* skeptic—watched you miraculously survive your own execution, thanks to the Life-Giver. You've always been shrouded in a bit of mystery, princess."

The succeeding matches were somewhat like the first. Although the Toryn were survivors and took their fighting skills seriously, most of the young men living within Calidar had never been tested in a real fight. Besides, they all had many other daily tasks to help keep their community alive. I could tell none of them had spent as much time practicing as Avrik had, and none had his training, even if mostly from books, or his instincts acquired from hunting—his quick eyes, taking in all his surroundings and easily predicting his opponents' next moves, his light feet, or his calm, confident focus. They were desperate to win, maybe too desperate. Avrik was relaxed, smiling and enjoying every minute. To him this truly was just a game.

When Iyleth left her seat to stand beside him, beaming and applauding with her people, I had to look away. It wasn't in Avrik's nature to let someone beat him in a competition, but I couldn't help wishing he'd let himself lose. He could have feigned incompetence. Stumbled through the matches. Pushed himself out of the competition as one of Iyleth's suitors.

At my side, Jennah squeezed my arm, and it only troubled me more that she recognized my discomfort. Layk noticed the gesture but looked away without a word. I could feel Narek's gaze boring into me from across the table. It seemed everyone but Avrik knew how I felt.

"Avrik leads our competition!" Captain Luiken announced, and in that moment, it was impossible to tell if he was pleased with the results or not. "Next is Jabek, then Torrilev, and Devron is last in our rankings." He gestured to the three young men standing beside him, away from Avrik and Iyleth.

Two more days and I can look for Gillen and put this frivolity behind me, I thought. *Two more days...*

Another long day passed in which I helped in the planting rooms. In the afternoon Jennah and I found some rare free time to spend together, so we slipped off to the library where she continued to help me learn Alrenian. At last, we went to the Common Room for dinner, where I answered countless questions about Misroth from a curious girl and boy, to the slight discomfort of their parents.

Near the end of the meal, as the Toryn again began to gather on the other side of the Common Room with instruments and dancing, Iyleth came toward me and pressed a hand to my arm. I'd already risen from my seat, hoping to slip away to my room. "Stay," she urged. "Show my people that you can be one of us and they'll warm to you even more."

I weighed the wisdom of her words and nodded. Turning in my seat, I watched as the Toryn musicians warmed up their instruments and then plunged into a sweet, vigorous tune, its notes pulsating off the rocks around us and spinning images in my mind of wild open plains and warm sunshine and flowers. The Toryn formed a circle and began their dance, twisting and turning about one another in a complicated pattern I could scarcely follow, but one that was breathtakingly beautiful in its rhythm and graceful movement. Women's long tunics and skirts swished about their ankles, and everyone's colorful attire shifted in countless different and dazzling hues.

With a soft laugh, Iyleth leapt to her feet and pulled Avrik into the circle, gently coaxing him until even his awkward, uncoordinated motions looked almost elegant. Her laughter was contagious, spurring Avrik to laugh and talk freely, his eyes glittering with their old light as he watched her. Daggers scraped across my heart and I looked away. Even Layk and Jennah had joined the dance now, imitating those around them as best they could. Jennah had a natural grace, falling easily into the rhythm as if she had known the notes and motions all her life, and even reserved, cautious Layk surprised me with how quickly he took to the dance. My friends had a carefree air about them I hadn't seen in a long time.

"Not one for dancing?"

I hadn't seen Narek amongst the crowd at the meal, but the quiet way he approached me and slid onto the bench didn't startle me, not anymore. His voice was smooth and level, his movements more lighthearted than I'd ever seen. When I turned to search his face, I even noted a glint in his eyes as he listened to the music.

"I take it you aren't either," I said pointedly.

His eyes slid to where Avrik and Iyleth danced and then back to me, and a look of understanding passed across his features. "You should dance, princess." His dark gaze was intense, drawing me in even when I did not want it to. But I understood his meaning, and as he rose and offered me his hand, I didn't refuse. I slid my hand into his calloused one, heart thudding while he pulled me toward the dance.

He was surprisingly gentle, his motions as fluid and easy as his fighting style. When he twisted me around, I lost myself to the rush of movement and the beat of the music, closing my eyes and savoring even this brief instant when my cares could fall away. And when he drew me closer to him, hints of blue and green from the cavern's glow flashing in the depths of his eyes, I didn't pull away. Instead, I longed to know Narek's secrets, to learn what motivated him and just what sort of threat he posed for my friends and me, if any. I recalled my vision as easily as if it were a memory, how he had once been a young boy as desperate for survival as I was. We weren't that different after all, our souls laden with the same ache of loss, our hearts bursting with the same longing to save what remained of all we loved.

"Iyleth has spent much time talking to me, at first because she was fascinated with the Zare'forith," Narek said in a low voice, keeping me close. "But lately it's been about the alliance."

I looked up sharply.

"She values my insight, someone who's lived in both kingdoms and, at least in her opinion, has ties to both."

I didn't like his smile.

"And?" I prompted.

"I think she's sincere about wanting the best for both kingdoms. Or at least she thinks she is." He glanced over at where Avrik and Iyleth were dancing together.

I wondered if Avrik would be angry at the sight of Narek and me dancing together, but I resisted the urge to look at him. Besides, he might never notice us, enraptured as he seemed with Iyleth. Even if he did, would it be jealousy that fueled his fury or simply fear for my safety due to his loyalty to his kingdom, and perhaps a lingering sense of loyalty to me, his old friend? Surely he didn't feel the same emotions that churned in my own heart, always tugging against my feelings of anger and betrayal.

My own emotions made the thought slide into place, and I smiled slowly, watching Narek carefully. "You wanted this distraction too," I said, "because you also wish Iyleth had chosen a different partner." I shot him a pointed look.

"No," he said quickly, but I allowed myself a self-satisfied smile, sure I'd found a chink in Narek's armor at last.

He seemed to be weighing his words. "After tomorrow," he continued. "What do you plan to do then? After sending men to go aboveground with you, the Toryn will likely expect something from you in return."

"Including you," I said. "You want the barrier broken as much as they do."

He didn't respond to my accusation. Instead, he asked, "What do you think they will do if you find Gillen?"

"You said Iyleth might be on my side."

"And she does have great influence over her father, but so does Haed. Besides, imagine the temptation for Captain Luiken, maybe even for Iyleth, if someone from Toryn found Gillen before you. Would the Toryn tell you? Or…" He let the thought drift away unfinished, letting my imagination fill in all the terrible possibilities.

It had been Narek who'd asked me when we'd first come to Calidar if I'd choose Gillen over my kingdom. Would the Toryn ever try to use Gillen to force me to break the barrier?

Fear clutched my chest as the song ended, its notes lingering as they reverberated throughout the room and at last faded into a whisper. Narek pulled away and I stood still, catching my breath. Our eyes locked. "Why are you telling me this?" I whispered. "Are you helping me or threatening me?"

Narek's face was, as usual, inscrutable. "I'm sharing with you how the Toryn are thinking right now, from the little insight I have. I'll let you decide my motivation."

I stepped back, realizing I was dangerously close to trusting a man who had long been my enemy. *He is probably using the same tactic as Iyleth and trying to build your trust*, I thought bitterly. I shook my head and broke my gaze with Narek. "Don't think this makes me trust you."

A mirthless smile twisted his lips. "I didn't expect it to."

Not wanting to pretend to enjoy the festivities any longer, I left the Common Room soon afterward. Besides, I had other thoughts to concentrate on. My entire being felt alive and alert at the thought of the next morning, terrified of what it may bring yet hopeful that it would at least lead to clues regarding Gillen's whereabouts. I clutched his pendant in my fist, sent up a fierce prayer for his safety, and wondered for the thousandth time what the Life-Giver expected me to do to control my gift and save my cousin.

We gathered after the morning meal in Captain Luiken's council room: Jennah, Layk, and I all in our Misrothian tunics; Avrik in an outfit given to him by the Calidans; and Haed, Narek, and another man named Emrod clothed in attire bearing the Toryn insignia. There we were outfitted with Toryn leather armor, which was sturdy, lightweight, and surprisingly comfortable.

Iyleth was there too, seemingly to bid us farewell. She nodded to me first, her smile reassuring as she uttered a Toryn blessing over me. "May the gods walk beside you."

I offered a tight-lipped smile in response.

Then she turned to Avrik, face beaming, and my heart hardened further. She reached out to clasp his hand and he didn't pull away, didn't waver. "I will look for your return," she murmured.

Captain Luiken surveyed us all carefully for several moments before directing us to the map sprawled across his table.

"You will return before nightfall," he commanded, and then indicated the river snaking a path across the length of the Toryn kingdom. "Your safest route would be along the Elhalin, but that is also the route least likely to bring you to your cousin. If he is still alive, one of the only other places outside of Calidar that he could seek refuge would be within Haemil, which has also become an underground city. But it is located far too near to the Wasteland border for me to sanction a journey there. Not without any evidence that journey is worth the risk." He gave me a pointed look. "If you find any evidence suggesting your cousin has traveled to Haemil on this excursion, then we can prepare to send men in that direction. For now, you scout the area near Calidar and that is all. Haed, Narek, and Emrod will provide protection and ensure you return to us safely."

Pressing my lips into a firm line, I nodded my understanding. Calidar was our only haven for miles, making any escape attempt by my friends and me a foolish idea, yet it was clear Captain Luiken was not taking any risks. The Toryn could sense my desperation to find my cousin, and the men accompanying us were as much for our protection as they were to watch us and prevent us from leaving Calidar and their hopes for an alliance.

A day seemed like hardly enough time to help me find Gillen at all, but I would take what I could. Anything was better that wasting another day confined to the underground. Grasping his pendant once more, I followed Haed toward the cave's entrance.

We filed into the first of many tunnels gradually winding their way toward the surface. My heart pounded with anticipation. I couldn't give up the hope I'd clung to for so long. Jennah stayed by my side, reaching out more than once to squeeze my arm or shoot me an encouraging glance. Her gaze buoyed my soul and strengthened my steps.

At last we were at the docks again, filing into two canoes and rowing toward the cavern's exit. Daylight sparkled along the water and then blazed in our eyes as we emerged into the open world. The smell of earth and damp gave way to a fresh breeze carrying the scent of grass and wind and sunshine. I inhaled deeply and studied the sky as if I hadn't seen it in years. It was brilliant blue and cloudless, looking vaster and more beautiful than I'd remembered it.

Seated ahead in the canoe, leaning on his oars, Haed met my gaze. His eyes were alert and wary; his muscles taut and ready for anything. Wind rippled through his hair and for the first time in the daylight I was able to see the traces of brown within its deep black tones. "You have one day," he reminded me.

We disembarked on the opposite side of the Elhalin and at my request, made the long, weary trudge toward the underground tunnels leading toward Delgoth.

"Venturing into Delgoth is extremely dangerous," Haed said gruffly. "The nestrae are always prowling…"

I cut him off impatiently. "I know. But that is where I found Gillen's pendant, so that is the best place to start searching."

We'd been in the tunnels for a couple weary hours when we stopped at the stream I remembered from our retreat from Delgoth. After taking long swigs of water and washing our grimy faces, Layk turned to Haed.

"How have the nestrae not found your cave beneath Calidar if they already know about these tunnels?"

Haed grinned slowly. "They hate water, which means that although they are probably searching for more tunnels around Calidar, they haven't yet ventured much through the Elhalin." His face grew grim. "But every excursion comes with the risk of revealing ourselves. If we are seen or attacked in Delgoth, we can*not* let them see us return to Calidar."

"Tell us what we don't already know," Avrik muttered under his breath.

When we finally exited the tunnel, pulling ourselves up into the courtyard where the nestrae had attacked my friends and me, we found the city eerie and still. The afternoon sun was already high in the sky, so I knew our time was short. Daggers in hand, Jennah stood close to me while the men spread out, scanning every direction for enemies, before deeming it safe to continue. I asked Narek to retrace our steps from our first night in Delgoth, and we walked for a while in silence.

Focus, Halia, I thought as Narek led us through the empty streets. Could I conjure a vision at will? I let my mind wander back across the years to when I'd lived at the castle with Gillen, spending days studying with my tutor or playing with my cousin, taking occasional etiquette lessons from my mother or earning criticism from my father. Most days, my uncle and aunt had offered me more warmth and affection than my own parents, welcoming me into their private family gatherings. How I'd longed for my father's approval and love… Unbidden, my fingers strayed to my armband, caressing its familiar markings.

I cringed, trying to swipe away the memories and bring back thoughts of Gillen, but it was already too late. The bright world around me vanished and a new sight took its place. I was child again, back at the castle, before my life had changed forever. Immediately I recognized this moment: the night the nobles of the capital had approached us at court to offer both their condolences and their blessings on the eve of my uncle's funeral and my father's coronation.

Seated at my vanity, staring into my mirror, I waited for the maid to finish combing my hair when a knock sounded at the door. My heart jolted as two servants answered. The door swung inward to reveal my mother's silhouette in the entryway, standing still and proud in a flowing lavender gown. Her dark hair was half plaited on her head, half spilling down her back in a long curtain. In the dim mixture of candlelight and moonlight bathing my chambers, her eyes shone like emeralds. My throat felt swollen, a familiar longing taking hold that I'd learned long ago to mask. I knew better than to expect warmth and affection from my parents.

Mother strode in, dismissing the servants with a graceful wave of her hand. She stopped behind me, our eyes meeting in the mirror. An emotion fluttered across her stoic features and disappeared. Wordlessly, she lifted the comb from the vanity where the maid had left it and began running it through my waves of hair. She worked smoothly and efficiently in the heavy silence that enveloped us, until my hair was glossy beneath the light and she had pulled it up into a tidy knot. Then she laid a cool hand on my shoulder.

"I know tonight will not be easy for you. Grief lies heavily on us all, but…" She hesitated. "There is strength within you, just like it is within your father."

Surprised yet pleased at the comparison, I tried to meet her gaze in the mirror once more, but her eyes were downcast. Her face was pale and drawn with weariness; her shoulders slumped. It was the most vulnerable I had seen her in as long as I could remember. She drew a deep breath.

"I know it is difficult to believe in your own courage or fortitude when everything inside of you feels weak and shattered. But do not believe what you feel. You will not be easily broken."

The vision ended abruptly, melting away to Delgoth's ruins and leaving me aching and breathless.

"Did you see anything?" Jennah asked from my side, her eyes wide with wonder and hope. She kept her voice low so Haed and Emrod, walking at the rear of our party, could not overhear.

I shook my head and impatiently brushed strands of hair away from my face. "Nothing useful." To my dismay, my voice came out low and hoarse.

"You could try again."

I commanded my heart to stop pounding. "Yes," I said. "I can try again."

Again, I struggled to focus my thoughts on Gillen. *I need a vision that helps me find him,* I pleaded with the Life-Giver. *Something, anything...*

What if he is already dead, his body burnt like Gare's, like my uncle's, like my mother's...

"Iyg kurik vouren..." I couldn't tell if the whispers were memories echoing in my head or the beginning of another vision. Or were they here, in the real world? I opened my mouth to ask Jennah...

Another vision pulled me under. Flames flashed across Gillen's pallid face and burned in his eyes, lending him a look of life where otherwise he had none. The Misrothian flag snapped in the cool autumn breeze and men and women alike openly wept, lifting their faces to the sky or offering their fallen king, stretched across the pyre before them, their final salutes. I reached out to grasp Gillen's cold hand and squeezed his fingers, even if my own trembled. My father shot a sidelong glance at me, a silent reminder to resist the urge to cry, and I clenched my jaw. The pain was unending, but it also felt unreal and distant, like some other Halia was standing at the edge of the sea bidding farewell to her beloved uncle and trying to comfort her cousin. Like someone else was about to watch her father's coronation.

Then the vision changed. Snippets of fireside conversations with my uncle darted in rapid succession through my mind: his laughing face, the familiar crinkles by his twinkling eyes, and his low, soothing voice as he told stories or encouraged me after a troublesome day of lessons. There was my mother again, holding me close and singing old Alrenian lullabies in my ear when I was just a child and frightened by the crashing, stormy sea outside the castle. My past in Misroth City faded and gave way to memories of Lyanna and Rev. I listened to them share about their days or converse about the Life-Giver and our time spent in the garden that week. Weak and frightened, I lay in bed while Lyanna read aloud. I heard Rev introduce me as his daughter for the first time.

Pain lanced through my chest, but the visions did not stop. They flitted faster and faster, spiraling my emotions into a torrent until my head throbbed. I was with Avrik again as he held me close; I was standing beside Gare as he set a reassuring hand on my shoulder; I was racing with Gillen through the castle halls and darting around servants just before we collided into them.

Stop, stop! I pleaded. I couldn't bear the constant reminders of everything I'd lost, everything my fight for my kingdom had taken from me.

The visions slowed at last, melting into overwhelming darkness. Cold air ruffled through my clothes and snaked down my back. Overhead, the stars were cold and far away, many shrouded by wispy grey clouds. Whispers rent the air: "*Iyg kurik vouren…*" Gillen pressed himself against a building, clammy hand clutching his sword hilt while his lips moved in a silent prayer.

Life-Giver… I began, as if I could cry out for Gillen's safety across time and distance.

Flames burst against the night and shadowy, smoke-wreathed forms emerged from the ruins surrounding my cousin. They marched slowly, confidently, scraping steel against steel and pounding their heavy boots against cobblestones to instill blinding terror. Their tactics were efficient. Brutal.

The nestrae launched themselves at Gillen and he disappeared amongst them, consumed by fire and smoke.

CHAPTER SEVENTEEN

I JERKED MY EYES OPEN with a violent shudder, my body numb.
"What is it?" Jennah's voice was frantic, her brow drawn with
concern.

"I…nothing." It was disorienting to return to the real world after
such a powerful series of visions had consumed me, and it took me a
second to understand only moments had passed.

Jennah was scanning the buildings surrounding us and I realized both
of her daggers were at the ready, as if she were expecting a foe to charge
us at any moment. Every one of our companions was doing the same:
Layk and Avrik with arrows strung to their bows, while the Toryn men
had their blades out. They all gazed in different directions, searching
frantically.

A chill settled in my bones. "Did you…*hear* something?"

Jennah's lips were a thin line, the closest I'd ever seen her to looking
afraid. "We need to get out of here."

The sun was already low on the western horizon as we turned and
raced back toward the courtyard, every sense alert. But despite our fear,
we made it back to the tunnel without sight or sound of the nestrae.

I couldn't decide if I felt safer in the tunnels or not. They were dim
and cramped, with nothing but the light of torches Haed and Emrod held
aloft to guide us. Haed took the lead while Emrod continued to prowl in

the back, always watching us like he expected my companions and me to bolt at any second.

"We should never have come here," Haed growled. He threw me a look over his shoulder, so I could see the venom in his eyes.

It was a long, tense journey back through the tunnels. We stole like thieves back into the Toryn countryside, looking everywhere for signs of the nestrae. By the time we reached the Elhalin, the distant cry of an ichgor sounded in our ears.

But Haed, Emrod, and Narek were already shoving canoes into the river, waving at my friends and I to board quickly.

Narek caught my eye and nodded once, as if to say, *We will make it back before it finds us.*

I refused to look at Haed as we climbed into our canoes and began to row across the Elhalin.

My fear was already melting into concern for Gillen, and I found it hard to concentrate on any of the whispered words that passed between my companions as we rowed back. Our return to the depths of Calidar was a blur of dank, narrow tunnels, echoing footsteps, and flickering torchlight. We entered the Common Room as the Calidan were gathering about the tables and preparing for the evening meal, but before anyone could stop me or insist I sit and eat, I shouldered my way past our group, through the crowd, and to my room.

It wasn't until I'd sat on the hard bed that I let myself truly consider my latest vision about Gillen. It had looked like he'd been overwhelmed by the nestrae and their fire. It didn't seem possible for him to survive what I'd seen.

Have the nestrae already killed Gi?

The strength I'd drawn upon at my father's bidding for years felt like it was crumbling. My world lurched and shrank away.

Gil can't be dead.

Numb, empty, I collapsed back onto the cot. I scarcely registered anything, scarcely even breathed.

"This is not a day I feel strong." My last memory of him was vivid, relived countless times when I'd ached for his company and prayed for his safety. Despite the starkness of his grief, he'd still looked so vibrant, so *alive*.

He can't be dead. Pain throbbed through me and fell away into disbelief.

Four years of clinging to the final thread of my past, to my first friend and one of the last remaining members of my family, four years of hope…they could not end like this. I'd faced impossible odds and tasted death itself to claim victory over my father. How could he win now, even in death? *He cannot have Gil.* I wanted to scream the words in rage, but my throat already felt raw. I reached up and felt tears trailing down my cheeks. And that was when I realized I was already weeping, already letting weakness overtake me.

There was a soft knock echoing off the wall outside my room. I swiped at the tears streaking my face. It would be Iyleth pestering me with her attempts to build trust and friendship between us, or Captain Luiken and Haed demanding a recount of the day's occurrences, perhaps prepared to accuse me of putting the entire underground city in jeopardy with my trip to Delgoth. Or perhaps Narek, who could finally insist that he'd already named me Queen of Misroth. I wanted to tell whoever it was to leave me in peace, but I didn't have the breath. I cast my eyes downward, letting my hair fall across my face and hoping it would hide my distress as someone pushed my curtain aside.

"Halia?" His voice was gentle, a memory of warmer, friendlier times.

I jerked my head up in surprise and my hair fell back. Avrik blinked at the clear signs of grief marring my face and stepped near. He smelled of wind and grass from aboveground and his hair was still disheveled from our excursion. His bow and quiver were strapped to his back and his hands were covered in his worn leather shooting gloves. All comforting, familiar sights.

"I know I said I'd stay away, I know I shouldn't have come and Iyleth would wonder and it could hurt the alliance," he rambled, his cheeks warming. It was strange to see confident Avrik so unsure. "But I saw the pain on your face. I know you had some sort of vision when we were in Delgoth and you wouldn't tell anyone. No one else would know and I couldn't let you sit here alone in pain when, when once we were…"

In an instant he was seated beside me on the bed, his arms enveloping me in a warm embrace. It felt natural to press my face against his neck and breathe deeply, inhaling the smell of leather from his jacket as it mingled with the fragrance of the outdoors, scents that sharpened the memories of our time in Evren. For a little while I was Elena again, mute and lonely, but Avrik's best friend. No matter what the past had done to us or the future held before us, we had each other. My heartbeat steadied, and my breathing fell into an even rhythm. The tears dried on my cheeks and on his jacket, but he didn't seem to mind. He held me like we were trusted companions again, like we were friends again, like we were far more than that and the hundreds of unspoken words between us had all been said long ago, tying us together for the remainder of our lives. He held me like the rest of the world had fallen away and time had stopped, like all our hurts and fears had been eased and nothing could harm us ever again.

I could feel his warm breath on my neck as he reached up and gently brushed his fingers through my hair, an old gesture from months gone by. My heart ached and I willed this embrace to never end, keeping us in a place where, no matter the attentions he received from the other Evren girls, he spurned them all for me. When his touch against my cheek had whispered possibilities for a future. Hope pulsed in my chest: surely he felt what I felt; surely his heart pounded the same way mine did.

Never let go, I thought, echoing my silent plea from our flight through Delgoth, but the moment couldn't last forever. My shock and grief were too fresh and powerful to be ignored, and I wasn't Elena. We were a bereaved princess and an angry, grieving son, trapped underground with people who were more our enemies than our allies. Our pain was still real. There was still a barrier of uncertainty and hurt between us, and the future

I'd once dared to dream of seemed like it belonged to another world, to another girl. To Elena. Never Halia.

Avrik pulled away and I glanced down, suddenly uncomfortable again in his presence.

"You saw Gillen in your vision," he murmured, "but it was worse than the others." It wasn't a question. I dared to lift my eyes to meet his warm brown ones, steadily watching me with the most sympathetic expression I'd seen on his face in a long while.

Gulping, I struggled for words. In my mind's eye, I could still see the flames bursting around Gillen's form. "I—I saw Gillen die." My voice sounded hoarse, and I hated it.

Avrik furrowed his brows and reached for my hand, curling his warm fingers about my cold ones. "Are your visions really *always* true?"

I knew he was scrabbling for hope: the old, optimistic Avrik was back, unwilling to accept despair. Blinking my stinging eyes, I nodded.

"Maybe there was some mistake…something…" Avrik's words trailed off as he realized his attempts at reassurance were empty.

"My visions have always given me the truth," I whispered. I dropped my head, a cold sensation filling my being. My numb disbelief threatened to fall into despair.

When I looked up, pain and helplessness had leaked into Avrik's eyes. "I'm so sorry."

I glanced away. There was nothing to say, nothing to do.

"Do you need anything?" Avrik asked after another long moment.

Shaking my head, I struggled to speak. "Just…to be alone."

He nodded, stiffening suddenly as if remembering himself. Remembering his pledge to remain distant from me and his acceptance of Iyleth's offer of courtship. He stood and watched me awkwardly. "I know I said we couldn't even be friends anymore. But…" He shrugged, at a loss for words. Regret and sorrow softened his eyes. "I wish the alliance didn't depend so much on Iyleth's favor," he blurted out. "Forgive me." And with that, before I could even think of how to respond, he pressed his fist to his heart and slipped away as swiftly and quietly as he'd arrived.

In my memory, my mother had called me strong. *You will not be easily broken.* That was a lie. Here I was, with grief shredding open my chest, shattered into countless pieces. Everything I'd clung to for so long had slipped through my fingers, and the cousin who had once been my best friend, my constant companion, was gone forever. Never would I be able to ask for his forgiveness for leaving him four years ago. For hiding rather than facing my father and ending his tyranny sooner.

I'd returned to save Gillen…four years too late. His death was at my father's hands, but it could just as easily have been at mine. He was dead because of me.

I fell back against my bed, curling my legs against my chest, pressing my eyes shut tightly against the harsh world around me, and willed everything to fade away.

It could have been minutes or hours or even days later when I heard another knock outside my entryway, this one sounding harsher, insistent. Before I could even gather my words to respond, Haed forced himself into the room. My heart jolted in response and I sat up quickly, straightening my back into a rigid line and folding my hands in my lap. I settled myself into a composed attitude, though I couldn't mask the animosity flaring up inside me.

"What happened up there?" he demanded. His eyes spat fire.

"What do you mean?"

Haed stalked toward my bed, looming over it like a menacing shadow. His face twisted into a sneer. "Did you not hear the nestrae?" A vein pulsed in his forehead. "You risked my men—and the safety of my entire city—on your foolish hopes."

I shot him a cool glance. "Your father agreed to this alliance."

"We've already given you enough," he snarled. "How can we build an alliance if you only take from us? *When will you bring down that barrier?*"

I kept my mouth in a firm line. "How can we build an alliance if you're so untrusting?"

Iyleth barged into the room, her eyes narrowed into thin slits. "Haed," she said, her voice a low threat. "I could hear you outside! If you dare to threaten or intimidate our *guest* again I will call for guards to escort you away."

Haed stiffened, his demeanor shifting from fury to frustration. "Iyleth, I have not—" he began, but she waved him away.

"Leave," she ordered. When he hesitated, she lifted her chin and stood to her full height, still at least a half foot shorter than him, and yet no less fearsome in that moment. "Now."

Muttering, Haed shuffled toward the entrance, casting one last spiteful look over his shoulder at me before he vanished.

"I'm sorry about my brother's short temper," Iyleth said. Her tone was soft again, her face warm and inviting. I wondered how the same person could manage to be so imposing and so inviting all within the space of a few minutes. She tossed her long, dark hair over her shoulder. "He doesn't always think his actions through. He's passionate about wanting to help our people, to save our land. When we lost our mother a few years ago, he became…angry…bitter." Her brows pinched together. "I will not let him trouble you again."

My throat felt raw. "Thank you," I murmured.

"Will you join us for dinner?"

Feebly, I shook my head. "I don't feel well," I said, grateful that my gift only prevented me from lying, and not from withholding the truth.

Iyleth quirked an eyebrow at me, studying my face for a moment, but she let the question fade from her gaze and nodded instead. "I'll leave you alone, then. Let us know if you need anything." She turned to leave. "Our healers are quite skilled," she added with one last look over her shoulder.

And she left me to my grief.

The night passed in a miserable haze, a strange mixture of sleeplessness and forgetfulness as I somehow dozed off and on through the hours, sometimes tossing, sometimes sinking into sleep, sometimes staring into nothingness, and sometimes pacing the floor. Grieving for Gillen was far different from grieving for my mother, whom I'd begun to mourn four years ago, years before she'd died. The pain was even fiercer and more poignant than I'd thought it could be, because I was not only devastated from the loss of my cousin but also from the loss of the hope and purpose that had driven me to cross Toryn's nightmarish countryside.

When I woke in the morning, the gaping hole within me threatened to crush me, to throw me back into the oblivion that had claimed me the night before. It was like a knife digging deep, giving me a new wound for each memory of Gillen that flickered through my mind.

But I drove myself from my bed and began to dress. I held the tears at bay as I secured my armband over my sleeve. There was a heaviness over my limbs, but I kept my head held high and squelched my grief. *The Toryn will not know Gil may be dead. I will not give them any advantages to hold over me in their supposed alliance attempts,* I resolved.

I joined Avrik, Jennah, Layk, and Narek in the Common Room and forced some mushy porridge down my throat, bite after bite, until every fragment was cleaned from my plate. No matter what had or hadn't happened to Gillen, I would need every ounce of my strength in this land.

"Feeling better, I see." Iyleth's voice was warm and breezy, as always, though there was a hint of something in her undertone—suspicion? annoyance?—that could have been my imagination, or perhaps not. Either way, it set me on edge. But when I looked up into her eyes, they were friendly as ever, reflecting the violet and gold glow of vines hanging above her.

"Yes," I said.

She slipped onto the bench beside me. "I understand not finding signs of your cousin and having no idea where to look must be discouraging," she said. She laid a hand on my shoulder and I blinked at her, for the first time taken by surprise at her attempts toward friendship. Leaning closer, she lowered her voice to a whisper. "Don't lose hope."

My mother's old words darted through my brain again: *You will not be so easily broken.*

Drawing a deep breath, I sat up straighter and shot Iyleth a grin. "Thank you." Comforted, she smiled back at me and then turned to engage Avrik in conversation. Their light tones and her musical laughter dropped away as my world narrowed to one thought, one obsession: I had not yet seen Gillen's body. No matter what my visions had shown, no matter how dark circumstances seemed, I would be stubborn. Maybe there had been some sort of mistake in my vision. In my heart, I couldn't give into despair yet. My visions hadn't stopped me from hoping before, and without hope, there was nothing.

I will keep searching, and I will find him, whether he is alive or dead. I clutched the pendants that hung against my chest, letting their cold surfaces offer me the barest of comfort.

I won't lose hope. I won't be broken.

CHAPTER EIGHTEEN

I FOUND THAT WRESTLING WITH grief made time move differently. Days and nights melted into one another as I tried to hold sorrow at bay with my decision to hope. Iyleth's words rang in my ears every morning as I pulled myself from bed and dressed, and I reminded myself if these people, robbed of nearly everything they loved, could find hope and manage to survive within this broken land, then I could too. Each day I set aside time to wander the fields where the grated ceiling offered glimpses of the sky. When the space cleared of people at night, I would gaze up at the stars, praying to the Life-Giver and attempting to force my visions to come and offer me more information. But my emotions and thoughts were a vicious tangle, and the few times a vision did come, it was a scrap of an old memory from times long past or people I'd lost.

I ached to venture out again, to leave the suffocating cavern behind and continue my search for Gillen, but I knew Captain Luiken and Haed would never agree to send out more of their men so soon. Though it was necessary for the Toryn to travel beyond Calidar's tunnels occasionally for supplies, they never undertook a journey lightly. Each was carefully planned and taken only when it was deemed of utmost importance.

"It's not simply the risk to my men who leave," Captain Luiken almost growled at me when I'd cornered him at an evening meal in the

Common Room to ask about another expedition, "but the fact that they could give away the location of our underground city if we are constantly traveling in and out."

Silently, I nodded and backed away. Impatience prodded my every step, every day, yet I knew if I insisted too fiercely, Captain Luiken and Haed might refuse me altogether and my friends and I could become their prisoners. Already I could see that Haed's suspicion that I would never cooperate with their terms for alliance had strengthened Captain Luiken's. At every Common Room gathering, he watched me carefully, as if continuously weighing my value as an ally versus a prisoner.

Aboveground, the month of Mareth arrived, ushering in the start of spring and one of the biggest celebrations in Misroth: the Feast of Peace, the day Eldon's war against the Alrenian Empire ended and Misroth finally untethered itself from Alrenor's rule. It was hard not to long for home as the holiday approached. I knew the capital streets would be decorated with countless colorful ribbons and banners. Everyone would wear their best attire, filling the streets and courtyards with food, music, dancing, and cheer. My aunt would officiate the royal ceremony for the court, wreathed in her finest silks and a gauzy veil, and someone would stand before the crowd and sing the history of Misroth's fight for freedom.

When I was a child at court with Gillen, we had managed on that day alone to make even the impassive guards stationed about the castle burst into grins with our antics. Everyone was cheerful on the feast day, even my father, who would drink Brev wines with the noblemen and councilmen as if he didn't have a care in the world.

More than the celebrations in Misroth City though, I longed for the quieter gatherings in Evren. Selna would be bustling about Wanderer's Rest, calling out to her husband in the kitchen to hurry as she darted to and fro with plates for her guests. Her tables would be pushed to the far walls to make room for dancing and music. But, if the weather permitted, the largest celebrations would take place outside, where the town gathered to sing and dance and take turns sharing stories of our history. Avrik and I would sit with Bren and Shilam and Jaren, talking and eating and partaking in some of the games. Occasionally the boys would ask me or another girl to dance. Often, we prodded Avrik into dancing and sat back to laugh at his clumsy attempts.

But Toryn did not celebrate the Misrothian holiday. Instead, Iyleth came to my room that morning chattering about a different sort of event, Thyrenna. It gave the Toryn the opportunity to thank Thyred, god of provisions, for the beginning of a new planting season and to seek his generosity for the future harvest. "Tonight we'll dress in our finest and sing to the gods for favor and to celebrate all they've given us," she said.

I finished combing through my hair and turned to Iyleth, trying to reign in my desperation. "But when can we scout aboveground again?"

Iyleth's excited face softened. "Nothing happens until after Thyrenna. Our people will not send our men above without partaking in this sacred day. It would stir the ire of the gods."

I sucked in a deep breath and tried again. "Tomorrow morning?" I suggested.

She patted my shoulder in what could have been an attempt to be comforting, but to me felt condescending. I tempered my anger. "I will speak again with my father," she said.

"Please."

"In the meantime, you should spend the day with me." A mischievous grin flitted across her face. "And Avrik…could he come too?" She looked down at the ground as if she'd suddenly become shy.

Iyleth, shy! I scoffed at the thought.

"Yes," I agreed. "He can come."

Iyleth took Avrik and me to the open planting rooms with the grated ceilings, where we strolled in the sunshine for a while. It was grating to see the way Iyleth flirted with Avrik, but I tried to ignore it and concentrate on the warmth of the sun on my back. I remained as silent as I could, content to try to pretend they weren't with me. Or, at least, that

Iyleth wasn't.

"I can't believe you've never been allowed aboveground," Avrik said.

"Couldn't you convince your father?" I asked, my curiosity overpowering my desire to avoid speaking. "You seem to be able to persuade him about almost anything."

"It's not that simple," she said. "You see, my father may be the Captain of Toryn and my brother may be his heir, but women are looked to as the pillars of strength and hope in Toryn. Especially me, as the Intercessor. If anything were to happen to me…" She shook her head. "My father and brother lead my people. As Father explained, it is my duty to go before our deities in the temple each day and plead for our people. It is *my* voice that is believed to hold the greatest power, the one everyone believes the gods will listen to the most. Women are most favored by the gods, in part because the goddesses comprise many of the most powerful of the deities."

I had never known much about the Toryn religion. Iyleth must have noted the confusion on my face, for she added, "Do the Misrothians still worship the Alrenian god? I suppose this is all…very different to you."

"You don't seem pleased with your responsibilities," I said.

Iyleth's lips tightened into a firm line. "The gods have not listened to my requests for help. I wonder if they are even listening at all, or if they have forsaken us like everyone else. All except Nesrelle. Sometimes it seems she is the only deity ruling this land." Her words reminded me of Narek and his own bitterness. "I've asked them many times to destroy the barrier or to bring us someone who could. But…" Her voice faltered. "As much as I hope for an alliance between us, I believe you when you say you don't even know how to break the barrier. My father thinks you'll find a way. But I…I'm not so sure. It's hard to hold onto hope for long in this place. And as much as we need the barrier to fall, I don't believe risking your kingdom is the right way to save ours."

I swallowed, unsure of what to say. For once, I believed she might be sincere after all. Maybe Narek had been right.

"I'll show you the temple," Iyleth said. She wound her way through the great planting room and through several smaller adjoining ones, taking us through various tunnels and past many more until the tunnel we were in spilled into another huge space.

The room was vast, with white, rounded walls and a ceiling made of surprisingly smooth rock. A waterfall emerged from a tunnel set high in the far wall and drained into a wide pool filling almost half the room. Everywhere tangling vines of silver and gold made complex, interweaving patterns over the white rock, giving the entire space an ethereal glow that set the water blazing with beautiful light. It was hard to decide if the room was more breathtaking or blinding, a place that felt equal parts serene and overwhelming.

"This is where I come each day to beseech the gods for favor and blessings, for salvation," Iyleth said, and her voice danced off the walls around us like a melody.

"It's…beautiful." Avrik studied everything as if transfixed. Under the silver-gold light, his eyes were bright, and his smile took me back to Evren. I forced my gaze away from him and glanced at Iyleth, who was watching Avrik with open admiration.

"It's my favorite part about being the Intercessor," she admitted.

Iyleth led us toward the pool, kicking off her slippers and lifting her skirts to her knees to wade in its shallow waters. Avrik followed, but as soon as I stopped, my muscles taut, he glanced back at me, searching my face.

It's shallow, you fool, I tried to tell myself, yet I couldn't move closer. I stared, watching half-disgusted and half-mesmerized as the silver and gold drops of water fell like glass shards from Iyleth's feet and legs as she splashed. She tossed a look over her shoulder and noticed my distress.

"Are you…?"

"She'll be fine," Avrik said, swift to sense my emotions, even now. "It's just against Misrothian custom for royalty to…swim."

My heart warmed at his defense of me, then just as suddenly, the feeling faded away. He stood tall and unyielding beside the pool, his eyes focused on Iyleth and never sparing a look toward me, standing quiet at his side. No matter what kindness he showed me, it was that and nothing more. Whatever we had shared, whatever we had felt last night had vanished the instant he'd left. Or, even if he still felt it, I knew what he had to do. Risking Iyleth's displeasure could put us all in jeopardy. He was Iyleth's suitor now, and I felt like less than a shadow beside him.

The thought made me chasten myself. *It doesn't matter what he thinks of you.*

Iyleth quirked an eyebrow at us, her eyes darting from Avrik to me and then back again. Her eyes always seemed to drift toward him. "You Misrothians are rather formal." She waded back out of the pool, dropping her dress so that it swayed about her ankles once again and stepping back into her slippers.

We spent time wandering around the temple, listening to Iyleth as she recounted stories about the gods and various Toryn customs. She described what the Toryn temples had once been in their grandeur, or at least what she'd heard they were like. The creatures of the Wastelands had destroyed most of her kingdom before she was even born. "They exist only to destroy, to watch us suffer," she whispered, her voice ragged with sorrow.

At last she led us back toward our rooms, bidding Avrik a warm farewell. "I will see you tonight, for the dancing," she said with a dazzling smile, squeezing his hand.

Turning away, she grew quiet as she accompanied me toward my own room. "There isn't…anything between Avrik and you?"

An old memory rose in my mind, one of me standing in Jennah's kitchen and being asked a question by her daughter: *Do you love him?* I brushed it away. Those were girlish dreams, ones I didn't have the luxury to entertain anymore.

I drew a deep breath. "We were close friends, once."

"Nothing more?" Iyleth cocked her head to the side as we stopped before my room. I resisted the longing to avoid her gaze and met her eyes with an even stare. "I could end our courtship, dismiss him as one of my suitors," she said quickly. "It was meant to strengthen the ties between Misroth and Toryn, not shatter them. I never thought there might be…you didn't seem close, but today you seemed…" It was strange to see Iyleth stumbling over her words, when usually she was so self-assured in her conversation. "I just thought maybe there was something." She studied me earnestly. "I don't want to hurt you. I want to be friends."

There was something almost pitiful about her in that moment, about the way her blue eyes looked wide and pleading. As the Intercessor, did she feel set apart from her people? Too revered to have close friends? Was she greatly loved, but only from a distance?

I shook my head. "There's nothing between Avrik and me. Don't avoid him for my sake."

That evening Iyleth came to my room laden with clothes and accessories the like of which I'd never seen before, all to help me prepare. She herself was dressed in Toryn purple and green, hidden bells on her legs jingling as she moved, ribbons braided through her hair and over her brow, and her long dress swirling about her legs and trailing along the cavern floor with every step she took. With a grin, she tossed me a red dress that shimmered with hues of silver and blue—Misrothian colors. I caught her eyes and returned her look with perhaps the first true smile I'd ever given her.

"Try it on," she urged.

The dress was made of the same comfortable material all Calidan clothing seemed to be composed of; unlike my royal gowns at home, this one flowed to my ankles in gentle, light waves that made movement effortless. No wonder Iyleth walked the cavern's tunnels with such light-footed grace. Iyleth kneeled and began to wrap red, blue, and silver ribbons adorned with small silver bells about my ankles. She stood and added more to my wrists, wrapping the ribbons in intricate patterns halfway up my forearms. Then she waved me toward the chair on the other side of the room, nudging me into the seat and promptly attacking my hair.

Iyleth pulled my hair back into a loose yet elegant knot. Finally, Iyleth brought out a case of glistening powder, brushing it across my eyelids so that they glittered silver in the shifting candlelight. I glanced back at Iyleth and realized she'd applied golden powder to her own eyes. This was completely new: I knew about the Teramese tradition of lining women's eyes with kohl and the Brev custom of applying rouge to lips and cheeks, but this shimmering substance was as foreign as the strange yet beautiful Toryn clothing.

She lifted the looking glass she'd brought so I could inspect myself while she stood back and beamed. Mentally I conceded that my hair did look elegant, with a few loose waves framing my face, while the rest shone with silver ribbons Iyleth had woven within the locks. My dress clung to my body in a way that made me look taller and shapelier, and I realized I truly wasn't the Evren girl or timid princess I'd once been. This reflection revealed a woman, one with a cool gaze weighed down by sorrows and fears she tried to lock up inside, but one that looked beautiful, maybe even as beautiful as Iyleth. I couldn't lie: Iyleth had arrayed me in such a way that I truly did look like a princess…no, like a *queen*. Was this an indication that she didn't believe Gillen was alive? A signal that she looked to me to lead my people in an alliance with hers? I shook the painful thought away.

With every movement I made, the bells jingled, and I bit back my urge to cringe. A rush of homesickness overcame me, and I ached to turn back to the mirror and see a different reflection, one of a girl with loosely flowing hair, a comfortable wool dress, and worn leather boots. One who'd almost put her sorrows behind her and embraced a new home, a new family.

But that girl was a coward, I thought darkly. *She never truly put grief and fear behind her. She only ran from it.*

"Do you…do you like it?" Iyleth's uncertain expression looked alien on her face. She always appeared so self-assured, so untroubled. She too had learned to set pain behind her. "You look stunning. Don't you want to look beautiful for Thyrenna?"

Turning back to study myself within the mirror, I once again thought of Gillen: dead or alive, he was lost as long as I was deep within the belly of this cave. I thought of Iyleth with her confidence and charm, and of Jennah with her fierce strength and courage. Then I remembered my father, who had used terror and deception to gain power, his own fear only ever a display of weakness. Beauty didn't matter here in a world where loved ones could vanish in an instant, where trust could shatter even after years of being painstakingly built, where impossible choices had to be made, and where real, waking terrors were worse than nightmares. I considered my words carefully, knowing Iyleth could misunderstand me and our fragile alliance could bend. "I want to be beautiful in the way a blade is beautiful: graceful and deadly."

A flicker of understanding crossed her face, and just for an instant I saw something harden in the lines of her jaw and the set of her mouth. She was no stranger to grief either.

"It's time. Come with me," she murmured, and she led me from my room, through the maze of tunnels, and to the gathering crowd within the Calidan temple.

The other Toryn women were arrayed similarly to Iyleth and me: they wore ribbons and bells in their hair, on their ankles and wrists, or around their waists and necks. Women wore their hair in extravagant plaits cascading down their backs or in elaborately styled knots and coils atop their heads, and their eyes glittered with the same silver and gold powder that covered Iyleth's and my eyelids. Some people clustered together talking, but most were already immersing themselves in dancing and merriment, a strange blend of celebration and supplication like nothing I'd ever seen before. The Calidans took turns joining group dances around and within the pool, dipping low toward the earth and moving in slow, sweeping gestures both captivating and humble, spinning and twisting their bodies and then uplifting their hands in silent pleas toward their gods. Those in the pool somehow made the dance even more graceful, with the silver- and gold-tinted water rippling in vast circles around them and dripping in glistening beads from their bodies. Others engaged in more lighthearted activities, jesting and laughing with friends, coupling off to dance, or gathering at one of the long tables, laden with countless foods and drinks.

Off to one side, musicians played instruments I'd never seen before: drums fashioned with metal and leather, wind instruments crafted in Toryn colors, graceful stringed instruments whose notes echoed off the cavern walls and seemed to expand endlessly within the space until the music felt all-encompassing, consuming everything. Voices lifted to the Toryn deities in wordless chants and prolonged, vibrant notes the singers held for so long that at times their voices sounded more like wails, hauntingly beautiful as they beseeched blessings from their gods.

I didn't want to, but it was impossible not to stare at Avrik once I caught sight of him standing near one of the tables, leaning casually against the wall and chatting with Layk. The two grinned like a pair of old friends and once more I noted the change in Avrik, the way he held himself confident and upright again, the way the gold and silver light flashed in his warm brown eyes, the way his cheek dimpled when he smiled. He was dressed in a Toryn shirt and trousers whose colors rippled in shades of red, the hues so bright in the shifting light that even he stood out in the sea of colorful clothes. As if sensing my gaze, his eyes slid toward mine and for an instant he froze, his smile hovering in place uncertainly, the barest shadow darting over his features. My heart throbbed unpleasantly against my rib cage. Then he saw Iyleth at my side and his demeanor slipped effortlessly back into his usual charm, and I quickly dropped my stare.

"Your other two companions aren't bad-looking either," Iyleth said, studying the crowd and giving me a playful nudge. Then, with one last smile in my direction, she pressed through the crowd to meet Avrik.

Distracted as I was, it took me a moment to realize she had been looking at Layk and Narek. As usual, Layk stood out amongst the dark-haired Calidan crowd with his golden hair. His eyes were bright and merry and his expression, normally set so carefully in disciplined guard fashion, was surprisingly carefree. He stood laughing and talking with Jennah, who was clothed in a pearlescent dress that set off her golden-brown skin. Gold ribbons and bells were tied around her waist and neck. I couldn't help but return the smile and started to move toward my friends.

But my path converged with Narek. His dark Toryn eyes were as inscrutable as ever. With his lithe, self-assured movements, he brushed through the crowd, speaking now and then to his fellow Toryn, but remaining apart from everything. He was one of them, and yet…he wasn't. He watched Thyrenna's dancers with a cool gaze, his face schooled into an impassive expression, whether by his nature or his years of training, and I wondered what he was thinking. Despite his desperation to save his people, they didn't seem especially happy he had returned to them, and unless they lived outside Calidar, he didn't appear to have any family or close friends left alive. Was he glad to be back in Toryn amongst his people?

Something in me ached—a painful blend of loneliness and grief that mingled with sympathy as I watched him. Before I registered what I was doing, I found myself tracing a path to him, where he stood near the edge of the pond, arms crossed as he watched his people dance.

"Do the gods even hear us?" he muttered once I was within earshot, not bothering to look at me.

I knew he meant the Toryn deities, gods and goddesses that the Misrothians believed were only myths dreamed up by the Toryn people long ago. While Misroth had rejected the Alrenian culture and language, we had clung to our own version of belief in their Life-Giver, though for most it was a faith of empty rituals and formalities. But the Toryn had spurned anything at all to do with the Alrenians and had refused to consider that an Alrenian god could be more than another source of imprisonment. They'd held fast to their own ways and only worshipped their ancient gods.

Now, as I watched the Toryn dance in supplication, hoping for an answer from one of many gods who had long been silent, I hurt with pity. The Life-Giver was still a mystery, his plans confusing, but I had seen him. Spoken to him. His gift flowed through me, through Jennah, and perhaps through countless others if only we could stop long enough to see it. He had led me through death itself, holding me as my blood had poured from my veins, and stitched me back together. Despite the times I felt abandoned, I knew in my bones he was still with me, the man in the woods who spoke in riddles and smelled of pine and earth.

"I saw what happened to you in Misroth City, when you should have died." Narek's voice was low and raw, and his shoulders slumped. I had never seen him look this vulnerable, and to my surprise, my heart lurched in sadness for him. "Your Life-Giver saved you. But here…my people continue to die, to suffer, to live in this endless darkness." He waved his hand at the tons of rock hemming us in. "You claim to have seen him, to have spoken with him, while all my people have is silence."

I rubbed my hands up and down my arms. From cold? From sadness?

"You have a gift that could help us, given to you by your god," Narek continued. He turned to me, his dark eyes searching mine. Gold and silver specks sparked in them, intermingling points of flame and hope, loss and fear. *Enemy or friend?*

I reached out and touched his arm. He watched my fingers clutch at his sleeve, but he didn't pull away.

"I want to help your people, Narek, and I hope to find a way, somehow. But right now I can't even find a way to help my own. How can I save your people if I can't even save my own?"

Narek drew a deep breath, holding my gaze. I didn't move my hand from his arm. "You are like your father, but not in the ways you think," he said at last. His voice was gentle, his expression soft, reminiscent of the boy I'd seen in my vision, fighting alongside the girl Reylinn. Was this what lay beneath his armor, forged through loss and horror and bitterness? "You remind me of her, sometimes."

He didn't need to speak her name. I knew. I could see in every taut muscle in his body, in the crinkles between his brows, and in the crooked curve of his lips how much he mourned for her. Perhaps Toryn, full of people who tolerated more than accepted him, was all he had left.

"I'm sorry," I whispered.

Then he drew back, slowly, his arms falling limply at his sides and his eyes flitting toward where Iyleth and Avrik were dancing. My heart clenched at the sight, at the way her hand entwined in his and the way he smiled when he spoke with her. She was beauty and grace itself in that moment, throwing back her head and laughing while her skirts twirled around her. With every misstep or clumsy movement Avrik made, Iyleth only giggled and redirected him, her arms constantly pulling him closer, closer.

"Love doesn't always end well," Narek said.

I straightened hastily, hating that Narek had read me so easily. "He was only a friend," I protested lamely. "We didn't…"

"So you kept silent," he interrupted. "Does that take away the pain?"

I dropped my eyes.

Narek offer me a calloused hand. For a moment I stared dumbly, then reached out to grasp it. Firm but warm, his fingers encircled mine. "Toryn still sees me as an outcast. My loyalties have always been with my kingdom and my people, but you have proven yourself to be more than what you first appeared. And more than what your father was. For whatever it's worth, you have my loyalty." He withdrew his hand and offered me a tight-lipped smile. "Now, let's humor Captain Luiken and Haed and pretend we are enjoying ourselves, and tomorrow we'll hopefully be searching for your cousin again."

Nodding, I watched him enter the crowd, finding a group of men and women talking and laughing and joining in. At first they looked disconcerted, but whether out of genuine kindness or forced pleasantry, they fell into conversation with him. I wandered away, at a loss. I couldn't see Layk and Jennah in the gathering anymore. Maybe they were dancing and enjoying themselves. Avrik certainly was.

I wandered toward one of the far walls, off at a quiet corner of the room where only a few people lingered: two men muttering quietly to each other, nibbling on cheeses while they stood straight and tall as if locked in a business discussion; a boy and girl a little younger than me tangled together against the wall as they kissed passionately; a young woman seated on the floor nursing an infant. The entrance to another tunnel gaped at me, its floor sloping upward, its walls—more of the smooth white stone comprising the temple—nearly covered in a tangle of vines and fungi glowing muted shades of blue and purple so deep it was nearly black. Without a backward glance, I crept out of the room and began climbing the tunnel, my slippers skidding along the slick floor.

After I'd climbed a short while, the boisterous noises of the temple became muted and the gentler sound of running water took their place. I rounded a bend and found myself facing a dark, rushing stream. Its waters looked almost black in the dim lighting and flowed swiftly yet quietly, like a stealthy animal slithering through the cavern. The cave's walls and ceiling turned narrow and low here, just tall enough for me to stand.

Here I stopped to sit near the stream and lean against one of the cool, damp walls. My pulse skittered at the sight of water, but if I closed my eyes and drew a deep breath, I could concentrate on the way the sound of the stream could be soothing. More than anything, the distance from the tumult of Thyrenna was welcome. Perhaps here I could focus and bring myself a vision, like information about Gillen's location or a way to return to Misroth. Anything but the painful reminders of what I'd lost, what I couldn't change or escape.

A footstep startled me upright. I turned, wondering who else would have wandered this far from the celebrations, and was surprised to see Avrik. With shadow shrouding half his face and his eyes reflecting the blue and violet light around us, he stood with his hands in his pockets and his brow furrowed.

"What are you doing all the way back here?" he asked.

It hurt to look at him, but at the same time, it was hard to turn away. Looking at him was like looking at our happy past, our dreamt-up future, and the painful reality of our present all at once. The air between us was tense not only with memories of laughter and friendship and my old hopes that he shared my feelings, but also with memories of betrayal and my empty longing that he would return to me.

"I could ask the same of you," I said, my eyes scanning his grave face, his uncertain posture.

"I came to see…" His voice faded away and he hesitated. "I saw you leaving and came to find you. You can't build an alliance if you keep distancing yourself from the Toryn people." He shook his head. "After your vision… I know you're worried about Gillen, and I know you haven't told anyone else, but..."

Slowly, I stood, my hand gripping the wall for support. I kept the distance between us. "So are you," I cut in, and instantly regretted the words. What point had I meant to make? Why had I let my churning feelings make me rash? Avrik had a way of drawing my emotions to the surface and making me face everything I tried so hard to hide, even from myself.

His eyes dimmed and his jaw clenched at the reminder of his father's death. Not that grief, our constant companion, ever needed a reminder. Its presence entombed us wherever we went: its cold fingers snaked around our arms as it leaned in close and whispered memories and achingly impossible wishes in our ears. But my words were a swift reminder of the divide between Avrik and me, and I could see in the way his body stiffened that his emotions were the same whirlwind that I was experiencing.

To my surprise, he didn't respond to my comment. Instead, his eyes focused on the stream, his voice gruff, he said, "The Toryn will want to see you participating in their holiday to show you're interested in building an alliance. Otherwise they may not agree to let you go aboveground again."

I didn't answer his statement either. "The Avrik I knew wasn't very fond of dancing," I said instead. I dared to meet his gaze, and his eyes burned into mine.

He sighed and stepped nearer, closing the gap between us. My heart jumped, and I wasn't sure if I wanted to step backward or forward. Frozen, I stared up at his face, watching the way his lips pressed into a thin line while his eyes traced my face, as if he were memorizing every feature. Or as if he were searching for something, like he was trying to find his friend from Evren in the face of a stranger. "The Elena I knew didn't keep secrets. Or I thought she didn't."

His words stung, giving voice to something I'd wished to ignore. "I was being hunted," I said, fighting to keep my tone even. "If word had gotten out about who I truly was..."

"You couldn't trust your closest friend?"

I grimaced and stared down at my feet. "I don't mean that. I was afraid, then. I had wanted to leave my old life behind. To really be Elena."

It was true: I'd tucked away the fragile, painful parts of my past, longing to forget them. But it had become impossible to forget them, not when my kingdom needed me. I had been Elena to him, never Halia, and now we were in a world where Elena had no place.

But as strong as my guilt and sadness was, my anger was just as fierce. If Avrik was listing every wrong I'd committed against him, I could not hold my tongue.

"I understand what it feels like to be betrayed by the one who was supposed to never disappoint you, never shatter your world," I said, slowly lifting my head. "I told you the truth and you left me."

I was surprised to see that he was still watching me.

"Was it because I was mute?" I continued. "As soon as I started speaking, I shared the truth with you and you rejected it. You left me when I needed you most." My voice broke this time, but I forged onward. "Do you prefer your mute friend, the one whose sorrow and troubles were her own, never yours? Was that easier for you?"

His expression turned stormy. "I heard every single word you ever spoke to me, Elena. Even when you were mute. Even when you held all your secrets in. I saw everything you ever shared with me, in your eyes, in your smile, in your silent laughter." He drew a breath. "The problem lies with everything you held back." There was a sheen in his eyes, perhaps from the glowing plants around us, perhaps from tears. He reached out and grasped my arm, his hand warm and gentle, firm and desperate all at once. No amount of anger or hurt could keep me from leaning into his touch. My thoughts felt foggy; my emotions were a tangled thread.

"But I'm sorry I left you." His words seemed to surprise him as much as me. He blinked, but he didn't stop. "I wasn't ready to give up on my father." He frowned, pain heavily etched across his brow. "I had to try to save him, the only family I had left."

"You had me."

"I was not so sure of that. I was hurt and angry and afraid. I didn't believe the Elena I'd known would keep secrets from me. And if she could withhold the truth…what if she could also tell a lie? I was forced to choose between my friend and the last of my family. And I made the wrong choice, but…I wasn't sure at the time. I was afraid. Confused. Angry."

I hung my head. "I'm sorry too. Can we be Elena and Avrik again," I asked bitterly, "just for a little while?" Reaching out, I grasped his hand.

Slowly, he shook his head, but more in pain than refusal. "I know in many ways I've been a fool. Elena was everything to me," he said, cradling my hand in both of his. "My closest friend. My confidant." He hesitated. "The future I hoped for."

As abruptly as he'd stepped forward, he dropped my hand and

moved away, his face pale and taut with sadness. "But now you are Halia, and perhaps my queen. I don't know who to be around you anymore. I want to—but I can't..." He sighed. "Even if..." His voice trailed off again. "I'm Iyleth's suitor. And with her favor toward me and Captain Luiken's desire to build ties, I think even if I fared badly in the upcoming competitions against her other suitors, they would still overlook their customs and betroth me to her."

I drew a long breath, trying to drown my pain. "Would you accept a marriage proposal?"

Avrik shrugged hopelessly. "What choice do I have? She is kind and a good friend, but can I risk the wrath of her father? The alliance is so fragile." He stepped back quickly. "I'd...better go before she asks where I went."

And with that he disappeared back into the tunnel.

I stood there for what could have been hours, could have even been an eternity, and listened to my blood thundering through my veins and the gently rushing stream drown out the distant sounds of Thyrenna. Then, shattering the peace and shaking me from my confusion, screams rent the air.

CHAPTER NINETEEN

I RACED BACK DOWN THE tunnel, nearly tumbling down the slope. My heart was a pulsing drum in my ribcage, louder than any of the Toryn drums that had been playing only moments before. The screams continued to echo throughout the cavern, men's and women's and children's all rising in a terrible chorus. With it came the clanging of weapons and a rushing, roaring sound that mingled with the steady pulse of the waterfall.

I rounded the final turn at last. The nestrae were everywhere. Flames licked at their armored bodies as they grappled with Toryn guards and unarmed citizens alike. Fires consumed the tables of food. Billowing clouds of smoke swirled through the temple, making it hard to see and almost impossible to breathe. Nearby, a woman and her son sprinted from a nestred, but they weren't fast enough. The nestred reached out an arm, glistening beneath the flames engulfing it, and dug its claws into the woman's arm. Fire sprang onto her sleeve as she tugged and screamed and tried in vain to shove the nestred away.

The Toryn guards trying to form a blockade at the temple entrances were severely outnumbered. Nestrae still surged into the temple, pressing toward the Toryn citizens, who were clustering within the pool to escape the flames and carnage.

Out of habit, I reached for my bow before remembering I wasn't armed. As I crept forward to search for my friends, the bells around my ankles and wrists tinkled. *Curse this dress, and curse these bells!*

That's when I saw Layk and Jennah, who had prepared for the celebration without the help of a Toryn ally. They held daggers they must have concealed on themselves and were fending off nestrae at the edge of the pool. Layk moved with practiced precision, clearly in his element. Fighting side by side, they had a small pile of bodies already laid out at their feet. Narek was nearby, armed with one of the nestrae's black axes, swinging into the weak spaces at the neck of an enemy's armor.

Hope bloomed in my chest, but died quickly. With our exits blocked by the nestrae army, we were trapped and outnumbered. And if we didn't escape to fresh air soon, we'd suffocate even before the nestrae or flames could kill us. Slowly, I crept into the tunnel and scanned the chaos for a weapon, any weapon.

My eyes landed on a gleaming point amid the smoke: a sword lying beside a dead Toryn guard. I tore into the fray, darting around a nestred that charged with its axe swinging. Another circled around behind, lunging for me with its flaming hand. I dove forward just as its fist closed, latching onto the folds of my dress and setting them aflame. With a cry, I wrenched away, tearing fabric, slamming into rock, and rolling over bodies. My face smacked a rock when I came to a stop and I blinked away the pain. Thick tendrils of smoke wove through the air and stung my eyes, almost concealing the forms of the two nestrae bearing down on me. Staggering to my feet, I raced forward and seized the sword.

I spun just in time to meet the first nestred's attack. Axe and sword scraped together with a fierce screech, and the nestred growled and pulled back. The second charged forward and plunged its sword straight for my neck, while the first attacked my legs. I ducked and leapt backward, cradling my sword close to my body. The nestrae didn't expect me to be bold, so I responded by unleashing a quick onslaught of strikes on every weak patch in their armored bodies I could find.

They parried my attacks easily and then circled around, trapping me between them. Through the shifting smoke and swirling flames encircling their bodies, their eyes were vast pits of emptiness, showing no emotion. With a roar I darted forward, trying to use my speed to my advantage. I sliced at one nestred's neck then deflected the other's attack. To my relief, the first toppled backward, blood pouring from its wound. The second stomped over its companion's body with a snarl, drawing so close I could feel the heat of the flames on its body.

"*Iyg kurik vouren,*" it hissed, and suddenly, inexplicably, I knew what its taunt meant.

You are ours.

"No!" I shouted.

Something deep and awful sounded from its chest, almost like a low chuckle, but too inhuman. Despite the heat and the sweat dripping down the back of my neck, a chill shuddered through me. The nestrae stared over my shoulder, and though I didn't want to turn away from my enemy, though I feared it was some sort of trick, I couldn't resist the compulsion to glance back.

That was when I saw Avrik, and every sane thought fled my mind. Two nestrae were dragging him from the fray, and kick and struggle as he did, they were far larger and overpowered him. Flames leapt along his arms, licking at his sleeves and searing flesh until his yells became screams of pain. His enemies shoved him to the temple floor, one aiming a kick that sent him sprawling face first but extinguished the flames. A nestred paced in front of him, tossing its double-bladed axe from hand to hand and staring at Avrik hungrily. Firelight reflected across the blades' surfaces, glowing like greedy eyes.

Heart lurching to my throat, I was sprinting across the temple floor before I could think, before my desperate cry had even left my lips. The nestred behind me was still emitting that awful, soul-shuddering sound. Almost lost in the noise of battle, I heard its boots crunch over gravel and fallen bodies in pursuit.

More nestrae approached Avrik with other figures in their clutches. Through the smoke I couldn't recognize them at first; I blinked and realized they had kicked Jennah and Layk down beside Avrik. My lungs burned and my vision blurred. *Hurry.* I couldn't move quickly enough. Someone was screaming—or maybe everyone was—but in my ears it all melded into one all-consuming, heart-shattering roar. I couldn't hear anything else, yet I could sense the nestred still in pursuit of me, like an animal instinct had flared to life in my fight for survival.

The smoke was so acrid and thick I couldn't always be sure of what I saw. Was that Iyleth shouting at her brother, rivulets coursing down her cheeks as she fought to hold him back? Was that Narek, leaning on the axe he'd stolen and watching the carnage impassively? I was drowning in smoke; I was tripping over bodies; I was being hunted by monsters faster than me.

Clawed hands seized my arms, piercing the skin until warm blood spilled, and I cried out. A kick dropped me to the floor, grit and gravel biting at my face. Gasping, I scrambled to sit up and fight back, but the claws raked along my skin again and thrust me to the ground while something heavy crushed my legs.

Only able to move my head, I lifted my chin to find that nestrae had restrained my friends in a row on the ground before me, so close that I could see the defiant sheen in Layk's clear blue eyes, the fierce tilt to Jennah's mouth…and Avrik… Avrik watched me with eyes that reflected regret and pain, the face of someone, like me, who knew death all too well. Someone who did not fear for himself, but for those who would be left with only grief. His eyes met mine, and in them I saw all that had been and all that could have been swallowed up by what was.

When my friends tried to struggle against the claws biting at their arms, the nestrae kicked them, cracking ribs, breaking noses. The nestrae with the axe paced before them all the while, licking its lips and fidgeting with its weapon.

"No," I choked out, my voice raw and terrified. "Kill me! Kill me instead!" My pleas were the inane, hopeless ramblings of someone who had nothing left to bargain with.

Behind my friends, leaning against a wall, I saw Narek, away from the chaos. With his arms crossed and his axe lying at his feet, he watched the destruction of his people indifferently. Surely he couldn't be this cruel. He wouldn't let his enemy win again, not after how much he had lost, how much he had suffered. And my friends…even if he could claim us as enemies, surely his desire for an alliance to save his people wouldn't let him stand by and watch them be slaughtered. Even if he didn't care at all for the Misrothian people he'd struggled and fought alongside, even if there wasn't an ounce of compassion within him, he had to know the value in keeping them alive. For his people's sake. For his sake.

"Narek." My voice was still hoarse with smoke and tears. "Stop them, Narek, please. Save them!"

His eyes met mine and I felt like I was staring into a void. An icy chill swept through my veins. There would be no help from him.

Layk gave me a firm nod. I could remember the instant he'd embraced his siblings, holding them close to comfort them as he'd said farewell. Leaving them in the hope he could give them a better future. In the hope he could someday return. He spoke, and even through the din of metal on metal and consuming flames, of dying screams and gasps, of roars of rage and sobs of loss, his voice rang out strong. "If you survive, tell them—" His words faded out, as if he realized there were no words that would comfort his siblings now.

The axe fell. It clanged off the floor as it finished its bloody arc, a sound that echoed mercilessly in my head.

My scream was more animal than human, a savage cry half-strangled by sobs. I was half-aware of claws tearing at the back of my dress and peeling it from my skin as the nestred stalked toward Jennah.

"Help!" I screamed at Narek, unable to let go of my last shred of hope. Narek didn't move, didn't even flinch.

The nestred stalked toward Jennah and I felt the claws on my back again, driving into my flesh in slow, agonizing movements. I bit my tongue to hold back a yell of pain as blood oozed from the wounds. The nestred's boots thudded along the floor as it swung its axe back and forth, back and forth, drawing out each death a little longer to relish in its victims' rising terror and grief. The tang of blood filled my mouth. Again the claws pierced and tore at my skin. Jennah's brown and gold eyes reflected fire—and yet, somehow, she looked peaceful. Ready. The world grew hazy around me. Pain and horror and sorrow mingled until I could barely breathe, barely see. My teeth chattered and my limbs shook as blackness collected along my periphery.

"*Ivanah meryk,*" she murmured, closing her eyes and bowing her head.

The nestred's axe fell again. Then it turned on Avrik.

I couldn't even scream anymore. My throat was raw; my tongue clinging to the roof of my mouth. Avrik's and my eyes met, but there was nothing we could say. Nothing we could do. The black spots were dancing in front of my eyes now. Did Avrik's lips move then? I couldn't see clearly. Couldn't hear beyond a shrill ringing in my ears.

Another claw dug deep. Pain lanced through my body. Narek blinked impassively. The Toryn died all around me.

And the nestred dropped its axe one last time.

I was sure I was drowning now—in smoke, in blackness, in blood. The nestrae restraining me pulled back and slammed my face into the stone floor. For one aching moment I managed to lift my head, and as darkness consumed my vision, I saw Narek strolling toward me.

Head pounding, body aching, I startled awake to find myself in my room in Calidar, lying in bed on my stomach. Muted hues from the glowing fungi and vines along the walls and ceiling lit the bedsheets around me and the air smelled faintly of smoke, like the memory of flame. At the scent, horror washed over me anew as I remembered the nestrae's attack.

The screaming, the bodies, the blood…

Layk and Jennah. My body trembled with horror, with grief. *Avrik. They're dead. All dead.* I choked back a sob and clutched at the bedsheets desperately, like they were my anchor in a tumultuous storm.

When I tried to move, my head throbbed and my back felt like it was alight with fire, and I remembered my injuries. But who had survived to bring me here? And why had the nestrae spared my life?

A soft knock made me sit up quickly, despite the ache in my head and sensation of fire on my skin. Iyleth slipped past the curtain, a tray in her hands. Her hair was pulled into a tight knot, a green cloth tied around her forehead. I couldn't tell if she wore it as a bandana or for an injury. Rather than her usual dress and slippers, she wore a sleeveless tunic, leggings, and sturdy boots. But most shocking of all were the jagged wounds, like claw marks, marring each of her bare arms in matching cuts. There was a fierce set to her mouth and a hard look in her eyes.

"My friends," I croaked out.

Hands shaking, she set the tray, laden with bandages and ointments, on the table and approached my bed. "I'm sorry," she said, her tone broken and defeated. "I'm sorry for what happened to your friends."

I was dumbstruck, my mind still trying to grapple with the horror of everything that had happened.

"They found us, after all of our time in hiding and all of our precautions." Iyleth's voice still shook but she set her chin, trying to look brave. "They killed…so many… They killed Father…" She paused to compose herself. "We finally managed to drive them back. Those of us who survived sought shelter from the smoke in our open rooms. We've been tending to the wounded and burying the dead for days, recovering where we have shelter from the ichgor… We finally moved some of the wounded, like you, to places where we can better help you clean up." She nodded at my dress, torn and coated in grime and blood. "We—we cannot stay in Calidar. We're leaving today. I came to dress your wounds and help you get ready."

My lungs felt constricted and my throat ached with tears I would not cry. I had a thousand questions, but my mind was too numb and my mouth too dry to even begin to ask them. I wasn't sure I wanted to know the answers, anyway.

Dazed and lost, I moved like I was underwater while we gathered my belongings. Iyleth helped me bathe and dressed my wounds with fresh ointment to soothe the pain.

"They are markings," she said bitterly while she worked.

"What?"

Iyleth paused to hold up one of her arms for me to inspect. Her eyes glistened with unshed tears, yet her tone never wavered. "They're words in the nestred language. Even if we don't understand it, these runes hold power over whomever they mark, like a message only the marked can read and feel. And...hear." She swallowed. "You can hear them whispering it to you, sometimes, in your mind."

She turned me so that my back was to the washroom's looking glass, then drew another hand mirror from the cabinet and passed it to me. I held it up, at first only seeing my pale, drawn face and wild eyes in its reflection. Moving it to change its angle, I caught a glimpse of my back and my breath hitched. Two rough lines curved down the small of my back and intersected near their ends, while a third slashed across their tops and a final jagged line ran down the middle. As if the nestrae were right there beside me, once again holding me where there were gashes and burns along my arms from their attack, I could hear their hissing voices in my head. But this time I understood the word they spoke: *Condemned.* It repeated in my mind, recalling images of my friends' deaths and searing me with guilt. Shuddering, I shoved the mirror back into Iyleth's hands and closed my eyes until the word faded from my thoughts.

But my grief and guilt never would.

"They know our worst sorrows and fears," Iyleth continued. "Whatever haunts us, they discover and use."

Coldness trickled down my back and arms. "What do you mean?"

Iyleth lifted bandages from her tray and began to wrap my wounds. "As you have probably learned, they worship the goddess of fear and death; therefore, their mission is to inflict chaos, terror, and death as sacrifices to her. This means they don't merely kill. They torment and terrorize first, relishing our pain as Nesrelle does."

Rage and sorrow slammed through me. I mashed my hands into fists and closed my eyes to quell the emotions. Before memories of Avrik or Layk or Jennah could overwhelm me, I made myself focus on something else. "And we only know what our own markings mean?"

Iyleth nodded somberly and glanced down at her arms again. "Mine mean *Daughter of the Dead.*"

I had nothing to say, no comfort to offer her. She stepped back and silently gathered her supplies, so I turned and slipped on my Misrothian tunic and leggings. When I was dressed, Iyleth turned to go. "I have to help my people. Meet in the Common Room in no more than an hour."

When she left, grief descended on me like a weight. I sat and pulled my knees to my chest. There was nothing to keep me company but silence, cold cavern lights, and the scent of old smoke.

They're all dead. There's nothing left. My friends had risked everything on a fool's mission. For me. Layk would never return to his siblings; Jennah would not see Marke or her mother or daughters again on this earth. And Avrik… He'd never see Evren's garden or beautiful rolling hills again. He wouldn't laugh and joke with his friends or compete in archery competitions; there would be no more teasing him about his clumsy dancing or quirk of carrying his bow everywhere he went. He wouldn't have a chance to heal from his parents' deaths and start his own family, or travel around the world like we used to dream about. His future had ended before it began. Because of me.

And what was left for me? All the anger and hurt and uncertainty I'd felt around him vanished. There would never be a chance for us to reconcile. I'd been a fool. My mind taunted me with memories of our last conversation, my last chance to make things right and explain how much he meant to me.

Do you love him? Jennah's daughter had asked, at a time that now felt ages ago. *Yes,* I thought desperately. After everything, I still did. My heart ached with an emotion I felt in vain. In my old habit, I reached for my armband and traced the sythrel carved into its leather face. *What do I do now?* I wondered. *How do I go on? Where do I go? What if Gil really is dead too?*

Footsteps outside the washroom jolted me to my feet. "Who's there?" I demanded.

Narek stood in the entryway. Fury sliced through me, and without a second thought, I seized my bow and an arrow from where I'd stored them against the wall. Hands trembling, I strung an arrow and aimed for Narek's chest.

"You," I snarled. "You let them die."

He stood still for a long moment, his hair disheveled and his eyes shadowed with dark circles. "I don't know what you mean."

I pulled the string tauter, until my knuckles brushed my cheek. My fingers strained with the urge to release the arrow. "Don't play with me. We had an agreement. You would bring me to Gillen. You would help me *save* my kingdom and my people, not kill them. And here I am, trapped in Toryn without hope of finding my cousin alive, and here you are, the man who stood by and allowed my companions to die and who hasn't found Gillen or any sign of where he could be, alive or dead. You knew your life would be forfeit if you threatened any of us." Sweat beaded at the nape of my neck. "It seems you've outlived your usefulness."

Narek's dark eyes narrowed. "Your father killed those who weren't useful to him. Is this who you want to be?"

My anger was a rushing, roaring storm in my ears. "Don't talk to me about morality!" I cried. "You let them *die!* You stood by and watched! You did *nothing!*" Tears blurred my vision, but I blinked them away. Everything appeared hazy and distant and my head was still pounding. "Give me one reason not to kill you."

Narek stepped forward, his face firm. "Because this isn't who you want to be. And I did *not* kill your friends."

"You didn't stop the nestrae, either."

"I tried. Don't you have a gift for the truth? Can't you call on a vision to see what *really* happened?" Narek's voice was heavy with emotion. This, more than his words, gave me pause. Ever so gradually, I lowered my weapon, sending the arrow clattering to the floor.

"What happened?" I asked.

He wiped a weary hand across his forehead. "The nestrae can give you…visions. Perhaps like what you see, but rather than a gift, they are weapons used to torment. The nestrae use your weaknesses and force you to experience your worst fears." He stepped closer. "When the nestrae caught you and began torturing you, Layk and I tried to stop them. Layk…your friend died trying to save you." The pain on his face was unmistakable.

Grief squeezed my heart. "And what happened to Jennah?" I asked tremulously. "To Avrik?"

Narek watched me steadily. "They're not dead. At least, they weren't killed during the fight."

I stared at him, uncertain. "How can I know what I saw wasn't the truth?" I demanded, terrified to hope.

"No one is exactly sure what transpired, since the nestrae can affect everyone's perception of reality, but Iyleth and I both saw the same things." He continued to study me carefully, perhaps waiting to see if I would reach for my bow again. "The nestrae took Jennah and Avrik, to torture and sacrifice them to Nesrelle."

"But…" Head spinning with a strange mixture of sorrow and hope, I almost couldn't form the words. "They're not dead yet?"

"We can hope."

Against my will, tears spilled over and trickled down my cheeks.

"I'm sorry," Narek said, and before I had time to be surprised, he wrapped me in an embrace.

"But there is hope," I said. "For two of them, if I can find them."

"The nestrae have taken many people over the years. They took more Toryn along with your friends. We will find them," he growled.

Blinking, I pulled back to look at him. "You'll help me?"

In his eyes I could see the memory of the youth he'd once been, terrified and helpless as he'd tried to save Reylinn. As he'd watched his people suffer and die. This was a man who would never stop fighting to ensure something like that didn't happen again. This was why he'd thrown a girl into the sea to drown, why he'd carried out my father's biddings in the threadbare hope that Zarev would keep his promise and assist the Toryn people. This was why he'd accompanied me through the mountains and across the Toryn countryside to once again face its horrors.

Without a word, Narek unbuttoned the top of his shirt and peeled it back to reveal an ugly scar marring his chest, just over his heart. The marks were in a familiar jagged pattern—it was another nestred rune. As I studied it, I wondered what word haunted. "They've marked and robbed from me too. It's time to stop them," he said darkly.

This time, I believed I could trust him. *Not enemy. An ally after all,* I thought.

"How?" I demanded.

"You're gifted with the truth. You will find them."

Steeling myself with a deep breath, I nodded. *I will,* I vowed.

CHAPTER TWENTY

TOGETHER, WE GATHERED MY BELONGINGS and ventured toward one of the planting rooms. The glow of a pale morning through the vent softened the air and gave the space an otherworldly feel, too peaceful for the devastation it now represented.

The crops were burnt and gone. In their place were endless rows of memorials, plain rocks rolled over the spaces where the remains of the dead had been buried. Layk's was not hard to find. His name was painted on a smooth stone, too humble of a memorial for someone who had died for his kingdom in a foreign land.

Layk of Misroth
Perished Year 201, Age 18

I stared at the memorial numbly. The light suddenly felt too harsh in a world where my friends had been torn so cruelly from me, from their families. What would happen to little Dalen and Fia without their brother?

"This was in his room," Narek said after a long moment.

My eyes were frozen to the memorial, but I reached out my hand for Narek to drop something into my palm. Finally, I looked down at Layk's oval locket, plain silver on a heavy chain. Fingers trembling, I opened it.

Inside were paintings of a blond boy and red-haired girl grinning back at me.

We entered the Common Room in silence. The Calidan survivors gathering there were a ragged, miserable band, severely shrunken in their numbers. Men, women, and children wore packs full of as many goods as they could carry. Haed and Iyleth, the former with bloodied bandages wrapped around his head, stood before the crowd, silently assessing the people.

"Our journey toward Haemil will be slow and dangerous," Haed was saying, "especially with all of our wounded." His gaze slid to the far end of the room, where healers were tending to the wounded, some standing, others lying on stretchers. "But we won't give up! We'll continue to fight, and our enemy will *not* win!"

He was met with resounding shouts from his people, far heartier than I would have expected from the bereaved, discouraged gathering.

I cast a sidelong glance at Narek. "Haemil?"

"Haemil is one of the final standing refuges in Toryn, or at least it was the last time they and the Calidan people were able to communicate. Journeys between the two cities are rare. No one's certain about what's left of Haemil."

"It's close to the border of the Wastelands," I pointed out. "Traveling to one of their strongholds is probably our best chance to find our friends."

Narek gave a curt nod. "There are other strongholds throughout Toryn, but I agree that a force like that probably came from somewhere well-fortified. Either somewhere close to the border, or Delgoth. So which direction do you want to go first?"

"Toward the border," I said without hesitation. Whether it was intuition or a feeling based on my gift, I felt in my bones that we needed to move closer to the Wastelands. Somehow it seemed inevitable that we'd eventually have to travel that way.

He met me with a searching gaze. "Are you ready?"

I did not waver. "Yes."

Haed marched swiftly through the lines of his people, as if doing a final inventory check. Were there enough supplies to last the journey? Were there enough if the Toryn arrived to find Haemil had long since been destroyed?

Ignoring Narek's look, I stepped through the crowd, pushing my way past several disgruntled people, until I reached Haed. "We may find shelter in Haemil," I said, causing him to look up from the elderly woman he was comforting to stare at me, "but we can't forget that the nestrae took our people hostage."

The old woman gaped at me, her eyes watery and her lips quivering with sorrow.

Haed watched me for a full minute, until I felt my courage transform to anger. "I'd do anything for my people," he said slowly. "But when the choice becomes whether to protect those who remain or risk all for the small chance I might rescue others, I have to make the hard yet necessary choice. I know you don't understand that, since you abandoned your people and chose your cousin over an entire kingdom."

I glared at him. "What sort of ruler would I be if I were not willing to risk my wellbeing for even just one of my people? If I turned my back on my king, or on my friends now?"

"Return to your castle, princess," he growled, turning on his heel to join his sister, where she waited at the front of the crowd. "Those outside of Toryn know nothing of sacrifice or danger. Don't you understand that if it were not for *you*, the nestrae never would have attacked?"

"What?" I demanded. Everything before the attack felt hazy and distant now. My brain was too overwhelmed with the memories of the sights, the sounds, the smells…the *death*…

He turned back to glower at me, his voice low and dangerous. "The nestrae found Calidar because we ventured aboveground, for *you*, on your fool's mission to find your cousin. All those people who have been killed and captured—it happened because of *you*. So don't speak to me about what *I* should or should not do for my people."

I balled my hands into fists, repressing the urge to snap at him or to crumble into further guilt and grief. I remembered the whispers I'd heard in Delgoth the day we'd ventured aboveground. *My fault.* I trembled. *They died because of me. Because I put Gil before everyone else…*

But I couldn't let the feelings overtake me, so I blinked and forced them away. I started to turn back toward Narek, and a vision took over.

The Common Room disappeared and I was back in the temple during the nestred attack, surrounded by piles of bodies, screaming women and children, and Toryn struggling to fight back against the flood of enemies. The pungent scents of smoke and blood merged and burned the back of my throat. Just ahead, Iyleth was running and screaming, her long hair streaming around her tear-stained face, her flowing dress charred and torn.

"Haed! Haed, no!" she shouted.

Heart in my mouth, I looked ahead and saw her brother. Covered in blood, his eyes wild, he swung a nestred sword at everyone around him, both nestrae and Toryn. The Toryn shouted at him and tried to flee or defend themselves, but he fought furiously, fueled by the rage that gleamed in his dark eyes.

"Stop!" Iyleth screamed. The nestrae were everywhere, slowing her progress. She ducked to avoid the swing of a mace and sprinted around a tangle of Toryn guards and nestrae. "Haed, what you see isn't real!" But her words were hard to hear over the roaring fire and clanging weapons. Nestrae hissed and whispered, making bumps rise on my arms.

Haed turned and Captain Luiken was there, armed with an axe. "Son!" he cried. "It's me. You have to stop!"

Haed stared at him for a moment, a look of bewilderment crossing his face. Then his expression hardened and he snarled. "It's a trick. You won't fool me, you monster!" He plunged his blade toward his father's heart, and the captain scarcely had time to dodge the blow.

"Haed, please!" Captain Luiken said. "I can't fight my son! Stop! They're lying to you. It's me; I'm here!"

But Haed did not falter. In one swift move, he plunged his sword into Captain Luiken's chest and then pulled it out. Blood spilled from the wound and the captain's face turned ashen. "Haed…" he breathed, more blood dribbling from his mouth.

Starting, Haed blinked, studying his father in horror. Iyleth's screams were terrible, but not as terrible as Haed's expression. "Father?" he said. He dropped the sword with shaking hands. They were red with his father's blood. "*Father!*" Weeping, he cradled Captain Luiken in his arms, but his father was already gone.

Iyleth ran to him, sobbing. Too late. Far too late.

Mind reeling, I spun around in time to see the nestrae overtake me in the temple. Their claws shredded my dress and dug deep into my lower back, slowly carving their rune into my skin. I struggled and shrieked, my eyes staring distantly at the vision they'd entrapped me in.

Seeing me, Layk charged forward, his weapon dripping blood. Nestrae swarmed him, cutting off his path. They chanted and snarled behind their face guards, then three attacked him at once.

A nestred swung a mace for his head and Layk ducked. Another creature lunged, and he sidestepped, parrying as a third nestred's axe sliced for his neck. But he didn't see the next attack, aimed at his head, until he heard the clang of axe against sword, stopping the enemy blade just inches from his face. Layk turned to see Narek fending off two of the nestrae that hemmed him in.

"N-Narek," Layk stammered, slicing at the weak spot near a nestred's neck and abruptly ending its attack.

"The Royal Guard never leaves one of their own alone in a fight," Narek said. He kicked an enemy back and sprang toward another.

"You're not—" Layk began, still at a loss for words. He stopped himself to defend against two nestrae at once.

The rush of nestrae seemed unending, more constantly racing forward to take the place of the ones they fell. Some were armed only with weapons, but others were alight with greedy tongues of flame.

Narek closed in toward Layk to offer him more support. "We've fought too many battles against these monsters for me to not help you now."

Shock and gratitude mingled on Layk's face. "Thank you," he said, and a smile flashed across his lips. "My almost-captain."

Narek smiled too as he shoved his blade into the opening of a nestred helmet, spraying blood, and kicked the dead creature down to face the next.

My screams for help pierced the din of battle.

"But I'm not worried for myself," Layk finished. "We have to help Halia!"

A flaming nestred leered at Layk and seized his arm, tearing fabric, drawing blood, and burning flesh. Layk shouted and jerked back, but the nestred's claws held firm.

"No," I whispered, as if anyone could hear me speaking in my vision. As if I could stop what was about to happen—what had already happened. I stood by helpless, watching the demons overtake men, women, and children throughout the temple. But my horror grew to its greatest pitch seeing my friend pulled, fighting and shouting, into the fiery fray of his enemies. Their flames were everywhere, white-hot and all-consuming.

"Layk!" Narek shouted, desperately trying to drive the nestrae back to reach him.

Hot tears cascaded down my cheeks as the vision disappeared. I could still smell flame and ash, blood and sweat. The tang of battle was bitter on my tongue, a sharp reminder of all we'd lost.

I closed my eyes, fighting back my grief before the Toryn saw my brokenness. *Life-Giver, carry Layk into the afterlife,* I prayed. *Keep his siblings safe without him.* I wiped away the tears. Layk had died trying to save me.

Feeling sick and empty, I glanced back at Haed, who stood with his jaw set, looking out at his people. "There's no time to waste!" he was saying.

And with that, we left our refuge behind. The long trek through the tunnels felt darker and more cramped than usual with the echoes of dozens upon dozens of footsteps and the somber mood hovering over everyone.

"Halia?"

I looked up to see Iyleth at my side, her voice uncertain.

"No matter what my brother says, you're welcome to travel with us. Aboveground, our numbers might provide us with more protection."

"Or with more danger," Narek muttered from his place on my opposite side.

I offered Iyleth a feeble smile. "Thank you, but I have to find my friends."

Understanding crossed Iyleth's face. "You *do* love him," she said. "But why didn't you— All this time you let me…"

"It's complicated," I interrupted.

Iyleth's gaze was wistful. "I wish you all the best. If…you need anything…" Her voice faltered.

I shook my head.

"Farewell," she said.

Without another word, she disappeared amongst the people ahead, perhaps to rejoin her brother.

Our numbers were so great that Narek and I had to wait a while to board a canoe in the outer tunnel. When it was finally our turn, my eyes watered in the brilliant sunlight awaiting us. It was a warm spring day, with a pure sky and a fresh, sweet-scented breeze fluttering through the long grasses on the riverbank. Several men ferried us across to the southern side of the river, where we disembarked quickly so they could return for more people.

"Narek," Haed called, striding toward us. He shot a brief, contemptuous glance in my direction. Knowing the pain beneath his anger, I couldn't blame him for how he felt about the Misrothian people. Especially toward the one he believed could end his people's sorrow. "I expect you to stop associating with the Misrothian scum. The alliance—if you could ever call it one—is broken." His eyes darted to me again. "I will not threaten her life…*yet*. But I will no longer harbor her or risk my men to protect her. She has refused to help us and brought danger to our doorstep, so from now on, she is an enemy, unwelcome among us," he spat. "My father was a fool to think we could ever find a way to be allies."

"Haed…" Iyleth said, her voice a warning as she pressed her way through the crowd to join us.

"Be silent!" Haed snapped.

There was fire in Iyleth's eyes, but Narek spoke before she could.

"I understand," he said in a cool voice, "but I'm going with her."

"You'll turn your back on your own people?" Haed's eyes narrowed with an unspoken threat.

Narek didn't budge. "No, they *are* my people. The men and women—Toryn and Misrothian—that the nestrae took are *my* people. All enemies of the nestrae are *my* people. I will not abandon them to their fates to seek my own safety."

"You have allied yourself with one of the very people who brought this fate upon us," Haed snarled, his hand flying to his sword hilt.

I watched him warily, unwilling to show fear.

"Haed!" Iyleth said firmly, grasping his shoulder to hold him back. "She is a *friend.*"

My gaze snapped to her.

"Anyone who stands in the way of saving my people is an enemy." He withdrew his hand slowly, reluctantly, and instead coiled it into a fist. "If we ever meet again, know that we meet as enemies."

Narek nodded once. Every muscle in his body looked taut, even though his arms hung loosely at his sides. I was familiar enough with his mannerisms to know that he was watching Haed carefully. His fingers twitched near his sword hilt but never touched it.

"Now leave," Haed spat, "before I change my mind."

"Of course," Narek said, stepping back.

For a brief instant, Iyleth's eyes met mine and I could read the regret and sorrow there. *Daughter of the Dead.* Maybe she had been sincere toward me after all, truly wanting what was best for both my people and hers. And despite her powerful position amongst her people and her tight-knit community, she was plagued with loneliness and grief. By being so revered among the Toryn, she was set apart. She'd lost her parents and now she would lose her chance at having a friend too. To my surprise, my heart ached with sympathy. Maybe we could have been friends, under different circumstances.

Narek and I walked past the silent Calidan people. Some watched us with looks of regret, mourning the lost alliance; others showed their anger and contempt plainly. But whether they had heard Haed or not, they seemed to understand we were not to be touched and let us by peacefully.

The Toryn people disappeared behind us, taking a slower, more westerly route, while we pressed toward the southern border. As we walked, I tried to force a vision to come, but it felt impossible. Guilt and pain clung to me like a cloak. All my hopes teetered on fragile plans. Make my visions guide us. Save the nestrae's captives. Survive and escape Toryn.

The landscape stretched wide and flat, reminding me of our early days in the grasslands of Toryn. Occasionally a rare copse of trees would offer us shade, or we would find ourselves ascending the slope of a gentle hill. Despite our constant wariness, forever scanning the horizon in every direction and studying the earth for footprints or scorch marks that could give us a hint regarding the nestrae's whereabouts, we saw nothing. It felt like we were alone in a vast world of open grass and sky.

"We'll continue due south and begin searching any strongholds still standing along the border," Narek said at last, "unless we have any reason to change our path." He cast me a sidelong look.

I averted my gaze and avoided the subject of my visions. All I could do was hope we were traveling in the right direction, since I wasn't sure my gift was going to help. Not when I didn't have control of it. "I expected to see tracks from their army."

Narek's eyes returned to the sky, even though we both knew it held no threats yet. "They don't leave much to track. They put their fires out to travel. And they can pass like wraiths through the grass. They're surprisingly light on their feet. We can hope, but…I wouldn't hope too much."

I growled my frustration. What advantage did our enemy *not* possess?

Time dragged when my thoughts were consumed with fear for my friends. As the western sky blushed orange and gold and the air grew cooler, I asked at last, "Why have you decided we're your people now?"

"Fighting alongside you earned my respect," Narek said after a long pause.

"You tried to save Layk," I whispered, my voice tight. "I saw it in a vision. He was my friend and—and for that I owe you my gratitude."

Narek's lips were in a tight line. "I'm sorry I couldn't save him," he said softly. "He deserved better."

I bowed my head. "So do his siblings."

"So do we all."

We were silent again for a long time, each of us lost in our own thoughts.

At last, Narek broke the silence. "For so long, I hated all Misrothians, especially Misrothian royalty." His eyes flicked briefly to me. "I wanted revenge perhaps even more than I wanted my people to be saved."

"And so you didn't mind working for my father, even if you hated him too," I said.

"But traveling alongside you helped remind me of my passion to help my people. As much as I want you to bring down the barrier, I realize I can't ask you to risk your people for mine. I can see that we aren't that different, like I told you. I respect you, Halia." A muscle in his jaw twitched. "Besides, my own people scarcely trust me, as you saw, while you and your friends are the ones I've fought and suffered beside for weeks. And I know what it is like to lose someone you love before telling them how you feel." His voice wavered a little, and I knew he was remembering the horror of Reylinn's death. "I want to help you. No one deserves to suffer that."

I stared down at my feet.

"I'm no fool," he insisted. "I know you love him. What I don't understand is why you refuse to admit it."

"Because he abandoned me." My voice cracked, but I pressed on. "And yet…and yet he is my best friend, and I broke his trust too. And now that he could be gone, my hurt doesn't seem so important anymore." I swallowed. "Even if…even if we save him, I don't know if he could forgive me or ever trust me again. Perhaps…perhaps my father was right about some things." My throat burned. "Love is impossible in this world. It's business for Misroth and a game for Toryn and for me…only a distraction from keeping my people safe." *And so perhaps it is only weakness after all.*

Narek toyed with his sword hilt, his eyes darting over the evening sky like he already expected ichgor even though the light hadn't faded. "No," he said, shaking his head. "Love is pain. But as hard as it is, love fuels survival. What else do my people hold on to? What brings them courage when hope fails? What else has kept any of us going, but love of someone or the memory of that love?"

The memory of Reylinn's face rose before my eyes, and I blinked it away. Would Avrik become nothing more than a memory to me as well?

I changed the subject. "So you are saying, when we near the border, that you won't force me to destroy the barrier?"

His hand still close to his hilt, Narek tapped a finger on his belt, beating out a quick rhythm. "You understand my desperation for my people, Halia." He wasn't looking me in the eyes this time, but staring straight ahead, his shoulders tense. "But I mean what I've said. I can't ask you to risk your people or I'm as bad as…well, as I believed all Misrothians to be." He hesitated. "That doesn't mean the temptation isn't still there."

"At least you're being honest with me now," I murmured.

He shot me a glance over his shoulder. "I withheld information before." One of his familiar smirks flitted across his lips. "That is not quite the same as dishonesty."

Some would differ, I thought, thinking of Avrik.

Later, another thought came to me, one that brought such relief and hope I almost couldn't bear it. "If the nestrae can give people visions," I said slowly, "perhaps there is hope. For Gillen."

Narek studied my face. "You speak as though you had doubts." He raised an eyebrow.

"I—I saw a vision of him being killed, when we went aboveground to Delgoth. But…"

"The nestrae had been nearby," Narek finished for me in understanding.

"I didn't want to believe it. But now I have a reason not to. Maybe it wasn't one of my visions. Maybe it was one of *theirs.*"

Narek was watching the sky restlessly. "Whatever lends you strength to keep going," was all he said.

Night descended and still we walked. The bandages around my torso felt constricting with every breath I took, and my head pounded. I was exhausted and every inch of my back and arms burned, but I forced myself to keep my senses alert.

The air turned cool and soothing; the world was calm and quiet—perhaps too quiet. Other than the rustling of wind in the grass and our own cautious steps, there were no sounds. It seemed like we were the only living creatures for miles, and that made me uneasy. Not even an insect stirred.

Narek, too, was uncomfortable, constantly scanning the horizon.

The world slipped away gradually, like a cloud had slithered over my eyes, and then everything looked different. It was summertime in Evren, the sky pure and cloudless, the air thick and lazy with heat.

"Are you even watching, Elena?"

Avrik and I were fifteen. Seated in the grass outside Kyrin and Avrik's cabin, Avrik was trying to teach me how to start a fire, first with the materials from a tinderbox and then by hand.

A breeze finally stirred the heavy air, cooling me after all this time sitting in the hot sun. My eyes were trained on a pair of rabbits bounding toward a nearby hill, pausing now and then with their noses twitching. I shifted restlessly.

"How could you let your attention wander when you have *me* to teach you?" he asked, his tone light and playful.

And indeed, it was hard not to smile when I saw Avrik's familiar grin, mischief sparkling in his eyes. The breeze ruffled his chestnut hair. His dimple stood out on his tanned face, which was shaded with stubble. With his shirtsleeves rolled up, the muscles in his arms stood out more than usual. There were many reasons the girls at school had always admired him, but now he was a young man, not a boy, and those reasons seemed to multiply every day.

Cheeks flushed, I grasped my journal and pencil, at my side as always, and began to write. I smirked as I held the page up for him to see. *What a lofty opinion you have about yourself.*

He laughed outright. "But really, if you want to travel someday, don't you think learning to start a fire would be useful?"

I rolled my eyes. *When would I travel anywhere without a tinderbox?*

Avrik shrugged. "What if you lose it? My father made me learn this when I was young. He said a hunter should always know how to survive in the wild...in case..." His voice trailed off and he laughed again. "Well, in case I was hopelessly lost and tossed my tinderbox in a stream, I suppose." He looked at me, almost pleadingly. "What about seeing all of Misroth? And even beyond, if someday it's no longer forbidden?"

Or we could just sneak across the borders.

He grinned. "What a rebel."

All right, I'm watching.

"See?" he asked, after demonstrating again how he rubbed the stick between his hands. "Now you try—keep your palms flat. Now twirl it like this." He placed his hands over mine and I felt my heart jump.

My thoughts went wild. *What if... What am I thinking? He's your friend...*

I glanced up to find him watching me, so I quickly dropped my gaze back to our hands, pretending to focus on the task.

"What are you two up to?" It was Kyrin approaching us, leading his horse toward home. His clothes were dusty, his shoulders stooped with weariness from his latest journey.

Avrik's face lit up. "Father!" he called. "I'm teaching Elena how to build a fire." He leapt to his feet and raced to greet his father.

"In case she wanders off into the forest?" Kyrin chuckled, embracing his son.

"We'd like to travel someday—see the world." Avrik shrugged. "It seemed like a useful skill for her to have."

Kyrin scrubbed at the dirt on his face and clapped a hand on Avrik's shoulder. "Your mother would have been thrilled. I'm glad you have dreams like that for yourself. This village isn't enough for you."

Then the vision changed. Sunny Evren winked out and I was in a world of darkness and distant screams and whimpers. The hair on my arms rose and I shivered. The space I stood in was dank and smelled of earth, blood, and filth; but it was too dim to see anything clearly.

"*Iyg kurik vouren. Iyg kurik nestryk,*" the nestrae's voices hissed, and I ground my teeth to keep them from chattering, suddenly terrified that they might hear me too.

Light flared. I saw Avrik, hunched and chained against a stone wall, surrounded by nestrae. For once, the flames didn't come from them but from torches they held aloft.

"No…" Avrik was saying weakly. My heart twisted at the sound: strong, confident, optimistic Avrik sounded broken.

One of the nestrae lowered its torch, hovering it over his arm, and he began to scream. I squeezed my eyes shut to block out the sight.

"Halia! *Halia!*"

I opened my eyes to a vast starlit sky and Narek's face hovering over me. He was shouting my name and shaking me. My throat felt raw—I was screaming. I gasped and blinked at Narek, struggling to reorient myself to the real world. The grass was cold against my back; the night wind was a soft melody, in stark contrast to the screams I'd heard. Slowly, I relaxed my muscles.

Narek's face was intent but sympathetic. "What did you see?"

Sitting up, I wiped my clammy palms on my leggings and reached for my bow, stroking my fingers along its curves as if it could bring me comfort. It would if I could use it to kill Avrik's captors. To save Gillen and Jennah. To avenge Layk and Gare.

"I saw Avrik in a prison, I think, but I don't know where it is," I said, swiping my damp waves away from my face. Ignoring Narek's proffered hand, I stood. My legs trembled from fury, from enough adrenaline pummeling through my veins to kill a hundred nestrae. But they were far off, unreachable, and I was helpless to rescue my friends. For now.

Narek studied me. "Exactly how do your visions work?"

"I've always visited moments that show me glimpses into the past, whether it's distant or something that took place only minutes ago."

"Do you see the future?"

I shook my head. "I'm not an oracle."

"And they're random, always coming unexpectedly?"

Thinking, I closed my eyes, trying to revisit moments when visions had come. "They're usually related to what I'm thinking about, but they feel out of my control."

Narek spoke in a low voice. "You saw Avrik just now. Maybe your emotions are controlling your visions. You felt afraid and guilty before we even arrived in Toryn, and maybe that has made your visions seem uncontrollable."

"How…how do you know I felt guilty?"

"Do you think I'm not familiar with guilt?"

I considered his theory. The words the Life-Giver had spoken, in a time that now felt ages ago, ran through my mind: *Your emotions both help and hinder you.* Was this what he had meant? "Perhaps…" I said slowly. "If I can concentrate my feelings on how it would feel to find them…"

"Your visions will lead us to them," Narek finished.

CHAPTER TWENTY-ONE

SEVERAL DAYS PASSED MISERABLY. OCCASIONALLY we found signs the nestrae had left behind: trampled grass or a few stray footprints, but they never led us far before we lost the trail. The spring rains arrived and left our clothes soaked and our bodies numb with cold, though it kept the ichgor at bay. We took rest whenever we could, which was in the rare times we found a safe space to seek sanctuary, day or night. One evening we found shelter in the ruins of a lone cabin, finding some warmth even though its roof leaked and the wind howled through crevices in the walls. Another night we burrowed into a small cave with a cozy dirt floor. We started out trying to take turns on watch, but eventually we were both far too weary to do much more than tumble into our bedrolls and fall into restless sleep.

Sometimes we saw ichgor in the distance, but the land was now full of craggy hills and ancient trees, so we took shelter in crevices among the rocks or beneath clusters of trees.

I used the scraps of energy I had left whenever I was awake to focus on bringing a vision to myself. I pictured my friends' faces and believed Narek and I would find them. But my thoughts and emotions were not easy to control. I still tried to push them away, like my father taught me, but the pain of loss was becoming too hard to ignore.

My dreams became more vivid as my worries grew. Most often they were nightmares full of nestrae lurking toward us or murdering my friends. I woke in a cold sweat more than once, clutching at my armband or reaching for my bow. Whenever Narek heard me cry out, he sprang from sleep, blade drawn, ever on the alert.

Other times I dreamed of Avrik and home. One night, Avrik and I were at Wanderer's Rest. Cozy and content, we shared a large armchair by the hearth and sipped mugs of Selna's tea, all the while laughing about our latest competition or the antics of some of our classmates. Suddenly Avrik's face grew serious; he set down his mug and cupped my cheek, brushing my hair behind my ear. "Do you know how much you mean to me?" he murmured, and then he kissed me, his mouth warm and comforting and passionate all at once, a taste of home and hope.

I woke with the dream still hanging in the air, the feeling of his lips on mine lingering, as if the kiss had been real. Sitting up, I drew a deep breath and told myself for the hundredth time to focus. I had to find him.

"We *will* find them, we will," I said, squeezing my eyes shut.

I pushed my grief and fear to the recesses of my mind, turning off every feeling until I felt empty.

I saw a flash of Avrik's face, contorted with pain, but as always, he was in chains and shrouded in darkness while nestrae tormented him. The image filled me with fury, and I opened my eyes, chest heaving with emotions. I knew that my feelings would render it impossible for me to concentrate again.

Narek and I spoke little as we traveled, too discouraged and tired to waste energy in needless conversation. When the rain cleared, our fear of the night grew stronger; we often had to press ourselves low to the earth as distant shadows crossed the horizon, wing-beats carried on the wind thudding dully in our ears.

Enveloped in desperation, the hours blurred and bled into one another as we crossed grasslands and small forests, hills and valleys, creeks and ponds, decrepit homes and plundered ruins. The closer we drew to the southern border and the Wastelands beyond, the fewer animals we saw and the sparser the plant life became. Our supplies, already meager since the Toryn remnant had little to spare after the nestred attack, dwindled. We had to pause more frequently to scavenge for fruits and nuts, or the rare bird or squirrel. I worried that once we reached the southern border, we would have to walk its entire length, searching countless strongholds and facing endless enemies, before we found the one in which our friends were held prisoner. Unless I had a vision that guided us straight to them.

"How can I stop feeling when there is nothing left but pain and anger?" I bit out one day as we huddled beside a mossy pond. Another attempt at bringing a vision had failed.

Narek sat across from me, sharpening a dagger. Beside him, the pond water was so limpid it reflected his form against the blue sky above. "Did your god say you had to stop feeling?"

Earlier, we'd climbed in fully clothed and sank on our haunches in the shallow water to cool and rise off. Tired yet clean, we'd climbed out and collapsed on the grass, not yet ready to move on. My hair hung limp and wet in my eyes as I considered Narek's words.

"You said the grief and guilt interfered. And he said…"

"Your father taught you to repress your emotions so well that when you feel anything at all, your first response is to dismiss it as weakness. But if guilt and pain have brought you visions, then maybe your emotions fuel them. Maybe it's not about turning your feelings away, but focusing on the ones you need."

I sat silently, contemplating what he'd said.

Happiness, hope, love—maybe my father hadn't believed in those feelings, maybe the nestrae had nearly stolen them from me, but I had to trust them now. I sat up straight, drew a deep breath, and told myself my emotions were *not* a sign of weakness, no matter what Father had said.

For perhaps the thousandth time, I closed my eyes and pleaded with the Giver of Life. *Let me see them. Let me save them.* I dared to let hope seep into my bones gradually, like the slow approach of dawn after a long night.

This time, the vision came easily.

Ichgor swirled and swooped in the night sky as the nestrae swept over the grass, their feet unnaturally light in their leather boots. Amongst the black mass of armored skin and weapons and claws, I found Jennah and Avrik, looking dirty, wounded, and weary. Nestrae dragged them forward in chains.

The nestrae crept up the slope of a rocky plateau, its edges so jagged they looked like teeth jutting from the earth. To the east, I could see the Haemil Mountains piercing the sky. In the south, over the plateau's edge, a barren landscape of brown rock and sand stretched beneath an overcast sky. Perched close to the precipice, overlooking the Wastelands, was a tumbledown, flame-scorched stone fortress. Its gaping entrance awaited them. From one of the crooked, half-fallen battlements fluttered a solid black flag with a forked tail. Below, two armed nestrae flanked the entrance. I could hear screams coming from somewhere deep within the fortress, making me shiver with disgust and horror.

The vision vanished, and I turned to Narek. "I saw them."

Narek's eyes were wide. "What did you see?"

I described the rundown fortress and surrounding landscape to Narek, who nodded grimly.

"Then we head toward a fortress near the mountains. We're not far."

As we closed in on the nestred fortress, we began constructing a plan to infiltrate it, find the captives, and safely lead them out. The more we developed and argued over details, the more I realized what a foolish, impossible mission we had undertook. And yet when I paused, frustrated and uncertain, I knew that *not* attempting to save our people was equally impossible.

At last the landscape changed. The hills grew craggier and larger and thickets of ancient, gnarled trees dotted the countryside. On the distant eastern horizon, the purple Haemil Mountains pierced the sky.

"We're close," Narek said. "We should reach the fortress tonight."

The wind whispered through the trees. I focused on keeping my mind clear for what came next. As night fell, we came upon a thicket. Raindrops pattered on the leaves, a warm spring rain that made the ground slick and visibility difficult. Through the ceiling of branches, I could see the moon, cloaked in clouds. Its light glanced off the new leaves of old trees.

"Ahead," Narek said at last, pointing. The rain had slowed, the clouds clearing from the sky and bathing the world in dim light.

Through a break in the trees, I saw where the thicket ended and a rocky slope began. I traced a path with my eyes up the plateau to the fortress. It looked as it had in my vision: a black, foreboding mass against a star-studded sky. Its stonework was impressive even in its charred, decrepit state. A heavy iron gate, bordered by two nestred guards, secured the yawning entrance. Towering ramparts, even if they were crumbling in places, gave the imposing sense that no one could enter or leave the fortress without its occupants' consent. Despite the distance, I could hear faint screams borne on the wind, as if the fortress itself had a tormented voice that was never silenced.

We crept forward, crouching near the edge of the thicket to better study the fortress.

"Are you ready?" Narek asked.

I checked for the dozenth time that my bowstring was secure and my quiver was full of arrows. I nodded.

We worked quickly, gathering as much kindling as we could to form a huge pile, one that would create a fire large enough to be seen from the fortress even at night. Enough to draw out the nestrae. As Narek knelt to start it, I crept away, hiding among the trees. And I waited.

When the fire flared to life, lit by the precious oil Narek carried, I crouched down and watched the fortress. It didn't take long for nestrae to pour from the fortress entrance. As soon as the last nestred crossed into the forest, I shot one of the guards through its helmet's visor, dropping it instantly. The second drew its bow in a flurry, but not before my next arrow pierced its throat.

Rising, I lowered my bow and sprinted for the fortress. Cool air rippled through my hair, yet the adrenaline thrumming through my blood made me feel like a living flame. Below, the rocky slope was steep and unforgiving; above, the sky was velvet and open, an expansive sea of stars and darkness reaching for me; ahead, the fortress lay like a sprawling beast with its gaping mouth waiting eagerly to swallow me whole. The nestred flag snapped in the wind and my own ragged breathing filled my ears, and all the while I could sense my enemy's quiet pursuit. At least one of the nestrae had spotted me and was giving chase.

Claws tore at my cloak, shredding the fabric as they yanked me back. My cloak ties dug into my neck, gagging me while I struggled to pull away. The cloak gave way with another ripping sound and I collapsed, my head smashing onto the rocks underfoot. White sparks flashed before my eyes and a rushing sound filled my ears. I heard my bow clatter to the ground and arrows spill from my quiver. Blinking, I shook off the dazed feeling and flipped over to face my attacker, already hovering over me with an axe pointed at my neck.

It snarled and raised its axe. I scrambled, rolling to the side and clutching my bow while reaching for an arrow. The nestred's blade bounced off one of the rocks I'd been sprawled across just an instant before. I turned, nocked an arrow, and aimed. My enemy growled and swung again, but I was faster. With a thud and a spray of blood, my arrow found its mark in the nestred's neck, toppling it down the slope toward two other nestrae.

There was no time to waste. I scooped up more arrows from the ground and dumped them back into my quiver as I ran. The entrance opened right before me, without a guard in sight. Plowing past the iron gate and under a stone archway, I entered a dank, empty hall dimly lit with flickering torches.

For only the briefest of moments I hesitated, until another shriek shredded the air and directed me to a narrow entrance on my left. It led to a slick stone staircase descending into darkness. I drew an arrow and held it in one hand while I clutched my bow tightly in the other. But other than the faint drip of water nearby, I heard nothing else. Hands clammy, I hurried down the steps.

The air was heavy with the stench of filth, blood, and burned flesh. There was no sound of chase from above and no sound of approach from beneath. Even my own breaths began to seem loud. Every step I took echoed along the walls as I twisted deeper, deeper into the belly of the fortress.

At last, the thought couldn't be ignored. The two nestrae that had been pursuing me must have stopped, and however many had stayed within the fortress were not trying to hinder me either. *They're letting me in. They want me here.* Trembling, I froze for a second as my brain screamed at me to turn back and flee.

"*Iyg kurik vouren…*" the voices hissed from somewhere below me, or above me, or perhaps even in my mind. I couldn't tell. The words bounced off the walls and ceiling, leaving a heavy sense of dread.

I'm going to die down here, I thought. *I'll be another prisoner, with no means of escape.* The idea flitted through my mind that perhaps Narek had sent me here on purpose in that very hope, playing off my desperation in order to kill me. But that idea was born of the paranoia steeping the atmosphere of this place rather than any rational thought, and I shook it away.

Think of Avrik and Jennah and Gil, I urged myself, and continued down the steps. Even if this was a trap, I couldn't turn around and abandon them.

At last I reached the bottom of the steps. A cool draft breathed across my right temple and I turned to peer into further darkness and quiet. I crept forward, listening to nothing but dripping water and the soft echoes of my movements, until I noticed a light flaring far ahead: a torch ensconced on the dripping stone wall. It illuminated a puddle beneath it and a long stretch of empty hallway, interrupted only by a few rats scurrying over broken stones. As I drew closer to the flickering light, I noticed more torches lining the walls on the left side, while on the right, rusty iron-barred doors blocked the entrances to deep, cavernous cells full of shadows.

I reached for the first door and nudged at it. The door creaked open. For a moment I froze in place.

It's a trap, my brain hissed, yet I couldn't turn back. Avrik was in danger, and I would face any threat in the world to find him. Trap or not, I couldn't leave any space of this fortress unsearched. Despite the anxiety humming in my bones, I strung an arrow to my bow, pushed through the cell entrance, and stepped into darkness.

I felt blind, unable to see beyond the few feet the torches lit. Swiping the sweat from my brow, I stepped forward once, twice. The stone floor was gritty with rubble, dirt, and—my breath hitched—*bones*. Aside from sections of slick, half-crumbled wall on either side, I saw only a vast space of shadow that left me feeling small and vulnerable.

"Avrik?" I whispered. "Jennah? Gil?"

They're not here, I thought. *It's an ambush. Get out before it's too late. Find another cell.*

But something glistening on the ground caught my eye, and I kneeled to inspect it. My heart twisted. There lay Jennah's and Gare's pendants, the two items Jennah had worn day and night, never letting them leave her sight. His was a gold circle; hers a silver, diamond-studded piece in a rendering of Shyla, the warrior constellation.

And with that rush of emotion, I was plunged into a vision. As with so many others, I was in this dark fortress, surrounded by charred, crumbling rock. The walls were lined with torches that revealed the filthy floor, littered with bones, ash, and chittering rats. In the center of the vast room were several stone tables, some layered with ashes, some with piles of wood, and one, surrounded by a cluster of chanting nestrae, with a pyre. My eyes quickly found Jennah in the fray, her eyes wide yet her jaw set bravely. Her clothing was dirty and torn, while every exposed patch of her arms and legs bore scratches and burns and bruises, endless injuries covering her body. The nestrae held her before the flaming table for several terrible moments, chanting loudly to their goddess while the sweat gathered on Jennah's forehead. Despite the silent prayer on her lips, her eyes betrayed her fear.

Then the nestrae shoved her into the flame and her screams filled my head.

Two more nestrae pulled Avrik toward the pyre next. There was a determined set to his shoulders, as if even in his last moments he refused to stop hoping. The nestrae pushed him forward and blinding light overcame the vision.

I jolted back to reality and bit back a sob. *It's not real,* I insisted. *It's not real.* Snatching up the pendants, I discovered with surprise that their chains were still intact. Perhaps Jennah had left them behind on purpose. I swallowed back tears and slipped the chains over my head to hang beside the other pendants and Layk's locket.

The scrape of steel on steel behind me sent a shudder down my back. I spun to see several nestrae hulking toward me, the one in the middle armed with dual blades it continued to scrape together. My mouth tasted coppery, a mixture of adrenaline and fright that I forced myself to swallow back as I lifted my bow and aimed at the central nestred. The arrow landed an inch too low and ricocheted off its armored body, falling harmlessly to the floor. Shaking, I drew another arrow and shot again, yet this time the nestred was prepared and sliced it in two mid-flight, leaving me with no choice but to back away into the dark depths of the cell. My third arrow hit its mark in the creature's neck, but there was no spray of blood, no hint of weakness or injury as it continued to advance. I must not have struck the right place, or maybe this one was as inhuman as they all seemed. Undying, or already dead. A demon from the deepest depths.

I tried to quell my rising panic. My brain was giving into the fear the nestrae thrived on.

There was a hissing sound behind me, the barest hint of words whispered in the dark. I hazarded a glance over my shoulder and saw more forms shrouded in shadow, their eyes alight not with anger, not with passion, but with a calculated, detached patience. I was outnumbered, trapped just as I'd feared.

The nestrae continued to close in on me. I shot arrow after arrow, felling two nestrae before I reached back to find my quiver empty. With a growl of frustration, I threw down my bow.

I scanned my surroundings, my eyes landing on a sword lying near one of the fallen nestred, but I would have to push past the enemies encircling me to reach it. Just as I had in the capital when I'd fought my father, I imagined what Avrik would say. *Trust your advantages. Remember, you're fast.*

Ducking to avoid a blade, I lunged for the sword. I dodged a strike from another nestred and twisted to evade a third, but a hit from a mace smashed into my boot. The blow pulsed through my leg and toppled me to the floor. Right in front of the sword.

I reached out and grasped its hilt. I tried to yank myself to my feet, but my right leg was numb and refused to move. Fear trickled down my back: the nestrae were closing in on me. With a groan, I ignored my useless leg, clenching my teeth against the first stab of pain bursting within it, and shoved myself up with my free hand, balancing on my one good foot.

The nestrae saw my weakness and ugly smiles darted across their faces. I narrowed my eyes at them and grasped the sword with two hands. The weapon felt large and unfamiliar, an unwieldly tool for someone weak with pain. But I was determined, and my determination lent me strength.

I swung the sword toward the first nestred to charge me, smacking it in the face guard and nearly losing my balance. The nestred stumbled backward. Another swung for my arm and I ducked, teetering precariously for an instant before drawing myself back up to full height and responding with an attack of my own. The nestred jumped back before I could hit it, but I didn't stop. Another nestred plunged its blade at me and I swung my weapon for a weak point at the crook of its elbow. The strike pierced soft skin and the nestred grunted in pain, dropping its weapon. Sweat streamed into my eyes and my strong leg began to tremble with exhaustion. Pain coursed through my right leg like fire.

I looked around and shouted in a voice that sounded more like a feral animal than a human. "Come on then!" I screamed. "You have nothing left to take from me, nothing left to offer your demon goddess!"

"Unworthy," the nestrae hissed back in eerie unison. "Guilty. Condemned."

More sweat snaked down my back. My body trembled with pain. *Don't listen to them,* I thought, pushing aside the guilt that threatened to swallow me. *Don't let them win.*

Then I blinked, and the world shifted. My father stood before me, his greying hair sweeping neatly to his shoulders, his eyes clear and bright. Clothed in scarlet and blue, he looked like the regent king my people had once welcomed with hope to the throne. The man I'd once bowed to with unquestioning obedience and timidity, always eager for the smallest offering of love or approval.

"Halia," he said, his voice low, almost gentle.

The blade slipped from my sweat-slick hands and clattered to the floor.

"You have become the strong daughter of kings I raised you to be." There was a note of pride in his tone, and despite myself, I could feel my heart rise to my throat with longing, with hope. Tears pricked my eyes and I blinked them away, knowing I couldn't afford a show of weakness now. Not for him.

He is dead, a voice prodded inside of me. *This is another lie.* But it felt so real. The tangle of hope and doubt, pain and desire made my soul ache, as if I could shatter at any moment.

"You did not let defeat stop you," he continued. "You understood that sometimes those weaker than yourself, your subjects, must suffer casualties for you to accomplish what is necessary and right."

All my childish wishes fell away in the face of this reminder of who my father truly was. *No. I don't want the approval of a murderer. I am not like you!*

"I no longer wish to make you proud," I said, though my throat ached and my vision swam. "Everything you value comes with the price of blood."

"You already have made me proud," he insisted. "You are my daughter and my blood flows through your veins." The cell seemed to dim even more, and his eyes looked darker and more ominous in the shadows. "Everything I have been, you will become too. Their blood is on your hands. My blood is in your heart. You are *mine*."

"Condemned, condemned," the nestrae chanted in agreement, stomping toward me. My father vanished in the overwhelming flood of enemies rushing toward me. In my mind, I saw my friends' faces. The nestrae drew closer, chanting, chanting, chanting.

I screamed, throwing my arms up over my head and crumpling to my knees as if I could block out the noise or the horror pulsing through me. "No! No!" I shrieked, over and over, wishing my words could erase the truth of theirs. But their words continued to echo infinitely in my ears.

Eyes squeezed shut, I was still crying out when they dragged me, chained me to the wall, and left me in the cell.

CHAPTER TWENTY-TWO

THE NEXT VISION COULD HAVE come moments or hours later. In this space of endless darkness, I could only mark the passage of time by the increasing pain in my leg and the intermittent screams and sobs emanating from the places beyond my cell door. Maybe some belonged to my friends, or maybe my friends were long dead. Maybe I was alone in this fortress, surrounded only by the enemy and the sounds they wanted me to hear.

However long it had been, I was unprepared for the change from darkness to thrilling, living light. It filtered in through barred windows set high in the wall to my left. I was still in the same cell, but it was swept clean and empty of rats, nestrae, and prisoners. This was the fortress as it had once been, when Toryn still kept it, holding their enemy at bay on the border. Somewhere on a floor high above me men talked and moved around, while I sat on the floor, unchained, facing a man seated composedly across from me. The Life-Giver.

Anger claimed me.

"Why are you here *now*?" My voice was tremulous with emotion. "You're too late."

The man studied me. "Am I?"

His composure infuriated me. "Gillen is dead, and I've killed all my friends in pursuit of him. I'm no better than my father, and I...I've lost *everything.*" I swallowed, struggling to control my rush of feelings. Tears trickled down my cheeks anyway, tears I was ashamed of, tears I wasn't sure I even had the strength to shed anymore. Yet still they fell. "I thought this was what you wanted me to do, and that my gift was supposed to guide me to Gillen. Not guide us all to our deaths."

The man watched me soberly, his dark eyes reflecting a hint of…something. Sadness? It couldn't be. "Did your fight with your father end without any pain or loss?"

I swiped a tear away. "No, but… I came all this way for nothing. My friends' lives could have been spared. I could have remained in Misroth rather than abandon my people…for nothing."

"You could have remained in Evren and spared yourself the heartache of becoming Halia again and leaving your loved ones behind. You could have avoided the pain of the past, and death itself, and left your father on the throne. Or yes, you could have stayed in Misroth and ignored your visions of Gillen. There are many things you could have done, but they aren't what matter now."

"Is this what you wanted?" I demanded. "All of this suffering? This death? How could you let this happen? Why didn't you save them?"

As soon as I spoke the words, I regretted them. A muscle in the man's jaw twitched and I noticed the tears shining in his own eyes, ones he did not try to hide. I remembered his concern when he'd saved my life in the woods after Kyrin had left me to die. I remembered the way he'd held me and wept as I'd nearly died on my father's orders. I remembered the old stories of his sacrifices to save the hurting and dying, and my cheeks burned with shame.

"Forgive me," I said huskily.

"I'm sorry for your pain," the Life-Giver replied, and the tears in his own eyes made his words sound so sincere, my heart ached in response. "Did you expect to avoid sorrow and death in an imperfect and dying land?"

Another tear trailed down toward my chin in response.

"Do not weep for your friends. I was there with them in their final moments to comfort them and lead them on their next journey."

I longed to ask about the afterlife, to know if my friends were happy. But my throat ached. I opened my mouth to ask about Gillen and Jennah and Avrik, but he spoke first.

"Your gift can still help you."

I pushed back my frustration. "I can't even tell truth from lies anymore."

He reached forward and gently touched my leg where it throbbed and pulsed inside my boot. There was a sudden spike in pain, shooting from my foot all the way up my leg, and then just as swiftly, it vanished. Cautiously, I wiggled my toes and found I could move them again. I eased a sigh of relief and stared into his eyes.

His gaze was steady and assured, his tone calm. "You will be able to know the truth. Your fear skews your own visions and lets the nestrae in to show you their lies."

My vision vanished. The Life-Giver was gone. Shadows descended on me and I was a desperate prisoner again, but my leg was still healed. That much, at least, must have been real.

There was scarcely time to ponder the Life-Giver's words before footsteps sounded in the tunnel and my cell door clanked open. Several nestrae hovered in the entrance, silhouetted against the torchlight. I tensed, preparing myself for whatever new tortures they would inflict.

They slunk forward noiselessly, two grabbing the manacles on my wrists while the third stood before me, a ring of clinking keys dangling from its claws. I squeezed my eyes shut, imagining fire and knives, screams and whimpers, but the nestred merely reached forward and unlocked my chains, first from my wrists and then my ankles. The two on either side of me clutched my arms roughly, their claws drawing fresh blood along my skin.

With a grunt, the first nestred led us out into the tunnel, along the passageway flickering with intermittent torchlight. The fortress was eerily quiet, the earlier screams having fallen silent, so the only sounds were my boots scuffling the floor and the rats darting back from our approach. After passing several empty cells, we turned down into another narrow stairwell dimly lit with more torches, and descended until nestred voices reached us from below. We emerged into the large room I'd seen in my vision of Jennah and Avrik.

There were nestrae everywhere, hissing and chanting while flames gleamed on their armored skin. Their claws dug into the arms of countless prisoners, so injured and thin they looked skeletal. Most were too filthy for me to tell them apart, but I didn't recognize any of them. My hope fell.

The nestrae leading me pushed their way through the crowd toward the stone tables in the center. The tables were full of kindling, ready to be lit for sacrifices. Instead, three nestrae stood in the middle of the crowd facing down a lone prisoner who looked less dirty and broken than the others: Narek.

He glanced over his shoulder as the nestrae shoved me to his side. I dared to step closer to him despite the dark stares from the trio in front of us. I longed to ask him if he'd seen our friends, but I didn't risk a word. It was strange to find solace in the presence of a man I'd once feared.

"Princess." The gravelly voice was such a surprise that it took a moment for me to realize it came from the mouth of the foremost nestrae. It was the only one whose visor was lifted, revealing leathery skin around its eyes. Three jagged claw marks ran down one of its armored shoulders, perhaps a token of battle or a symbol of a nestred leader. I wondered if it could truly speak my language, or if this too was a trick from the nestrae's ability to fool minds and tamper with reality. "Our goddess has revealed that you are of great importance to us."

"How?" I snapped.

Narek settled a hand on my shoulder, whether as a warning or for support I wasn't sure.

"You are no stranger to Nesrelle," it rumbled on. "You've felt the touch of death and despair many times, despite any favor your god has gifted to you."

I shuddered at the words but forced myself to stand firm. Narek's fingers dug tighter and I knew this time he was trying to encourage me. Despite our differences, we had only our similarities here in this dark place.

"She said you can free us and open the way to further glory for her. You are an heir of Eldon and can remove the barrier he placed around Toryn, trapping us within its borders so that we can never return home or conquer more lands."

Fury quaked through me. "I will never remove the barrier," I said through my teeth. "What sort of ruler do you think I am? Do you think I'll bow to the will of your demon queen?"

A slow, nasty smile spread across the nestred's bloated, pale lips until they parted to reveal four slimy yellow fangs. I turned away in disgust. "You won't bow to her," it agreed. "But you would to another. One who will ensure you obey our demands."

Two nestrae from the ring surrounding us shuffled forward, dragging a male prisoner into the center with Narek and me. His long hair hung in tangled strings before his eyes, so filthy it could have been mistaken for brown rather than blond. Clothes bearing the Misrothian insignia were shredded almost beyond recognition and revealed the patchwork of scars, burns, and freshly bleeding wounds marring his skin. But when the boy pushed the hair from his eyes with a trembling hand, his eyes were the same bright blue I remembered, his jaw still the strong line he'd inherited from his father.

"Gil," I whispered. I didn't think I had any tears left to cry, but the sight of him gave me such hope and fear that I ached.

"Yes," the nestred said, its hideous smile growing wider. "Your dear, lost cousin. We'd hoped that he would break the barrier, but since he is not gifted with visions like you are, he couldn't learn how to."

Gillen raised his head to stare at me, his eyes widening in recognition.

Years and countless miles may have separated us, but we were too close to forget one another's familiar features. "L-Lia?" he rasped. He passed a weary hand over his eyes, shaking his head. "No, this can't be real. I can't tell what is real anymore." His voice shook. "Too many times I've seen you..."

"It's me, Gill!" I cried. "I'm here. I've found you."

"And you can guarantee his survival," the nestred cut in, "if you break the barrier." It turned to the nestrae at its sides. "Take them back to their cells."

"No! Gill!" I shrieked, struggling to pry myself from the nestrae's claws. They pulled me away from Narek and Gillen, back through the crowd, back to my cell. I shouted and fought the whole way, desperate to see Gillen again, to speak with him and reassure myself that he was alive, if suffering. To find a way to save him.

"Don't trouble yourself too much," the nestred leader chuckled as others fastened my manacles around my wrists. I lifted my head, startled to see it standing at the entrance to my cell, its form framed with flickering torchlight. "You can still consider yourself reunited with your cousin, because we are putting him in the cell beside yours." Another ugly smirk crossed its face. "You can listen to each other scream."

All sense of time disappeared, hours or days or weeks blending into one endless nightmare. Hunger gnawed at my stomach and pain haunted me, waking and sleeping, but none of it matched the torment of listening to the sounds of Gillen's screams and whimpers coming through the wall.

The nestrae never came to torture us at the same time, ensuring that one of us was always silent and alone when the other was screaming, so we could always hear one another. They burned flesh and pierced skin with their claws; they kicked and bruised and battered and deprived me of food and water for so long, I was sure I was on the edge of death. But worse were the visions, the taunts, the memories of all I'd done and failed to do.

"Condemned," the voices would hiss, sometimes when I was sure I was alone, until I was half-convinced they emanated from the walls themselves.

My mother emerged from a shadowy corner, blood pouring from her wound and bubbling on her lips. Her eyes found mine and she whispered, "You are guilty. Guilty! You let others die to achieve your own desires, to do what *you* decided was best for our kingdom."

I squeezed my eyes shut and willed her to disappear, but the voices did not stop. Over and over they chanted, and I could hear hers rise and mingle with theirs. They went on until I was screaming at the walls to stop, screaming for the Life-Giver to take me.

When my tormentors left me alone, I could hear them wreaking havoc on Gillen until his shrieks echoed down the passageways and filled the dark, empty spaces of my cell. Sometimes I could hear the nestrae taunting and torturing him; other times I couldn't hear anything but his own voice, shouting, "No! Stop!" Occasionally he screamed for his mother or father, or even me.

But when I shouted for Gillen, my voice raw and ragged, he never responded. Was he too lost in his pain and illusions? Did he simply think my voice was another trick, offering false hope in his endless nightmare?

Sometimes my father came and sat with me, chuckling and marveling at how proud he was of me. He would review my friends' deaths, reminding me in painful details just what had happened to them until I was sobbing, begging him to stop. His hand clutched my arm, his fingers gripping so firmly I gasped.

"That is what it means to have power," he said. "To choose when others will live or die. To convince them to die for you. They died for you, for your mission." He sneered at me. "But why all this effort to rescue Gillen at all? What a queen you could be. So powerful. Gifted and strong like me. And a fighter, with such a drive to persevere until you achieve your desires. All you need is to focus your desire on the throne…"

"You're not real!" I shouted, tears spilling down my cheeks.

I closed my eyes and when I reopened them, he was gone.

What is real anymore? I asked myself, my pulse roaring in my ears.

The chanting began again until I dissolved into screams. Then it was Gillen's turn to scream. A horrible cycle, going around and around.

Would they let me die before they forced me to break the barrier, or were they waiting until I was so insane I could no longer resist?

Finally, I saw Velaire, her eyes full of tears. "Bring him back to me," she begged. She knelt at her bedside, her head bowed in prayer. "Bring back my son. For me, for my people."

"Now they'll die if Gil lives, and Gil will die if they live," I argued, realizing the insanity of speaking to this vision. The insanity of speaking to any of the people who had appeared in my cell. Velaire was not here, and yet she was. I could smell the perfume on the silky folds of her dress, see the wrinkles gathering around her eyes and along her forehead, hear the way her voice wavered and broke. My heart swelled with pain to see her so desperate, though I feared the way my emotions responded to the sight of her. What if this was another illusion from the nestrae, conjured to confuse and fool me into doing their bidding?

"I've pled so many nights with you," she whispered. "Misroth needs Gillen. You've shown me this, Life-Giver. If he dies, we are lost. You must help Halia save him. You must let him live, let him save his people."

She vanished as abruptly as she'd appeared, and I was left sweating, pain and fear and confusion crowding my mind.

"It's time." The nestred leader's voice rumbled through the air.

I lifted my head weakly from my chest and blinked up at the forms releasing my manacles and yanking me to my feet.

They dragged me through the passageway and up the staircase, up into the startlingly bright sunshine of a spring afternoon. I saw Gillen ahead of me, pulled by two nestrae as well.

"Gil," I croaked. My voice didn't carry far, and he didn't respond.

He was silent the whole way, his head hanging low as he swayed on his feet. His captors dragged more than led him through the grass.

"Let me speak with him," I said, the words rasping through my parched throat and dry lips.

The nestrae holding me only hissed in response. Behind us, the nestred leader strode forward. His visor was back in place. "Speak with him? You hardly have room to bargain with us, princess," he laughed. He gave me a shove, and the nestrae continued onward.

We settled on the plateau edge, its drop off marking the edge of Toryn. Behind me, more nestrae poured from their stronghold with prisoners. I shuddered at the hopeless sight of the overwhelming odds our enemy held over us. I found Narek, but there was no sign of Avrik or Jennah.

As we neared the edge, the wind picked up and rustled through my hair. The Wastelands stretched out beneath me. The home of my enemies. Somewhere between them and me, the barrier crackled with energy, like a thrumming beneath my skin, vibrating through my bones and accelerating my heartbeat. The two nestrae holding me forced me to my knees, and the rocky ground dug into me like needles.

"Break it," the nestred leader snarled behind me. "Or your king dies."

I glanced back at Gillen, his face despondent and his eyes wide as he stared back at me. The nestrae had him on his knees as well, with a long black dagger pressed so hard into his throat that a scarlet trickle was already running down his neck. He gave the smallest shake of his head, and I knew exactly what he expected of me.

How can I destroy the barrier and doom my people to the horrors the nestrae bring? I thought. *But...how can I let Gil die?*

I imagined Lyanna and Rev, Velaire and her rebel guards, Bren and

Shilam and Jaren, Selna at Wanderer's Rest, Benor and his wife, Marke and his daughters, Layk's siblings, and Gare's widow and son. Every life I could lose if the barrier no longer barred the nestrae's path. My memories flooded back in an overwhelming rush and there, again, were all the lives I had lost, the blood that was already on my hands. I could see my mother moving her lips to try to speak and Gare draw his last breath; I could hear Layk's final plea, whether given to me by the nestrae's false vison or not; and I could feel Avrik's warm mouth on mine, even if it had only been in a dream. I saw Avrik in the dark as the nestrae tortured him and I felt helpless, lost, my heart screaming with longing to find him alive somehow. An image of Jennah on the pyre opened before my eyes again, and I could feel the heat of the flames leaping toward her body and sense her sorrow as she reached in her mind's eye for one last glimpse of her husband and daughters, one final picture to carry with her into the afterlife.

I saw Gillen racing me to the beach on horseback or stealing away with me to stargaze. I was seated beside him as he tenderly lifted a baby bird from where it had fallen from a tree, as he looked at me with his soft, thoughtful eyes and told me he could nurse it back to help. I could still hear the thud from my father's hand as he slapped him across the cheek when Gillen had insisted it was *his* influence that had me parading about the castle, against proper etiquette. Though it was rare that the Crown Prince was disciplined for anything, he had always taken whatever punishment he could for me. He would just as gladly lay down his life for the kingdom he'd spent a lifetime preparing to lead and sacrifice for.

A nestred lifted its claws and scraped them slowly along Gillen's cheek, drawing an angry trail of bloody gashes, but he didn't even scream. His eyes looked dead. Beaten.

"Sing for us, King of the Hopeless, King of the Weak," the leader growled, and drove its claws deep into Gillen's side. Gillen's mouth opened wide in pain; his shriek was like a battering ram in my skull, echoing until I was so full of fury I saw sparks dance before my eyes.

"Don't kill him!" The nestrae's claws were buried in my arms, digging, scraping, burning.

Guilty, the voices hissed. *Another will die because of you. Will you sit there and watch the light fade from his eyes as you do nothing?*

I could feel guilt marring me as clearly as the scars disfiguring my back. No matter what choice I made, blood would be on my hands.

Gillen was the hope I'd clung to for so long, the chance at redemption for abandoning both him and my kingdom years ago, the chance at saving a people I wasn't sure I could lead. Here was the one who had never made me feel unwanted or unworthy throughout all those long years when I'd fought so hard for my father's approval, my mother's time. If I let him die, he would be another in a long string of failures, another tally in an ever-growing count of people I could not save.

He was a true leader, worthy of Misroth. He was the one our people needed, not me. Not the one who had led a band of friends into enemy territory and watched them perish, one by one.

Condemned. Killer.

"No," I groaned. Pain lanced up and down my arms where the claws were digging in.

The nestrae clawed Gillen, tearing at flesh, pouring blood. His groans and whimpers were worse than his screams. One kicked at his ribs, his leg, his arm, and I heard bones cracking. He was so frail, so helpless against them. And Velaire believed our people needed him. Could I trust that vision, or was it a nestred trick? It felt true.

I trusted my gift. I trusted my aunt. And I trusted that Gillen would save our people.

Give me a sign. Help me know.

Whether from the nestrae's influence or my own horrified imagination, I could see the terrors the Toryn monsters would inflict in Misroth. I saw Velaire cornered in the castle by a sedwa stalking her through the halls; Evren's fields consumed by fire as Bren and his family were hopelessly overwhelmed; Rev and Lyanna weeping in sorrow and fear as their home erupted in flames. Grief and guilt were knives twisting into my heart. But even if I could have stopped the images, I wouldn't have. Unflinching, I watched them come, letting sorrow claim me as it needed to. I embraced the pain as a familiar friend. I needed to remember what was at stake.

Gillen would never break the barrier to save his own life over those of his people. But it seemed a cruel thing to watch him die. Was this the sort of sacrifice a leader must make to help her kingdom survive?

He screamed again, the sound making my stomach tighten.

Tears streaked down my cheeks. My overwhelming emotions launched me into a vision.

In it, the world was bright, the sky pure blue, much like it was today. Eldon kneeled in the snow of Landari Pass and lifted his hands to the heavens. "Life-Giver," he whispered, "I need you to use my gift to defend my people again. Build a barrier around Alrenor, Toryn, and the Wastelands, so that no human or beast may leave their lands. Keep Misroth safe from conquerors and invaders bent on destruction. Protect my people. Let only myself or my heirs pass through this barrier, and let it only be destroyed at our hands. Through my sacrifice, my blood."

He drew a dagger from his belt and slashed it across his palm. Blood welled from the injury. Stretching out his hand, he held it over the ground, letting his blood drip onto the earth. The barrier thrummed to life.

I opened my eyes. It was that simple. And yet, it was not. Trembling, I stared out over the Wastelands. Gillen's screams echoed in my ears, but so did the imagined screams of all my other loved ones. My people.

"Thank you for showing us the way," the nestred leader said, its mouth stretching in a smile. With a guttural laugh, it slashed its claws down my arm, drawing blood. My breath hitched. It had never occurred to me that they could not only influence my thoughts, but also see into them.

You fool, how else would they know to send you visions of your father? Of Mother dying?

Struggling in vain, I watched in horror as the nestred leader lifted its claws toward the barrier, letting my blood run down them and drip onto the grass.

The wind rustled and the nestrae behind me were still and silent. Then an almost imperceptible flash sparked through the air along the plateau's edge and the thrumming sensation inside of me died away. Hesitantly, I reached forward, stretching my fingers through the place where the barrier should have been. They slipped through the air easily. The nestrae roared and cheered, chanting in their eerie language.

The barrier was gone.

TO BE CONTINUED

Thank you for reading *Forsaken Kingdom*! If you have a moment, please leave an honest review on Amazon.

ACKNOWLEDGEMENTS

I'm always afraid when I begin to write my acknowledgements that I'll leave someone out. So many people had a hand in this effort, even if it was just through their support and encouragement. Shout out to my awesome parents in heaven for all your love and the ways in which you shaped my passion for reading and writing. Because you believed in me, you made this possible, even if you're not here to see it! Also, thanks to my husband for his support, even though he's not a big reader. And finally, thank You, God, for giving me this love of words and stories, and the skills and abundant resources to make dreams like this come to fruition.

Once again, I am endlessly grateful to YA author David Estes for being a beta reader and offering phenomenal constructive criticism. You've helped me grow as a writer in so many ways.

Of course, I have to thank Sheree Whitelock and Julienne Calhoun, fellow book-lovers and friends, for all their input and constructive criticism. I cannot thank you both enough for everything you do to support my dreams and for being the best of friends.

Many, many, thanks to my mighty beta reading team: Jenny Dickerson, Kimberly Fisher, Rebecca Isley, and Destinee Owens. You are AMAZING!

Last but not least, thanks to you, readers, for taking the time to venture into my world, cheer on my characters, and watch me grow as a writer.

ABOUT THE AUTHOR

Rachel L. Schade was born on the first day of summer in a small town in Michigan, only to end up in another small town in Ohio. She attended The Ohio State University to learn how to write obnoxiously long papers, cite people who use big words, and discuss her passion: books. She has a great love for the color blue, sunshine, chocolate, and not folding her laundry. Currently she lives with her husband and surrounds herself with books, coffee, and furry creatures on a regular basis.

You can email Rachel at rachelschade@gmail.com, or find her on Facebook and Goodreads: Rachel L. Schade, and on Instagram and TikTok: @rachelschadeauthor.

www.rachelschadeauthor.com